Praise for

her
one
mistake

"I flew through this book, desperate to unravel the secrets within. A chilling, captivating story of friendship, motherhood, and deceit, *Her One Mistake* kept me guessing until the very end."

—Megan Miranda, *New York Times* bestselling author
of *All the Missing Girls*

"A terrifically suspenseful and intriguing novel that hooked this reader from beginning to end."

—Liz Nugent, internationally bestselling author
of *Unraveling Oliver*

"*Her One Mistake* is a breathtaking, bone-chilling work of psychological suspense. An outstanding debut that had me guessing right up to the very end."

—Cristina Alger, *USA Today* bestselling author
of *The Banker's Wife*

"[This] domestic suspense debut is sure to be a hit. . . . Once the pace takes off, the twists come fast. Perks is an author to watch, and this examination of true female friendship will appeal to many."

—*Booklist*

"Gripping . . . realistic . . . Fans of domestic thrillers will look forward to Perks's second outing."

—*Publishers Weekly*

"Perks lays down a major twist halfway through, but the book is also a clever, thoughtful study of the fraught power dynamics between women—as well as the people they love (and, sometimes, fear)."

—*Entertainment Weekly*

"In the vein of *Big Little Lies*, Heidi Perks's latest thriller gives domesticity a biting edge when a mother's only daughter goes missing, vanishing under the watchful eye of her best friend, Charlotte."

—*InStyle*

"This psychological thriller is one you can't afford to miss."

—*PopSugar*

"The narrative is full of twists and turns . . . the ending is shocking and totally unexpected."

—*New York Journal of Books*

her
one
mistake

HEIDI PERKS

POCKET BOOKS

NEW YORK LONDON TORONTO SYDNEY NEW DELHI

Pocket Books
An Imprint of Simon & Schuster, Inc.
1230 Avenue of the Americas
New York, NY 10020

Copyright © 2019 by Heidi Perks

This Pocket Books paperback edition July 2021

POCKET and colophon are registered trademarks
of Simon & Schuster, Inc.

For information about special discounts for bulk purchases, please contact Simon & Schuster Special Sales at 1-866-506-1949 or business@simonandschuster.com.

The Simon & Schuster Speakers Bureau can bring authors to your live event. For more information or to book an event, contact the Simon & Schuster Speakers Bureau at 1-866-248-3049 or visit our website at www.simonspeakers.com.

Interior design by Davina Mock-Maniscalco

Manufactured in the United States of America

10 9 8 7 6 5 4 3 2 1

ISBN 978-1-9821-7218-3
ISBN 978-1-5011-9423-8 (ebook)

For Bethany and Joseph.
Dream big and believe in yourselves.

NOW

M y name is Charlotte Reynolds." I lean forward to speak into the microphone, though I'm not sure why. It just feels imperative that I at least get my name across clearly. Reaching out for the glass in front of me, I grip it between my fingertips, pushing it slowly in counter-clockwise circles, watching the water inside ripple.

The clock on the otherwise bare white wall flashes 9:16 p.m. in bright red lights. My children should be in bed by now. Tom said he would stay the night and sleep in the spare room. "Don't worry," he told me when I called him earlier. "I won't go anywhere until you're home." That isn't what I'm worrying about, but I didn't say as much.

Home feels so far away from this airless, white-washed room with its three chairs and desk and the microphone balanced on one end of it, and I wonder how long I'll be here. How long can they keep me before they decide what comes next? Ever since the school fair two weeks ago I've dreaded leaving my children. I'd do anything to be tucking them into bed right now so I can breathe in their familiar smells, read them that one more story they always beg for.

"They're not holding you, are they?" Tom had asked me on the phone.

"No, they just want to ask me a few questions." I brushed off the fact I was in a police station as if it were nothing. I didn't tell Tom the detective had asked if I'd wanted someone to be with me, that I'd refused and had told her as breezily as I could that I didn't need anyone as I'd happily tell her what I knew.

My fingers begin to tingle and I pull them away from the glass to hide them under the table, squeezing them tightly, willing the blood to rush back into them.

"So, Charlotte," the detective starts in a slow drawl. She asked me if she can use my first name but hasn't offered me the privilege in return. I know her name is Susanne because she said as much for the recording, but I expect she knows I won't call her that. Not when she introduced herself as Detective Rawlings to reinforce who is in control.

My breath sticks tightly in my throat as I wait for her to ask what I was doing there tonight. In many ways, the truth would be the easy option. I wonder if I told her, if she'd let me leave now so I can go home to my children.

The detective is interrupted by a knock on the door, and she looks up as a police officer pokes her head into the room. "Captain Hayes is on his way from Dorset," the officer says. "ETA three hours."

Rawlings nods her thanks and the door closes again. Hayes is the Senior Investigating Officer of what has become the Alice Hodder case. He's been a constant fixture in my life for the last two weeks, and I wonder if they'll keep me here until he arrives because I assume he will want to speak to me. The thought that I could be cooped up inside this room for another three hours makes the walls close in tighter. I don't remember ever feeling claustrophobic, but right now the sense of being trapped makes me feel light-headed, and my eyes flicker as they try to adjust again.

"Are you okay?" Detective Rawlings asks. Her words sound rough. They give the impression it would annoy her if I weren't. She has dyed blond hair scraped back into a tight bun, which shows the black of her roots. She looks young, no more than thirty, and has plastered too much bright red lipstick onto her very full lips.

I hold a hand against my mouth and hope the nausea passes. I nod and reach for the glass of water to take a sip. "Yes," I say. "Thank you, I'll be okay. I just feel a little sick."

Detective Rawlings purses her red lips and sits back in her chair. She's in no rush.

"So," she begins again, and asks her first question, but it isn't the one I was expecting. "Let's start by you telling me what happened thirteen days ago. The day of the fair."

CHARLOTTE'S
STORY

BEFORE

CHARLOTTE

At exactly ten o'clock on Saturday morning the door-bell rang, and I knew it would be Harriet because she was never a minute late. I emerged from the bathroom, still in my pajamas, as the bell sounded a second time. Flicking back the curtains to be sure it was her, I saw Harriet hovering on the doorstep, her arm tightly gripped around her daughter's shoulders. Her head was hung low as she spoke to Alice. The little girl beside her nodded as she turned and nestled her head into her mother's waist.

My own children's screams erupted from downstairs. The two girls' voices battled to be heard over one another. Evie was now drowning out Molly with a constant, piercing whine, and as I fled down the stairs, I could just make out Molly crying at her younger sister to shut up.

"Will you both stop shouting!" I yelled as I reached the bottom. My eldest, Jack, sat oblivious in the playroom, earphones on, zoned into a game on the iPad that I wished Tom had never bought him. How I sometimes envied Jack's ability to shut himself in his own world. I picked Evie off the floor, wiping a hand across her damp face and rubbing at the marmalade smeared upward from both corners of her mouth. "You look like the Joker."

Evie stared back at me. At three she was still suffering from the terrible twos. She had at least thankfully stopped bawling and was now kicking one foot against the other. "Come on, let's play nicely for Alice's sake," I said as I opened the door.

"Hi, Harriet, how are you doing?" I crouched down in front of Alice and smiled at the little girl who continued to bury her head in her mum's skirt. "Are you looking forward to the school fair today, Alice?"

I didn't expect an answer, but I plowed on regardless. Besides, once Molly took Alice under her wing, she would happily follow my daughter around like a puppy. In turn, my six-year-old would have an air of smug superiority that a younger child was finally looking up to her.

"Thank you again for today," Harriet said as I straightened.

I leaned forward and kissed her cheek. "You know it's a pleasure. I've lost count of the number of times I've begged you to let me watch Alice." I grinned.

Harriet's right hand played with the seam of her skirt—balling it up, then pressing it down flat—and for a moment I couldn't take my eyes off it. I'd expected her to be nervous; I'd even thought she would cancel.

"But with four of them, are you sure—" she started.

"Harriet," I cut her off. "I'm more than happy to take Alice to the fair. Please don't worry about it."

Harriet nodded. "I've already put sunscreen on her."

"Oh. That's good." That meant I now had to find sunscreen for my own. Did I have any?

"Well, it's so hot and I don't want her burning . . ." Her voice trailed away, and she shifted her weight from one foot to the other.

"You *are* looking forward to your class today, aren't you?" I asked. "You don't look like you are, but you should be. It's exactly what you need."

Harriet shrugged and looked at me blankly. "It's bookkeeping," she said flatly.

"I know, but it's what you want to do. It's great that you're planning your future."

I meant it, even though I'd originally turned my nose up when she'd said it was bookkeeping. I'd tried to convince Harriet to do a gardening class instead because she would make a lovely gardener. I could picture her running around town with her own little van and told her I'd even design a website for her. Harriet had looked as if she was mulling the idea over, but eventually said gardening didn't pay as much.

"You could do my garden for me," I'd said. "I need someone to come and give me some new ideas. I would—" I stopped abruptly because I'd been about to say I'd pay her more than the going rate, but I knew my good intentions weren't always taken in the right way when it came to money.

"How about teaching?" I'd said instead. "You know how wonderful you'd be. Just look at the way you were with Jack when I first met you."

"I'd have to train to be a teacher and that won't get me a job this September," she'd replied, and averted her gaze. I knew her well enough to know when to stop.

"Then bookkeeping it is," I'd said, smiling, "and you'll be great at that, too." Even if it wasn't what I'd do, at least Harriet was thinking past September when Alice started school and she could concentrate on something for herself. I had another two long years until Evie started and I could get back some semblance of a career instead of the two days a week I worked now for the twenty-something who'd once reported to me.

"Oh, I haven't packed a lunch or anything," Harriet said suddenly.

"I'm not bothering with lunches." I brushed a hand through the air. "We can get something there. The PTA invests more in food stalls than anything else," I joked.

"Right." Harriet nodded but didn't smile, after a moment adding, "Let me get you some money."

"No," I said firmly, but hopefully not too sharply. "No need."

"It's not a problem."

"I know it isn't." I smiled. "But please, let me do this, Harriet. The girls are excited Alice is joining us and we're going to have a great day. Please don't worry about her," I said again, holding my hand out toward her, but she didn't take it.

Harriet bent down and pulled her daughter in for a hug, and I watched the little girl melt into her mother's chest. I took a step back, feeling like I should give them some space. There was such a tight bond between Harriet and her daughter that felt so much more raw than anything I had with my children, but I also knew what a big deal today was for her. Because despite Alice being four, Harriet had never left her daughter with anyone before today.

I'd been thrilled when I'd first left Evie overnight with my friend Audrey, when she'd been barely two months old. I'd had to coax Tom into coming to the pub with me, and even though we were home by nine thirty and I had crashed on the sofa half an hour later, it was worth it for a night of undisturbed sleep.

"I love you," Harriet whispered into Alice's hair. "I love you so much. Be a good girl, won't you? And stay safe." She lingered in the hug, her arms pressing tighter around her daughter. When she pulled back, she took Alice's face in her hands and gently pressed her lips to her daughter's forehead.

I waited awkwardly for Harriet to eventually pull herself up. "Do you want to go play with Molly in her bedroom before we go to the fair?" I asked Alice, then turned to Harriet. "Do you still want me to drop her back at your house at five?"

Harriet nodded. "Yes, thank you," she said, making no move to leave.

"Please stop thanking me." I smiled. "I'm your best friend, it's what I'm here for." Besides, I wanted to watch Alice, and Harriet had been there for me more than enough times over the last two years. "You know you can trust me," I added.

But maybe we were a little more on edge than usual since a boy had been taken from the park last October. He was nine—the same age as Jack had been at the time—and it had happened only on the other side of Dorset. Close enough for us to feel the threat, and still no one had any idea why he'd been taken or what had happened to him.

I reached out and took hold of my friend's arm. "Don't worry," I said. "I'll take good care of her." Eventually Harriet stepped off my doorstep and I took Alice's hand and brought her into the hallway.

"You've got my number if you need me," Harriet said.

"I'll call if there's a problem. But there won't be," I added.

"Brian's fishing. He has his phone with him but he rarely answers it."

"Okay, well, I'll get hold of you if need be," I said. I didn't have Brian's number anyway. I wanted Harriet to hurry up and go. I was conscious I was still in my pajamas and could see Ray from the house opposite staring as he mowed his front lawn in painfully slow stripes. "Harriet, you'll be late," I said, deciding I needed to be firm with her now or I'd find her dithering on my doorstep for the rest of the day.

WHEN HARRIET EVENTUALLY left, I closed the door and took a deep breath. There was a time when I would have called out to Tom that Ray was watching me and we would laugh about it. It was at the oddest times it struck me that I had no one to share those moments with since we'd separated.

"Ray caught me wearing my pajamas," I said, grinning at Jack as he emerged from the playroom.

My son stared at me. "Can you get me a juice?"

I sighed. "No, Jack. You're ten. You can get your own juice, and can you say hello to Alice, please?"

Jack looked at Alice as if he had never seen her before. "Hello, Alice," he said before disappearing into the kitchen.

"Well, that's as good as it gets, I'm afraid." I smiled at Alice, who had already taken Molly's hand and was being led up the stairs. "Everyone, I'm going to have a shower and then we'll get ready for the fair," I called out, but my words were met with silence.

When I reached the bedroom, my cell was ringing and Tom's number flashed up on the screen. "We agreed seven p.m.," I said as I answered.

"What?" he called out over the noise of traffic.

I sighed and muttered under my breath for him to

put the damn car roof up. "I said seven p.m." I spoke louder. "I assume you'd forgotten what time you were coming to sit with the kids tonight?" Even though I'd only told him yesterday.

"Actually, I just wanted to check if you definitely still need me?"

I closed my eyes and gritted my teeth. "Yes, Tom, I'm still planning to go out." I didn't ask him often. I didn't go out enough to have to. In the two years since we'd separated I had gradually realized I didn't need to show him I was still having fun, and most of the time I wasn't anyway. Now I was comfortable enough in my single life to only go out when I wanted to. Though if I were being honest, I didn't really fancy drinks with the neighbors tonight, but I wasn't going to give Tom the satisfaction of letting me down at the last minute.

"It's just something's come up with work. I don't have to go, but it would look better if I did."

I rubbed a hand over my eyes and silently screamed. I knew what my night would be like: awkward conversation over too much wine with neighbors who I had little in common with. Yet I should go. Not only had I promised them, but I'd let them down the last time they'd had a party and probably the time before that.

"You told me you were free," I said flatly.

"I know, and I'll still come over if you really need me. It's just that—"

"Oh, Tom," I sighed.

"I'm not backing out if you still want me. I was just checking you definitely want to go, that's all. You never usually want to."

"Yes, I want to go," I snapped, hating that he still knew me so well. I wouldn't get this hassle if I used a babysitter, but I knew the kids loved having him over.

"Okay, okay, I'll be there," he said. "Seven o'clock."

"Thank you. And come on your own," I said before I could help myself. I knew he would never bring his new girlfriend. He hadn't even introduced her to the children yet.

"Charlotte," he said. "You know you don't have to say that."

"I'm just making sure," I said sharply, before putting the phone down and feeling irritatingly guilty because, despite the way he still annoyed me, I couldn't fault Tom's parenting. And we muddled through surprisingly well.

As I turned on the shower, I tried not to think about why I was rattled by his latest relationship news. It wasn't as if I wanted him back. Fifteen years of marriage hadn't ended on a whim, we had gradually grown too far apart. Maybe I just didn't like change, I thought, stepping into the shower. Maybe I had gotten too comfortable with the easy flow of my life.

THE TEN-MINUTE DRIVE to the school took us through our village of Chiddenford toward the outskirts where the small village park and quaint little shops made way for expansive areas of countryside. St. Mary's school grounds rivaled that of some private schools. Opposite the school sat its impressive field, which backed onto parkland.

It was here that I first met Harriet five years ago when she was working as a teaching assistant. I'd always thought she'd end up sending Alice to the school, but the drive from their house was a nightmare. It was a shame because it would have helped Alice's confidence having Molly two years above.

It must have been well past noon by the time we finally arrived for the fair, joining the long snake of cars as they approached the corner of the field that had been cordoned off as a makeshift parking lot.

Underneath the brightly colored bunting across the entrance was Gail Turner waving cars through as if she ran the school rather than just the PTA.

When Gail saw me she gestured to wind down my window, her white teeth flashing brightly in the sun. "Hello, lovely. How lucky are we with the weather?" she called through my open window. "I feel like I've been personally blessed."

"Very lucky, Gail," I said. "Can I park anywhere?" Four-by-fours ahead of me were already squeezing into tight spaces they'd unlikely get out of easily. "Why's it so busy?"

"My marketing, probably." She beamed. "I tried to speak to as many parents as possible to make sure they were coming."

"So where can I park?" I asked, flashing my own patient smile back.

"Hold on, my lovely, let me see if I can find you a VIP space." She turned away and I rolled my eyes at Jack, who sat beside me. When Gail turned back she pointed to a spot at the far end. "Go over there." She smiled. "No one will block you in."

"Thanks, Gail," I said as I slowly pulled away. Being friends with her did have some advantages.

It was the hottest day on record for May, the DJ on the radio had said that morning. As I climbed out of the car, the pink sundress I'd plucked from the closet was already starting to cut into the skin under my arms and I regretted not wearing flip-flops. Lifting my hair up, I tied it into a ponytail and riffled through my bag for my sunglasses, rubbing at a scratch on one of the lenses before putting them on, promising myself I'd look for the case when I got home. "Two-hundred-pound Oakleys should not be shoved to the bottom of your bag," Audrey had once sighed, and I agreed with her but still had no idea where the case was.

"Mummy? I need the toilet," Evie cried as soon as we made it onto the field.

"Oh, Evie, you have to be kidding," I muttered, grabbing my dress out of her hands. "And please don't tug on my clothes, darling." I pulled the top of my dress back up and looked down to see if she'd revealed my bra.

"But I need to go. I can go on my own."

"No, Evie, you really can't," I sighed. "You are only three."

"I can go with Jack."

I turned back to Jack, who was dawdling behind me, his head still stuck in his iPad, brow furrowed in deep concentration as he fought dragons. Jack was ten now and had accomplished major skills for flicking and tapping and swiping anything that posed a threat. I knew I should make him spend less time on gadgets—I'd even been told it wasn't conducive to the much-needed improvement of his social skills—but despite all that, I also knew my son was happiest when he was in his own private world.

He looked so much like Tom with his thick, dark hair and the way his eyes scrunched up when he was concentrating hard. I smiled at him, even though he remained completely oblivious, and when I turned back to Evie I realized I'd lost sight of the other two. "Where are Molly and Alice? They were both right here. Evie?" I questioned impatiently. "Where have Molly and Alice gone?"

Evie pointed a chubby finger toward the cake stall. "Over there."

I let out a breath as I saw them idly staring at the sugar-topped fairy cakes that had been delivered in hundreds by the mums. My daughter had a hand grasped tightly around Alice's arm and was talking at her and pointing out cakes as if she were about to reach out and pinch one.

"Girls! Stay with me," I called. Streams of people wove in and out of the stalls, and Molly and Alice were momentarily lost behind a family—a large father with a T-shirt that read LOS POLLOS CHICKEN, and his equally large wife stuffing a doughnut into her mouth. I edged toward the cake stall, peering between the legs of the kids trawling behind the couple.

"Molly! Come back here, now." The two girls finally appeared. Meanwhile Evie was now bouncing from one foot to the other and tugging on my dress again.

"When can we get cotton candy?" Molly asked. "I'm starved."

"And I really, really need the toilet, Mummy!" Evie shouted, stamping a little pink shoe into the grass. "Urrrgh, I've got mud all over my feet," she cried, shaking her foot and kicking me in the leg.

"It's a bit of soil, Evie, and I did tell you it was going to be muddy, but you still insisted on wearing those shoes," I said, wiping the dirt from her foot and my shin. "And try and watch what you're doing. You hurt Mummy."

"I'm dirty!" Evie screamed, falling into a pile on the ground. "I need the toilet." I looked around me, praying no one was watching. A couple of mums glanced in my direction but turned away again quickly. I could feel the heat spreading rapidly to my cheeks as I decided whether to walk away and leave her writhing on the ground or pick her up and give in just to save face.

"Oh, Evie," I sighed. "We'll go behind the tree." I waved my hand toward the side of the field.

Evie's eyes lit up.

"But do it subtly. Try not to draw attention to us," I said as I pulled her over to the tree. "Then we can go and get cotton candy," I called behind me. "And we can find the bouncy castles too, would everyone like that?" I asked, but if they answered, I didn't hear them above the noise of the crowd.

DESPITE THE START of a niggling headache, I ordered a coffee from the cotton candy stall. It felt inappropriate to get a glass of Pimm's when I had four children to watch, and coffee was almost the next best thing. I looked around and waved at friends I spotted in the distance. Audrey tottered across the field, wearing ridiculous high-heeled sandals. Her hair was piled high on her head, a shawl draped over her shoulders, and a long satin skirt swished behind her as she walked. Audrey was completely not dressed for either the weather or a school fair, but she didn't care. She waved back at me, grinning and gesturing at all the children huddled beside me with a look of mock horror. I shrugged as if I couldn't care less that I was on my own with so many children to look after.

I saw Karen and smiled to myself as she stood outside the beer tent waving her arms dramatically to get her husband's attention as he tried to ignore her.

"So the bouncy castles next?" I asked, when each of the kids was happily picking at the sticky pink sugar. We began walking toward the farthest side of the field, where I could make out the tip of an inflatable slide. "Look how big that one is."

"I want to go on that one instead." Molly's eyes widened as she pointed to a huge inflatable that stretched back to the very edge of the field. It was bright green with inflatable palm trees swaying on the top and the words "Jungle Run" running down the side. Molly ran over to look inside its mesh windows, and for once Jack was close at her heels.

"It's awesome," she cried. "Come and have a look, Alice." Alice ambled over obligingly and peered through the window. My heart went out to Alice as it often did, seemingly happy to go along with whatever the others decided, but sometimes I wished she would speak up. I rarely knew if she was happy or simply didn't have the confidence to say otherwise.

"Can we go on, Mum?" Jack asked.

"Yes, of course you can." It was the kind of thing I would have loved as a child, and would have reveled in dragging my sister through.

Alice pulled back and looked up at me.

"You don't have to go on it if you don't want to," I said.

"Of course you want to, don't you, Alice?" Molly piped up.

"Molly, she can make up her own mind." I pulled out my purse to count out change. "Would you rather stay with me?" I said to Alice.

"I'm not going," Evie interrupted. "I'm going on the slide."

"Would you like to go on the slide with Evie?"

"No, I'll go with Molly," she said quietly, and I realized those were the first words she'd said to me all day.

"Right, well, stick together all of you. And Jack,

watch out for the girls," I called behind him, though I doubted he'd heard me. He was already halfway down the side of the Jungle Run.

I passed the money to a mum I didn't recognize and when I looked back, they were already out of sight around the back.

"Come on, Mummy." Evie tugged at my dress again.

"Five minutes, Evie," I said. "They've got five minutes on this and then we'll go on the slide." I needed to sit down in the shade. My head was starting to thump and the coffee wasn't making it any better. "Let's go and watch that magic show being set up, and then I promise you can go on it."

EVIE WAS ABSORBED in watching the magician, which meant she was momentarily silent. I pulled my phone out of my bag as a matter of habit and checked my messages, reading a text from my neighbor about the party that night, asking everyone to come around the back so we didn't disturb the baby.

I looked at my email and pressed a link that took me to Facebook, reading some inane quiz and then scrolling through posts, getting caught up in everyone else's lives.

I glanced over and saw the children tumbling down the slide at the end of the Jungle Run and then running around the back again before I or anyone else had the chance to tell them their time was up. I commented on a picture of a friend's holiday and updated my status that I was enjoying the hot weather at the school fair.

When I eventually got up and told Evie she could go on the slide, we went back to the Jungle Run, laughing as Jack hurled himself over the edge at the end and fell onto his back at the bottom.

"That was awesome," he cried, picking himself up and coming to stand next to me.

I threw an arm over his shoulder and pulled him in for a hug, and for once I didn't feel him tense. "I'm glad you enjoyed it. Where are the girls?"

Jack shrugged.

"Oh, Jack. I told you to look out for them."

"They should have kept up with me," he said smugly.

We watched Molly throw herself over the top and plummet down. "Ha! I beat you by a mile." Jack laughed.

"That's because you pushed me at the start. Mummy, Jack hurt my arm."

"You'll be fine," I said, rubbing her elbow. "Where's Alice?"

"I thought she was behind me."

"Well she isn't, Molly, she's probably stuck somewhere and she might be scared. One of you'll have to go in again."

"I'll go," Jack said, already sprinting around the side, eager for another turn.

"Me too." Molly disappeared just as quickly, both of them out of sight again. I waited. I glanced around the field, marveling at the amount of people, noticing Audrey again, but she was too far away to call out to. I needed to ask her if she could take Jack to football for me that Monday, so I'd try and catch up with her at some point.

Jack appeared over the tip of the slide again. "She's not in there," he called, landing at my feet.

"What do you mean she's not in there? Of course she's in there."

He shrugged. "I couldn't see her. I went all the way through, and she wasn't in there."

"Molly? Did you see Alice?" I called out to Molly, who had now appeared at the end too. Molly shook her head.

"Well, she has to be. She can't have just disappeared. You'll have to go back on again, Jack," I said, pushing him around the back. "And this time make sure you find her."

HARRIET

Harriet was told to switch off her phone at the start of the class. She looked around the room and wondered why no one else seemed reluctant as they clicked off their cells and carelessly tossed them into bags and pockets. Surely there were others there who had children?

Of course Harriet knew it was unusual that her internal reaction to turning off her phone bordered on neurotic. *But I've never left my daughter with anyone before*, she protested silently. *How can you possibly expect me not to be reachable when someone else has Alice?*

In the end she decided to switch her phone to silent and balance it carefully on top of her handbag so she would catch it flash if anyone called or texted. With the decision came a tiny burst of relief that she had gotten around this small issue. She pulled out her own notepad and placed it in front of her so she could take notes.

As she listened to the teacher, Yvonne, make her introductions to the world of bookkeeping, Harriet considered that maybe she should have listened to Charlotte and done something she was interested in. Her friend was right, after all. Harriet would make a good teacher and it'd be nice to put her English degree to better use. *But this is about the money*, she reminded herself as she tried to focus.

THE MINUTES SLOWLY ticked into hours, and by early afternoon Harriet felt like she'd been folded into that small desk for most of her life. The room was incredibly stuffy, filled with too many people, making it difficult to breathe. Fanning herself with her notebook, she wished Yvonne would open a window, but the woman seemed oblivious to her mounting discomfort. Now Harriet's right leg was cramping, and even though they were surely due another break, she wondered if she could escape to the bathroom and dampen her forehead with cold water. Then she could check her phone, too. It had somehow slipped into her bag and without making a fuss of looking for it, she couldn't easily see if there were any missed calls.

Making a snap decision, Harriet picked up her handbag and squeezed past the people at the next table. Keeping her head down, she left the room for the bright, airy corridor. Already she felt herself breathing more easily.

"You had enough too?" a voice rang out behind her.

Harriet turned around to see a young girl from class had followed her out.

"Sorry?"

"I'm done with it in there. It's too hot, isn't it?"

"Yes it is."

"And too dull." The girl sniggered. "So I'm leaving." She stared at Harriet, her gaze drifting toward her mouth.

Harriet brushed a hand across her mouth self-consciously, but the girl continued to stare under thick false eyelashes, barely blinking.

"I can't listen to that woman, Yvette, for one more minute," the girl carried on.

"Yvonne," Harriet said before she could stop herself.

"Right." She shrugged. "You should leave too, unless you're enjoying it." The corners of her mouth twitched up.

No, Harriet wasn't enjoying it, but she also knew she could never leave. She couldn't possibly walk out before it had finished.

With one last smirk the girl trotted off down the corridor, disappearing around the corner, and Harriet slipped into the bathroom.

Letting out a deep breath as she ran the cold water over her wrists, Harriet stared at her reflection. Her cheeks were red from the heat and her neck was blotchy. Her hair was escaping from its bun, and as she scraped it back she caught sight of the gray hairs glistening at her hairline.

Harriet frowned. At thirty-nine she was aging fast—though it's not like she did much to help herself. She didn't wear makeup and her haircut was shapeless. Charlotte was always suggesting places to get it trimmed, but thirty-five pounds seemed far too excessive. Though maybe a bit of mascara would highlight the fact she had eyelashes and make her look less tired. Still, her clothes did nothing for her. Her entire wardrobe was gray or dark brown. She'd borrowed one of Charlotte's bright pink scarves once, winding it around her neck to keep the chill out at the park, and she couldn't believe the difference it made.

Once she had cooled down, Harriet grabbed her phone and tapped the button to light up the screen. When nothing happened, she pressed the side button to turn it on, but the screen remained black.

"Come on," she muttered, her stomach clenching by

reflex. She pressed it again and again, but nothing came on. The phone must have run out of battery, but she didn't know how. She'd plugged it in last night as she always did when she went to bed. Harriet remembered doing so because she knew she'd need it today more than ever.

Maybe she had forgotten.

No, she definitely didn't forget. She'd made a point of charging it, just before making a cup of tea to take to bed. She'd remembered because she'd checked it again on her way out of the kitchen. Yet somehow the phone was dead.

Harriet threw it back into her bag. Now she had no idea what was going on at the fair and no one had any way of telling her. And suddenly the stupidity of the phone's lack of battery made her want to burst into tears.

She gulped back a sob. It pained her to be away from Alice. It made her heart quite literally burn, but no one understood that. So Harriet had learned to play down how much she wanted to hold on to her daughter, how she hated the thought of letting her out of her sight. She saw the way Charlotte's friends glanced at each other when she'd admitted she'd never been away from Brian or Alice overnight.

"She'd cope without you," Charlotte would say. "Doesn't Brian want you all to himself for the odd night?" Harriet tried imagining what Brian would say if she ever suggested it. He'd probably be thrilled at the idea.

"Or leave her with Brian and come away with the girls instead?" she'd persisted.

She couldn't see herself doing either, so she mostly played down how she felt because she despised the fact she was like this in the first place. No one knew what it took to leave Alice with Charlotte today. But Charlotte had been thrilled she had asked her, even though Harriet didn't have to tell her there was no one else to ask.

"You have to let them go one day," a woman in a shop had said to her once. "One day they grow their wings and just fly away. Like a butterfly," she added, flapping her arms in the air. Harriet had resisted the urge to slap them back down.

Alice would want to fly away one day, just like she had. Harriet's own mum had held on to her, too much so, and Harriet was well aware how destructive it could be. She'd promised herself not to be like that with her own children and yet here she was. Somewhere along the line she had become the mother she never wanted to be.

She should forget the phone and go back into the room and suffer through the rest of the course. It didn't matter, she told her reflection. It was only another she checked her watch—two hours at most, and she'd be home at four thirty as planned.

Or she could slip away like the other girl had.

Harriet tapped her fingers against the sink. She really should be able to make simple decisions.

CHARLOTTE

As I peered through the mesh window of the Jungle Run, all I saw were screaming children tumbling over each other, barely realizing they were stepping on others in their excitement. Alice could be crouching in a corner and most of the kids wouldn't give her a second glance. I had to go on it myself—I couldn't rely on Jack to search for her properly.

"Come on, girls," I said, trying to keep my voice even. "Let's go see where Alice has gone." I grabbed the girls' hands and as we ran to the back of the Jungle Run, it crossed my mind I wouldn't have been worried if it were any of my children. They were prone to hiding from me or wandering off. But Alice? I couldn't imagine her doing either. There was something so fragile about her that wasn't like any other child I knew. And there was something so horrific about losing someone else's child.

Five feet from the back of the run was the fence that separated the field from the parkland, and in the distance a line of trees partially hid the golf course beyond. I slipped off my shoes and, holding them in one hand, crawled through the Jungle Run, both girls close at my heels.

I called Alice's name as we clambered over ramps and crawled through tunnels, looking at every child we passed, hoping to see a flash of her pink frilly skirt.

"Where could she have gone?" I called out to Jack, who was waiting at the end. He shrugged in response as I inelegantly swung a leg over the final slide and pushed myself down and climbed off. At the bottom I held my hands out to Evie who was giggling behind me, lost in a bubble of excitement that I had crawled through with her.

"God, this is ridiculous." I looked around, slipping my shoes back on and turning to the children. "Did she say anything about wanting to go anywhere else? Did she mention the magician, maybe?" I hadn't seen her come into the tent, but she could have wandered off in the wrong direction and gotten lost. "Surely I would have seen her," I murmured to no one in particular.

"Molly, did you actually see her get on this thing?" I asked, my voice rising an octave as I gestured behind us at the inflatable.

"I think so."

"You *think* so?"

"Well." She paused. "I think she came on after me."

"But you don't know for sure?" I said, trying my hardest not to shout.

Molly shook her head. I went over to the woman who had taken my money and was now talking to another mum about the cake stall. "A little girl came on this with my children," I interrupted. "About ten minutes ago now, but there's no sign of her."

"Oh?" I doubted she'd noticed which children were getting on and off. She'd barely lifted her head when I'd placed the coins in her outstretched hand. "Sorry, I don't know," she said. "What does she look like?"

"About this high." My hand hovered at the top of Molly's head. Alice was tall for her age. "She's only four, though. She's wearing a white T-shirt and a pink frilly skirt."

The woman shook her head as her friend stared at me blankly. "No, sorry," she said. "I don't remember seeing her. I'll keep a lookout, though."

"Oh God." I felt sick. This couldn't be happening.

"What do we do?" Jack looked at me, biting the edge of his thumbnail as he waited for an answer. He wasn't worried, why would he be? He assumed I'd sort out the problem and then, when we found Alice, we'd move on to the next activity.

"We start looking for her." I took hold of the girls' hands again. "We'll search the whole field. She has to be here somewhere." But my pulse raced a little faster as we started walking, Jack close behind us, weaving through the crowds across the field, back toward the car park. And the more time that passed, the quicker it beat.

We stopped at every stall, looked under trestle tables, between the long legs of the adults, all of us calling Alice's name with varying degrees of panic. Past Hook-A-Duck and the soccer shoot-out, the lines of dads cheering when one of them missed. The tombola spitting out raffle tickets, the cake stall again. As we passed each one, the grip on my daughters' hands tightened, my head constantly swiveling around to check Jack was following.

"Have you seen a little girl?" I stopped just past the cake stall and called out to a mum from Molly's year who was manning the toy stand. My voice was louder than I'd intended. "Blond hair to here." I pointed to just below my shoulder. "White T-shirt, pink skirt."

Her expression was grim as she shook her head. "Where have you looked?"

"Everywhere," I cried out in a tight breath.

For a moment I couldn't move. My hands started to tremble, and I didn't realize how tightly I was gripping on to my girls until Molly yelped as she tried to pull away. I needed to do something, but what? Put out an announcement? Call the police? I'd lost track of how long it had been since I'd seen her. Didn't every second count in these situations?

"Why don't you see if they'll make an announcement?" the mum said as if reading my thoughts. She pointed to the far end of the field. "Mr. Harrison's usually over there somewhere."

I stared back at her, not knowing how to answer. The truth was I didn't want to. Because as soon as I did, I would be admitting this was serious. I would be admitting I had lost a child. And someone else's child, at that.

"Charlotte?" A hand clasped my shoulder and I turned, coming face-to-face with Audrey.

"Oh God, Aud." I dropped the girls' hands and clamped my own over my mouth. "I've lost Alice. I can't find her anywhere."

"Okay," she said calmly, automatically looking about. "Don't panic. She's got to be around somewhere."

"What do I do? I've been around the whole field." I needed Audrey to fix it in the no-nonsense way she's so good at.

"We'll find someone in charge," she said. "Maybe they can close down all the exits." She looked over toward the car park and I followed her gaze. Streams of cars continued to meander in. The fair was getting busier.

"Who?" There was no one in charge. I'd not once

seen the headmaster, Mr. Harrison, with his loud-speaker. He was supposed to be here today. He always attended the fair. But apart from Gail, no one was acting as security or even manning the gates to the car park and the perimeters of the field. Alice could have gotten out in any one of four directions had she wanted to. Is that what she had done at the back of the inflat-able? Had she, for whatever reason, climbed over the fence and headed toward the golf course?

"We've lost a little girl," Audrey called out to anyone who would listen. "We need everyone to look for her." She turned to me. "Maybe we should call the police."

I shook my head as a couple of other mums came up to us. "Are you okay, Charlotte?" one asked. "Who have you lost?"

"My friend's daughter," I cried. My hands pressed the sides of my face, fingers stretching to cover my eyes. "Alice. Her name is Alice. She's only four. Oh God, this isn't happening."

"It's okay," Aud said as she took my arm and eventu-ally pried my hands away. "Everyone can help look. Don't worry, we'll find her. How long has it been?"

"I don't know," I said, my heart beating rapidly as I tried to think how long it was since I'd last seen her. "Maybe about twenty minutes."

"Twenty minutes?" one of the mums asked.

"Okay," Audrey announced. "I'm calling the police."

THE NEWS OF a missing child spread rapidly. A whisper passed through the crowd, kicking up a burst of activity as everyone looked around them. The threat of danger, an unspoken murmur of excitement that everyone had a role in finding her, no doubt had people wanting to be the one who could call out that she was hiding beneath their stall. I doubted any of them were imagining the worst. Children get lost and it was never long before they were found and the terrified parents gushed their thanks to the person who happened to come across the child.

In a daze I let Audrey lead us to the edge of the field by the car park, where she had agreed to meet the police.

I rested my back against the fence, the glare of sunlight pounding down on us. People in front of me were beginning to blur and as my eyes flickered to refocus, a wave of nausea surged through me.

"Drink some water." Audrey pressed a bottle into my hand and I took a large gulp. "And for God's sake, move into the shade. You look as if you're about to faint," she said, nudging me toward a tree. "Alice will turn up," she went on. "She's just run off and gotten lost."

"I hope you're right." After all, nothing awful happened in the sleepy Dorset village of Chiddenford. "But I just don't think Alice would run off."

"All kids do from time to time," Aud said. "Alice is no different from any other four-year-old."

But you don't know Alice, I thought. Alice *is* different. Audrey had never taken the time to get to know Alice, most likely because she'd never gotten a word out of her. She'd never really taken the time to get to know Harriet, either.

"I should call Harriet," I said as she ushered my children to a patch on the grass where they obediently sat.

"Talk me through what happened again."

"I don't know what happened. Alice just vanished. She went around the back of the inflatable and never came off it. What do I tell Harriet?" I took another sip from the bottle. "I can't tell her I've lost her daughter, Aud," I cried.

"You need to try and keep calm," she said, grabbing my arms and pulling me around so I was facing her. "Breathe slowly. Come on. One, two—" She started counting slowly and I fell into her rhythm. "Alice will be found soon, I know she will, so there's no point worrying Harriet yet. And besides"—her gaze drifted over my shoulder—"the police are here."

I turned to watch the marked car pull up alongside the field. Two uniformed officers got out and, as they walked toward us, the graveness of the situation smacked me once more. It was official. Alice was missing.

OFFICER FIELDING INTRODUCED himself and his female colleague, Officer Shaw. They asked if I needed to sit but I shook my head. I just wanted them to start searching for Alice.

"Can you tell us what happened, Charlotte?" Officer Fielding asked.

"The children were excited to go on the Jungle Run," I said, pointing to the large inflatable. "Well, not my youngest, Evie, she wanted to go on the slide, but the other three went," I said, though I knew Alice hadn't been excited.

"And you saw all three get on?"

I shook my head. "They ran around the back of it quickly and you can't actually see the start of the run."

"So you didn't go around and check?" he asked, one eyebrow slightly raised as he peered at me over the thick black rim of his glasses.

"No." My chest felt tight. "I assumed they had because they were begging to go on it."

The policeman nodded and made a note in his pad. I reached my hand to my throat, scratching at the heat that began to prick my skin. "Obviously now I wish I had," I went on. "But I didn't think I needed to because as far as I knew, there was nowhere else for them to go . . ." I trailed off. Of course I wished I had now. I wished to God I'd never let them go on it in the first place.

"And what did you do next?" he asked, nodding to Officer Shaw, who wandered off and began speaking into her radio.

"I sat down in the shade with my youngest, Evie. She didn't want to go on the Jungle Run and I had a headache," I told him, watching the policewoman and wondering what she was saying and to whom.

"And could you see this Jungle Run from where you were sitting?"

"Yes, I had my eye on the end of it the whole time," I told him, nodding to convey more certainty than I felt.

"And did you see them at all after they'd run around the back of it?"

"I—I did," I faltered. "I saw them coming off and running around again."

"All of them?" He looked up from his pad.

"I saw Jack first," I said, remembering my son grinning from ear to ear because I'd felt a surge of happiness that he was enjoying himself. "And then Molly." Her mouth had formed a wide O as she had gone down the slide, her pigtails flying into the air behind her.

"And Alice?" he asked with a hint of impatience.

I paused. I'd thought I'd seen her at the time. Or maybe I'd just assumed I had. I couldn't actually remember her dropping down the slide like the others. "I thought so," I said, then added, "I can't say for sure."

"So when did you notice Alice definitely wasn't there?"

"When my two came off. They said she wasn't with them and they couldn't remember if she got on." I looked over at my children, already dreading the moment the police would want to question them.

"What about her shoes?" This came from Officer Shaw, who was walking back toward us.

"What do you mean?"

"Well, don't kids usually take off their shoes to go on these things? Were Alice's still there?"

"Oh." I paused and tried to think. "I don't know. I didn't see." I didn't even notice my own children taking off their shoes or putting them back on again.

"You'd better go check," Officer Fielding said to Shaw, who nodded and walked off briskly in that direction.

My heart was beating so hard it rang through my ears. I looked over at Audrey and the kids, then back at him. Why wasn't he promising me she'd be found soon instead of asking me more questions? Now they were about Harriet and Brian, and he needed me to give him their phone numbers.

I fumbled through my bag and pulled my phone out, scrolling until I found Harriet's number. There was no point in looking for Brian's. I'd never had it, but I made a pretense of checking anyway.

I described Alice's pink frilly skirt with its little birds embroidered around the hem that I'd seen her wear so often. It was getting shorter against her growing legs, but it was obviously one of her favorites. I told him she had a plain white T-shirt and white ankle socks and light blue shoes with Velcro straps. The shoes had tiny stars pinpricked into a pattern on the toes. I was relieved I could so accurately remember what she was wearing.

I told him Alice was roughly the same height as Molly, with blond, wavy hair that comes to just below her shoulders. She didn't have any clips in it and wasn't wearing a hairband. I scrolled through the photos on my phone to see if I had any of her, but I didn't, and even though the image of Alice was as clear in my head as if she were standing right next to me, I wasn't sure how well I'd managed to get it across.

"We need to be out there looking," I said. "She could be anywhere by now."

"Don't worry, there are officers out there," Officer Fielding said. "Where are the parents?"

"Her mum is taking a class at a hotel." I couldn't tell him which one. There are a number of small hotels scattered along the coast, and I'd never thought to ask Harriet.

"And Dad?"

"Fishing. He goes every Saturday morning."

"Do you know where?"

I shook my head. Fishing was as much as I knew.

"Okay." He beckoned to Officer Shaw, who was returning. "We need to get hold of the parents. Find anything?"

She shook her head as she reached us. "No shoes, and the woman manning it says none have been left behind."

Officer Fielding looked at me blankly. He didn't have to tell me what he was thinking: the mood was heavy with the sense of my incompetency. "So, very possibly she didn't get on in the first place," he said.

• • •

I JOINED AUDREY and my children while Officer Shaw tried to call Harriet. I stared at the woman's back as she paced away from us, straining to hear if the call had connected, imagining my friend on the other end listening to the officer tell her that her daughter was missing.

"You're shaking," Audrey said. "Sit down. I'll go and get you another bottle of water."

I shook my head. "No, don't go anywhere." A ball of bile lodged in my throat and I desperately didn't want Audrey leaving me.

"Alice is going to be fine. You know that, don't you? They're going to find her."

"But what if they don't?" I cried. "What if it's the same guy who took little Mason last year? And if we don't find her, and we don't know what's happened . . . Jesus!" I sobbed, feeling Audrey's arms catch me as my legs buckled. She pulled me into a hug. "I couldn't live with that. I couldn't live with myself if she never comes back."

"Don't," she said. "Don't do that. She will be found. This has nothing to do with what happened to Mason. Alice just wandered off and got lost. No one's taken her, for God's sake. If that happened, someone here would have seen something."

"We can't get hold of the mum," Officer Fielding said as he walked back. "I need to ask some more questions, if you don't mind, I'd like you to come over to this Jungle Run with me, if that's okay?"

While Audrey stayed with the children, I followed the officer across the field. He wanted to know more about Alice's family—asking me again if Harriet and Brian were still together, which I confirmed they were. Did any grandparents live nearby? I told him they didn't and the questions stopped when we reached the Jungle Run, where a couple of policemen were hovering around the back.

"There's no gap or gate in the fence," one said, walking to meet us. "The other side of the trees is the golf course and the parking lot to the golf club, which is pretty busy."

"Any CCTV?"

"That's being checked out."

"Good." Officer Fielding nodded, looking around. The crowds had clustered into small groups huddled by stalls, those nearby watching the commotion around the inflatable with undisguised interest. "She could have slipped off in any direction," he murmured.

Alice wouldn't do that, I wanted to say, but I held my breath as I waited for him to decide what to do next. She wasn't the type of child to just slip off. But if I was right, then I couldn't think about what that meant.

HARRIET

Harriet drove home, wondering if she'd done the right thing. She hadn't told anyone she was leaving the class, but as soon as she'd walked into the fresh air of the parking lot she was relieved to be out of the hotel. After a twenty-minute journey home, she could plug in her phone again.

The drive passed quickly, but as soon as she turned onto her street, her foot slammed hard on the brake. Blue and red lights flashed ahead, and even though the road was long and lined with cars on either side, she knew the bursts of light were directly outside her house because they were immediately in front of her neighbor's wretched van.

Cautiously she eased her foot onto the accelerator until forced to stop again to let a car pass. "Come on," she muttered, craning her neck to see if she could see anyone outside the house. Her fingers drummed impatiently on the wheel. The other car slowly trundled by. She could feel her heart pounding and pressed a hand against her chest. One. Two. Another missed beat.

Eventually Harriet pulled into the small space between the police car and Brian's silver Honda and saw her husband standing in the front garden, one hand clutching tightly around his fishing rods, the other roughly rubbing his stubbly chin.

A policewoman stood on the grass beside him. Harriet could see her lips moving, but her face was impassive. She held up both her hands and indicated with one toward the house, but Brian stayed stubbornly rooted to the spot.

Now Harriet could only see the back of his head, but he was shaking it and had raised it high, looking up to the sky, his shoulders clenched tight.

Harriet didn't move. She didn't want to get out of the car. She could hear her breaths filling the silence, too deep, too fast, but as soon as she stepped out she'd have to listen to what Brian had been told. She didn't need to see her husband's face to know the police-woman had told him something bad. Just the way his body was arched, taut with tension, she knew.

Harriet's fingers shook against the key as she slowly turned it and the engine cut out, the policewoman and Brian turning to look at her. Still she didn't move.

Brian mouthed her name slowly, as if it suddenly dawned on him that whatever he had just learned he was going to have to pass on to his wife. His eyes were wide with fear as he stared at her, before he slowly walked down the sidewalk toward the gate, dragging his fishing rods behind him.

Harriet shook her head at him from behind the safety of the glass. Don't say it, don't you dare say it, because if you don't then I don't have to hear it.

The day she'd turned up at the hospital and saw her mum's empty bed, she'd run from the ward and huddled in the corner of the hallway with her hands clamped over her ears. She knew her mum had passed away. Harriet had been told to expect it for weeks, but still she didn't want to think it had finally happened. And she figured if no one actually told her, then she just might be able to believe her mum was still alive.

Harriet hadn't taken her eyes off Brian, yet the click of the car door still startled her when he opened it.

She closed her eyes. "What's happened?"

"Come out, my love." His voice was lifeless but unnervingly calm. "Please come out of the car."

"Tell me what's happened. What is she doing here?" Harriet nodded toward the policewoman.

"Let's go inside," he said, holding out his free hand.

"No. Tell me now."

"Mrs. Hodder?" The policewoman appeared by his side. "I think we should go into the house."

"I don't want to," Harriet cried, but she took Brian's hand and allowed him to pull her out of the car.

He gripped her tightly, brushing his thumb across the top of her hand. "Darling, I really think we should just get inside," he said, managing to get her onto the front stoop before Harriet stopped. Her legs felt like they would give way beneath her if she carried on.

"Will one of you just tell me what's happened?"

The policewoman stopped beside her. She had a pudgy face and small eyes that flicked nervously between her and Brian. Harriet looked up at her husband. Over the years she had learned to read him well. She knew every expression by heart. Before he'd even opened his mouth she'd known when something was worrying him, but never more so than in that moment.

"Mrs. Hodder." The policewoman cleared her throat as she spoke again. "I'm afraid we've had some bad news. Mrs. Charlotte Reynolds has reported that—"

"Alice is missing," Brian interrupted, throwing the words out. Harriet could almost see the letters spilling out of his mouth, reshaping in the air, making no sense. Then slowly her husband's words trickled down until one by one they landed on her.

"No." Harriet's voice was a whisper. "No, don't say that." She shook her head almost manically, even though her body was so tense it pained her to move.

"Let's go inside," Brian said quietly.

"Alice," Harriet said, looking about as if she might find her in the front yard and all of this was some sick joke. "Alice!" She cried her name, this time in an ear-splitting wail, and with it her legs buckled and she fell to the ground. To anyone watching it looked like the air had been sucked out of her in one breath as she crumpled into a ball on the hard concrete of her front path.

"It's okay, Mrs. Hodder," the policewoman was saying.

Of course this is not okay, a voice screamed inside her head. *How could it possibly be okay?*

Brian's precious fishing rods clanked against the path as he threw them down, looking from the police woman to his wife, his face startled and searching for one of them to tell him what to do. He didn't know whether to drag Harriet into the house or leave her there to punch out the ground as she had started doing.

"What happened?" she cried. "What happened?"

"I really think we should get inside," Brian urged, looping his arms under his wife's and pulling her up and into his chest. Harriet allowed herself to sink into him; his arms swallowed her up as he tugged her along. With one hand he searched for a key in his back pocket and fumbled it into the lock. "This is Officer Shaw and she's going to tell us everything," he said.

• • •

THE HODDERS' HOUSE was unfailingly dark. Despite the bright afternoon, Brian needed to switch on a light in the hallway. The door to the kitchen at the far end was closed, as was the one on the right, making the small hallway even pokier.

Brian opened the door on the right, gently maneuvering Harriet into their neat, square living room and onto the sofa. Officer Shaw followed them, and even with only the three of them in it, it felt cramped.

"Will someone just tell me what happened?" Harriet said.

The policewoman sat in the armchair and shuffled to its edge so she could face Harriet and Brian, who were now side by side on the sofa. "Your friend, Mrs. Reynolds, was looking after your daughter today?"

Harriet nodded, feeling her husband wriggle awkwardly next to her. Out of the corner of her eye she could see him looking at her quizzically but she kept her gaze on Officer Shaw, who had paused momentarily, distracted by Brian's jerky movements. "I'm so sorry." She turned back to Harriet. "I know how difficult this must be to hear, but Alice has disappeared from the school fair. We have officers looking and—"

"When? When did she disappear?" Harriet asked.

"We received the call at one fifty this afternoon."

"And what happened?" Harriet demanded. She felt her hand shaking inside Brian's tight grasp.

Officer Shaw inhaled loudly through her nose, and didn't appear to exhale. "Your daughter had gone on an inflatable obstacle course. She ran around the back and that was the last Mrs. Reynolds saw of her."

"I don't understand," Brian said. "You mean like a

bouncy castle? What was she doing at the back of it? Alice wouldn't do that."

"No, it wasn't a bouncy castle. It's called a Jungle Run," the policewoman said.

"But Alice hates anything like that." Brian shook his head. His grip on Harriet's hand tightened. "She's never been on such a thing. Why would she go on one today?"

Officer Shaw pressed her lips flatly together. It was obvious she couldn't answer his question.

Brian continued to stare at her. "She probably got scared," he cried. "She'd have hated it." Harriet felt his shoulders rise and dip with his deep breaths. "But maybe that's a good thing?" he said. "It means she probably ran off rather than someone took her?"

"We are trying to ascertain what happened, Mr. Hodder."

"I want to go," Harriet said. "I need to see it."

The policewoman shook her head. "It's better if you're both here right now."

"No. My wife's right," Brian said. "I want to see this thing too. None of this makes sense."

"Mr. and Mrs. Hodder, please," the policewoman urged, "you'll be helping much more if you stay put. We need you at home for when there's news."

Brian tensed beside her but he didn't persist. "Where was Charlotte when all this happened?" he asked instead, his gaze drifting over to Harriet and then back to Officer Shaw. "When she was supposed to be looking after our daughter. I mean, how did Alice even manage to go anywhere without her seeing? She should have had her eyes on her the whole time." Harriet could almost feel his rising panic; his breaths had become more rapid. The thought of a mother not watching a child—it was something she knew filled Brian with dread.

"Charlotte couldn't see the back of it from where she was," the officer said. "And when Alice didn't come off, they searched the fields and then raised the alarm. I believe she did everything she could to—"

"To what?" Brian cried out. Officer Shaw dropped her eyes. "She did everything she could to look for her, is that what you were about to say? She should never have lost her in the first place!" He shook his head and slumped back into the sofa, pulling his arms away from Harriet and cradling his head in his hands.

"I'm sorry," the policewoman said. "I didn't mean to upset you, Mr. Hodder. The area is being thoroughly searched and everything is being done to ensure Alice will be brought home safely." She paused, her eyes flicking nervously between the two of them again, making Harriet think the officer didn't believe her own words. "We are doing everything we can," she said more quietly.

Brian's body was hard and heavy and uncomfortably close against Harriet. She could feel the tightness of his muscles. Fear seeped out of him and bled into her until she wanted to move away so she didn't have to feel it. Every so often his eyes glanced toward her. She knew there was something he needed to get off his chest.

Instead he placed his right hand over her knee and said, "They'll find her, my love. They will. They have to." His hand squeezed her and he eventually turned back to the policewoman. "Oh God, you don't think it's the same guy, do you?" he asked suddenly. "The one who took that little boy?" Harriet felt the pressure of his hand harden against her leg. She tried to inch away from him. She couldn't bear that he was asking this already. Her left hand gripped the leather cushion beneath her until her fingers began to burn from where she was holding so tight and she had to let go.

Officer Shaw drew another deep breath. There was already too little air left in the room to go around.

"We don't know, Mr. Hodder. At this stage we are still assuming Alice has wandered off from the fair on her own." She gave a thin-lipped smile and dropped her gaze so she was no longer looking either of them in the eye.

"Do you really think that?" He inched forward until he was perched on the edge of the sofa. "Or are you already linking this to Mason Harbridge? Because seven months have passed and no one has any clue what happened to him."

Harriet saw flashes of little Mason, the boy the press had described as having vanished into thin air. "I'm going to be sick," she cried, and rushed to the kitchen where she leaned over the sink and retched into the basin.

Any moment Brian would be right behind her, rubbing her back in an attempt to soothe her. She wiped a hand across her mouth and rinsed it under the tap. She wanted to be left alone, just for a bit, before he started asking questions she didn't want to answer.

"Just a moment, Mr. Hodder." Officer Shaw's voice murmured through the open door of the living room, obviously stopping him on his way out. Their voices were low, but once Harriet turned off the running water she could just make out what they were saying. "I know this is a shock for you."

"It is."

"How well do you know Charlotte Reynolds?"

There was a pause. "Personally, not well. She's Harriet's friend, not mine."

"And is she a good friend of your wife's?"

"Well, clearly not."

"I mean, are they close?"

Harriet waited for him to answer, and eventually he spoke. "Yes," he said. "I suppose they are."

NOW

"Tell me more about your friendship with Harriet,"
Detective Rawlings says. "How did you first meet?"
It's hard not to forget we aren't on the same side when
she softens like this.

"Harriet was working at St. Mary's," I say. My mouth
feels dry and I sip the last drop of water from the glass,
hoping she might offer me more. She told me I can take
breaks, but I haven't yet found the courage to ask.

"The school where your children go?" she asks. "The
same school that held the fair?"

"Yes. Before Harriet had Alice she worked part-time
as a teaching assistant." I tell her I had been called into
the school because there had been an issue with Jack,
but I resist the urge to tell her it wasn't anything my son
had done. "I'd seen Harriet around before then, but
that was the first time we spoke."

An image of Harriet flittering nervously across the
playground pops into my head and I can hear Audrey's
voice saying, "She scuttles around like a mouse." I may
have sniggered because, as always, Aud's observation
was spot-on, but I had also felt something else as I
watched her. Pity, perhaps?

"She's probably just shy," I'd muttered, looking back

at Jack's small head. Another note had circulated about lice and Jack had already had them four times. I wasn't prepared to accept a fifth. "Or she doesn't want to be bothered by any of the parents."

"Hmm. She's a little odd," Audrey had said. "She doesn't look anyone in the eye."

At that I'd looked up to see Harriet darting into the main building and wondered what she must have made of us mums all huddled in a group, heads close together as we gossiped and laughed loudly. We were a pack, and most of us took comfort from that, even if we didn't say it aloud.

I didn't tell the detective any of this. Instead I told her that Harriet had been honest and open with me and very easy to talk to. As she told me about her concerns for Jack, I had watched her fingers play with the seams of her A-line skirt. Her fingernails were bitten low, a hard nub of dry skin clutched onto her thumbnail. At one point I had focused on that, willing her to stop talking about my son with unsettling accuracy, for fear I would start crying.

"Charlotte?" Harriet had said softly. "If you think I've gotten this wrong, then please tell me."

I shook my head. "No, you're not wrong," I'd said. She had been the first person to get it so very right, to see Jack for the little boy he was.

"He's very bright," she went on. "Academically he's miles ahead, but socially he doesn't always cope with things as well as he should at this age."

"I know," I'd said with a nod.

"There are assessments we can look into, help we can get."

"I don't want any labels," I'd said. "I'm not embarrassed, but—"

"It's okay, Charlotte, you don't have to make any decisions right now, and you certainly don't need to worry about considering a different school if you don't want to."

"She was so caring about the children," I tell the detective. "She gave me time. We talked and I realized we had things in common."

"Like what?" she asks. It's not the first time I've been asked this.

"At first it was our pasts," I say. "We spoke about—" I stop abruptly. I was about to say we'd spoken about our fathers, that we had shared confidences. Even though the meeting had started off about Jack, I'd somehow veered into the course of my own childhood and shared with Harriet the story of my father. Well, some of it. But I'd told her more than I had anyone else. I told her how he'd walked out on us when I was still a child.

But then Harriet told me hers had died when she was five and I immediately felt a pang of guilt, because surely that was so much worse than what I went through?

"It was years ago," she'd said as she pressed her hand into mine. "Please don't feel bad."

But despite her smile and the way she looked at me so assuredly, I had seen a glimmer of tears in her eyes and knew she was just trying to reassure me I hadn't upset her. Deep down I could sense she was still hurting at the loss and, even then, right at the start of our friendship, I'd felt guilty.

"Time is a great healer, isn't it?" she'd said. "Don't they say that?"

"They do, but I'm not entirely sure I agree," I'd mumbled.

"No." She'd smiled. "I'm not sure I do either."

It was only after the briefest of pauses that I'd found myself asking her to join me and my mum friends for coffee the following week. Harriet looked taken aback and I'd assumed she would turn me down.

But instead she had thanked me and told me she'd love to, and while I smiled at her and said that was wonderful, I immediately wondered if I'd been too hasty with my invite. The other mums wouldn't like that they couldn't talk freely about the school, and Harriet would be my responsibility, and I didn't think I needed any more of those.

When I told Audrey what I'd done, she'd raised an eyebrow.

"Give her a chance. I think you'll like her," I'd said. "Besides, she doesn't know anyone else in the area."

Harriet didn't have any other friends, I'd realized early on. Tom had called her another of my pet projects, which had disproportionately annoyed me, but there was something about Harriet that made me want to take her under my wing. I'd decided I could help her. First step—she needed to meet more people.

"Harriet had only moved to Dorset a few months earlier," I tell Detective Rawlings. "I wanted her to feel welcome."

"And how did she settle into your group?" the detective asks.

"Well." I pause. "She didn't, really. Whenever she came along she always looked so uncomfortable that in the end I stopped inviting her. I didn't want her to feel awkward when it obviously wasn't her thing."

Detective Rawlings's eyebrows flicker upward and I fidget on my hard seat. "I knew she didn't want to be there," I say defensively. "I knew she wasn't that keen on some of them."

"But you carried on your friendship with Harriet?"

"Yes, although not so much at the start. I still chatted to her whenever I saw her, but it wasn't until she had Alice and I had Evie that we started meeting up regularly. By then all my other friends had school-age children and were doing different things with their days. Harriet and I kept each other company."

Harriet had stopped me from going crazy. She became a friend at a time when I needed someone like her more than ever. When everyone else I knew could go back to work or to the gym or spend hours in coffee shops without feeling drained from a night of no sleep, and who very quickly forgot what it was like to have a newborn.

"I wasn't happy after Evie was born, and Harriet was a good listener," I say. "On top of that, my marriage was struggling and I used to offload to her." Much more so than Audrey back then, but Harriet had always been so eager to help.

"Would you consider yourself best friends?"

"She's one of my best friends, yes," I say, thinking of Aud and how the two of them couldn't be more different. But don't friends play different roles in our lives?

"How would Harriet answer that?" she asks.

Harriet would say I'm her only friend.

"She'd say the same," I tell her.

I imagine what Rawlings must be thinking, but she doesn't ask the question that hangs on the edge of her lips.

What would Harriet say *now*?

BEFORE

HARRIET

Brian and Officer Shaw's murmured voices blended into the background as Harriet stared at her backyard through the kitchen window. She'd always loved the space. It was nothing like Charlotte's—it didn't have room for a wooden climbing frame and double swings, or a fourteen-foot trampoline and a playhouse. But she'd only ever known a life of living in flats and making do with strips of balconies.

The backyard was the only thing Harriet had liked about the house when they'd first moved in. Five years ago, when Brian had pulled up outside the thin semi he'd bought for them, her heart had plummeted. Their move to Dorset had been sold to her as her dream—a house by the sea. Harriet had imagined opening the windows in the morning and smelling the sea air, hearing the squawk of seagulls circling overhead, maybe even glimpsing the water from a bedroom window.

She hadn't actually wanted to leave Kent, but Brian's

portrayal of life by the coast had finally persuaded Harriet. It was, after all, what she'd always wished for as a child. So as they followed the moving van south, Harriet warmed to the idea to the point that she allowed herself to get a little excited.

Besides, it was their chance to start fresh. Brian was trying to put the past behind them. He'd gotten a new job in Dorset and found them a house. Her husband was making an effort, so the least she could do was try and put her heart into it too, and on the drive down, Harriet considered that relocating her whole life might not be such a bad idea. So she'd have no friends and would have to find another job, maybe none of that really mattered. If it meant them being together in her house by the sea, then it would be worth it.

When they'd stopped outside the house, Harriet thought there'd been a mistake. They'd turned off from the coast road at least ten minutes earlier. She couldn't even walk to the beach from where they sat in the parked car, let alone see it. She'd peered up at the house and back to Brian, who'd unclicked his seat belt and was beaming at her.

The house was nothing like the picture in her head—the one with its large windows and wooden shutters. All the homes on this road looked like they had been squeezed in and no one had bothered finishing them. The house itself looked embarrassed by its appearance, with its peeling paint and roof tiles stained with yellow moss.

Brian squeezed her hand. "This is it. The next chapter in our life together. What do you think?"

It crossed her mind her husband must have known this wouldn't be the house she'd dreamed of. But then she looked at his face and immediately felt a rush of guilt, pushing aside her worries that he was still upset with her and told him she loved it.

She didn't.

Brian led her inside and showed her each of the rooms, while Harriet held back the urge to scream. Everywhere was so cramped and dark. She wanted to rip down the walls of the characterless, square rooms just to let the sunlight in.

Yet the house was still bigger than what she'd grown up in. As a child Harriet had lived with her mum in a two-bed, first-floor flat that had overlooked a concrete park. The flat could have tucked quite nicely inside the semi twice over, so she knew she shouldn't complain, but she couldn't shake the feeling that she'd never be happy here.

The back garden was her haven though, kept immaculately by its previous owners. Harriet soon learned the names of all the flowers that ran up the left-hand side along the fence that still needed repairing. It had blown inward during the winter winds and Brian was adamant it was the responsibility of the neighbor, though she knew he would end up repairing it rather than get embroiled in a disagreement.

On warm days Harriet always took her first coffee on the patio bench while Alice played in the sandpit at the far end of the yard. "I made you a sand pie, Mummy," her little girl would call out.

"Wonderful, darling, I'll enjoy that with my coffee."

"Do you want a blueberry on top?"

"Oh yes, please."

Then Alice would totter across the grass, fixed concentration on the pile of sand, making sure it reached her mum in one piece. And Harriet would take the pie and pretend to eat it, rubbing her tummy as she laughed.

The memory hit Harriet with a surge of dread that made her double over at the kitchen sink. She could see her baby so clearly—and yet she was gone.

Officer Shaw's voice broke through her thoughts and the image of Alice fractured into a thousand pieces before dissolving completely.

"Mrs. Hodder, are you okay?" the policewoman persisted.

Harriet turned to see the woman waving a photo of Alice that Brian had plucked out of an album. She took the photo and traced a finger over her daughter's face.

"This isn't a good picture of her. She wasn't happy here." Harriet remembered that Alice had dropped her ice cream and Brian had stopped Harriet from getting her another one. Alice had to be persuaded to smile for the camera, which meant her eyes weren't sparkling like they usually did.

"We just need one to circulate. Is it a good likeness of your daughter?"

Harriet nodded. "Yes, but—" She was about to say she'd prefer to find a better one, when the doorbell rang. She looked nervously at the officer and then through to the hallway where Brian was already emerging from the living room.

"I expect it's Angela Baker," the officer said. "She'll be your FLO. Family Liaison Officer," she added when Harriet looked blank.

Brian opened the door to let the visitor in. The woman introduced herself as Detective Angela Baker, telling Brian he could call her Angela, a fact she repeated when she came into the kitchen and met Harriet.

Angela had a sensible, neat, brown bob that didn't

move when the rest of her did. She wore a gray suede skirt, flat brown shoes, and a cardigan that she took off and carefully laid over the back of a kitchen chair. "I'm here for you both," she explained. "You can ask me anything, and I'll be your main point of contact so it doesn't get too confusing for you." She smiled again. "Maybe I can start by making us all a cup of tea"— Angela gestured to the kettle—"and we can go through everything that will help us find your daughter as soon as possible. Will you come and sit down?"

Harriet obligingly sat at the table, blankly watching as Officer Shaw murmured a good-bye and left the kitchen. She wondered what the arrival of a new detective meant for them. Meanwhile Brian had insisted he would make a cup of tea for everyone, as he pulled out a chair for Angela.

"Thank you very much, Brian." She smiled at him, and Harriet immediately wondered if she shouldn't have been so ready to let their new guest make the drinks, but she had no desire to do it.

"So you're a detective?" Brian asked her.

"I am," she said. "I'm here to keep you updated, and if there's anything you need, you just ask. We find families prefer having one person to speak to, someone they can get to know."

"But ultimately you're a detective?" Brian asked again.

"Yes. I'll be liaising with the officers who are looking for Alice," she said.

Harriet knew that wasn't what Brian meant, but he didn't respond as he dropped tea bags into mugs, took the milk from the fridge, and gave the bottle a little shake before carefully pouring it in. They both knew Angela was also there to gather information from inside their four walls that could be fed back to the officers at the station.

"I feel like we don't know anything," he said when he carefully placed mugs in front of Angela and Harriet. "Officer Shaw didn't tell us much. We don't even know who's looking for Alice."

Brian had always had a light tan on his face and his cheeks usually wore a ruddy tinge above his neatly trimmed stubble, but right then they were drained of color. Harriet was grateful for him making conversation. If she opened her mouth she was afraid she might break down again and that wouldn't get them anywhere.

"Well, right now there are many officers looking for her," Angela said as Brian joined them at the table.

"Where are they looking?" he asked. "How many people are out there?"

"As many as we have. We're treating your daughter's disappearance with the highest priority."

"Will you find her?" he asked, his words cracking as they left his mouth.

"We will," Angela replied, and she looked so certain that for a moment Harriet believed they would.

"But you haven't found the other one," Brian continued. "He's still missing after months."

"There's no reason to think the two cases have anything to do with each other at this stage."

"But they might," he persisted. "That kid went missing exactly like Alice, so they *could* be linked."

"Mason," Harriet said softly. "His name is Mason."

They both paused and glanced at her, as if they'd forgotten she was there. Mason Harbridge wasn't just a kid, he was a boy with a name and a mother who'd publicly fallen to pieces. Harriet knew everything about the case, having pored over the news, becoming obsessed with the story as it had unfolded bit by bit. The fact he had gone missing from a village like theirs in Dorset made it feel so close to home.

More than once, fingers had been pointed at the parents, but Harriet didn't believe they were involved. Her heart went out to them when she saw the press invading their lives, exposing everything about their family for the world to see. No one thought that seven months would pass and there'd still be no news of little Mason.

"Like I said, there's nothing at all linking Alice's disappearance to Mason's," Angela said. "As far as we know, your daughter walked away from the fair on her own volition and is lost."

"I just can't believe no one saw anything," Brian seethed, shaking his head as he sat back in his chair. "There must have been crowds of people there." He looked from Angela to Harriet. "I don't get it. I don't get it at all." Brian stood up and walked to the sink, leaning his back against it and holding his hands together in front of his lips as if in prayer. "God, I mean *why*, Harriet?"

"Why what?" she asked, although she knew exactly what he meant.

"Why was Alice with Charlotte? Why wasn't she with you? Where were you?"

Harriet bit her bottom lip. She felt Angela's eyes on her.

"I was taking a class," she said.

"A class? What do you mean 'a class'?" He rested his hands on the counter as if he was trying to steady himself. "Harriet?" he said again. "What class are you talking about?"

"A bookkeeping class," she said finally.

He stared at her, his whole body frozen, until his lips eventually moved but they didn't make a sound. When they did, his voice was soft. "You never mentioned a bookkeeping class to me."

"I did," Harriet said slowly, keeping eye contact with him. "I told you about it last week."

Brian's eyebrows furrowed deeper as he came back to the table and sat down next to her again. She could sense his confusion, but she also wanted to remind him that none of this mattered.

"No, my love," he said softly as he held out his hands to her, palms upturned on the table. "No, you definitely didn't." Harriet lowered her hands into his as his fingers curled around them. "But it's not relevant right now, is it? Finding Alice is paramount." He turned back to Angela. "I want to be out there looking for my daughter. I feel useless sitting here."

"I understand your need to be out there, but honestly, this is the best place you can be right now." She turned to Harriet. "Tell me about Charlotte," she said. "Do you leave Alice with her often?"

"No," Harriet said. "I've never done it before." Her hands felt hot and sticky as she pulled them away from Brian and ran them down the front of her skirt.

"So who would you usually leave her with?"

"I've never left Alice with anyone."

"Never? And your daughter's four?" Angela looked surprised. It was a reaction she was used to.

"Harriet doesn't need to leave Alice with anyone," Brian interjected. "She's a full-time mother."

Angela gave Brian an inquisitive look but didn't respond. Harriet presumed that if Angela had children herself, then she probably left them a lot, especially with such a demanding job.

"But today you needed someone to look after her?" Angela asked. "Was Charlotte your first choice?"

"Yes," Harriet said. She didn't add that her friend was her only choice.

"So is Alice happy with Charlotte? Does she know her well?"

"She's known her since she was born," Harriet said. "I met Charlotte before I was pregnant."

"And, Brian." Angela turned to face him. "You were fishing today? Where do you go?"

"Chesil Beach," he said. "But why do you need to know this? Surely I'm not under suspicion?"

"No. It's just crucial we build a complete picture of everyone close to Alice. But Chesil Beach is a lovely spot," Angela said. "My dad always went there. He said there was nothing better than sitting alone on the beach with a bottle of beer and a fishing rod. Do you go alone?"

"Yes. And I don't drink."

"My father used to go out on a boat too. There's a lovely spot just past—"

"I never go on boats," Brian said. "I don't leave the beach. But if you need to verify I was there with someone, you can ask Ken Harris," he said. "He was out on his boat today. He would have seen me."

Her husband had never mentioned anyone he fished with before. She always presumed he kept to himself.

"Thank you, Brian." Angela smiled. "And I'd like some details about your class, too, if that's okay, Harriet?"

Harriet nodded and stood up to get the enrollment papers from her handbag.

"And I wonder if you wouldn't mind getting me Alice's toothbrush?" Angela said as she jotted notes on her pad.

"What?" Harriet stopped still and turned to look at Angela.

"Her toothbrush. It's just standard procedure so I have something of hers."

"Oh Christ," Brian muttered, pressing the palms of his hands against the table and pushing his chair back so it screeched across the floor. "You're thinking this already?"

HARRIET SLID OUT of the room, up the stairs, and into the bathroom where she could no longer hear Brian talking to Angela. Her hands shook as she clutched the sink. She knew they wanted Alice's toothbrush for DNA. That meant they were already thinking the worst—that they would find a body instead of her daughter.

Alice's princess toothbrush slipped through Harriet's fingers as she reached out to take it, tumbling into the basin.

The two remaining ones didn't look right on their own. His navy, pristine brush and hers with its bristles sticking out in every direction. She grabbed Alice's brush and stuck it back in the pot. Angela could have a new one, an untouched one from the drawer. There were two still boxed in there, she thought as she ran her fingers over the hard plastic.

"What are you doing?"

Harriet looked up and saw two faces in the mirror. Hers was wet with tears that streamed down her cheeks in rivers. She hadn't even noticed she had been crying. And Brian's, whose reflection loomed over her shoulder as he turned her around to face him. Wiping away her tears with one stroke of his thumbs, he left a trail of dampness across her cheeks.

"They need this toothbrush, Harriet," he said, and

reached over to pluck it out of the pot and take it back down to Angela.

She stared at the empty space he left behind, wondering how he was able to function so easily. A carelessly picked photo that was probably the first one he came across and now he was readily handing over their daughter's toothbrush. But Brian was good at holding it together. He was doing what was necessary to help the police find their daughter, meanwhile Harriet was left replaying the memory of Alice brushing her teeth that morning.

"Finished, Mummy," she'd said, automatically opening her mouth wide for Harriet to check.

"Gorgeous," she'd told Alice. "The tooth fairies will be pleased with how sparkly they are."

A fresh wave of tears left Harriet clinging onto the sink again as if it were the only thing holding her up, until eventually Brian reappeared and pried her hands away, leading her back down to the kitchen where Angela was patiently waiting.

"I need to know what she was doing when our daughter went missing," Brian demanded as he ushered Harriet into a seat and sat down next to her. "I want to know what Charlotte was doing, because she obviously wasn't watching Alice."

"I believe she was waiting in a tent right next to the Jungle Run with her youngest daughter," Angela said.

"So," Brian went on, "not watching my daughter, like I said. She was probably on her phone. You see it all the time—mothers ignoring their children while their faces are stuck elsewhere. Half the time they have no idea where their kids even are. This is why I don't understand it, Harriet. I don't understand why you asked her to watch Alice. You always say she's wrapped up in herself, that she lets her children run feral."

"No," Harriet said, aghast, "I never said that."

"I'm sure you did."

"That's not true," she argued. Charlotte's children weren't feral. They were boisterous, full of life and energy. "Feral" wasn't a word she would ever use.

"You told me once you wouldn't trust her with Alice." He looked at her pointedly. "That her head's not in the right place."

"No," Harriet cried, a flush of embarrassment heating her face. "I never said that." She could feel Angela looking at her intensely as Harriet tried to recall when she might have said something that Brian had misconstrued, but even if she had, she wouldn't have meant it.

Brian took a swig of his tea, grimacing as he placed the mug back down. It must have turned cold by now. "I'd just never have expected you to trust her with Alice," he said.

"There's a few more things I really need to ask you both," Angela said, and Brian nodded for her to go on. "Let's start with families. Alice's grandparents, aunts, uncles."

"There aren't many," Brian replied. "My dad died fifteen years ago and my mother—" He broke off and straightened his shoulders. "My mother left when I was young. I don't see her. Harriet's parents are both dead."

"Siblings?"

"Neither of us have any," he answered.

"So your mother, Brian?" Angela asked. "When was the last time you saw her?"

He shrugged. "Years ago, I'm not sure exactly."

Harriet watched her husband attempting to pass off his mother's abandonment. She remembered exactly when he'd last seen her and she knew Brian did too. It was nearly eight years ago. He'd taken Harriet to meet her a month after they'd met.

"And does she know where you live? Could there be any reason for her to come looking for her granddaughter?"

"I doubt she even knows she has one."

"You doubt? Do you think she might?" Angela asked.

"She doesn't know," Brian said. "I wouldn't have told her." He looked away and Harriet wondered if maybe he had once told his mother about Alice. She could imagine what reaction he'd gotten if he did.

Angela continued to ask about other family and close friends, but it was clear their circles were painfully small. Harriet told her that she didn't keep in touch with past colleagues and she saw some of the mothers very occasionally, but only because they were friends of Charlotte's. It was sadly obvious there was only one person in her life whom she saw regularly, and that was the person who'd just lost her daughter.

Brian's life was no more interesting. He left the house at eight every morning to go to work at the insurance company he had been at for five years. He was back in the house by five thirty without fail. He didn't do drinks, or Christmas parties, or attend celebrations, and wasn't remotely bothered that he had no one he could call a true friend.

Every Saturday Brian went fishing. He left early and came back at some point in the afternoon and, until today, had never mentioned anyone he met there by name.

LATER ANGELA MENTIONED an appeal to the public, which would most likely happen the following morning and air on all the major news channels.

They also discussed the possibility of Harriet and Brian meeting up with Charlotte.

"I can't do that," Harriet said. The thought of sitting opposite her and seeing the guilt slashed across Charlotte's face drove a knife through her stomach.

"That's fine," Angela told her. "You don't have to if you're not ready."

"You'll feel differently soon," Brian said. She ignored him—she knew she wouldn't change her mind.

But while thoughts of Charlotte and the appeal spun in her head, it was the idea of spending a night without Alice in the bedroom next to hers that gnawed deeply. How would she get through it? How would she function during every second that Alice wasn't with her? Life without her baby girl was not a possibility.

All she could see was her daughter's face, pale and frightened. "Mummy? Where are you?"

Harriet was trapped. Inside her own body and inside their house, with no idea what she should be doing for her daughter. Sheer frustration ripped through her like lightning, jolting her upright and onto her feet, unleashing from within her a raw, guttural scream.

Brian leapt out of his chair and to his wife's side, holding her tightly, shushing her and telling her it would all be okay. "This is all Charlotte's fault," he hissed to Angela. "After all, this isn't the first child she's lost."

CHARLOTTE

At seven o'clock on Saturday evening I had a call from Captain Hayes. He phoned to say Harriet wanted to see me, despite telling me earlier she was refusing to.

"Of course I'll go," I said when he asked if I was prepared to see them at their house, even though I'd been through every possible scenario of meeting Harriet, and none of them came out well. "I'll just need to get someone to look after the children."

"Of course," he said. "I can send an officer round."

"There's no need," I told him. A policeman babysitting the children would only frighten them. "I can be there in an hour, if that's okay?" I told him and hung up. I'd called Tom as soon as we'd gotten home after the fair, so I knew he'd come over when I needed him to.

I'D MET CAPTAIN Hayes earlier that afternoon after Audrey had insisted I leave the fair and she'd driven me and the children back in my car. I'd stared out the car window as she shunted the gears into reverse, muttering under her breath that she "wouldn't be able to get out of the sodding parking lot."

HER ONE MISTAKE   69

"I shouldn't be leaving," I said. "I should be searching with everyone else." Makeshift groups of parents were forming in clumps on the field despite police requests not to get involved.

"No, you need to be with your children," she said. "They need you more than ever right now and this isn't a place for them to stay."

I knew she was right, but as Audrey negotiated her way between the parked cars, I felt as empty as the extra car seat wedged behind me. The space between Molly and Evie was a gaping reminder that I'd not only lost Alice, but I was now walking away from her too.

We drove out of the car park, turning the corner with the field on our right, the tips of the inflatable palm trees on the Jungle Run no longer swaying. No one would let their children near it now since it had become a crime scene.

"And there are enough people out there," Aud continued. "The police don't even want them looking. Look at this place," she said in a whisper. "No one must want their children here now." Two more police cars passed us, their blue lights silently flashing. "Let's get you home," Aud said quietly.

Hayes arrived at my house at 4:30 p.m. That was when he told me Harriet was refusing to see me.

"I've tried calling her," I said. "I tried as soon as I got home, but her phone must be switched off." I picked up my phone and stared at its screen, a photo of my children smiling back at me. I'd tried Harriet a number of times. Each time I held my breath until her voice mail kicked in and I could hang up, able to breathe again.

"She must have questions," I said to the detective. "She must want to hear from me what happened. I know I'd want to." I'd want to scream at me if I were her, pound fists against my chest until I broke down. Demand an explanation, beg me to find her daughter or to turn back time and change what happened.

"Everyone's different," he said, and I nodded because it couldn't have been more true.

When Hayes phoned again at 7 p.m. I was in the middle of running the girls a bath. I finished the short call, turned off the water, and dialed Tom's cell.

"Any news?" he asked.

"Not yet," I told him.

"Oh, Charlotte. Are you sure there's still nothing I can do?"

"Actually, I need to go see Harriet. Can you come sit with the kids?"

"Yes, of course. How is Harriet?"

"I haven't spoken to her yet. When can you get here?"

"I don't know, um, half an hour?"

"That's fine," I said.

"So you've heard nothing about Alice at all?" he asked again.

"No, nothing."

"It's been on TV. I just saw it on the news."

"God," I sighed. I'd already had two calls from journalists, but as Captain Hayes advised me, I told them both I had nothing to say.

"I'm sorry, Charlotte—I don't know what to say."

"Don't say anything. Just come round so I can get over there."

I sat on the edge of my bed and waited for Tom as the bath water slowly went cold in the bathroom next to me. My phone flashed again with another text message from a class mum. "Is there any news? Is there anything I can do to help?" I threw the phone behind me. Sooner or later I was going to have to respond to all the messages I'd had since I'd left the fair, but I couldn't do anything until I got through this evening. With the curtains pulled, I was in semidarkness as I brooded over one question: What the hell did I say to Harriet?

I would have to look them both in the eye and tell them I had nothing that could make it any easier. No explanation, no excuses. Not even one suggestion that might bring them relief. They'd ask me what happened to Alice and I'd have to confess I didn't have a clue.

She ran behind the Jungle Run with Molly.

Then what? they'd ask.

I don't know. I just don't know what happened to your daughter then.

Molly and Jack had since told me they'd taken their shoes off behind the inflatable, but in their excitement neither of them stopped to help Alice, waited for her, or even noticed whether she'd gotten on. "You're ten, Jack," I'd cried earlier. "Why didn't you check the girls were safely on it like I'd asked you to?"

Jack had looked at me with a dolefully blank expression. I knew I couldn't expect my son to consider other children. Jack has a heart of gold, but he's the last kid you give responsibility to.

"Molly." I'd turned on my daughter. "She was running after you. Why didn't you help her on? What did you do, literally race on after Jack and forget she was even there?" I knew I shouldn't've transferred my guilt onto them, but still the words spilled out of my mouth.

Molly's eyes filled with tears. "I'm sorry, Mummy," she'd cried.

I pulled her to me and said that no, I was sorry. This was not her fault. "I'm not saying you did anything wrong," I'd told her, though of course I had implied it.

There was only one person whose fault this was. Who had lost themselves in texts and Facebook and maybe looked up occasionally but never enough to spot Alice. I knew deep down I hadn't seen her tumble down the slide. It was only ever my two I'd spotted from the shade of the tent. Which meant, as Officer Fielding said, she most likely had never gotten on in the first place.

AS SOON AS Tom arrived, I kissed the children goodnight and told them I'd see them in the morning. Then I tried leaving the house before we could get into a conversation, but he stopped me before I got to the front door.

"Are you okay?" he asked.

I shook my head, pressing my fingernails into my palms so I didn't start crying. "Of course not, but I don't want to talk about it."

"It was the lead story on the news." Tom rubbed his hands together uneasily. "To be expected, I suppose."

"Yes, well, it would be. Something like this—" I stopped. "I really just need to go, Tom."

He nodded, and I knew there was something else he wanted to tell me but I opened the front door, not wanting to give him the chance. "I just saw Chris Lawson as I was coming up the drive," he said. "He told me they'd called off their party tonight."

"I really couldn't care less if they have or not."

"No, I know, I'm just saying. They're still your friends and neighbors. They want to support you." I stepped out and onto the front lawn and he followed.

"Where are you going with this, Tom?"

"I just—" Tom paused and ran a hand through his hair, making it stick up in tufts. "Chris mentioned some things have been said on the internet. I don't want you suddenly coming across them."

"What kind of things?"

"Stupid people with nothing better to do, that's all. Not your friends. Not anyone who knows you, Char."

"What kind of things?" I asked again, feeling my throat burn with dread.

"Just . . ." He sighed ruefully. "What were you doing when she went missing? How come our kids are okay?"

I stepped back as if he'd slapped me.

"Oh, Charlotte," he said, reaching out and taking hold of my arms.

"I can't do this now," I cried, jerking myself out of his grasp.

"I'm sorry." Tom gaped at me remorsefully. "I should never have said anything."

"Well it's too late now, isn't it?" I snapped, and ran to the car before he could utter another word.

I'D RARELY BEEN to Harriet's house because she always preferred coming to mine. She'd often sit at my kitchen island and run her hands gently across its oak surface as if it were made of the most precious wood.

"Harriet, you don't need to worry," I'd said once, laughing as she carefully placed her coffee mug down, checking for rings under it when I hadn't given her a coaster.

"Habit," she'd murmured, smiling sheepishly.

"Well, I'm not worried about stains," I'd told her. "The kids make plenty of those." But still she would swipe her hand across the surface and tell me everything she loved about my home, while inside I was begging her to stop.

In contrast, Harriet's house was small and unbearably dark. The first time I visited she had apologized for its lack of light, leading me quickly to the kitchen at the back.

"Don't be silly, it's lovely," I'd told her. "I can't believe you painted all this yourself."

"Well, there isn't much to paint, really. It's not very big," she had said. "Not like your beautiful home."

The next time Harriet was at mine I found myself pointing out the chipped skirting board, the table that needed fixing, and the crack that ran along the length of the living room ceiling.

I made things up, too. Little harmless stories to show the perfect life she thought I had wasn't really that perfect. I complained that Tom was always working too hard and I never saw him, how I hated my job some days and wished I could leave. I told her she was so lucky to be married to Brian, who was always home by 5:30 p.m. so they could have tea as a family.

I wasn't lying when I told her dinner wasn't an enjoyable experience in our house. None of the children liked the same food and most nights I ended up giving them fish fingers or pizza because they were the only meals none of them complained about. But I omitted that Tom only added to the suffering at mealtimes, so it was easier for me to endure them alone. I didn't say that the idea of him walking in the door at five thirty every night without fail would actually be my idea of hell.

But Harriet had seemed to be placated when she said, "Yes, I'm very lucky that Brian never works late."

I turned off the main road out of town to where the houses were packed much tighter together. "Crammed in," Tom would say. Even at that time of night, Harriet's road was busy. I was forced to drive past the house to find a parking space between two dropped curbs on the other side of the road.

There were a handful of journalists hanging around outside Harriet's front lawn, so I'd been given the number of the liaison officer to call when I arrived, who would come out to meet me. I looked back at the house, its windows darkened by pulled curtains. The thought of them sitting inside, engulfed in a misery that I had created, made me want to restart the engine and speed off. But I didn't have that luxury. Swallowing the lump lodged in my throat, I tapped out the number and told the woman who answered, Angela, that I was there.

AS SOON AS I walked into the room the air felt heavy with misery. Inside the boxed walls, its stuffiness did nothing to suppress the shiver running the length of my spine. "Someone has stepped on your grave," Tom would have said.

Angela maneuvered me toward an armchair in the corner of the room that faced the sofa. On that, Harriet and Brian were glued together. In his lap Brian had his hands protectively wrapped around one of Harriet's. His fingers played, pressing into her hand, splaying then scrunching like a nervous child.

As I stumbled across the room and awkwardly perched in the seat, Brian's eyes followed me. His body was curved around Harriet's, a wall of protection to shield her from me. Within his enclosure, Harriet was deathly immobile. Her glassy eyes stared out of the window and didn't once venture in my direction.

The silence was cold until Angela broke it. "Can I get you a cup of tea, Mrs. Reynolds?" she asked.

I shook my head. "No thank you." My voice was little more than a whisper.

"Maybe it would help if you could tell Harriet and Brian what happened," Angela said softly. "What was going on when Alice went onto the Jungle Run?"

I nodded. I could sense Harriet and Brian both tensing, and my own muscles ached as I hunched uncomfortably in the chair. I had no idea how to start.

"I, um—" I broke off and swallowed loudly, inhaling a large gulp of air that hissed through my teeth. "I'm sorry," I said. "I know nothing I say will mean anything." I paused again. Brian's eyes continued to bore into me as if he could see right through my skin, but still Harriet wouldn't look over.

The skirt of my dress was damp beneath me. I shifted on the leather chair, the wetness of my thighs making it squeak, though any extra embarrassment wouldn't show on my already blotchy face.

"I'm sorry—" I started again.

"Sorry is not going to bring back our daughter," Brian interrupted, his voice quietly controlled. "So we don't want to hear your sorries. We want to know what happened today. How you lost Alice." His fingers continued to unfurl and then clamp back around Harriet's hand. Beside him she took a deep breath.

Brian leaned forward, moving his weight toward the edge of the sofa. I could see his eyes more clearly now, red lines creeping out from the edges. He must have been crying, but now he just looked angry.

"What happened?" he growled. "Because we need to know how you lost our daughter."

I felt my breath stagger in my chest. "I'm so sorry, Brian. I don't know what happened."

"You don't know?" He gave a short laugh, one of his

hands flinging into the air, which made Harriet jump. Brian moved his body, wrapping himself around Harriet more tightly, and despite how awful I felt for him, I wished he would get out of the way so I could see my friend.

"I don't mean it like that," I said. "It's just that everything happened so quickly. It was a split second. Alice went around the back of the inflatable with Molly and Jack, but then she didn't—" The words caught in my throat, making me gulp down another large breath. "She didn't come off it. And as soon as I knew that, I went on it looking for her myself. The children came with me, but"—I shook my head—"she wasn't there." I knew I sounded too shrill and my excuses hung awkwardly in the air as I waited for Brian to answer.

But it was Harriet who spoke, her voice rupturing into the room like it had no place being there. "How long had she been gone before you noticed?" Still she continued to stare out the window. It was a question I'd expected.

"I think it was maybe five minutes," I said quietly, willing her to look at me around her husband's shoulder. I inched forward in the seat, the squeak of leather making another unpleasant noise. My hand flinched as if it wanted to reach out for her, but almost by instinct she withdrew farther into the sofa. Eventually she turned her head and found my eyes.

"Five minutes doesn't seem very long," she said. "She can't have gone far in five minutes."

"I—well, maybe it was a little longer. I'm not sure exactly, but it wasn't long, I promise you."

Harriet turned away again, staring out the window once more.

"I don't know where she went; I'm so sorry," I said. "We looked everywhere and—"

"And what exactly were you doing?" In contrast to the softness of Harriet's voice, Brian's was fiercely powerful. "When she went missing, what were you actually doing that meant you weren't watching my daughter?"

"I was waiting for them at the front."

"But I want to know what you were doing," he said. "Because it wasn't what you should have been."

"I was with Evie," I said. "I was just waiting."

"Were you on your phone?" he barked. "Did you get distracted?"

"I, erm, well, I looked at my phone, but only for a moment. I was still keeping an eye on the children and—" I stopped. Of course I hadn't kept an eye on the children or none of us would be here. If I had, Alice would be asleep in her bed upstairs.

"But you weren't watching her, were you?" Brian's words felt like they had been screamed at me, but in reality they were tense and quiet as they hissed through his teeth. He'd moved forward until he was almost hanging off the sofa. His face was now only inches from mine, and as much as I wanted to recoil, I couldn't move. "And you didn't see a thing," he said, and all I could do was shake my head again, while tears now sprang out of my eyes and slid down my cheeks. His gaze was drawn to them trickling down and I rubbed at them roughly with the back of my hand. He looked like he was about to comment, when Harriet spoke timidly from behind him.

"How was she?"

Brian inhaled a large breath through his flared nostrils.

"Sorry?" I leaned to one side so I could see past Brian.

"How was Alice? Was she happy?"

"Yes, she was perfectly happy." I tried a weak smile. I knew Brian had every right to be there, but how I wished I could take hold of Harriet's hand and speak to her alone. Just her and me. "She was playing with Molly," I said. "She seemed absolutely fine. She wasn't upset about anything."

"What did she have to eat?" Harriet asked.

Brian swung around to look at her. "'What did she have to eat?'" he repeated.

"Yes," she said quietly, her gaze drifted up to meet his. "I want to know what Alice ate at the fair. Before she—" Harriet stopped.

"She had some cotton candy," I said quickly. The tears continued to run down my face. I stopped bothering to wipe them away as I remembered how carefully Alice had picked at her treat.

"Oh!" Harriet threw her hand to her mouth. "She's never had cotton candy before."

My heart plummeted. Harriet's eyes were wide and wet with tears. I wanted to tell her that Alice had enjoyed it; I was sure she would want to know that, but already Brian was speaking again.

"You mean you didn't give her lunch—" he snapped, suddenly cut off by the sound of an eerie, painfully long wail filling the room.

Harriet slumped forward, her hands gripped tightly to either side of her head. "I can't bear this anymore. Get out, Charlotte!" she screamed. "I need you to go. Please, just get out of the house."

Brian immediately grabbed her rocking body in his arms, whispering words I couldn't hear. "Please just leave, Charlotte," she sobbed.

I stood up, my legs shaking. I couldn't bear this anymore either.

In the doorway Angela held out a hand as she stood to one side. Numbly I edged toward her. "I'm so sorry," I whispered, tears now cascading down my cheeks unchecked.

"Don't tell me you're sorry again," Brian said over his wife's head. His cheeks were blotched in patches of fiery red. "You can go back to your children now. You managed to take *them* home safely."

"I think you'd better go," Angela said as she led me into the hallway.

"I'm going to do everything I can," I sobbed. "I'll do whatever it takes to get Alice back. Can you tell them that? I'll do anything."

NOW

"And you hadn't heard from Harriet at all after that evening you went to their house?" Detective Rawlings asks.

"That's right."

"Not until this morning," she says, "Thirteen days later."

"No." I feel my chest getting tighter. "Not until she called me today."

I can feel the ground start to soften beneath me and the air feels heavier. I expect her to ask me more about the call but she doesn't, and I realize there's no point in me trying to second-guess why.

"You said you would have liked the chance to talk with Harriet on her own. Why?"

I shift uneasily. "I guess because it's Harriet who's my friend and I didn't know Brian. I wanted—" I break off and slump in my seat, looking up at the clock. Its bright red digits blur in front of me. "I wanted the chance to tell her on her own just how dreadful I felt," I admit eventually.

"I hoped that if I could talk to Harriet, just the two of us the way we used to, then I could get her to see I hadn't done anything wrong, like Brian was implying.

Yes, I'd let them out of my sight and I wished more than anything I hadn't, but I was still there, I was a few yards away, and Alice really did just vanish. I wanted Harriet to understand I was looking after her like I'd promised, only—" Tears prick at my eyes. "Only I also knew I wasn't."

Detective Rawlings looks at me, confused.

"If I had been looking after her properly, then she wouldn't have disappeared," I say. "But I also knew I didn't do anything any other parent wouldn't have done. Yet no one else saw it like that. Already I was being blamed. People were saying I wasn't responsible." I wipe my eyes with the back of my hand.

"Who was blaming you?" Detective Rawlings asks as she pulls a tissue sharply out of a box and passes it across the table. I take it from her and dab my eyes, keeping the tissue scrunched in my hand.

"Friends. Strangers," I say. "Everyone jumps on the bandwagon, don't they? They think it's their right to comment on what I'm like as a mother, even if they've never heard of me."

"The power of the internet," Rawlings states.

"It was the people I thought of as my friends, though, they're the ones whose reactions sting the most. In the days after the fair, their silence became deafening."

"And Harriet's reaction must have been difficult to handle too?" the detective asks, steering the conversation as if I have no right to feel sorry for myself. "Her silence must have left you wondering what she was thinking."

"It did. I wanted her to shout at me and tell me she hated me, but she didn't and that made it worse. Harriet refused to see me." I look Detective Rawlings in the eye. "And that was so much harder," I admit. "I watched her crumble in that living room and there was nothing I could do to make it better."

"But Brian was more forthright?" she says. "Is that the reaction you expected from him?"

"I didn't know what to expect. I'd only met him a few times, and hardly at all in recent years." I always suspected Harriet felt like she couldn't bring Brian along after Tom and I had split up, even though I'd assured her he was welcome.

"So even though you became such good friends with Harriet, you never got to know her husband?" Detective Rawlings asks, leaning forward in her seat. Her eyes are unnervingly still as she stares at me.

"No. Our friendship didn't involve him or my ex-husband when we were together."

"That's unusual." She continues to look me in the eye as she lays her hands out flat on the table. "Don't you think?"

I open my mouth to respond that I didn't think it was, but instead I say, "Can we take a break now, please? I'd like to use the toilet."

"Of course." Detective Rawlings pushes her chair back and gestures toward the door. "And help yourself to a tea or coffee too," she adds, and for a moment I'm grateful for her kindness. It isn't until I walk out of the room I realize she's really just telling me there's still much more she wants to know.

BEFORE

HARRIET

That first night Harriet did not sleep, or if she did it was only minutes before she woke, soaked in sweat and disturbed by images she couldn't shake.

She lay on top of the covers throughout the interminable dark hours, staring at the ceiling, all the time thinking of Alice's empty room next to hers. Not one night had passed when she hadn't tucked her daughter into bed, kissed her goodnight, and crept in to check on her before she went to bed herself. It was no surprise she couldn't sleep.

Earlier in the evening, while Brian was still downstairs, Angela had come up to Harriet's bedroom, offering to call the doctor to see if he could prescribe some sleeping tablets. Harriet shook her head vigorously—she definitely did not want pills. She would rather be awake all night torturing herself than knocked out, miles away from reality.

"Thank you for staying so late," she said to Angela, grateful she was still there.

"Of course." Angela brushed off her gratitude. It was her job, after all, Harriet thought sadly, but still she was comforted by Angela's presence in the house. It took her mind off Brian pacing the floorboards below.

"I promised Alice I'd always keep her safe," Harriet said quietly. "But I haven't been able to, have I?"

Angela leaned over and touched her arm. "Try not to do this, Harriet. This is not your fault." Harriet wondered if Angela could tell Brian that too, because she could feel his blame hovering over her, his confusion that she'd left Alice with Charlotte. He knew Harriet would never have let Alice out of her sight.

Were her anxieties about Alice innate? she wondered. Would Harriet have been a different kind of mother if her dad had still been there, smoothing the path of parenting for her mum? With only her mother to learn from, was it any wonder she'd become overly protective?

"I see flashes of Alice's face." Tears pooled uncomfortably in the crook of Harriet's neck, but she made no move to wipe them away.

"Guilt is a very destructive thing," Angela said. "You mustn't let it take hold. You couldn't have changed what happened. No one can foresee something like this."

No matter what Angela said, the guilt would continue to bury itself deep into her skin, scratching away until one day soon she would be driven mad by it. She was sure of that.

But when Harriet wasn't thinking of Alice, unwanted thoughts of Charlotte filled her head. Charlotte in her warm, large bed in the cozy bedroom with the deep teal walls and fluffy cushions. She wondered how Charlotte felt, knowing her own children were safely asleep in their rooms; whether she derived comfort from that, even if she wouldn't admit it.

Charlotte's friends would rally around her. They'd line up outside her house with warm casseroles in Le Creuset dishes and Tupperware boxes of homemade muffins. It was no surprise Charlotte had so many friends, but it widened the trench between them now. That Harriet had not received one call from a worried friend was evident. Angela must have noticed she had no one else in her life.

She wondered what Angela thought of Charlotte. Did she feel sorry for her? Harriet knew her tears were real, but she couldn't bear to look at them. If she'd looked into Charlotte's eyes, she would have seen her pain and she couldn't bear to take that on too. "Charlotte feels guilty," Harriet murmured to Angela. "I can't tell her not to."

"Of course you can't. No one expects you to."

"Do you think she wasn't watching the children properly?"

"I'm sure she was," Angela said. "But she could never have expected this to happen."

Harriet rolled over on her bed. She hated to think that Charlotte hadn't been looking after her daughter, yet none of that really mattered anymore. Nothing but Alice's safety mattered.

"Brian said something earlier," Angela said. "Something about this not being the first child she's lost."

Harriet inhaled deeply and shook her head as she nestled into the pillow. "It was nothing like that," she said, and despite everything else she was feeling, Harriet was still ashamed that she'd betrayed Charlotte by telling Brian.

How she wished she hadn't listened to Brian about

Charlotte coming to the house. It wasn't a good idea like he'd insisted it would be. If he did it again she would have to refuse. There was no way she could bring herself to see or speak to Charlotte again.

Angela eventually left, and when Brian came up to the bedroom, he found Harriet lying in semidarkness. The only light that filtered into the room was from the moon, slicing through the small gap in the blinds. Harriet preferred it that way. Suddenly, the ceiling light flooded the room with its harsh white bulb as Brian flicked it on and slumped onto the edge of the bed.

Neither of them spoke until he got back up and paced to the window, where he peered through the slatted blinds onto the street below. "The journalists are still outside," he said. "Is there nothing I can do to get rid of them?"

Harriet said nothing.

"There are two of them right outside our wall. What the hell do they think they're going to get doing that? Angela told them we had nothing to say. They just want to look at us, like we're animals."

Harriet buried herself deeper into the covers, hoping he would either turn off the light and get into bed or preferably go back downstairs. She didn't want to talk.

Brian remained a while longer and then let the slats flick back, running a hand through his hair that now sprang out wildly from his scalp. Then he strode into the bathroom, leaving the light on. Every sound he made echoed harshly through the walls. Harriet covered her ears but could still hear the splash of him urinating into the toilet, the toilet flushing, faucets being turned on, water violently splattering into the basin.

"Why didn't you tell me about the class?" Brian reappeared in the doorway.

Harriet held her breath until her throat burned. She didn't want to have this conversation. "I thought I had."

"You definitely didn't. I would have remembered something like that. Why a bookkeeping class, of all things?"

"So I could do something when Alice starts school," she said. If he went on to ask why, she would tell him she knew they could do with the money. She'd seen the final notices hidden in his bedside drawer in the hope she wouldn't come across them.

"Did Charlotte put you up to it? Tell you that you needed to earn some extra money?"

"No. Charlotte never—"

"Is it because she's a career woman?"

"She works two days a week."

"But that's still not a full-time mother," he said. "And you know that's what you want to be, my love. She's trying to do both and be good at it, and you know you can't do that," he went on, his voice rising higher. "Christ, we both know that now, don't we?" he cried.

"Brian," Harriet pleaded. "Stop it, please." She couldn't deal with this. Not now. Not tonight. Surely he must see that? "The class had nothing to do with Charlotte."

"I worry," he said evenly. "That it's happening again, Harriet. You—you trust people too easily."

"I don't, Brian," she said in no more than a whisper.

"Just promise me you'll forget about this bookkeeping idea," he said, sinking onto the bed beside her. "You must know how it makes me so uneasy that you're even considering it."

"I'll forget about it," she told him. It's not like she ever believed it was a real possibility anyway.

"I care about you," he said, inching closer. "You know

that, don't you? You know I'm only thinking of you. After what happened before—well, I just worry we'll go down that path again."

Harriet sighed inwardly. How many times would he bring up the same thing?

"I hate to bring this up," he said, looking at her with angst. "But you have been taking your medication lately, haven't you?"

Harriet pushed herself up and stared at her husband.

"Oh, Harriet." Brian closed his eyes and took a deep breath, carefully trying not to sigh out loud as he exhaled. "Your medication. The tablets the doctor gave you two weeks ago. I had a horrible feeling you'd stopped. Please tell me you haven't?"

"Brian, I don't know what you're talking about. I don't have any medication."

"Okay, okay," he said calmly, holding his hands in the air as if he didn't want a fight. "Don't worry about it now. I'm sure it's not important."

"Of course it's not important," she said, "because there isn't any medication to take."

Brian smiled patiently. "We don't have to think about it tonight. It just worries me that you think you'd told me your plans and you clearly hadn't. But like you said, it doesn't matter right now, not with everything else going on. We'll talk about it in the morning." He stood up and ran his hands down his shirt. "You need to sleep." He walked out of the room, leaving the light on, and was down the stairs before she could say any more.

CHARLOTTE

One whole night passed and the following morning I spoke to Captain Hayes, who told me what I feared—that there was still no news.

"I'm sorry, there's nothing I can tell you, Charlotte," he said.

I pictured him and his team standing around their whiteboard, rubbing their chins, glancing at each other in the hope there was something they had missed. *Surely the child couldn't have vanished without anyone seeing anything,* they must have said. I wondered if they knew more than they were telling me, or were at least suspecting it. There had to be stats about these kinds of things, probabilities to determine what had most likely happened. Did they think Alice was already dead?

But he told me there were still no leads yet and couldn't even reassure me they were inching toward finding her.

The day before, Audrey had patiently listened as I clawed at the empty space between last seeing Alice and realizing she wasn't there. I hoped that by dissecting it enough times something would come to me. If Aud went home and told her husband she couldn't bear to hear any more, then she didn't let on.

Karen and Gail had both called to see if there was anything they could do. Many friends had texted messages of support, a few asking if there was any news, and even mums I barely knew from Molly's and Jack's classes had found ways to tell me they were sorry about what had happened.

As much as I needed their support and was initially relieved that I wasn't being judged, I began to begrudge relaying the story just to feed their curiosities with first-hand details. Each time I closed the door or hung up the phone I felt as if someone had taken away another piece of me.

On Sunday morning a neighbor had loitered on my doorstep, telling me, "I can't even imagine what I'd do in that situation."

I tried to remain patient as I nodded along with her.

"Still, I suppose you have to be thankful it wasn't your own child."

I looked at her in disbelief. "What?"

"I mean, it's awful, obviously, but losing your own child—well, isn't that worse?"

"No, it's not worse," I'd cried. "How can anything be worse than what's happened?"

"Oh no, I don't mean it isn't horrendous," she'd blustered. "I just think if it was one of yours, then . . ." she trailed off, looking desperately over my shoulder. "Where are your lovely ones, anyway?"

"Thank you for coming by," I said. "But I really need to get back in." I closed the door on her and pressed my back against it, shutting my eyes and silently screaming. I'd thanked her, for God's sake. What was wrong with me? Was I so afraid of pushing people away that I was letting them eject their unwanted thoughts onto me? Was I scared of what they would say about me if I didn't?

I was tired. Exhausted. I should never have opened the door. I'd barely slept, and when I had fallen into a confused mess of dreams, I was woken that morning at 6 a.m. with a piercing scream. I flung myself out of bed and raced into Molly's room where, the night before, Tom had laid mattresses on the floor for Jack and Evie to sleep on.

When I'd gotten home from Harriet's house I'd looked in on my sleeping children, my heart filled with love and grief.

"Thank you, Tom," I'd whispered.

"For what?"

"I don't know, just being here. Looking after them."

"Of course I'm going to. I'm here for all of you," he told me. "Anyway, they wanted to be together. Evie said she was scared and I found Jack hovering on the landing not knowing what to do with himself, so I told him to go in with the girls. By the way, he could do with some new pajamas. The ones he's in are skimming the top of his ankles."

How Tom thought pajamas were a priority right now was beyond me, but I told myself to let it go.

Evie was still screaming when I crawled onto her mattress and pulled her in for a hug. "What is it, Evie?" I whispered. "Mummy's here, what's happened? Did you have a nasty dream?"

"A bad man was coming to get me," she sobbed. "I was scared."

"Shhh. There's no bad man," I said, though by then I was certain there was, and he'd been feet away from my children.

"What's happened to Alice?" she asked innocently.

I put a finger over my lips and gestured toward her sleeping siblings. Molly stirred and rolled over but didn't wake. "I don't know, honey, but the police are doing everything they can to bring her home."

"Will she come back today?"

"I don't know, my darling. I don't know. I hope so."

"Did someone take her?" she asked, solemnly looking up at me with wide eyes. I furiously fought back tears. How I wanted to reassure her that Chiddenford was still a safe place to live and she had nothing to worry about, that her dream was just a nightmare she could forget about by the time she'd finished breakfast.

"I don't know what happened, but I promise you—" I inhaled a lungful of air that burned my chest as it sank through my body. "I promise I won't let anything bad happen to you."

I had no right to make such promises, but I knew I would never take my eyes off my children again. I would never let them run through the trees where I couldn't see them or play hide-and-seek in the sand dunes where the grass was so high it devoured them. I would never trust anyone not to be lurking a breath away from me, ready to snatch my children.

AUDREY CAME BACK to the house when I was making breakfast, at a point when we had temporarily fallen into a chaotic normality. When I opened the door to Aud, I realized how it must have looked.

"Oh, Aud," I blustered. "I'm sorry, we were just trying to get breakfast sorted and the kids, well, you know what it's like." I stepped aside to let her in, taking in the view of my hallway. Molly sat crying at the bottom of the stairs, while Evie hovered in the doorway to the kitchen, dangling a sodden night nappy in one hand.

The TV blared out from the playroom, where Jack had turned up the volume to drown out his sisters.

"It's how it should be," she said as she gave me a hug and carefully folded her cardigan on the hallway table. "I should have brought the boys round to sit with Jack. Anyway, you mustn't stop their lives going on as normal."

"I know but—"

Audrey held up her hand to stop me. "I'll make us both a coffee while you sort out whatever this is about."

I smiled gratefully and waited for Aud to head into the kitchen. "Now, Molly, what's wrong?" I asked, crouching next to my daughter on the bottom step.

"Evie kicked me," she sobbed.

"Evie? Is that true?"

"You forgot this," Evie said, hurling the wet nappy across the hallway.

"Jesus, Evie, come pick that up."

"I want my breakfast!" she said, balling her fists against her hips.

"I said come and pick this up, Evie." I pointed to the nappy, rising to my feet.

"I want Shreddies, not toast."

"Evie!" I shouted. "Do as you're told. And tell me why you kicked Molly."

"She kicked me first."

"I didn't, Mummy, I promise," Molly cried.

"God!" I clamped my hands over my ears. "Will you stop arguing? What is wrong with you both? Do you really think any of your petty squabbles are important right now?"

Jack glanced over from the sofa and then back to the TV. "And will you turn down the volume, Jack?" I shouted. "I can't hear myself think."

"Why do you need to?" Molly asked.

"What?"

"Hear yourself think."

I gripped the banister so tightly my knuckles went white. "Don't talk back at me, Molly."

Her bottom lip wobbled, and then she flung her hands over her head, dramatically curling herself into a ball and crying.

"Come and have a coffee," Audrey said, appearing in the kitchen doorway. "Girls, why don't you go watch some TV with your brother? I'll bring you breakfast in there today."

"Really?" Evie's eyes shone as she skipped into the playroom, and eventually Molly unfurled herself and followed her in.

"Have you eaten?" Audrey asked as we went through to the kitchen. The smell of coffee drifted from the pot. "I'm making you toast if you haven't," she said, popping two slices of bread into the toaster.

I shook my head. "Thank you, but I'm not hungry."

"You have to eat."

"I will later." I smiled at her gratefully and realized how good it was to have her here again, taking control. We hadn't done this enough in the last couple of years, and we'd drifted apart since Tom and I hadn't been together. Audrey had been supportive throughout our separation but had always made it clear she thought we should stay together for the children, so I'd stopped confiding in her. Not like I did with Harriet.

We sat on stools at the island in silence. She had folded back the doors to the backyard and a light breeze blew in, the sun shining daggers of light across the stone tiles.

"So tell me more about last night," Audrey asked

after a while. I'd called her once Tom left but had only given the briefest details.

"It was awful."

She nodded. "How were they?"

I sighed, stretching my arms in front of me, my hands wrapped around the mug of coffee Aud had pushed in my direction. "Brian took over, really. He was the one asking all the questions and getting angry."

"Really?" Audrey asked. A teaspoon of sugar hovered over her mug as she looked up at me.

I nodded. "It frightened me. I know that's a daft thing to say, given what he's going through. I suppose I should have expected it."

"And Harriet?"

"Harriet," I sighed, taking a sip of my coffee. "You put sugar in mine?"

"I thought you could use it."

I frowned but took another sip anyway. "Harriet very obviously didn't want to see me in the first place."

"I thought she asked for you to come?" Audrey said.

"She did. The detective made a point of telling me she'd changed her mind and was asking for me. I don't know, maybe she changed it again, or maybe just seeing me was too much for her. Whatever it was, she couldn't bear to look at me." I winced at the memory, still raw with its ability to slice through me as if it were happening now. Audrey sucked in a breath. "What is it?" I asked, looking up.

"I just can't begin to put myself in her shoes," she said softly. "The first time she's ever left that little girl and the unthinkable happens."

"I know. And I was always encouraging her to let me have Alice. That's what makes it so much worse," I added.

"She must be thinking she was right to be so bloody paranoid all along."

"Aud, she wasn't paranoid."

"Oh, she was. The poor woman is plagued by worries. She makes me nervous just talking to her."

"She was never that bad," I sighed. "You just didn't know her, didn't want to know her."

I could feel Aud staring at me, but I couldn't bring myself to look up. "I never disliked Harriet," she said. "You know that. I just wondered why you two got so close. She's very different to us. She never wants to do the same things."

I didn't want to get into this now. How Harriet had genuinely wanted what was right for me and I could tell her anything. How she'd never judged me. But right now it was Audrey I needed, and I was so very grateful she was here.

"Harriet might not know it right now, but she'll want to see you again."

"No." I gave a short laugh and shook my head. "I'm the last person she needs and I can't blame her."

"Charlotte." Audrey leaned across the countertop. "You can't give up trying. Tell me honestly who you think is going to get her through this?"

I sank my head into my hands. "Brian? You could see how much he was trying to protect her."

"She's going to need a friend as well as her husband."

"I know," I cried. "Don't you think I realize I'm the only friend she has? And that that's what makes all of this so much worse? The guilt that I have because Harriet left Alice with me," I sobbed, placing a hand over my heart. "Me," I said, balling it into a fist, this time slamming it hard against my chest. "She'd never wanted to leave her before, you're right, but I was always telling her she should, and I know she has no one else, Aud, but what can I do about it when I'm the one who's done this to her in the first place?"

"Oh, Charlotte." Audrey came to my side, folding her arms around me. "I'm sorry; I'm so sorry. Maybe you're right and Brian will be what she needs," she said, straightening up.

I raked my hands through my hair. "I know you don't believe that, but I really don't know what I can do when she doesn't want me in her house. Harriet isn't as weak as you think," I said, when Audrey reached for the coffeepot and refilled her cup. I held a hand over my own mug and shook my head.

"I've never said 'weak.' Fragile, maybe."

"I felt worse after being in their house."

"I'm not surprised."

"Not just because it was so hard, but I felt this despair as I was driving home," I said, my voice breaking at the memory. "On the one hand they were both clawing at hope and desperate for me to tell them something that would give them an answer. But on the other hand it felt like there was no hope left. I walked out of there feeling like the worst had already happened."

"That doesn't make any sense."

"I know." I thought back to the dark oppressiveness of the living room and the way the walls had felt like they were closing in on me. "Oh God, Aud." I buried my head in my hands again. "How's this going to end?"

"Alice is going to be found," Audrey said, looking at me over the rim of the mug.

"But what if she isn't?" I whispered.

"She will be." Aud was resolute, and I willed myself to believe her.

"How was Tom?" Audrey asked me after we'd fallen into a brief silence.

"He's . . . Tom," I said dismissively, and then shook my head. "No, that's not fair. He's been very good; he just doesn't always get it right." I needed to change the subject. "I want you to be honest with me. Would you leave your children with me again?"

"Oh, for God's sake."

"I need you to tell me the truth," I insisted.

She rolled her eyes. "You know I would."

I didn't answer as I sipped my coffee.

"Charlotte," she said, her voice firm, "there are friends you trust with your children and ones you don't. You are definitely one I would. You know that."

We had talked about it once at a barbecue at Audrey's. She and I were both tipsy when Aud gestured toward Kirsten, a neighbor of hers who was never less than fifteen minutes late picking her children up from school.

"I left the twins at her house the other day," Audrey had told me. "When I went to get them, her oldest, Bobby, was on the glass roof of the conservatory. They'd laid a mattress on the grass and he was jumping onto it. Thankfully my two weren't being so stupid. Or maybe I just got there in time." She'd laughed. "I won't be leaving them with her again. Even if my leg's falling off, I'll wait for you to come over before I go to the hospital."

Audrey smiled and said, "I'd still wait for you first, if that's what you're thinking."

"Thank you," I murmured, though I wondered if she might be the only one.

HARRIET

On Sunday morning Brian and Harriet sat in silence in the back of Angela's car as she drove them to the hotel for their public statement. Harriet's stomach clenched in knots as they passed the familiar landmarks that blurred in a haze.

In the small parking lot, Harriet looked out the window and saw the hotel was one of the generic boxes built away from the coast that always appeared to be filled with suited businessmen rather than vacationers.

Her door opened and she stepped out, shivering, even though it wasn't remotely cold. Brian took her arm and, with Angela on her other side, she was led up the concrete steps and into the reception area.

There was nothing attractive about the orange bricks or the mass-produced paintings that hung behind the reception desk, and the air-conditioning blasted through the conference room, making her wish she'd worn something warmer.

The room was already filled with rows of people, chattering among themselves, oblivious to her and Brian. Angela pointed to the front and told her they would be sitting at the table, where microphones were strategically placed and cameras were facing.

Harriet stood rigidly in the doorway. "I don't think I can do it," she said in a whisper.

She felt Brian move closer, could smell a fresh waft of his aftershave. "We can do this together," he said, never taking his eyes off the front of the room as he slowly walked her past the rows of people who began to lull into silence when they saw them approaching.

A flash of light made Harriet startle, as journalists began snapping photos before they'd even sat down. "Come sit over here," Angela told her as she directed Harriet to a chair, depositing her into it.

"Are you going to be next to me?" she asked.

Angela shook her head as she directed Brian to the chair on Harriet's right. "No, Captain Hayes will be," she said and crouched down. "You'll be fine," she said quietly. "Just remember what we said earlier."

Harriet nodded and glanced over at the young media officer who had come to the house that morning. Kerri had told Harriet she was there to advise them both about the statement, and confidently reeled through a list of instructions that Harriet had only half listened to.

"We should find you something to wear," Kerri had said, looking pointedly at Harriet, who in turn waved her hand toward the wardrobe. Kerri could choose something and she'd wear whatever it was. Though now she felt exposed in the thin white blouse that clung to her skin, and wished she hadn't been so careless that morning in her attempt to shut out what was happening.

The magnitude of the next hour was overwhelming, absorbing all her thoughts. Harriet knew exactly how important this was. She'd been the one sitting at home watching Mason's parents last October and had seen the mother's raw grief seeping from every bone in her body. But then she'd listened to the journalists who'd picked apart the parents' gestures, twisting them and suggesting the unimaginable. His father hadn't looked worried enough, according to one website. His eyes had shone bright with fear, as far as Harriet had seen, but it hadn't taken long for the trolls to label him aggressive. The mother had been caught smiling at her baby when they left the public appeal. Surely that meant she hadn't been affected by her son's disappearance, one paper had said.

People who knew nothing of Mason or his family wondered anyway, "Do you think it was one of them?" How frightening that the media can turn on you in an instant. So Harriet knew exactly how important their appeal for Alice was, and knew it was about much more than looking for her daughter.

Brian fidgeted next to her as she watched the room. The journalists had started chattering among themselves again as they waited for the news conference to start. A burst of laughter arose from the back before the room descended into a guilty silence.

Brian continued to squirm in his chair as though he were uncomfortable. His hands were splayed wide on the desk in front of him as if he were trying to ground himself. A night of no sleep and his usually pristine stubble had turned into the clumsy start of a beard. The gray hairs near his mouth glinted pure white in the false light of the hotel. Her eyes drifted to his hair that tufted up on top and then down to his eyes, heavy from a night of pacing the house. Despite all that, he still looked effortlessly handsome, she thought. The public would like that.

Harriet looked down at her shirt, one of its buttons

straining slightly where it was too tight. She could feel herself sweating where the underwire of her bra cut into her, and feared she might see a damp streak across her chest. Brian had told her she looked beautiful as they all left the house that morning, but she knew she didn't. They'd see he was well turned out, but she had no idea what they'd make of her appearance.

How did Brian still look the same as when they'd first met? She'd overheard Charlotte talking about him to Audrey once. She'd said she found Brian handsome in a way that she'd easily get bored of, but Harriet just thought he was conventionally attractive.

In the bookshop in Edenbridge, Harriet hadn't expected to meet the man she would marry eleven months later. Least of all the one browsing the fishing section. But when Brian had asked her if she came there often, Harriet had laughed at his awkward line and was immediately drawn in by his large brown eyes and cheeky grin.

After their first date he walked her home, taking hold of her hand and smoothly maneuvering around her until he was on the side of the curb. He made her feel safe, and she realized she'd been yearning for a man who would take care of her. Brian had rapidly filled the hole in her life her father had left.

"You are so beautiful, Harriet," he'd told her under the streetlight outside her flat. "I could shout from the rooftops about how lucky I feel." He'd pretended to leap onto a concrete boulder but she'd tugged him back, laughing, before he made a fool of himself. She had never met anyone before who was so effusive about her.

• • •

CAPTAIN HAYES INTRODUCED himself as the crowd settled. Brian's leg juddered up and down beside Harriet, knocking against her thigh, forcing his plastic seat to bump into hers. She had never seen him so nervous.

One of his clammy hands reached for hers under the desk and she could feel the wetness seeping into her palm. He took her hand and laid it on top of the table, clamped inside his. She wanted to pry it away and put it back into the comfort of her lap, out of sight, but she couldn't do that with everyone's eyes on them. *Did you see the mum pull away from him?* they'd say.

Instead she let his hand clutch hers tightly, burning into her skin until Brian eventually pulled away himself and placed his hands palms down on the table. She half expected to see a pool of sweat seep out from under them. Captain Hayes had introduced him now. It was time for him to speak, just as they'd agreed he would.

"I'll do this, Harriet," he'd said firmly as he speared a piece of bacon that Angela had cooked for them. She had pushed hers away, the smell of it making her feel sick. "I'll speak for the both of us so you don't have to worry about it."

"Actually, it would be good to hear from Harriet, too," Kerri had said.

"No, I'll do the talking," Brian continued. "It's what we've agreed."

"Harriet?" Angela had asked with a sideways glance at Kerri, who Harriet could see shaking her head out of the corner of her eye.

"I don't know," Harriet said honestly. "I don't know if I can—"

"I don't think you can either," Brian interrupted.

Harriet had looked up at Angela, who raised her eyebrows at Kerri. Did none of them think she was capable? That Brian should be the one to appeal to the public? "I still think she needs to say something," Kerri had muttered.

Brian's voice boomed into the room, making Harriet jump. "Yesterday afternoon our beautiful daughter, Alice, disappeared." He cleared his throat, straightening his tie with one hand. "I'm sorry," he said, much quieter. "This is very hard for me." He glanced over at Hayes, who nodded at him to continue.

"One minute she was having fun at a school fair and the next, she vanished." His voice was much calmer now as he continued, and Harriet felt herself relax ever so slightly, until he stumbled. "Harriet, my wife, she's, er, well, we—" Brian hesitated, looked down at the table and then back at the sea of faces. "We are begging anyone who knows anything about what happened to Alice to come forward and tell the police. Anything. Please. Because we miss her so much." His voice broke and he bowed his head again, shaking it from side to side. "We want her back. We just want our little girl back."

Harriet stared at him, willing him to keep talking. That couldn't be it. She had a lump the size of a football lodged in her throat, but she knew she needed to say something, because as soon as Brian had left the kitchen earlier, Kerri had implored her to. "You need to speak," she had said. "It's so important they hear you, too. As soon as Brian finishes you need to talk about Alice. Regardless of what he thinks is best," she'd added pointedly.

At the far end of the table Kerri was nodding at her. Harriet looked back at Brian, then at the crowd of strangers in front of her that were becoming uncomfortable in the silence, no doubt wondering if they could ask their questions yet.

"I want Alice back," Harriet blurted, echoing her husband's words as a bolt of heat flashed through her body. She could feel tears running down her face in hot, damp streaks. She didn't know where they'd come from, but they were flowing furiously, her body heaving and jolting as she sobbed.

Brian looked at her in alarm and for a moment both of them froze until he eventually reached an arm around her shoulders and leaned across her, telling Captain Hayes they couldn't say any more.

"We are now open for questions," Hayes announced, and the commotion of hands shooting into the air took the pressure off them and Brian's grip on her arm softened.

A tall man in the front row stood up and introduced himself and asked the detective the question they were told to expect. "Are you linking Alice Hodder's disappearance to Mason Harbridge?"

"We've no reason to suspect that the two cases are linked," Hayes said, "but of course we are looking into the possibility."

"Have you got any other leads?" a female journalist piped up from the back row. She had shoulder-length bobbed hair and cold eyes that hid beneath layers of makeup. She didn't look at Harriet and seemed only interested in the detective. "By the sound of it, there's nothing solid."

"There are a couple of lines of inquiry we're looking into, but nothing we can divulge right now," Hayes said.

Harriet's head snapped around. She knew nothing about other leads. What weren't they telling her? But the questions moved on. This time a man at the far end of the room stood, introducing himself as Josh Gates, who worked for the local newspaper, the *Dorset Eye*. "Mrs. Hodder, I wonder if you could tell me how you feel about the fact your friend was posting on Facebook instead of watching your daughter at the fair?"

"What?" Harriet said, barely audibly. She felt winded, as if someone had come along and punched her in the stomach.

He held up his iPad as if to prove a point. "At the precise time your daughter went missing, she was leaving comments on friends' posts and even wrote one of her own. Her attention was obviously elsewhere," he went on. "So, I just wondered how you felt about that, given she was supposed to be looking after your daughter."

She felt Brian's body press forward, nudging against the desk, certain he wanted to know more. Because if Charlotte was on Facebook, it was proof she wasn't watching Alice and was therefore a careless mother whose children ran feral. Just like he had said.

"I'm interested in what you think about your friend's actions, Mrs. Hodder," Josh Gates said.

"I, erm, I don't know anything about that," she said hoarsely, tugging nervously at her shirt. Charlotte had admitted she'd looked at her phone, but this man's suggestions made her distraction seem so much worse.

"If Mrs. Reynolds was—" Brian started, but Captain Hayes was already shutting the interview down, holding up his hand to stop the journalist and any more questions. Harriet wished he'd let Brian continue. She'd liked to have known what her husband wanted to say.

They were shuffled out of the hotel and back into Angela's car. Angela told them it had gone as well as they could have hoped, but Harriet wasn't listening.

Her head was spinning with what the last journalist had said, and now her window of opportunity to reach out to the world was over. She didn't know if she was supposed to feel something, didn't know if she had done enough, but she felt numb and exposed, and had no idea what to expect next.

NOW

The air-conditioning whirs slowly in the corner, but it doesn't generate enough air to cool down the room, yet instead of taking my cardigan off, I find myself wrapping it tighter around my body. I don't want Detective Rawlings seeing the vibrant blotches of red on my chest: the unmistakable marks of nerves. Pulling the woolen belt around my waist, I hold its ends between my fingers, rubbing them the way I did with my comfort blanket as a child.

"Let's talk a little more about your friendship with Harriet," the detective says. "You said that even though you were close friends you didn't get together with your partners?"

I shake my head. "Hardly ever. There was only one occasion I remember of Brian coming to my house and that was when they came to a barbecue." I don't offer any more. I'd barely spoken to Brian as I'd played host, skirting around groups of friends with offers of drinks and platters of kebabs. I didn't rest until everyone had eaten, and by then Harriet and Brian had already left.

I wonder if Detective Rawlings is skeptical we didn't do more together, because she's hard to read. Her blank expression could be disbelief or dislike for me, I have no idea. But this was the truth. Harriet and I met up during the day when we had the little ones, which suited us both. I had no need to integrate my new friend into the beginnings of my failing marriage and I liked that I had someone I could talk to who didn't know Tom. It meant she was solidly in my corner. I could tell Harriet how it was and I wasn't judged. I was listened to and sympathized with, and on occasion I would make it a whole lot worse than it was, just because it was nice having someone tell me they felt for me.

And yes, I admit I had no desire to spend time with Brian. I recoiled when Harriet told me that every night after Alice had gone to bed they would sit down together in the kitchen and discuss their days. How he would tell her the intricacies of his job in insurance and in return show much interest in her day with Alice. I couldn't tell you what Tom's job actually required him to do, and I doubt he had any idea if I'd taken the children swimming in the last week or if it was months ago. Harriet and Brian's marriage always felt a little too twee for me.

"Yet you must have talked to each other about your home lives," the detective says. "Isn't that what friends do?"

I bite my lip as I think about what I should say. Exhaustion hasn't just crept up on me, it's surging toward me like a tsunami, and I worry that soon I will say whatever I need to to finish this interview.

Rawlings's eyes look red. She must be tired too. Maybe she'd let me leave. Or maybe she knows more than she's letting on and as soon as I show signs of failing to comply, she'll arrest me and leave me no choice. In the end I decide it's not worth the risk.

"Of course. We talked about plenty of things," I say.

"Like what?" Her words sound aggressive, even if that's not her intention.

"Well, I talked about my marriage a lot. Even though Tom and I separated two years ago, things hadn't been good for a while."

I'm sure she isn't interested in the state of my marriage, but my flagging mind is drifting in and out of memories. When I see Harriet and me sitting on our usual bench in the park, the discussion that keeps invading my thoughts is the time I told her Tom and I were splitting up.

"Are you sure it's what you want?" Harriet had said. "You can't try counseling or anything?"

"We tried that," I'd told her. "Well, once anyway. But I found out there's someone else. It's not an affair," I added. "At least not yet, but he's gotten close to someone, sending her messages. You know, ones that are inappropriate if you're married."

I told Harriet that I'd asked Tom outright about the texts, my heart in my mouth, desperate for him to tell me they were nothing. But Tom has always been too honest, and the flush that engulfed his face told me all I needed to know before he stammered an apology that they had been flirting.

"How come you look so sad?" I'd joked to Harriet when the mood had darkened.

"I always thought Tom was a good man," she'd replied.

"He is in many ways. Just not one I can be married to anymore." I smiled.

Harriet reached over and took my hand. "The children will be fine," she'd said. "They have two wonderful parents who love them, and that makes them incredibly lucky. Besides, it's better to come from a broken home than live in one," she said. "Someone once told me that."

I was conscious of the tears building up, but I let them fall. Just to have her total support was all the strength I needed.

"Not many people have what you and Brian have," I'd told Harriet. It was the first time I realized there were benefits to the type of marriage she had.

Detective Rawlings is asking me if Harriet talked about her own marriage, and I tell her she didn't.

Rawlings stares at me, waiting for me to continue. When I don't, she suddenly says, "So tell me about the times you met up with Brian on your own?"

I look up, sitting a little straighter. I hadn't been expecting that.

I hadn't expected her to know. "It was just the once," I say eventually. "Or twice," I add when she continues to watch me carefully. "It was only two times."

"And what did he talk to you about?"

I take a deep breath and release it slowly. I don't know which time I should discuss. It's probably better to focus on the second. "Brian came to my house two days ago," I tell her. "I told Angela Baker," I say defensively. "She's the liaison officer on the case. . . ." I drift off because of course she already knows this. She probably knows about every conversation I've had with Angela and Captain Hayes over the last two weeks.

"Tell me about the other time," Rawlings says. "When was that?"

My fingers reach out for my empty glass, twitching as I grab hold of it. I need to ask her for more water but surely she'll know I'm wasting time, most likely think I've got something to hide. "Six months ago," I tell her, twisting the belt on my cardigan as tight as it can go.

"And why did you meet up?"

"Brian came to see me because he said he was worried."

"About what?" The detective leans forward.

"He said he was worried about Harriet." I shrug. "It was nothing much." I rub the heel of my hand against my right eye and glance up at the clock again. "Do you know how much longer you need me here?" I ask, my voice hoarse.

"It would be helpful if we could continue," she says, cocking her head to one side. We fall into an apprehensive silence.

Eventually I nod. "Brian said he was worried that Harriet was getting things wrong and forgetting things."

"'Forgetting things'?"

"Yes, like where she had been. It didn't seem to be anything major." I give a thin smile, but she doesn't smile back.

"Tell me what Brian said specifically."

I chew the inside of my mouth until I bite too hard and can taste the metallic tang of blood.

"'Specifically'?" I release another deep breath that comes out as a sigh. "He told me Harriet was suffering from postnatal depression. I thought it was ludicrous, because if all he was worried about was the fact Harriet was forgetting things he'd told her, then he only had to speak to Tom. He would tell Brian I forget most things he says because I'm not listening half the time."

I picture Brian standing in my backyard, running his hand across the oak table on the deck as he looked around, and I couldn't tell if he admired my yard or loathed it.

"I'm very worried about my wife," he'd said. "What I'm particularly worried about is that she puts Alice in danger. Yesterday she walked off and left Alice in the car on her own. She forgot she was in there."

Brian stopped running his fingers along the wood and turned to look me in the eye, and I instinctively took a step back.

"Harriet was so preoccupied with getting to the post office to renew her passport before it closed, that she completely forgot about her daughter. Charlotte, anything could have happened," he'd said. "My little girl could have been taken."

BEFORE

HARRIET

"Can I help you with that?" Angela pointed to the dishes on the draining board, taking a tea towel off the oven handle. "I always preferred drying when I was forced to help as a kid." She smiled.

It had been twenty-four hours since Alice had disappeared. Harriet had been trying to keep herself busy so she didn't have to think about how their appeal for their daughter had gone. "I don't mind washing. I've always liked looking out onto the garden while I'm doing it. I think I'd live outdoors if I could."

"Really? Where would your most favorite place to live be?"

Harriet liked that Angela was taking an interest in her, even though she understood the detective's underlying reasons. "By the sea," she said. "When I was little I dreamed of living in a house at the edge of the beach. It had an open porch at the front where I could sit and read and look at the water, and a wooden path that led through the dunes to the water's edge."

"Wow." Angela rested the towel on the draining board. "That sounds wonderful."

Harriet shrugged. "I used to draw it in my mind. I have a picture of it that's crystal clear, and if I close my eyes I can see every bit of it. The shimmering water, the ripples on the sand, the gaps between the boardwalk I can look through. I would picture myself sitting in a chair on the porch, looking out at the sea, imagining." Harriet smiled. "I can imagine anything when I look at the sea."

"I know what you mean," Angela said. "Though I love the forest, too. So is that why you moved to Dorset, to live by the sea?"

"Supposedly." Harriet quickly grabbed the scouring pad and began scrubbing the pan. If she rubbed much harder, the enamel would start chipping, but she didn't relent. Brian had wanted boiled milk and it had left a white layer of skin on the bottom. It was easier to use the microwave, but it wasn't a compromise Brian was prepared to make. He preferred it heated in a pan.

"So do you swim much?" Angela asked.

Harriet stopped scrubbing. She had momentarily lost her picture of the sea house and replaced it with the mundanity of Brian's milk. She'd almost forgotten they'd been talking about it. "No," Harriet replied after a beat. "I can't swim."

"Really?"

She knew this would surprise Angela. Who would want to live by the beach if they were afraid to go in the water?

"Tell me more about moving here," Angela persisted, but Harriet didn't know how to open up that can of worms. She wasn't sure this was even the right time—after all, she'd only known Angela since yesterday.

"You don't have to do this," Harriet said instead, nodding at the mugs and plates that were slowly piling up on the draining board.

Angela shook her head and flicked out the tea towel. "No, I want to help." She picked up one of the mugs and started to dry again. "Did you always live in Kent when you were a child?"

"Yes, I was born there. It's pretty, have you ever been?"

"Yes, I have an aunt who lives in Westerham."

"I know it. It's lovely."

"And it was just you and your mum, then? After your dad died?"

Harriet nodded. "Yes, just me and Mum since I was five. It was all I ever knew."

"That must have been hard," she said. "Your dad dying when you were still so young."

"Yes." Harriet paused. "I do wish I'd had him in my life," she said. "Somehow I think I would have liked him a lot."

Angela smiled sadly. "And what about Brian's mother?" she asked. Harriet looked over as Angela casually put the tea towel down and started wiping a cloth across the draining board.

"I only met her once," Harriet said. "Brian took me to her house a month after we met. He was so excited. He said he wanted to show me off, but his mother had no interest in me. When I left the room I overheard him telling her I was the girl he was going to marry and she laughed, told him marriage was a waste of time, and then said he had to leave because she needed to get ready for bingo. I never saw her again, and as far as I know, Brian hasn't either."

"That's very sad."

Harriet shrugged. "My own mum was different." She gazed out of the window. "We used to live in a two-bed flat that overlooked a park. We didn't have a garden and Mum hated that park. She said it was an accident waiting to happen. We saw a child fall off the monkey bars once and he laid at an angle that wasn't right at all." Harriet cocked her head to one side and stuck out her arm to show how distorted the boy looked. "Mum raced down there, screaming for someone to call an ambulance, shouting, 'Where the hell is this boy's mother?' Thankfully he was okay, but whenever we walked past the park after that, Mum grabbed my hand and sped past it. I don't think I ever went in it again." Harriet stopped and looked up at Angela. "She was a funny one, my mum. I was everything she had and I thought the world of her, but she didn't let me do a lot of things. She was always yelling at me to get down from walls that were only three bricks high in case I fell." Harriet raised her eyebrows.

"She was worried about you. It's what mothers do."

"It was more than that. She'd take my temperature every night just in case I was coming down with a fever. She was always the first mum at the school gate, and even when I went to middle school, she walked me to the bus stop because it was supposedly on her way to the shops. No one needs to go to the shops at eight thirty every morning."

"Why did you let her, then, Harriet?"

"Because I knew what it would do to her if I didn't. Like I said, I was all she had."

"That's a lot to put on a child."

"Maybe. Anyway, it meant I spent a lot more time in my bedroom than most kids and that's where I created my stories. These little alternative lives, like the house by the sea. Sometimes I used to dream I lived there with my whole imaginary family. Mum, Dad, and all my brothers and sisters. Crazy, isn't it?"

"Not at all. I had an imaginary sister. I'm one of four and the rest are boys. I was so desperate for a sister, I made one up!"

"I was one of five in my head. We all used to sit around this big wooden table at Christmas and laugh and make fun of each other. It was chaotic, but I always had someone to talk to if things got bad. It was totally different from reality. Some of the kids at school used to say I was mad. I sometimes forgot I was in public when I was talking to my family." Harriet smiled sheepishly.

"You shouldn't underestimate imagination."

"I didn't want Alice to be an only child," Harriet said, immediately wishing she could take it back. What did she expect Angela to say to that? Harriet turned back to the dishes and started scrubbing the pan again. She'd said far too much. Why had she even mentioned her imaginary family? "What are you all thinking has happened to Alice?" she asked.

"I think the statement this morning will help us gather more intel and put together what happened," Angela said carefully. "It's going to make people think about who they saw at the fair, and hopefully bring them forward."

"So you don't know anything yet, then?" Harriet asked. "Captain Hayes said you had some things you were looking into. Things he couldn't divulge."

"We don't have anything concrete," Angela told her. "I'm sorry."

Harriet nodded and dropped the scouring pad and pan back into the sink. A patch of milk was clinging determinedly to the bottom of the pan, but she could no longer be bothered.

"Harriet, I have to check in at the station in a bit, but I'll come back again after lunch. I'll be around as much as possible, but if there's anything else you need at all, you must let me know. That's what I'm here for." Angela laid the cloth on the counter, her gaze resting on Harriet expectantly.

Harriet nodded. "Thank you." Angela had no idea how much she could talk about.

"We're doing everything we can to get Alice back soon," she said. "I promise you."

"Angela?" Harriet looked up at the woman's face. "What that journalist said about Charlotte, you know, on Facebook when Alice disappeared. Is it true?"

"I believe so, but you shouldn't read too much into it. She may have been on it for mere seconds. Try not to think about that."

Harriet turned and stared out the window. "I don't know what else to think about," she said quietly.

WHEN ANGELA RETURNED to the Hodders' house later that afternoon, she had Captain Hayes in tow. They had news, they told Harriet and Brian. There had been a sighting at the fair. One of the mothers had seen an older man who'd looked suspicious, but she had apparently left the fair before she knew a little girl had disappeared. The grapevine hadn't reached her until she'd watched the news that morning.

"What do you mean acting suspiciously?" Brian demanded, moving in between Harriet and the detective as if sheltering his wife from bad news.

"The woman says she didn't recognize this man and

that he was on his own, wandering about at the start of the fair." Hayes raised his eyebrows in a way that made Harriet think he didn't hold out much hope for the sighting. "She seemed to think there was something not quite right about the way he was circling the field. We have a sketch we'd like you both to look at." Hayes held out a piece of paper that Brian took before Harriet got a chance to look at it.

Brian glanced at it briefly then handed it back to the detective, shaking his head. "I don't recognize him," he said.

"How about you, Harriet?"

Her hands trembled as she reached out for the paper. She didn't want to look at it for fear of what she'd see. What if she recognized the face Brian had so resolutely rebuffed?

"Look at it, Harriet," Brian said, and though he tried to sound calm, she could sense his impatience that she wasn't looking fast enough.

Eventually she dropped her eyes to the page. She shook her head.

"Nothing at all?" the detective asked, though he sounded like this was the answer he'd been expecting, and the whole "sighting" was a complete waste of his time.

Brian took it from Harriet and glanced at it again. "Maybe? There's something oddly familiar about him, I suppose. How much older are you suggesting?"

"Possibly late sixties," Hayes told him. "How do you mean 'oddly familiar'? Can you be a little more specific?"

"There's just something about him that looks like I might have seen him. But—" Brian shook his head. "I can't place him."

"And Harriet," he said, with the smallest hint of a sigh that Hayes had most likely not intended to let out. "Definitely not?"

"Not at all. Sorry," she added.

"Don't be sorry. It was a bit of a long shot. And I apologize for getting your hopes up too. Of course, it doesn't mean we won't be looking into this more," he added, flapping the paper in the air.

Harriet stood by the front door as Hayes left, feeling the welcome burst of outside air as it touched her face. It would be so easy to follow him. Apart from the short drive to the hotel that morning, she hadn't been out and the walls were closing in tighter than usual. She felt trapped, like she was in a coffin and someone was hammering in the final nail. Now she had the overwhelming feeling that if she didn't run out of the door right now, she might never be able to scratch her way out.

"I'm going for a walk to clear my head," she called toward the kitchen, where she could see Angela tidying the table. Brian appeared in the doorway as quick as a rabbit. Harriet grabbed her cardigan off a coat hook and slipped on a pair of shoes that were neatly tucked into the corner beside the fishing rods that still hadn't been moved.

"I'll come with you, darling." He was already reaching one arm across her for his jacket.

"No. Please. I just need to be on my own for a bit." She didn't want him with her, step-by-step at her side, clutching on to her hand as he led her around the block. That wasn't her idea of getting out and being able to breathe.

"Harriet." He held on to her arm like a child who wouldn't let go of his parent. "If you go alone I'll worry about you. I'll feel awful if I'm left here not knowing where you are."

How would she ever be able to escape now? With him looking at her, that forlorn expression hanging on his face. As soon as she stepped outside the house he would follow her, she wouldn't be able to stop him.

"Just let her go," Angela said softly from behind, wiping her hands on a towel. Harriet released a deep breath that made Brian stare at her. "It will do her good," Angela continued, nodding at Brian as she gently pulled his arm away. Harriet took the chance to step outside.

Brian remained rigid in the hallway. She felt him behind her but didn't dare look back. Instead she hurried down the path, running past the reporters, her heart beating fast, expecting any moment he would break free.

She could have cried with relief as her legs carried her as fast as they could away from that house.

CHARLOTTE

I couldn't face going into the office that week, and my manager quickly told me to take as long as I needed. *How long would I need?* I'd thought, putting the phone down on Monday morning. Two days had passed, but it already felt like weeks. There was every possibility that nothing would return to normal again.

For the next couple of days I twisted myself into knots over what I could do to help. I walked up and down the roads that surrounded the field in hopes that I would see Alice, even though I knew my search was futile—the area had been meticulously covered in the hours after she'd disappeared.

I called Captain Hayes and offered to find money to help the search.

"What for?" he had asked me.

"I don't know, PR, any kind of publicity. I can get whatever is needed," I said, sure my stepfather would hand over the money unquestioningly and without expecting a penny back. Funds had been set up for missing people before, appeals for contributions, surely the police would be grateful for the help.

Hayes told me there was no need, but I was getting desperate. I called my mum and asked if she thought we could pay for a private detective, but she told me I should let the police do their jobs.

"What can I do, Aud?" I cried into the phone. "I have to do something. I can't sit around waiting for news."

"I don't know," she admitted. "I think your priority has to be being there for Harriet."

"But she won't see me."

"Maybe ask Angela what you can do," Audrey suggested, and I wondered if I could hear the tiredness in my friend's voice or if I was imagining it. I'd lost count of the number of times I'd called her in the last few days.

"Yes, that's a good idea," I said. "I'm sorry, Aud."

Instead I focused on chores that didn't require thinking between taking Molly and Jack to school and picking them up again. I bought a new mop, a packet of dusters and spray for every surface, and I cleaned my house from top to bottom. I scrubbed the back of cupboards, emptied, cleaned, and refilled the fridge, and scraped away remnants of stickers that were still stuck to the insides of windows I'd replaced two years ago. I sorted through the children's clothes and bought Jack a new pair of pajamas.

On Wednesday I bought fresh food from the butcher and the grocery. But by the time it came to cooking dinner, I was so tired from cleaning that I couldn't concentrate. As I stood by the stove and prepared lasagna, I found myself thinking about Alice, the investigation, and what was in the press, and I ended up throwing everything into one pan and serving it as a pile of mush that the children refused to eat.

"This is really not nice, Mummy," Molly told me, pushing her plate across the table.

"It's 'sgusting," Evie added.

"I know it is," I sighed. "Don't eat it. I'll put a pizza in the oven." I swept up their plates and tipped the food into the trash, trying hard not to acknowledge that everything I did was screaming out failure.

With my back to the children, I tore into a pizza box and was only half listening when Molly said, "Mummy, Sophie said something horrible today."

"Did she, darling, what was that?" I traced my finger over the back of the box until I found the oven temperature.

"She said her mummy said she wasn't surprised you weren't watching Alice."

I spun around, attempting to put the pizza on the counter, ignoring it when I missed and it dropped onto the floor. "What did you say?"

"And she also said she wouldn't trust you to watch the cat. I told Sophie we don't even have a cat and they don't either, but she said I was being stupid and that's not what she meant. What did she mean, Mummy?"

"Nothing." I forced a smile. "It sounds like Sophie's just being silly."

"Sophie said that meant she won't be able to come here to play on her own again."

My fingers felt tingly. It spread quickly into my arms and down my legs. *Please tell me Karen didn't really say this,* a small voice whispered inside me. Karen would call me up after a weekend to tell me she'd had another hellish couple of days because her mother-in-law had popped in again, uninvited. We'd laugh about it until we had tears rolling down our faces, because she always made her stories so amusing.

But that wasn't the kind of thing a six-year-old would make up.

I picked the pizza off the floor, checked it wasn't

covered in dust, and put it in the oven. "I'm sure there's a mix-up," I said, smiling at Molly. "I'll speak to Karen and sort it out."

"I want Sophie to come to tea again," Molly said, hanging her head so I couldn't see her eyes.

"Of course she'll come again," I said, the smile still plastered across my face. "Now you've got ten minutes to go play and I'll call you back when dinner's ready," I said, my voice far too high-pitched. "Go on," I urged, practically pushing her out of the room.

My hands shook as they reached for the island to steady myself as I sat on a stool. I'd been doing fine hiding away, cleaning and scrubbing and doing mindless chores. One stupid remark and I was falling apart again.

Karen had sent me flowers on Monday with a card that said she was thinking of me. They were on the windowsill, tulips, in a variety of colors because she knows I like them.

I reached for my cell, my finger hovering over it. I wanted to hear Audrey tell me I was being stupid, that no one was talking about me. I wanted her to say that Karen would have likely said something else instead and Sophie misconstrued it and it was all a misunderstanding. I wanted to laugh and put the phone down with relief that my friends weren't talking about me behind my back.

But on Wednesdays Aud went to rugby with her boys, so I pressed another button and waited for the dial tone. I'd promised I wouldn't do this, but I couldn't help myself.

"Hey," Tom said when he picked up. "Everything okay?"

"No."

"Charlotte, what's happened? Is it Alice?"

"No, nothing like that."

"You're crying. Tell me what it is." So I told him what Molly had said.

"Oh, Charlotte."

The day we separated I swore I wouldn't rush back to Tom when things got hard. "You make your bed, you lie in it," my mother had said when I told her we were splitting up. "Your father left and tried coming back once, and I was stupid enough to let him. And you know what happened. Besides, the kids won't thank you if you change your mind."

But then again, my mother had never lost someone else's child.

"Call Karen," Tom said.

"I can't."

"Of course you can, she's your friend."

"And say what? 'Do you not trust me anymore?'"

"Ask her what she said."

"Tom, it's not that simple. What if she tells me she did say it? What if she says she means it?" I cried.

I knew I shouldn't have called him. There was no way I could ask Karen what she'd said. I'd sooner let the thoughts eat me up than confront her.

I stared at my phone, wondering what I should do. My cell no longer felt like a lifeline between me and my friends. The initial flurry of messages I'd received in the aftermath of the fair had reduced dramatically. In fact, it was *ping*ing with alerts much less frequently than it had before the weekend, and its silence was unsettling.

I clicked on my group texts again, something I'd been regularly doing in the last few days, but the last message remained fixedly on one that had been sent the day before the fair. I scrolled up and down the various groups: Molly's class, Jack's class, book club . . . there were always messages waiting for me to read. Not a day passed without someone asking about homework or a uniform or setting up a new group for a night out.

I pushed my phone away. I'd tried to ignore what was troubling me—the fear that new group chats had been set up without me, that my friends wanted to discuss things that didn't involve me. But after what Molly had said, I started to believe it was happening.

Since the journalist had pointed out I'd been on Facebook when Alice went missing, I hadn't been able to look at my account and even deleted the app from my phone. Somehow I'd convinced myself that even just logging on would create a trigger for my activity to be monitored. As if someone was waiting for me so they could say, "Hah, see. Here she is again. She can't keep off it." I'd passed my theory by Audrey, who'd told me it was ridiculous, but still I hadn't chanced it.

Once the children were in bed that night, I knew I couldn't hold out any longer. I needed to face whatever was being said. I needed to know. I poured a large glass of wine, which I took up to bed, and, taking a deep breath, I opened my Facebook page.

My pulse raced as I scrolled through posts about up-coming holidays and friends' high-achieving children, furiously searching—for what, I didn't know. A post that stated what a dreadful mother I was? A high number of likes and shocked-faced emojis attached to it?

The more I looked, the more my heart fell into an easier rhythm. I found nothing of the sort, but then I came across a Help Find Alice page that someone had started, asking others to share and post if they had any news.

It had been set up by one of the mums I barely knew, though at some point we'd become Facebook friends. I stared at the profile picture of her and her two girls. If I didn't know her, then Harriet wouldn't either, which made me wonder why she was pioneering this campaign. If anyone was going to do it, it should have been me.

I skimmed over the comments that others had left, but there were so many I couldn't read them all. Most were messages of support and concern. Warnings to others not to let their children out of their sight when there was a monster loose on our streets. Prayers that had been copied and posted attached with personal messages of hope that Alice was found soon. Some chose to share their opinions on what had happened. Many thought it was most likely the same man who'd taken Mason.

My name was mentioned a couple of times. People I didn't know relayed how sorry they felt for me.

"Just goes to show you can't take your eyes off your children for one minute," they said.

"You shouldn't trust anyone, not even at a school fair."

And, "Don't know if it's worse to lose your own child or someone else's."

I clumsily placed my glass of wine on my bedside table, almost knocking it over. I wanted to comment too. I had no idea what I'd say, but I wanted to let them know I was there, reading their thoughts, breathing, living this hell they were talking about.

I closed my eyes, leaning back against the headboard, tears trickling out from beneath my lids. I could read between the lines. They were careful with their words, but the sentiment was obvious: I was careless and I'd lost someone else's daughter.

I know that's what they meant because it was what I thought about myself.

I should have stopped looking then and put my phone away, happy that I hadn't found anything vitriolic, but instead I sat upright and tapped Alice's name into the Google search bar. It was with a strange determination to punish myself that I knew I wouldn't give up until the damage was done, and it didn't take long to find what I was looking for.

I first found my name in a comments section of the *Dorset Eye* website beneath an article written by Josh Gates, the journalist from the appeal. His vindictive piece had attracted the attention of locals. Names I didn't know, some anonymous, all thrilled at the chance to let rip and confirm I must be an awful mother.

I should never have been allowed to look after someone else's child, apparently. Mine should be taken away from me because quite obviously they weren't safe. If I'd lost their child they wouldn't be able to help themselves, one said. What he would do, he didn't explicitly say, but the threat was clear.

I balled my fist into my mouth, gulping large breaths of air that I couldn't swallow down. These were people who lived near me. They came from Dorset, maybe they were even from my village, and they hated me. Every one of them hated me.

I slid down under my duvet, pulling it over my head. Screwing my eyes tightly shut, I sobbed and screamed under the covers until I must have fallen asleep.

THE FOLLOWING MORNING I bundled the children into the car for school, hiding my red, raw, swollen eyes behind sunglasses. After leaving Jack at the school gate and taking Molly to her classroom, I was walking back across the playground with Evie when Gail called out to stop me. "Hi, I'm glad I've caught you," she said breathlessly as she struggled to catch up.

"Hi, Gail, how are you?"

She flicked a long, sleek black ponytail over her shoulder, pushing her own dark glasses on top of her head. After last night I was glad to have Gail seek me out. I even felt guilty for the way I sometimes moaned about her. Gail wasn't so bad, even if she could be high maintenance.

"Oh, I'm fine, my lovely, I'm fine."

"That's good."

"I just wanted to catch you because I don't need you to take Rosie to ballet tonight."

"Wh— What do you mean?" I stammered. "I always take Rosie to ballet."

"Oh, I know, but tonight she's getting a lift with Tilly's mum. She offered and, you know—well, to be honest, I didn't know if you'd be going or not so I said that would be fine." Gail flashed me a row of white teeth and took a step back, already preparing her exit.

"I'm still taking Molly," I said. "So it's not a problem for me to take Rosie, too. And Tilly lives on the other side of the village."

"Oh, well, thank you, Charlotte. But I might as well let her go with Tilly, as I've agreed to it."

"Right," I said. "I see."

"Well, I'll see you soon," Gail said, waving and turning on her heel.

"Gail!" I called before I had time to consider what I was about to say. "Wait a minute." I dragged Evie across the playground. "Do you really think you can't trust me to take your daughter to ballet? You're worried I might come home without her?" My voice cracked as I spoke and I knew I was going too far.

"No! God no, my lovely, nothing like that," she said, smiling that smile again that didn't reach her eyes. "Like I said, I just didn't know if you'd be going or not."

"You could have asked me," I cried. "That's all you needed to do. You could have just asked first."

"Yes, I know, I realize that now of course. Silly me." She gave a small, stupid laugh and I thought if I reached out I could slap the fake smile right off her face. I whisked Evie toward my car as quickly as her little legs would take her.

"SHE'S A STUPID bitch!" I cried on the phone to Audrey as soon as I got home. "What are they all saying about me? And don't say nothing, because I know they are."

"Take no notice of Gail. She's narrow-minded and neurotic. She's bound to overreact."

"You know that's not true, she's only saying what everyone else is thinking," I said, telling her what Karen had reportedly said. "Does everyone think I can't be trusted?"

"No. Of course not."

"Then why does it feel like that?" I said. "I've seen the comments online, Aud. Have you read them? I have. Look at them. Read the article on the *Dorset Eye* website. No, better still," I said, grabbing my phone and flicking up the internet, "I'll send you the link."

"Charlotte, you need to calm down. Whatever these comments are saying, they're just trolls. They're nasty people with small-town attitudes and nothing better to do. These are not the thoughts of anyone who matters, and you know that deep down."

"But it's about me. It's personal. They're talking about me." I slumped into a chair. "So it doesn't matter what I know deep down because this is my life they're discussing."

"I know, honey, I know," she said calmly. "But they aren't your friends. They aren't anyone who knows and loves you."

"Except they are. It's Karen and Gail."

"Who haven't said anything horrible about you," Audrey said. "They just act stupidly sometimes. They're putting their families first and maybe they don't even know what to do for the best, but they'll regret it if they know they've hurt you."

"Did they say anything about me before?" I asked. "Was I judged before Alice went missing?"

"Charlotte," Audrey sighed. "No, of course not. What happened to Alice could have happened to any one of us. It is horrific, but it didn't happen because of you or anything you did."

"Then how come it feels like it did?" I said in a whisper.

Before hanging up, Audrey reminded me about the school social the following Wednesday. "You should come along."

"It's another six days away," I said. "Anything could happen by then." I didn't want to think what I meant by that, but my hope was that Alice would be found. The thought of another week passing and still no news was unimaginable.

"Of course, and God hoping little Alice will be found safe and sound. But think of the social as a time for you to speak to the people you think are talking about you, and then you can put your mind at rest."

"Maybe."

"Seriously, Charlotte, you should."

I promised Audrey I would think about it, but I knew I wouldn't go. I'd rather continue hiding than face the mothers who'd be watching me with fascination. As soon as I put the phone down, it rang again. It was Captain Hayes asking if I would be in for the next hour. I told him I wasn't going anywhere and mindlessly watched *Sesame Street* with Evie as I waited for him.

When he arrived I took him through to the kitchen, making small talk as I made a drink for Evie, who was demanding a snack and asking if the policeman would play with her.

"No, Evie," I said, handing her a packet of raisins and an apple. "Go back to the playroom and I'll be in soon."

"Sorry," I said to the captain, once she was gone. "Do you have kids?"

"Yes, I have two," he said gravely. "Mrs. Reynolds, I have some news."

"Oh?" The look on his face told me it wasn't going to be good.

"I'm afraid we've found a body."

HARRIET

W hat does this mean?" Brian paraded back and forth in the small kitchen like a caged animal.

"We don't know," Angela told them.

"But the body wasn't that far away?"

"No," she said. "Less than five miles from where he was taken."

"And it's definitely Mason?" Brian asked.

"Yes, I'm afraid he's been identified."

"That poor family," Harriet cried. "I can't even imagine how they're feeling. I can't even think—"

"Then don't," Angela said. "There's still nothing that suggests what happened to Mason is linked to Alice."

"So what *did* happen to him?" Brian demanded. "How did he die? Was he killed straightaway?" He had stopped pacing, his hands gripping the back of a chair as he pressed forward, leaning toward Angela.

"I understand you want to know, but I can't give you the details yet."

"And I don't want to hear them." Harriet moved her hands to cover her ears.

Brian moved to his wife's side and carefully peeled her hands away from her head. "And you don't need to, my love," he said, kissing the back of them, his lips lin-

gering on her skin, leaving a moist patch when he
pulled them away. He slid into the chair beside her.
"You shouldn't have to be thinking about any of this," he
said.

He left her no option *but* to think about it, as he
continued to ask Angela questions about Mason that
she repeatedly told him she couldn't answer. Brian's
grip on her hands remained tight. His face was close;
she could feel his warm breath touch her cheeks in
puffs as he spoke. The scent of his day-old aftershave
trickled up her nose and into her throat each time she
breathed in.

Eventually Harriet extracted herself, making the excuse that she needed the bathroom.

Her heart broke for little Mason's parents. They had
no hope now—all they had was a finality that didn't
make anything better. She wanted to write and tell
them how sorry she was, and that she understood how
their lives must have shattered. Only she didn't understand. Because Harriet still had hope. So instead she
wrote down her thoughts in the little Moleskine notebook that she kept hidden under a floorboard in her
bedroom, and wished they were getting comfort elsewhere.

More comfort than Harriet was getting. She and
Brian swept like ghosts around the house that now
groaned with loneliness. He would reach out to touch
her, utter words in her ear, but they weren't comforting.
Each step she took on the wooden staircase echoed eerily back at her. In the hallway the Ikea lamp no longer
cast any warmth, just a long, menacing shadow along
the floorboards.

The living room looked as if it had been swept
clean of any trace of Alice. Harriet's fingers itched to

grab hold of the plastic toy boxes so perfectly stacked in a corner and overturn them, making it look like her daughter was still there. Had she been the one to hastily tidy them away once Alice had gone to bed last Friday night, or was it Brian who'd meticulously set things to order, restoring the room to a child-free area?

But Harriet knew she couldn't start throwing Alice's toys all over the house. She could imagine what Brian would say if she did. It would give him another reason to convince her she should have taken the medication she knew didn't exist.

At times she would just sit on Alice's bed, running her hand across the pink duvet embroidered with birds, still ruffled from her daughter's last sleep. Harriet would look for the indent in the pillow where Alice's head had last lain, imagining her blond hair splayed around her in a fan, but the image was rapidly vanishing.

Now there was just Hippo on the bed, where she had carefully placed him after finding him wedged next to Alice's car seat. It broke Harriet's heart into two clean pieces to think of Alice without the gray hippo that had always gone everywhere with her.

Over the week, the sense of Alice in the little girl's bedroom had diminished until Harriet was left wondering what was imagination and what was real. It was so frightening that Harriet started writing everything down in her book again.

Eventually she entered the bedroom less and less, but the thought of Alice somewhere else, sleeping in a place she couldn't imagine, opening her eyes and not being able to see her string of butterflies hanging in the window, was slowly and painfully killing Harriet.

• • •

ONE WEEK HAD passed since Alice had vanished and her disappearance was still hot news. A handful of journalists continued to hang around outside their gate now that Mason's body had been found, and there was more interest than before.

Harriet still read everything she could, however painful. Often she would lock herself in the bathroom with Brian's iPad and scour websites to see what people were saying. Then she would delete the search history. Brian wouldn't understand her need that had turned into an obsession. He would only point out how un-healthy it was.

Maybe he was right. She didn't need strangers voicing their opinions about them. It was Angela's opinion that counted. She was the person living Harriet's hell with her, yet she was giving little away.

Harriet liked having Angela in her life. She thought they could have been friends in very different circum-stances. Harriet wondered what Angela was feeding back to her bosses at the station. It was her job to watch and cast judgments on their tiny family, so she must have opinions. What did she make of them, danc-ing around each other like two strangers trapped in a prison of their own misery? Angela had eaten with them, waited while they slept, seen them at their worst. What was Brian telling her when Harriet wasn't in the room?

When Angela had left that evening, Brian turned on Harriet. "I'm not the only one who's worried about you," he said, shuffling far too close to her on the sofa, the smell of stale coffee drifting off his breath.

"What do you mean?"

"Other people have noticed, too," he said. "I'm only telling you this for your sake."

"What are you talking about, Brian?"

He sighed, rubbing his hands up and down his jeans. "When you went out for a walk the other day, Angela specifically told you she didn't want you going out on your own, but you ignored her and went anyway. Why are you doing this to me, Harriet?"

"Angela never said that," Harriet said, slowly shaking her head as she thought back.

"Yes she did, my love." Brian turned around to face her, furrowing his brow and cocking his head to one side as he studied her. His eyes drifted to her hairline and he reached out to gently push her hair back. "You said you needed to go out for a little walk, but Angela told you it wasn't a good idea and asked you to stay in the house. Yet you were insistent. Even when she told you it wasn't safe," he said, his hand remaining on her scalp.

Harriet stared at her husband.

"I just need to understand why you're doing this to me."

"I'm not doing anything to you. Angela didn't tell me I shouldn't go out," she said again.

"Oh, Harriet, you don't remember, do you?" he said, inching nearer still. He took hold of her arms, rubbing his thumbs across the fleshy skin above her elbow. "I knew this would be the case," he continued.

"Brian. I know Angela didn't say that to me. I would have remembered. If she had told me not to go out, I wouldn't have."

"Oh, Harriet." He shook his head again. "Do you have any idea how hard this is for me? I'm trying to deal with Alice and I can't worry about you, too." He gripped her a little harder. "There are things you choose to forget."

When Harriet didn't answer, he carried on. "We'll go

back to the doctor. I'll make an appointment for Monday morning."

"I don't need to see a doctor." She would be firm over this. She would not have a doctor brought in again.

With one last squeeze he let go of her arms and stood up, pacing over to the window. Brian's head hung low. She watched his shoulders heave slowly. Up, down, up, down.

When she couldn't bear the tension any longer she said, "Fine. I'm sorry. I believe you. I remember it now; I know what you're saying about Angela is right. So I don't need to see a doctor again, Brian."

"That's good, my love," he said, turning back and smiling at her, his dark, hooded eyes reflecting the light of the evening sun. "I knew you would."

NOW

It's clear Detective Rawlings has decided she doesn't like me, as she looks at me with scrutinizing eyes that frown under her thinly plucked eyebrows. I am not the kind of mum she would want to be friends with, though I doubt she has children of her own.

She is interested in the differences between Harriet and me. Not the glaringly obvious ones like money and houses, but the little nuances that separate us.

"You were happy to share everything about your life," she comments. "But Harriet didn't do the same with you?"

She already knows the answers to most of her questions. I'm sure her intent is to point out my shortcomings.

"I don't share everything," I say in defense. "Many parts of my life are private."

"But you talked about your upbringing and the intricacies of your marriage."

"With Harriet, yes," I say. "But Harriet is a friend, it's what friends do."

"Yet Harriet didn't open up to you in the same way?"

"Look, I don't really know what you're getting at." I don't mean to snap, and wonder if I have overstepped the mark.

"Don't you, Charlotte?"

"Harriet told me what she wanted to. I can't force someone to talk about their home life if they don't want to," I reply.

"Or maybe you didn't try," she says, and leans back in her seat as if satisfied with her trump card.

My fingers stop fidgeting with my belt and instead clench tightly until I can't stand the pressure. I know she thinks I wasn't a good friend to Harriet, that I took more than I gave, but her judgment angers me. She has comfortably positioned herself on Harriet's side, if there are sides to be taken. Before I even walked in this room she'd probably made her judgment.

"I'm going to have to take another break if you want me to answer more questions," I say sharply.

"Of course, of course. Take as long as you need." She gestures to the door but doesn't smile, and again I wonder if I should tell her I'm not prepared to stay any longer.

Once I get out into the fresh air of the courtyard, I call Tom. "How are the children?" I ask before he has the chance to speak. "Are they asleep?"

"Of course," he says. He sounds drowsy himself, as if I have woken him up, but if I have I don't particularly care.

"What about Molly?" I say. "Has her temperature gone down?"

"I think so," he says. "She's fast asleep though."

"Go check on her," I tell him. "If she feels hot, the thermometer's in the bathroom."

"Charlotte, I know where the thermometer is," he says. "Are you sure you're all right?"

"I'm fine. It's just taking longer than I thought it would."

"You're still at the station?" He sounds surprised. "I thought you'd be on your way home by now."

"Hopefully I won't be much longer. Obviously they have a lot they need to get straight," I say.

"But they're not, you know, suspecting you of anything?" he asks cagily. "I mean, they don't think you've done anything wrong, do they?"

"No." I feign a laugh. "Of course not. Like I told you earlier, I'm here to help them, that's all. It's better I get it done now and then hopefully they won't need to speak to me again."

"Yeah, of course. It just feels like you've been there a really long time."

"I have, Tom, it's been nearly four hours," I say, glancing at my watch.

"Right." I can tell he's trying to figure out what is really going on, wondering if there is anything I'm not telling him. But then Tom thinks I tell him everything. Just as the clever detective pointed out—people like me tell everyone what's going on in their lives.

"And is there any other news?" he asks. "You know—about—"

"No," I say as I rest my head against the wall. "Not that I've been told." I don't know if they would tell me anyway.

"Okay, well, look after yourself." I guess he's ready to go back to sleep. "Call me when you're out."

"I will. Thank you," I add, hoping he won't ask me what for, but I'm grateful he is there for me, caring for me in a way I no longer expect anyone else to.

Soon after Jack was born I remember Tom saying something to me that hadn't had much resonance at the time. "You'll always be the mother of my children now," he'd told me. "Whatever happens, I'll never stop caring for you."

I had brushed him off then, but now I know he meant it, and as reassuring as that is, it makes the distance between me and my family stretch unbearably further apart.

When I hang up I head back into the station, my heart feeling as heavy as my legs as I drag myself to the vending machine for another coffee. As I wait for the cup to fill, I catch sight of Detective Rawlings at the far end of the hallway, ushering someone inside through the front door. As the detective steps to one side and the bright lights flood the front entrance, I realize she's speaking to Hayes, who must have just arrived. And while I should be relieved to see a familiar face, I can't help but feel my heart sink a little lower.

BEFORE

HARRIET

On Sunday morning, eight days after Alice had disappeared, Harriet woke at 6 a.m. and walked out of the house. She had checked first to make sure Brian was still sleeping. He was, which was no surprise as he'd been scratching around downstairs for most of the night, only coming to bed in the early hours of the morning.

She noticed his sleeping patterns had changed in the last week. The previous day he'd taken himself fishing, but only an hour had passed before he'd come home to be with Harriet. And while she'd always been the first to bed, Brian usually followed shortly after. But this past week Harriet had lain in bed alone, barely sleeping while Brian stayed up until 2 or 3 a.m., prowling around beneath her. What he was doing she had no idea.

Harriet had crept downstairs, slipped on the shoes that were tucked under the coat pegs, and carefully opened and closed the front door behind her so she wouldn't wake her sleeping husband. She was grateful there were no waiting journalists this early as she took a deep breath of the morning air and climbed into her car.

As she drove along the nearest stretch of coastline, she glanced out at the cliffs. They were high and jagged with sheer drops to the sea below that would crash into the rocks when the wind picked up. The unlit road could be dangerous at night and there had been a few occasions where a speeding car had driven over the edge. A dented barrier ran parallel to the road, a sobering reminder in the daylight.

Harriet drove for another five minutes until she reached a sharp turn where she pulled off and headed down a stony track to a car park.

She loved it here. The beach itself was tiny and very pebbly. Alice always complained that she didn't like walking over the stones to the sea because they hurt her feet, but Harriet thought it was beautiful. The water was as clear as glass and she could sit at the edge and wiggle her toes while Alice filled up her bucket with stones.

Harriet opened the trunk, pulled out a small bag from under the picnic blanket, and walked to the beach. It looked so peaceful, she thought, as she pulled off her dress and laid it on the stones. Fiddling with the straps of her red swimming costume, she walked into the water one tentative step at a time, keeping her eyes on the horizon. The cold didn't bother her. It numbed her, and she needed to not be able to feel anything, even just for a moment.

With each pull of the tide, the water gradually built up over her body, as inch by inch it devoured her. It crept up her thighs and lapped around her waist, slowly edging up to her armpits until the rest of her body was submerged. Harriet plunged her head under and held it there as long as she could before she needed air. The release was instant. She felt anesthetized and it was a glorious feeling, but one that never lasted long enough.

Soon Harriet was swimming, farther out till she had to tread water to stay afloat and keep her blood circulating. Each time she sank her head under, only the basic desire to survive brought her back up again.

DESPITE TELLING ANGELA she couldn't swim, there was actually a time when Harriet swam in the sea every week of the year. Christie, her friend from university, had gotten her into it. Harriet loved the euphoria she felt when she let the water consume her. Nothing compared to that moment of pure bliss when she became part of nature and it a part of her.

Then one day she stopped. It was six weeks into her wonderful new relationship with Brian. He'd surprised her, showing up at her door with a large picnic basket and driving thirty miles to the beach.

"I know it's your favorite place," he'd said, and she'd felt herself falling even deeper. She remembered praying nothing would jeopardize their relationship. No one had ever made her feel so special.

On the sand Brian had laid out a checked blanket and they'd talked and laughed and fed each other strawberries.

"Doesn't it look inviting," she said, nodding toward the water as they held hands and wandered to its edge, paddling as the waves lapped around their feet. The tide pulled out, farther than before, and sent the water swishing back to them rapidly and much more forcefully. Harriet shrieked with childish delight, but Brian had leapt back, a look of ridiculous panic on his face.

"I'm going to sit on the blanket," he'd said and turned on his heel, leaving her no choice but to follow.

Back on the safety of the sand, Brian's face was flushed with embarrassment as he admitted that not only could he not swim, he also had a fear of the water. She begged him to open up to her, but the more she'd pushed, the more he'd withdrawn, until he'd eventually snapped, "I don't like to talk about it. But something happened to me as a child."

He'd looked away and Harriet hadn't said anything, just reached out to him, touching his leg. Brian had flinched and said quietly, "My mother wasn't that attentive. She thought it didn't matter if I went into the sea on my own when I was six years old. Didn't even notice I'd been dragged under the water till some stranger shouted out to her."

"Oh, Brian," Harriet had said. "I'm so sorry."

"It's really not a problem," he'd said with a sudden turn of tone and began packing up the unfinished picnic. Harriet knew she needed to do something. The day was turning sour and she could already feel Brian slipping away from her. With an overwhelming sense of pity and fear that she might lose him for good, Harriet told him the first thing that came into her head, which was that she couldn't swim either.

Brian had stopped packing away the food and turned to her. He'd cupped her face in his hands, and with a serious look told her, "I'm now absolutely certain that we're right for each other." He seemed so grateful at her little white lie that at the time she didn't think about its consequences—that while they were together she would never be able to go into the sea again. But then she was so in love with Brian, it seemed such an easy thing to give up.

Harriet had lived with her lie ever since. She'd lost touch with many of her friends, including Christie, not long into her relationship with Brian, so there was no threat of him finding out the truth by accident. The subject rarely came up now, but if it did, Harriet had simply gotten used to telling people she couldn't swim.

THAT SUNDAY MORNING Harriet drove home and was back in the house by 7:40 a.m. Brian was still asleep, so she crept into the bathroom, burying her wet suit at the bottom of the laundry basket where he'd never find it. The smell of salt water was hard to hide, and as she let the warm water of the shower cascade over her body, she wondered what Brian would actually do if he found out.

"All I ask is that you're truthful with me, Harriet. It's not too much to ask for, is it?" He always begged her for honesty. As if there were much honesty in their marriage.

The following morning Harriet's phone *ping*ed with the alert of an unexpected text.

"Everything okay?" Angela asked as Harriet stared at the message.

"Yes. I've just heard from an old friend."

"Oh?"

It was a surprise to her too. "It's funny," Harriet said, "I was only thinking about my university friends yesterday and now one of them has texted me."

"What does it say?" Angela asked as she filled a bucket with water. She'd offered to clean the kitchen floor, though it looked spotless to Harriet.

She read the text aloud. "'I don't know if this is still your number, but I saw you on the news. I want you to know I'm thinking of you. Let me know if there's anything I can do.'" Harriet looked up. "It's from my friend Jane. She was one of my best friends at uni. She, Christie, and I did everything together."

"That's nice that she got in touch with you."

"Yes it is. I haven't seen her for ages. Well, neither of them, actually."

"Why's that? Did you just drift apart?" Angela turned off the tap and heaved the bucket onto the floor. Harriet wondered if she was expected to help, but cleaning was the last thing she wanted to do.

"No," Harriet said. Angela paused expectantly, the mop poised in the air. "Well, maybe we did. I don't remember exactly," she said, absently running a finger over the phone. Of course she remembered every detail.

"I liked Jane and Christie a lot. I never had many friends at school. I wasn't one of the popular girls and I guess it didn't help that my mum kept me so—" She waved a hand in the air. "What's the word I'm looking for?"

"You mean the way she was so protective over you?" Angela asked.

"Yes. She didn't let me out of her sight, really. It's hard to make friends when your mum is always hovering nearby."

Angela dipped her head away before Harriet caught her expression. Did Angela think she was becoming her own mother? It was painfully clear there were more similarities than Harriet would have liked.

"Jane was like me," she went on. "Studious and sensible. Others probably thought we were boring." She smiled at the memory. "Christie was wilder, though. Not into clubbing or anything like that, but she was more adventurous. She had this crazy, curly, red hair. It was her who got me into—" Harriet stopped abruptly and fiddled with her top. How easily she'd nearly revealed the truth. It went to show how little she talked about her old friends. "Christie loved traveling. When we left uni she went backpacking; she wanted me to go with her."

"But you didn't?"

Harriet shook her head. "I've never even been abroad." She smiled sadly. "Can you believe it? I've never had a passport."

Angela dipped the mop into the bucket, splashing water over its edge. She looked up at Harriet. "Really?"

She could see Angela was shocked, but surely it wasn't that unusual.

"You really don't need to do that." Harriet pointed at the floor. "It's not that dirty."

"I just want to be helpful." Angela smiled. "So, do you miss your friends?"

"I didn't think so, but hearing from Jane now . . ." Harriet trailed off.

"Then text her back and tell her how nice it is to hear from her and say you'd like to talk. It's not too late to get back in touch, Harriet. Good friends will be there, no matter how much time has passed."

"Only I don't think I was all that kind to her," Harriet said softly.

"What happened?" Angela asked, genuinely surprised.

"It was a couple of months after I'd started seeing Brian. Jane used to invite me to stay at her flat, but the invitation never openly extended to him. I didn't mind because it was nice seeing her on my own, but Brian didn't like it. He said if she was such a good friend, she wouldn't be trying to keep me away from him." Harriet remembered how upset he was. She'd told him over and over that she was sure he'd be welcome too, but Brian had blankly refused to listen.

"The thing is, I don't think Jane would have wanted him, but she was too nice to say it. Only Brian wouldn't let it drop. He'd say, 'She doesn't like the fact you have a boyfriend, Harriet. Girls like her can't stand it when their friends are happier than them.'

"Schadenfreude, my love," he would say to her. "It's completely obvious Jane is jealous of you and will only be happy if you are miserable."

But that wasn't Jane. Jane had raced out of her exam when she found out Harriet's mum had died, scooping her up from the floor of the hospital corridor where she'd still been curled up in a ball half an hour later. She'd stood by her side at her mum's funeral, and when Harriet went onstage to accept a Promising Student award, it was Jane who'd sat in the allocated family seats, loudly whooping for her best friend.

"I took Brian's side and asked Jane if she was jealous of me. She said I was crazy, and I'd tried telling Brian he'd gotten it wrong, but he said, 'Of course she's saying that, she's completely manipulating you.'" Harriet took a breath. "I believed him," she said with a thin smile. "No, actually I never believed him; I just chose him."

"Oh, Harriet," Angela sighed. "I'm sure Jane will forgive whatever happened in the past. She obviously cares enough about you to get in touch, and besides," she said, resting the mop against the sink and reaching out to take Harriet's hand, "I think you could do with a friend right now."

Harriet shook her head. "I don't deserve her." She withdrew from Angela and began fiddling with cups in the sink.

"Do you keep in touch with anyone else from your past, from the school you worked at in Kent?" Angela asked.

Harriet shook her head, thinking of Tina. The reason they had moved to Dorset. "No. Everyone else disappeared from my life too," she said flatly.

Angela opened her mouth as if she were about to speak, but before she had the chance, her cell rang. "It's Hayes," she said, gesturing toward the hallway. "I'll take it in there." She answered the phone as she left the kitchen. "What the hell do you mean?" Angela murmured, disappearing into the living room and closing the door behind her.

Harriet stepped forward. Angela's voice was muffled, but Harriet could just make out what she was saying.

"Who? Brian? But why would he do that? No, you're right," Angela sighed. "This changes things a lot."

CHARLOTTE

When the doorbell rang on Monday morning I'd been lost in thought. None of us expected a whole week would come and go with no news of Alice. I had dropped the children at school, Evie at nursery, and phoned the office to explain I still couldn't face coming in, and as was frequently the case, my mind wandered to thoughts of Harriet and Brian.

When the bell blasted a second time, I answered the door to a man who looked vaguely familiar. He had a goatee and eyes that bulged under a fringe that hung slightly too long.

"Charlotte Reynolds? I'm Josh Gates," he said, holding out a hand, a gaudy, gold signet ring glistening on his little finger. I shook it tentatively. "How are you today?" he asked in the irritatingly confident manner of a salesperson. I told him I was fine.

"I'm with the *Dorset Eye*."

"Oh." Now I knew where I'd seen him. He was the journalist at the news conference who'd accused me of being on Facebook when Alice disappeared. The one who'd subsequently written a piece in the paper. "I have nothing to say," I said and started closing the door, but quick as a flash Josh's foot stopped me from pushing any farther. "Please," I said, "can you move your foot?"

"I wondered if you'd like to tell your side of the story? Make sure people know the truth?"

"I told you I don't have anything to say. Now move your foot." I pushed the door again but it wouldn't budge.

"Actually, I don't mean about this case. I mean the other story, Charlotte."

"What other one? What are you talking about?"

"Beautiful place you have here," he said, peering over my shoulder. "Must be worth a fair bit. Maybe I could come in so we can chat inside?"

"I asked you what you're talking about," I said through gritted teeth.

"Well, I've heard this isn't the first time you've lost a child."

"What?"

"And that one time your little boy, Jack, went missing."

"I don't, I—" I shook my head. In the corner of my mind, I saw a flash of the time Josh was talking about. I saw the only person who knew what I'd done, and I saw tiny pieces of my loosely-held-together world falling apart.

"Apparently he went off one afternoon and you didn't realize he was gone?" He raised his eyebrows in dramatic shock.

"Who have you been speaking to?" I cried, though of course I already knew. I just couldn't believe Harriet would do it.

"So it's true?"

"Get off my property," I said, and kicked Josh's foot out of the doorway, slamming it shut. "Get away from my house!" I screamed from the other side of my door. "I'm calling the police."

"I can always speak to the newsagent who found him, if you'd rather?" Josh shouted back.

"Just piss off!" I cried. I slumped back against the front door, sliding down it, burying my head in my hands. The room spun around me, bringing with it waves of nausea. Why was everyone so interested in me? They should be focusing on the monster who had taken Alice, but instead their attention was on me. Why was everyone so eager to make sure *I* was the one to blame?

IT WAS THREE years ago when Jack went missing. I'd walked home from the shops with the children, Molly asleep in the double buggy, her baby sister next to her screaming all the way, while Jack scooted a few feet ahead. As soon as I let us into the house, I needed to feed Evie before she woke Molly up.

"I hope you're not going to be this demanding forever," I'd murmured, lifting Evie out.

I pushed the stroller into the hallway and settled Evie on my lap in the living room. Jack was quiet and I'd assumed he was playing with his new set of trains.

With Evie latched, silence filled the house. I rested my head on the back of the sofa, closed my eyes, and let the exhaustion take over. My body ached with tiredness and it didn't take long for me to drift off to sleep while Evie fed.

When I woke with a start, Evie's eyes were fluttering closed in the early stages of sleep. I didn't want to disturb her, but I called out quietly to Jack anyway. He didn't answer, but then he didn't always, so I lay my head back and closed my eyes again.

When the phone rang I ignored it. I didn't want to

move and I was loath to transfer Evie to her crib. When it stopped and immediately started ringing again, I carefully maneuvered Evie onto the sofa and got up to answer it. As soon as I walked into the hallway, the first thing I noticed was that the front door was wide open.

"Jack, where are you?" I called out. I was sure I'd closed it behind me. Evie started crying again. I could see her squirming on the couch that I knew I really shouldn't have left her on, but Jack still wasn't answering. ·

"Jack?" I checked my watch. We'd been home for over half an hour. "Jack?" His name caught in my throat as I sprinted up the stairs, looking into each of the rooms. "If you're hiding, you need to come out right now."

The phone rang and stopped and began again. It must have been the fifth time when I picked it up and cried, "Yes?" into the receiver, only to hear the calm voice of Mr. Hadlow from the corner store telling me Jack was at his counter. Someone walking past had found him outside his shop.

"WHY DID YOU never tell me that?" Audrey asked when she turned up fifteen minutes after Josh Gates had left. I was still sitting on the hallway floor when she'd arrived.

"I didn't tell Tom, either."

I couldn't have told my husband because it would have confirmed I was failing. I couldn't have told my mother who would have reminded me three children was more than I could handle, and I didn't tell Audrey because she would have told me "these things happen," but I would have still seen the shock on her face. Audrey locks the door behind her, she doesn't leave car doors wide open all night by mistake. She doesn't lose her sunglasses case or her watch or her children, and Audrey would never ever lose someone else's child.

"But you told Harriet?"

"Is that the important bit right now?" I said, though I did feel guilty. I couldn't tell her I'd confided in another friend because I'd wanted someone who wouldn't've judged me. Not when Aud was the only friend not judging me right now.

"Yes and no," Aud said. "She's obviously talked to this horrible Gates character."

"I only told her to make her feel better about herself," I admitted.

"How?"

"She was panicking about something utterly unimportant. Forgetting to pack a spare nappy for Alice or something. I don't even remember what it was. It was a year after I'd lost Jack anyway. I wanted her to realize that mums aren't perfect, even the ones she seemed to think were." We both knew Harriet put me on a pedestal. "I told her to make her feel better and made her promise not to tell a soul."

"Well, she's done that all right."

"I even said, 'Don't tell Brian,' and she said, 'Oh God, no, I would never tell Brian,' so I didn't worry about it going any further."

"That's an odd thing to say."

"What is?"

"'God, no, I would never tell Brian.'"

"Maybe."

"I'd never say that about David."

"Oh, Aud," I sighed. "Does it really matter?"

"No, probably not," Audrey said. "But I still think it's odd."

"What am I going to do?" I asked, burying my head in my hands. "Harriet must hate me to speak to that journalist." Telling him this story did nothing but back up what he'd already implied about me. That I was irresponsible and couldn't be trusted. "I know she must be hurting, but this," I said, "it just doesn't feel right."

NOW

"Why do you think Harriet went to the press?" Detective Rawlings asks.

"I don't know that she did anymore," I say. My eyes are sore from rubbing them. I ache for the luxury of being able to place a cold pack on them, but all I can do is try to stop touching the tender skin.

"But she must have told someone?" The detective is relentless. "Even though you asked her not to. That must have made you angry?"

"Angry?" I could laugh at the woman who quite obviously has no clue. "No, it didn't make me angry. In some ways I thought she had every right to tell that journalist or her husband or whoever she wanted." I sigh. "I think it was Brian. I believe Harriet told him at some point and he was the one who spoke to Josh Gates."

"Why do you think that?"

"Because of what he said when he came to see me on Wednesday night, two days ago," I say with bite. I take a breath and then add, a little more calmly, "I'm struggling to see how this is relevant. What happened when Jack was young has nothing to do with any of this."

"We're just trying to build a picture," Rawlings says, and presses her lips into a perfect heart.

I look away and sit back, resisting the urge to fold my arms. She knows she's getting to me, and I have to be careful, but to say I'm exhausted is an understatement.

"Let's talk about the call you received this morning," she says. "Friday morning, thirteen days after you'd last spoken to her. It must have been a shock?"

"It was."

"What were you doing when she called?"

"I was supposed to be meeting Captain Hayes. He'd asked me to come to the station, but then the school called to say Molly was ill. So I was going to pick her up first."

"And the call from Harriet was totally unexpected?"

"Yes."

"How did she sound?"

"Frightened. Desperate," I say, remembering the sound of her voice with unnerving clarity.

"And why do you think she called you?"

"Probably because I was the first person she thought of."

"After what had happened, she still turned to you? Why would she do that?" Rawlings asks.

"I don't know," I say, my voice rising a notch. "She was afraid. Most likely it's because Harriet has no one else to call."

"So as soon as she called you, you went to help her?" she asks, pinning me with her eyes as she waits for me to respond.

"Well, no," I say. "Like I said, I had to pick up my daughter from school."

"So your close friend calls you, frightened and desperate, and for a while you did—nothing?"

"Not nothing. I had my daughter to look after—"

"But you didn't call the police?"

"No."

"Or tell anyone else?"

"No."

"Despite how desperate Harriet sounded?"

I nod silently.

"Then what I don't understand is why the delay in doing anything, Charlotte?" she asks. "Why did you sit around for what—an hour, more even—before deciding what to do?"

My mouth is dry regardless of how many times I swallow. I lean forward, my hands underneath my legs. My heart hurts it's beating so hard, and all the while she doesn't take her eyes off me.

But I cannot tell her the truth.

"Charlotte?" she prompts.

I wipe a thin streak of sweat from my hairline. I have to say something, but the harder I try, the faster words escape me. My voice is low and hoarse when I finally whisper, "I'd like to take another break, please."

BEFORE

HARRIET

Captain Hayes arrived ten minutes after Angela had hung up, and Brian quickly ushered him into the backyard. "Let's not worry my wife further," he snapped at the detective. "She's dealing with enough at the moment."

Harriet watched them from the window. Both men had their backs to her; Angela stood mutely at their side. She knew that if it was anything serious they'd have taken Brian to the station, but she was still desperate to hear what they were talking to him about. What had he done to make the detective come by so quickly?

When Brian eventually came back inside, Angela and Hayes stayed talking outside. He slammed the door and banged his fists on the table, snapping his head up when he noticed Harriet hovering.

"Why were they questioning you?" She continued to watch the detectives.

"They weren't," Brian replied curtly. "They had questions, yes, but they weren't questioning me." He hesitated as if he was thinking about how to continue. "Are you hungry?"

"No, I'm not," she said.

His body softened as he removed his balled fists from the table. "You haven't eaten anything all morning. I'll make you some toast."

"Brian, I don't want toast."

"I'll put some honey on it for you." He began hunting through the jars in the pantry until he found a pot of honey at the back. He knew she didn't like honey. He was the only one who ate it.

Harriet took a deep breath. "Why won't you tell me what they wanted to talk to you about?" She hated begging, yet it scared her that Brian knew something about Alice she didn't.

"Harriet." Brian slammed the jar hard on the counter. "I am going to have something to eat. As I have just told you, I will tell you everything after I've eaten. But please, will you listen to me for once and accept what I've said instead of trying to manipulate everything? You must see what you're doing to me."

The scream started in her gut, shooting up through her body like a bullet, as it often did. If she opened her mouth she wouldn't be able to stop it from coming out and filling the room with all the anguish inside her. She knew too well that if she screamed Brian would win, calling in Angela and the detective to tell them his wife seemed to be suffering a breakdown.

Brian wouldn't tell her what had happened outside until he was ready. Not until he had played with the situation a little more. Maybe not until she left the room, wondering if a conversation with the detectives had even taken place by the sandpit.

Resigned, Harriet squeezed her eyes shut to push back the threat of tears until the smell of toast wafted under her nose. "Eat up." He smiled, waving a plate of toast that was slathered in honey under her nose.

"I'm not hungry."

"Then why did you just ask me to make this for you?" he snapped, and threw the toast into the sink.

ONCE HAYES HAD left, Angela came into the kitchen and found Harriet sitting at the table with her head in her hands.

"I'm trying to get my wife to eat something," Brian said. When Harriet looked up at him he flashed her a smile.

"What were you talking about out there?" Harriet asked. She didn't care who answered, as long as one of them did.

"Have you not said anything, Brian?" Angela asked.

"Oh, Harriet." Brian shook his head and swept across the room toward her. Kneeling down beside her, he took her face between his hands, gently brushing her hair as he spoke. "Of course I've told her, Angela," he said without taking his eyes off his wife. "I've just been through it all with her while you were both outside. Have you forgotten already, my love?

"I told Harriet it would be sorted and it's nothing for her to worry about. Because I don't want her worrying anymore." He looked worried himself as he stood.

"Are you okay, Harriet? You do look a bit pale," Angela asked her.

"You haven't told me anything, Brian," she said. "So will one of you please tell me what's going on?"

Brian took another deep breath and gently nodded.

"Of course. I'll go through it all again if that will help," he said with feigned patience. "The detective wanted to know why my alibi had fallen through."

"Your alibi's fallen through?" Harriet repeated.

"Yes. Ken Harris," he said, rubbing her shoulders. "You know what he's like. You've said yourself the man forgets what day it is half the time." Brian paused. "Well, now it seems he can't actually remember seeing me the day Alice went missing."

"I've never even met Ken Harris," Harriet said slowly, watching Brian carefully for a reaction. When he didn't give one she went on. "So what does that mean, that he can't remember seeing you?"

"Nothing. Please don't look at me like that, Harriet. You know I'm telling the truth. I wouldn't lie about where I was."

Harriet chewed on her lip, unsure what to say as Brian leaned in closer. "Harriet, I'm not lying; you know that, don't you?" She could hear the desperation in his voice, feel the tremble in his hands, and see the beseeching way his eyes flickered over her. Harriet looked at Angela, who gave her nothing.

"I don't know what to believe anymore, do I, Brian?" she said quietly.

TEN MINUTES LATER, while Brian was still in the kitchen with Angela, Harriet crouched beside her bed and peeled back the corner of the carpet. She reached under the loose floorboard for her notebook, tucked it under her top and crept into the bathroom, carefully stepping over Brian's iPad that had strangely been left charging on the landing.

She locked the door and sat on the closed toilet,

opening up the thick, deep gray Moleskine notebook that she had treated herself to on a trip to Wareham. Turning to the next clean sheet, Harriet pressed it flat with the heel of her hand. Then she pulled the silver pen out of the spine and started to write.

In meticulous detail she wrote down what had just happened. What Brian had actually said to her while Angela and the detective were in the yard, her husband's promise to tell her eventually, his intent on forcing her to eat toast and honey. Then how he had calmly told Angela he'd already relayed the story of his lack of an alibi to her. When she'd finished, Harriet read through her notes and the discrepancies between what Brian said and what he tried to make her believe, until she was confident she knew the truth.

Before she closed the book she flicked through the pages that came before, ones that had become a lifeline to her since she'd started writing. Her first entry was dated May 18, 2016, almost twelve months ago.

The rest of the world may think she was losing her mind, and Brian might be trying to prove she was. But at least she'd found a small way of gripping tightly to reality.

THAT EVENING, WHILE Harriet ran herself a bath, she thought how Brian had been unnervingly calm. He seemed unfazed by the fact his alibi had fallen through, as he skittered around the house, tidying shelves, offering cups of tea, and casually flicking through an old copy of *Angling Times*.

She had run the bathwater so hot, it almost scalded her as she placed a foot in to test it, but Harriet couldn't stand baths that turned cold soon after she'd gotten in. As the bubbles soaked around her, she closed her eyes and felt herself drifting into the state where she was almost falling asleep, when there was a shriek.

She jolted upright to find Brian standing in the doorway as her phone, attached to its charger, slipped off the side of the tub and into the water. Harriet screamed and jumped out in horror, standing naked on the mat.

"What were you doing?" Brian yelled.

She stared at him wide-eyed, her shivering body dripping water into a puddle around her feet. "I didn't do anything," she said. She'd never felt so exposed as she did then, the thought of lying naked in the bath while Brian had crept in.

He took a towel off the radiator and wrapped it around her so tightly she couldn't move her arms. "You can kill yourself doing something stupid like that."

"But I didn't. My phone wasn't even upstairs. I wasn't charging it. I'd never pull it into the bathroom." She tried to untangle herself from the towel, but with every movement he swaddled her tighter.

"So tell me what it's doing here," he said, pulling her against him as they heard Angela racing up the stairs.

"What's happened?" she asked, looking from one to the other.

"Thankfully there's no harm done," Brian said as his eyes wandered to the bath where the phone lay sadly at the bottom, its cord still attached and snaking out of the door onto the landing. "Please just give me a minute to get my wife dressed," he said, and Angela nodded, silently backing out of the room.

"You were lucky I got there in time," he said, loud enough that Angela would hear. "I saw the phone plugged in and pulled it out of the socket before I found you in the bath."

"I didn't do it, Brian," she said as he wrapped his arms tightly around her and led her onto the landing where Angela hovered.

"It was an accident," he said, and she could have sworn she saw him furrowing his brow at Angela. "Thankfully everyone's fine."

"I saw your iPad charging. It wasn't my phone." Harriet looked over her shoulder, but there was no sign of Brian's iPad. *It wasn't me*, she mouthed at Angela, whose eyes flicked to the plug that had been pulled out of the socket just as Brian had said it was.

"If I hadn't been here," he said as they disappeared into the bedroom, pausing and shaking his head, "you'd be dead, my love."

HARRIET

It was Wednesday, eleven days after Alice had disappeared, and Harriet knew she had to get out of the house again. She called to Brian and Angela that they needed milk, but before she got to the front door Brian appeared at her side. Where he had sprung from this time she wasn't sure, but he was making a habit of skulking around corners, then pouncing out at her.

"But we don't need milk, my love," he said. "We only bought some last night."

"No, it's all gone," she assured him, standing her ground. "You can check if you like."

Brian's tongue whipped out, licking his bottom lip as he was about to protest, when Angela called from the kitchen. They both turned to see her shaking an empty plastic bottle. "Actually, we do need some," she said, and while Brian was looking the other way, Harriet took the chance to slip out.

She didn't look back as she hurried down the path, which meant she didn't notice him still waiting on the doorstep, watching her. When she returned half an hour later, he was still standing in the open doorway. Had he been there the whole time? She couldn't care less, she thought, as she tried to push past him. All she needed was to get inside so she could lie down, because all of a sudden she was feeling dreadful.

"And how was your walk?" He didn't budge as he held his ground, his eyes crawling over her face as he didn't let her pass.

"I was just getting milk," she muttered. Her hands were trembling and amid the hot flushes that ran through her, Harriet felt surprisingly cold. She hoped she'd be able to pass it off as coming down with something—Brian was already looking at her strangely.

"Are you okay?" he said, eventually stepping back so she could get inside. "You look very white." He reached out and took the milk from her.

"I don't feel well."

"Are you sick? You look as if you're going to be. I hope nothing's happened while you've been out?" His smile vanished.

"No," she whispered. "Nothing's happened, I just really don't feel well and I need to lie down." She slipped off her shoes and pushed them into the corner with her foot.

"Okay, let's get you up to bed. I'll come and lie down with you."

Harriet took hold of the banister. "No," she said. "I'll go on my own." She started to walk up the stairs when he grabbed her arm and stopped her.

"Everything okay?" Angela asked, stepping into the hallway. Her handbag was slung over her shoulder and a cardigan draped over her arm. "You don't look well, Harriet."

"She's not," Brian said. "But I'm taking care of her. Aren't I, my love?"

"Can I get you anything before I go?"

"No," Brian said. "We're fine. I can get my wife what

she needs. Thank you, Angela," he added as an after-thought, or maybe because Brian was never one to for-get his manners.

ALL HARRIET WANTED was to be left alone, but as she climbed the stairs Brian was right behind her. When she got to the bedroom, she asked him for a glass of water just so he had to reluctantly go down again. Curling up on top of the covers, Harriet found that every time she tried closing her eyes, they sprang open. The swirling patterns on the wallpaper danced in front of her until they blurred into one large fuzzy shape.

Harriet knew every inch of those walls by heart. Every change of color in the paper, all the bits that didn't quite match. She had loved it when she'd picked it out, her tummy swollen with her baby, wondering if they were having a girl or a boy. Brian was adamant he wanted a son. An heir, someone just like him, he was al-ways saying, and in turn Harriet found herself praying they'd be blessed with a girl.

Now she hated the wallpaper. Its swirling patterns made her feel even more nauseous, until Harriet thought she actually would be sick. She pushed herself up and held a hand over her mouth, waiting for the feeling to pass.

How happy she had been when she was expecting Alice. What a lifetime ago that felt like, wandering the aisles of Buy Buy Baby, promising herself she would al-ways protect her baby. She could never have foreseen this. The terror of not knowing where her daughter was and whether she was safe coursed through her veins until it paralyzed her. And for a moment, Harriet didn't register that something wasn't quite right in their bedroom, even though she was staring right at it.

When her eyes finally refocused, the silver frame on her dressing table eventually became clear. "Oh my God." Harriet shuffled to the end of her bed and reached out to pick it up. The day Brian had bought her the frame three years ago, he had put a photo of her and Alice in it. He'd taken the picture on a beach in Devon and given it to Harriet as a present. It was a beautiful picture of her baby girl, their cheeks pressed against each other's, Alice's wide eyes bright blue as they reflected the light. Her yellow dotted sunhat skewed at an angle on top of her head, tufts of baby blond hair poking out beneath it.

But now Harriet was looking at a very different picture. It was a photo of their wedding day, one she'd never liked because her eyes were half closed and she was looking away from Brian while he stared intently at her. "Look at you," the inexperienced but cheap photographer had said with a laugh. "You adore her."

"Of course I do, she's my wife," Brian had said.

"Yes, and she's not even looking back at you." The young man laughed at what he thought was a very comical situation.

Brian's head had snapped up to look at Harriet. "Well, she is a lot more beautiful than me." Brian smiled.

When the photographer had finished, Harriet had forced herself to drink the lukewarm champagne. "Why would you do that to me?" Brian had leaned in close as he spoke into her ear.

"Do what?" Harriet was genuinely baffled.

"Try and make me look a fool on our wedding day. That boy is laughing at me, no doubt telling everyone my new wife doesn't even want to look at me, while I can't take my eyes off you."

"Don't be silly, Brian, of course I was looking at you," she'd said. "I just saw that waiter spill red wine down this man's shirt." Harriet giggled. "He was so flustered, trying to mop it up as—"

"Well," he'd spat, taking her hand as he'd led her off toward the restaurant. "Isn't that just wonderful."

When he'd slipped into bed beside her that night, Brian had left a cold space between them. "You didn't take your eyes off him all night."

"Who?" Harriet had turned toward her new husband.

"The waiter, of course. You embarrassed me on purpose, Harriet."

"What do you mean? I wasn't looking at him all night," she'd pleaded. He'd caught her attention a couple of times because he was so incompetent, but that was all. Did it look like she was staring too much though? she'd wondered with a pang of guilt.

"You spoiled the day for me. How do you think you made me feel on our wedding day when you kept looking at another man?"

"I wasn't looking at him. Not like that," she'd implored. "Brian, I'm sorry, I didn't mean to hurt you. What you think happened just isn't true."

"You think I'm lying? That I'm making things up? I know what I saw."

"No, I don't think you're lying but—"

"You made me look like an idiot," he'd snapped, his face flushing with rage. "So don't start trying to pretend this is my fault."

"Brian, I'm sorry." Harriet couldn't believe she'd hurt him so badly. How stupid she had been. She'd reached over to touch her husband, moving closer, hoping that as it was their wedding night he could forgive her. He wasn't a big drinker, so maybe he'd had a little too much. But then she didn't remember him having any alcohol after the champagne on the terrace. "Come here," she'd murmured softly. She'd make him forget whatever he was working himself up over.

But Brian had rolled away and she'd been left looking at the back of his broad shoulders, rising and dipping with his sharp breaths.

Harriet had turned onto her back and stared at the hotel ceiling, tears sliding down her cheeks that their wedding night had come to this. It was nothing she had hoped for. She had never felt so alone.

"I'm sorry," Harriet had whispered to her husband's back. "I'm so sorry. I never meant to hurt you." She'd known he was still awake, but he hadn't answered.

"I'VE BEEN WONDERING why you swapped the photo." Brian's voice made her jump. "Did you not like the one I took of you and Alice?" He stood in the doorway with a tumbler of water that he carefully placed on the nightstand. His eyes never left Harriet's.

"You know I didn't swap it," she said, letting the frame drop onto the bed beside her.

Brian leaned forward and picked it up. "And you know I don't like this picture."

"I didn't change the photo, Brian," she said again, noticing the muscles twitching in his jaw.

"So she's gone," he said, waving the frame in front of her.

"What are you saying?" Harriet shifted nervously on the bed. "Brian, you're scaring me."

"Am I?" he said, getting closer until she could feel his breath on her cheek. "My love, I wouldn't do that." He reached out and took a tendril of her hair, stroking it between his fingers. "You must be getting confused again." And with that, Brian let go of her hair and walked out of the bedroom.

CHARLOTTE

By Wednesday evening Audrey had persuaded me I should attend the school social, though when Tom arrived to look after the children I was already regretting it because I really didn't want to go.

I'd fallen into a routine of making pleasantries at the school gate, keeping my eyes hidden behind sunglasses, my head down, and scurrying away again before anyone could stop me. I stopped returning messages and became completely reliant on Audrey acting as a go-between for me, thanking friends for whatever thoughts they were passing on to me.

Aud had removed Facebook from my phone again. She'd told me I was banned from reading anything online. I knew if I did I'd find myself talking to her about what I'd read, and then she'd most likely fulfill her promise to take away my phone. Strangely, I began finding it relatively easy to hide away from the world. What I didn't know wasn't hurting me.

But withdrawing had made the thought of the social even more terrifying. I was only going because of Audrey's insistence and my desire not to let her down after everything she'd done.

"I thought you said it was starting five minutes ago,"

Tom said, tapping his watch. "It's already eight fifty." He found me rummaging through the children's school-bags. I'd already laid out their uniforms and washed up the water bottles—jobs I'd usually leave till morning. "Just go," he said, practically pushing me out the door.

"When did the light stop working?" I muttered when the outside lamp didn't automatically come on.

"I'll have a look at it," Tom said, peering up before sighing. "Oh, I can hear Evie. I thought you said she was asleep. I'll see you later." He closed the door behind him, leaving me standing in the semi-dark walkway. As I walked toward my car a flicker of movement stopped me in my tracks, and Brian's face suddenly appeared above the corner of the bushes lining the walk.

"Brian, you made me jump," I said, wondering how long he'd been watching me. "Do you, erm, want to come in?"

"No," he said coldly. "I want you to come to my car." When I didn't move he added, "I don't think you have the luxury of refusing me, do you?"

I jangled my keys nervously, looking up at the house, hoping that Tom might be looking out, but there was no sign of him. Reluctantly I nodded and followed Brian to the silver Honda parked a few houses up. He held the passenger door open, and as I climbed in the smell of dead fish wafted from the trunk and into my nostrils.

Our cul-de-sac was quiet and eerily still. The click of the car doors locking was loud and sharp in the silence as Brian twisted to face me.

His mouth twitched at the corners and, tilting his head to one side, he spoke slowly. "Tell me what you know."

"What I know about what?" I asked.

"Tell me what you know about my wife."

I fidgeted uneasily. "Why are we talking about Harriet?"

"I do everything for her. She's my world," he continued. "I always have. But she doesn't treat me the same, though I assume you know that. She must tell you everything."

"No, actually, Harriet doesn't say anything to me," I said.

"It breaks me. She breaks me. Do you know that? Of course you do. You're her best friend." He laughed. "Despite what you say, you must know everything."

Brian's behavior was as disturbing as his appearance. His hair stuck out wildly in different directions, as if he'd grabbed it with both hands and ruffled it vigorously. His eyes were dark and heavy as they bored into me. I'd never seen Brian anything less than pristine and, despite the situation, I knew something else was wrong.

"Did she tell you she doesn't love me?" he went on.

I shuffled forward uncomfortably in my seat. "Harriet loves you," I said. As much as I didn't want to confront his anger about Alice, I still thought it would be preferable to whatever this was about. "Whatever is happening right now, you can't start doubting that."

"I know you were close, Charlotte. Why else would you tell her about losing your son?"

"What?"

"Make a habit of it, don't you? Losing children. Almost like it comes easy to you."

"Brian—" The air in the car was getting unbearably stale. "Can I open the door? Or even just the window?"

Brian ignored me as he slammed the palm of his hand against the steering wheel and turned to stare out the windshield. "Mothers like you should pay for what you do. But you don't," he carried on. "You never do."

"I need to go," I said, my voice shaking. "I want you to unlock the door now, Brian."

"I'll make sure they write stories about you," he said. "I'll make sure it's out there."

I wondered if I should scream, and whether anyone would hear me if I did. The air was getting closer and I could feel my lungs working harder, yet the only thing stopping me from hammering on the window was the thought that this was nothing less than I deserved.

"Tell me what she's told you!" he yelled.

"I don't know what you want me to say," I pleaded. Harriet had never uttered a word against her husband. "Harriet's only ever had good things to say about you—"

"You know I've always liked you, Charlotte," he said, his words suddenly sounding lighter and softer as he arched forward. "Of course I'm glad she has you as a friend, but I need you to be honest with me."

"Brian, what are you talking about?"

"I'm sure you can make her see sense," he said. "I need to go now."

"Brian, I don't understand what you're—" I stopped as he stretched across me to open the door, giving it a shove so it swung open.

"I'm sure you do, Charlotte," he said. "I'm positive you understand very well what I'm talking about. Now please get out of my car."

I stared at him incredulously as I backed out of the car. He pulled the door shut behind me, started the engine, and hastily drove away. All thoughts of the school social had vanished. It was with relief that I made my way back to the house.

I had no idea what had just happened. Whether he

and Harriet had had an argument, if this was Brian's way of taking it out on me. Wasn't it all any father would do in his situation? I didn't stop to think Harriet was in any danger because, despite his behavior that evening, I still didn't think Brian was to blame. His words were nothing compared to what the trolls had said they would do to me, after all. I should have expected much worse.

NOW

D o I have to go over the facts?" Detective Rawlings
says. "We have a missing person and someone died
tonight."

"I know." I press my fingers to my eyes, squeezing
them shut. "I know."

"And we still aren't getting to the truth," she goes on.

"I'm telling you what I know," I snap.

"Are you?" She sits back in her chair and stares at me.

"Yes," I plead, though even I know I don't sound
sincere.

Harriet had never told me what was going on in her
marriage. Yet as much as I can tell myself it was because she didn't want me to know, I can't ignore the
feeling I didn't look hard enough.

Maybe that's what the detective saw the moment I
walked into the room. That right from the start of our
friendship I was wrapped up in my own life. Isn't that
what the mums like us are like? The gaggle of women
who take over the playground with our raucous laughter, acting like the school owes us something for being
there?

I saw that in some of them over the days after the
school fair, the way they ushered their kids away from

me, afraid if I came too near that one of their children would disappear too. Not all of them. Not Aud, of course. But it made me realize how fragile the strings were that tied the rest of us together. How some friendships are built on so little they can fall apart at the slightest strain.

But I wasn't like them, I wanted to plead with Rawlings. I still feel the urge to persuade her that I wasn't, and that is why I was drawn to Harriet.

Harriet reminded me of the person I wanted to be, the one I still was in the heart of my soul. Harriet didn't kiss the air or gush over handbags like they alone would solve third-world problems. I could tell Harriet anything and I knew she cared.

She could have told me anything too. Only she hadn't.

"But you didn't see any clues?" the detective persists.

Looking back, there were possibly many clues, but I tell the detective I didn't. Yet as I sit here in the whitewashed room, with the microphone still recording and my mind dissolving, I remember a particular time when Harriet and I sat on our usual bench in the park.

Evie had been a baby and was finally asleep in the stroller and, while I hadn't been able to rest completely with the threat of her waking any moment, I'd closed my eyes and reveled in the moment's peace, when Harriet's voice rang out from behind me. For a moment, I'd felt my stomach sink. I hadn't thought we'd arranged to meet.

When I'd opened my eyes, I'd seen Alice toddling off to the sandpit where Molly was filling a bucket. Harriet had stripped off her cardigan and pulled a lunch box out, and I remember thinking it looked like she was there to stay. "What are your plans today?" I'd asked. "Are you and Alice off anywhere nice?"

"No, nothing special. I have to go back to the shops later."

"What, on a lovely day like this?" I'd said.

"Yes, I bought this jumper for Brian and I need to take it back." Harriet had reached into her bag and grabbed a handful of the top.

"Tom had one like this," I'd murmured, running my hand over the soft wool. "What's wrong with it? Doesn't Brian like it?"

"Oh, I think he probably does. I just got the wrong one. He said he'd asked me for red." Harriet had shrugged her shoulders. "I could have sworn he said green."

I sighed and folded the top back. They were hardly two colors you could mix up, and I had felt myself getting irritated by Harriet's mistake. My patience had almost been on empty, and in those times her carelessness annoyed me.

"I could do with going shopping," I'd said. "We should go one day, blow some money and treat ourselves." When Harriet didn't answer, I'd realized my tactlessness and said, "I mean, I'd like to treat you to something. You'd be doing me a favor just by coming. I'll dump Evie on my mum for the day."

"Yes, maybe."

I'd looked over at Harriet, who had been waving at Alice, holding up a packet of raisins to her daughter while she'd played obliviously in the sandpit. Nearby a mother had been raising her voice at her young son, her finger wagging an inch from his face as the little boy started sobbing.

"He didn't even do anything wrong," Harriet had said. "I was watching him. He only wanted another go on the swing."

The mother had shouted louder, the little boy slunk backward. Her hand drew back and the next moment she'd slapped him across the back of his legs and marched him through the park.

"We should say something," Harriet had gasped.

"Don't get involved," I'd said quickly, placing a hand on Harriet's arm.

"But he's in a dreadful state."

"I know and it's horrible, but no one will thank you for saying anything. About this shopping trip," I'd added, desperate to avoid confrontation with the mother who was by now at the gate. She had hard features that looked like she was permanently angry and I knew who'd come off worse if Harriet got into it with her. "When shall we go?"

I'd opened up Harriet's bag and was about to put the jumper back in when I'd noticed a necklace glistening at the bottom. "Harriet, I haven't seen this before." I'd pulled out the chain, holding its delicate gold leaf pendant in the palm of my hand. "It's beautiful."

"My necklace," Harriet had gasped and grabbed the chain from me. "Where did you— Where was it?"

"It was just lying in your bag. It's gorgeous." It really was, and I couldn't remember ever seeing Harriet wear it.

"I thought I'd lost it." Harriet had stared at it suspiciously, turning the leaf over in her fingers. "I thought—" She'd shaken her head and hadn't finished the sentence. "It was my mum's. I know it was in my jewelry box. I don't wear it because it's so precious. But then it was gone and I looked everywhere."

"Well, you have it now."

"But I searched the house." Harriet's voice had dropped as she continued to marvel at the pendant, and

I'd stared at her, wondering if she was talking to it or to me. "I don't get it. How could it even be in my handbag?" she'd said in little more than a whisper.

"Does it really matter, if you've found it?" I'd sighed, fearing I might have snapped at Harriet as I closed my eyes again. I could hear Aud's voice as clear as if she were sitting on the bench between us. "Charlotte, I'm sure your friend is very sweet, but she looks like she's away with the fairies half the time."

I remember turning to look at Harriet, who was then staring at a point in the distance, past Alice, past the trees that lined the park. Her lips had twitched; she was deep in thought. I had lost Harriet completely and Evie was stirring and I knew any minute she'd start screaming, and I'd felt the rise of irritation spreading inside me like a fire.

"WHEN YOU ASK me if there were any signs," I tell Detective Rawlings, "it's that bloody memory that comes to mind, and I think if that's all I had to go on, then did I really miss anything?"

When she doesn't answer, my body burns with the sheer frustration that we are going around and around in circles and somehow end up in the same spot every time.

My arms feel like jelly as they hang limply by my sides. My back slumps as I reach forward and my hands fall onto the table. "Please," I say, "I need to go home. I want to go now."

Yet I know that if I'd sensed what was going on behind Harriet's closed doors, I could have helped. I would never have convinced her to leave her daughter with me, promising that Alice would be safe. I knew, more than many, how controlling some fathers and husbands can be because my own dad was that way. Harriet understood that, yet still she didn't confide in me. She hadn't trusted me to help her.

And Brian knew so much more than she'd given him credit for.

BEFORE

HARRIET

On Thursday morning, twelve days after Alice went missing, Harriet woke knowing that, like it or not, everything was about to change. She was relieved that on that day Angela wasn't getting to the house until 4:00 p.m.

She'd watched Brian cautiously as he moved around like a ticking time bomb. He hadn't uttered one word since he'd walked out of the bedroom the night before, leaving her staring at their wedding photo. But she could see by the way he flitted about that he was still wired.

Above her, the floorboards of the bathroom creaked. It was already late morning and Brian still wasn't dressed. There had been plenty of times when she'd sat like this at her kitchen table with her hands wrapped around a cold mug of tea waiting for her husband to appear, though never so late in the day. She didn't know what to expect as her mind raced through thoughts of the previous night, trying to figure out if she'd done something wrong. Over the years memories had faded into a dark recess in her mind until she had no way of gripping on to them again. She knew she'd become reliant on Brian reminding her, because he'd told her often enough. Her husband's support had never wavered, though. Brian would always be there for her.

He'd told her that enough, too.

He'd promised that.

Threatened it.

At first Harriet hadn't wanted to believe she had problems with her memory, but Brian had been insistent. He took her to a private doctor two years ago, to a practice on the other side of Chiddenford. Harriet had sat mutely as her husband had described her problems, the many mistakes she made, how concerned he was for his wife and daughter's safety.

"I didn't have an issue as a child," she'd told the doctor when he'd asked if she knew when it started.

"Well, it often comes on in adulthood," Brian had said sharply.

Like the day I met you? Harriet now wondered.

The not knowing was frightening. Believing so adamantly in one thing but then having the one person she loved and trusted tell her the reverse was true left her fearful and worried. Harriet had once found herself standing in the middle of a supermarket, frantically trying to remember if Brian preferred the biscuits covered in milk chocolate or dark.

"I've told you so many times, Harriet," he'd said as she'd handed him the packet of milk chocolate cookies later that evening. "It's the dark ones I like."

The next time she went to the store, Harriet rolled his words around and around on her tongue. "Dark chocolate, dark. Remember it's dark, Alice."

They stood in the biscuit aisle, her fingers trembling as they hovered over the dark ones. "Alice, what did I say?"

"Dark." Her daughter nodded as Harriet cautiously put them in the basket.

When they got home and she laid one out next to his mug, Brian had picked it up and turned it over in his hands as if he'd never seen anything like it. Then he'd looked up at Harriet and said, "Oh my love, come here. You've done it again, haven't you? It's the milk chocolate I prefer."

Harriet was losing her mind. By then she was certain of that. She feared she would ultimately lose everything.

"You will lose Alice one day," he would often tell her.

He was right about that. Now she had lost her daughter.

THE CREAKING ABOVE her stopped and Harriet froze as she listened for his footsteps down the stairs. Of course, by now she knew she wasn't losing her mind anymore. She was well aware it was Brian trying to convince her she was. She had become sure of that over the last twelve months, since the day she'd started writing in her notebook.

Though it was also fair to say she had done something crazy.

When he came into the kitchen he looked at her, but still didn't speak. "Is everything okay?" she asked as calmly as she could.

"I need to go out. I need to speak to someone," he said, though he didn't move.

"Who?"

Brian gave a small shake of his head. He seemed uncertain about leaving her in the house, which made her wonder what was so important that he would go anyway. "Remember, Angela is coming round soon."

"Yes. I know."

"She'll be here in half an hour, so there's no time for you to go anywhere."

Harriet nodded. The clock behind Brian showed it was nearly midday. Angela wouldn't be here for another four hours.

"Twelve thirty, Harriet. She's arriving at twelve thirty," he persisted as if goading her to contradict him, but Harriet just nodded again. Eventually Brian tutted and walked out of the kitchen. "I won't be long," he called as he went out the front door.

IT CROSSED HER mind that Brian was going to see Ken Harris, the man who'd withdrawn his alibi, but she couldn't think about either of them right now. Wherever he was off to, it was the least of her problems. Harriet needed a clear head to work out what she was going to do next, because she only had four hours until Angela arrived and even less before her husband returned.

Closing her eyes, she pressed her fingertips to her temple. "Think, Harriet."

The past twelve months flickered like a movie behind her eyelids. The realization that Brian had created a life she and Alice couldn't escape from, the appearance of the ghost from her past, the sheer desperation that made it seem like her plan was a good idea.

Everything had changed in the last twenty-four hours and Harriet knew it was dangerous to leave, but

Alice was her priority. It was always about Alice. Only now she might possibly lose her daughter for good.

It was Harriet's fault her daughter had disappeared twelve days ago, because she was the one who had planned it. Every meticulous detail of Alice vanishing from the fair was so they could escape him.

HARRIET'S STORY

Wednesday, May 18, 2016

I'm worried I might have done something bad.

Brian came home from work last night and rushed straight upstairs, frantic. He asked me why I'd left Alice in the bathtub on her own. I told him I didn't. I can't believe he thinks I would—I'd never do that.

But he looked at me in that way he does when his head leans to one side and his eyes roll over my body. It makes me think I've done something wrong, only I can't remember.

He said Alice wouldn't lie. He's right—we both know she wouldn't. He told me he was worried, even though I pleaded that I didn't leave her for a moment—I could see myself in the bathroom, sitting on the footstool. I'd filled a jug of water and tipped it down Alice's back, making her squeal with delight. Then I got a clean towel from the radiator and wrapped her in it as she stepped out of the tub. I remember it all. I didn't leave the room. Yet, if Alice says I did . . .

The memory was so clear only moments ago, but a small black hole has appeared in the middle, slowly spreading like spilled ink. Now I'm left with a gaping blankness in the middle of the picture that I can no longer fill in.

Brian carried on talking at me, telling me Alice was frightened but that she would be okay. He told me not to cry as he wiped my tears with his thumbs, but I couldn't bear the thought that I did anything to hurt my baby girl. His next words cut through the air like a knife—all it would take was for Alice to slip under the water and she'd be dead. I screamed at Brian to stop, clamping my hands over my ears. I would never let that happen.

But what if I had?

I told Brian we would go see the doctor again. I'm supposed to call him today and make an appointment. He will take more notes, pen it in black and white that my daughter is not safe alone with me.

Maybe she isn't. All night I couldn't sleep because every time I closed my eyes I saw Alice disappearing under the water. Beside me, Brian lay peacefully still, his breath deep and content with his spotless conscience.

There are plenty of things I forget, but never before has it put my daughter in danger.

This morning I asked Alice if she remembered her bath last night and if she enjoyed it. She looked at me oddly, but then it was an odd question. I tickled her in the ribs until she giggled and told her I was just wondering if I'd left her on her own, saying I was very sorry if I had because I should never do that.

She said I hadn't, that I never leave her on her own.

My heart was beating so hard. It still is. I reminded her to always tell me off if I do and as an afterthought asked if maybe she'd told Daddy something about her bath.

Alice started giggling again, but not like she was when I tickled her. This time she was nervous and said Brian hadn't seen her last night because she was hiding behind the sofa. Apparently she stayed there until he came upstairs to talk to me.

Her little face paled when she asked if she did something wrong. I assured her she hadn't. Not at all.

I don't think either of us have.

I must remember to ask Alice why she was hiding behind the sofa. It seems a strange thing for her to do.

HARRIET

The day I left Alice with Charlotte I knew that if everything went to plan, my friend would not be bringing her home. On the drive to her house I couldn't take my eyes off Alice through the rearview mirror. I wanted to soak up every part of her because I didn't know how long it would be until I saw her again.

Under her left arm, Alice clutched Hippo tightly. Her head was bent toward him and every so often her right thumb slipped toward her mouth until she realized what she was doing and pulled it away again. We'd talked about how sucking thumbs wasn't good for her teeth. At some point between home and Charlotte's house, Hippo had slipped out of her grip and fallen between her seat and the door. I didn't notice she wasn't holding him as I led her up Charlotte's driveway.

I rang the doorbell and looked up at the bedroom window where the curtains were still closed. I'd been looking for signs that I shouldn't do this. Anything to tell me that even though I had gotten this far, my plan was ludicrous and wouldn't work. If Charlotte had forgotten she was having Alice, I thought, pressing the doorbell again, then that would be a sign. I couldn't do this without Charlotte.

Alice sank into my side and I pulled her tighter against me. Each time I inhaled, my breaths felt sharp, like they were stabbing the inside of my chest. "You'll be safe, Alice," I murmured for my benefit as much as hers. I was doing this to keep us both safe.

When Charlotte appeared, still in her pajamas, my heart plummeted with dread that it was all going to go wrong. I considered telling her I'd had a change of heart and was coming to the fair with them. She wouldn't bat an eyelid. She probably expected me to back out of leaving Alice anyway.

Charlotte gabbled away, unconscious of Evie yelling in the background as Alice sank deeper into me. But if I pulled out now, what would we do? I had been through it so many times. There were no other options.

I bent down and told Alice yet again she would be safe. I must have looked so jumpy to Charlotte, but she tried to brush over it, telling me they would all have fun and how exciting it was that I was taking a class in bookkeeping.

I knew she didn't believe that. Neither of us did. Being crammed in a hotel for a day-long class was nothing more than an alibi. It was also an explanation Brian would fall for when he'd demand to know why I hadn't told him I was leaving Alice with someone else. The police would find the final notices he'd hidden from me in his bedside drawer. They'd hopefully see the itemized receipts I'd needed to produce that were neatly folded under his pants. No one could question I was only trying to help. What they hopefully wouldn't find was the rainy day money I'd squirreled away in a box, buried under a tree next to the sandpit.

Eventually I let go of Alice and walked away. I didn't turn back. I couldn't let either of them see the tears that flowed down my face, leaking into my mouth. It was the bravest thing I had ever done, but I'd never felt so frightened.

AT 1 P.M. on Thursday afternoon, twelve days after the fair and three hours before Angela would arrive, I left the house with the bare essentials, which were little more than a small amount of cash, Alice's Hippo, a toothbrush, and my notebook. I still hoped I wouldn't have to make the four-hour journey to find my daughter, because I knew how much I was risking by leaving. I hoped I would track them down before I got out of Dorset. My phone wasn't working, thanks to it sinking to the bottom of the tub, so I was reliant on stopping at pay phones.

I prayed my call would be answered the next time I tried. I refused to dwell on the fact it had already been twenty-four hours since he hadn't picked up, and what that meant.

My hands trembled against the wheel as I drove. In my rearview mirror Hippo smiled back at me from Alice's car seat. She would be over the moon to get him back, but I didn't know if I could leave him with her. Would Angela notice he was missing?

"Shit." I thumped my hands against the steering wheel, stinging the flesh. This was all going horribly wrong. Whatever I did from now on, there would be too many consequences, and if I couldn't get ahold of him my head wouldn't be straight enough to think clearly.

After fifteen minutes I was almost on the outskirts of Dorset when I spotted a pay phone on a side street and pulled over. As I dialed the pay-as-you-go number I'd memorized, I knew that if there was no response I would need to drive all the way to Cornwall to find the cottage I had only ever seen pictures of.

The ringtone filled my ear, but it rang and rang until eventually it abruptly stopped. "Oh God, where are you?" I cried. None of this was right. He'd told me with such certainty he would always answer my calls and I'd believed him.

It was too late to ask myself why I'd trusted him. I had only known him six months. I had known Brian double that before I married him, and look how wrong I'd been about him.

I slumped down the side of the phone booth, balling my fists and hitting my forehead with the heels of my hands.

The plan to escape Brian had once seemed so certain in my head that even though I knew many things could go wrong, I never expected *this*. Now it was hanging together by loose pieces of tattered thread and, as I squeezed my eyes tightly shut, I knew that not only could my daughter be absolutely anywhere, but it was all my fault.

Monday, July 4, 2016

Brian was given a bonus at work. He's so excited, says it's an "overdue payment." I think it's embarrassing that he's never been shown any gratitude for his commitment before, but Brian has been easily mollified with this extra amount.

This morning he announced he wanted to give me a little something so I could treat Alice and myself at the shops. I gasped as I watched him count out twenty-pound notes and slide them into a long, white envelope. It looked much more than a little something.

Brian winked at me as he said he'd put three hundred pounds in the envelope, which he sealed and tucked on top of the fridge. He asked if I'd go shopping today and told me to get whatever I fancied.

I was almost jumping up and down like a little kid. I'd already decided to get myself something and let Alice choose a new outfit, and then we'd go to the toy shop. I even wondered if maybe all we needed was for Brian to be given a boost of confidence at work.

I kissed him good-bye and left him to finish his coffee while I got Alice up and dressed. By the time we came downstairs, Brian had left for the office.

I put the envelope in the inside pocket of my handbag. There was more cash in it than I'd ever had on me, and I was nervous as we walked through the shopping center. I kept a hand over my bag the whole time.

At the counter of the first store, I laid out two jumpers I liked for myself and a pink frilly skirt Alice hadn't been able to keep her hands off. It was a little big on her, but at the rate she was growing, I knew she would grow into it, and it really was beautiful. Alice couldn't stop stroking the embroidered birds that ran along its hem, asking if she could show it to Molly later, and I was so happy to see her bubbling with joy.

I told her Molly was at school and that maybe we could show it to Evie, but when I ran my fingers under the seal of the envelope and reached inside, I gasped out loud.

The girl behind the counter stared at me gormlessly, asking if there was a problem.

Yes, there was a big problem. Instead of the three hundred pounds I had watched Brian count out, there was now only a ten-pound note. My cheeks burned as I made some excuse that I would need to come back, and picking up Alice's hand, I hauled her toward the doors.

Her little feet were hurrying to keep up with me, but I didn't stop until we were outside. Already her eyes were glistening with tears as she asked me if she wasn't allowed to have the skirt anymore.

I crouched down and took her hands in mine, giving her the biggest smile my heart would allow. I said I was silly and forgot the money and I promised her—with a hand over my heart, I promised her—that one day I would come back and get that skirt for her.

Monday, August 8, 2016

I told Brian it would be hard to make nice meals every night with my allowance cut down, but he just retorted that I would have to be a little more creative. He grinned at me as he ruffled my hair.

I pulled away, fixing my hair, and asked why we had to budget if things were better at work.

Brian screwed up his nose and sighed deeply, telling me not to use the word budget and that we don't have money issues. I knew what was coming before he said it—he had to learn to trust me again.

I bit the inside of my lip. I would not rise to the bait. Patiently I told him I need more than what he's giving me to survive.

Alice already needs new shoes and I need to get her a coat for autumn.

Brian snapped back and asked how I could really expect him to hand over cash when I'd lost three hundred pounds. I pleaded with him that I didn't lose it, that the money wasn't in the envelope, but Brian only sighed and said he didn't want to go through all that again. He said money doesn't just disappear, and then asked me to keep itemized receipts for everything, and if Alice needs new shoes, then we can both take her on Saturday.

He said it would be fun for us to have a family trip out together when he got back from fishing. Then he reached out and ruffled my hair again.

HARRIET

I sat in my car, staring blankly at the unfamiliar road ahead, my handbag clutched tightly on my lap as I wondered if I had any other options. There was no choice. I had to find the remote hideaway where we'd planned for Alice to go.

From now on I would have to pay for anything I needed in cash, but I was still praying it wouldn't be long before I knew Alice was safe and I could turn around and go home.

Fear was spurring me on to Cornwall, but I was also filled with dread at what I'd left behind, and the longer I was away the worse it would be.

Was Brian home already?

I imagined his face when he'd walk in and find me gone. For a while he'd presume I had popped out, but how long until he realized I should have been back? How long before he alerted Angela to the fact I'd disappeared? Until he urged them to believe I was as unhinged as he'd been making out and they should track me down immediately?

I put my handbag on the passenger seat and started the engine. I couldn't waste any more time—I needed to get as far as I could as quickly as possible.

• • •

AS SOON AS I saw the flashing lights of the police car parked outside my house the day of the fair, I knew my plan had been carried through and Alice was gone. Brian had already been told that his daughter had disappeared and soon they would tell me. I couldn't back out now, I kept thinking as I watched from inside my car.

Brian had dragged me out of the car and up the sidewalk, his fishing rods clanking like boats in the wind. For a very short moment my heart went out to him. Despite all he had done, I wondered if he deserved to think his daughter had been taken.

"Alice is missing." His words screamed out into the still air. My legs were pulled from under me as I fell onto the ground as if my body had been taken along with her. That's when it really smacked me that in that precise moment, I had no clue where my daughter was. I could pinpoint on a map where she *should* have been, but even as I imagined it, every road and motorway between us stretched interminably until I feared I might have lost her forever.

Had I made a mistake? What if someone else took her at the fair? How would I know if she was in a car accident? I screamed out Alice's name, clawing my fingernails into the concrete until I was taken inside and forced to endure her last known whereabouts.

When Angela suggested it would be good to talk to Charlotte, I knew she'd be my downfall—I'd want to tell her everything. As adamantly as I refused, Brian was insistent, and eventually I caved. But as soon as my friend stepped inside my living room, I couldn't bear to look at her. I wanted to freeze time around us so I could crawl across the floor and whisper in her ear, "I know where Alice is. This isn't your fault. I'm sorry for what I'm putting you through, but I'm doing this for her." As fear and guilt dripped from Charlotte's words, I realized how stupid I'd been to convince myself she would one day understand why I'd done what I did.

Before that moment, I'd told myself it was only a matter of time before my daughter reappeared and Charlotte could move on with her life. Her abundance of friends would get her through the short term and no one would blame her. In fact, I'd not only thought they wouldn't blame Charlotte, I believed they'd feel sorry for her. How dreadful she must feel, they would say. Their hearts would go out to her. It could have happened to anyone.

What I didn't anticipate was that Charlotte would be posting on Facebook the moment my daughter was taken. That a journalist would pick that up and twist it until she looked like nothing more than a careless and inattentive mother who was ultimately as responsible as whoever had taken my daughter. To make it worse, every news report on Alice attracted comments from strangers lashing out at her, blaming her. Everyone was focused on Charlotte's failings, and I couldn't imagine how she was coping. Yet still I continued to reassure myself that as soon as Alice was back, everyone would forgive and forget.

But deep down I knew what I'd done. Because seeing Charlotte in my living room, trying to piece together how she could have lost my daughter, fractured my broken heart into more shreds. She would never get over it.

Later Brian paced the living room, loading every ounce of blame onto Charlotte, skillfully dodging it himself, as always. Of course, he could justifiably wipe his hands clean on this one, though it never stopped him when he couldn't. *This is your doing, Brian*, I thought, watching him prowl, smacking a fist into the palm of his other hand when Angela wasn't watching. *If you hadn't made it so impossible for me to leave, I would never have resorted to this*.

It was ironic that the reason I'd never confided in Charlotte about my husband was because I didn't want to lose her, when I knew now that I would anyway. When she came to the house that night, it was clear there was already too much separating us to be able to find our way back.

I'd had another friend once. After Jane and Christie and before Charlotte, I'd worked with a receptionist named Tina at my school in Kent.

Sometimes Tina and I would slip out and have lunch at the local bakery. She was in her early thirties and lived alone in a one-bed, purpose-built flat with two cats she wasn't supposed to own. She was always intrigued by married life and how it didn't seem to make people as happy as they should be.

"I'm happy," I'd told her during one lunch.

Tina had snorted, wiping a napkin roughly across her nose, making me wonder how it didn't catch the tiny stud that sparkled when she moved. She took a large bite of her sandwich. "No you're not," she'd said as sauce dripped onto her plate.

"Of course I am." I'd been married a year and had a husband who was forever telling me he loved me and how beautiful I was, how I was the only thing in his life worth living for. We had just enough money to get by and I enjoyed my part-time job at the school, even if I wasn't making the best use of my education. How could I not be happy?

"Really?" She opened her eyes wide. "Can you hand on heart say everything's great?"

I fidgeted and looked down at my untouched sandwich. Brian might not be the person I thought I'd end up with, and maybe I didn't always feel like I got things right. It was true I managed to upset him quite regularly. Just the night before, he'd questioned why I never showed him much affection.

"Why don't we ever see Brian?" she'd persisted. "He turns up to collect you, but he never comes out. Nor do you, much."

"I do," I'd protested. I couldn't tell her Brian couldn't stand Tina's brash sense of humor or how her loudness grated on him. "In fact, I'm coming to the end-of-term drinks on Friday," I announced suddenly, knowing I'd get away with it because Brian was, unusually, away overnight at a conference.

That Friday evening, as Tina downed her sixth glass of Pinot Grigio, she'd slurred at me, "Brian has a weird hold over you."

I brushed her off, though her words stayed with me, and a few months later when Brian and I had a row, I ended up walking out of our flat and staying at hers.

"I can't believe what I've just done," I'd told her. I was shaking. I'd never stood up to him before. Brian wanted me to cut my hours at school, but for once I wouldn't agree. I loved my job and had even just been offered a promotion. "Mrs. Mayer's job," I'd explained to Tina.

"What's the problem with that?" she'd asked. "And you should totally go for it. You could do that job with your eyes shut."

That was what I'd thought, only Brian wanted me home more.

Tina choked on her wine, managing to spit a mouthful back into her glass. "You're kidding, right?"

I wasn't. He told me I should be more of a homemaker than a career woman, and asked me if I wanted our marriage to work, because if I did, I was going the wrong way about it.

But as Tina had continued to vilify Brian, I found myself drawing away from her, unable to defend my husband but increasingly anxious to do so. He was still the man I loved, and I didn't think he was as controlling as she said. I needed to believe he was only worried for my sake, because if I didn't, then what else was wrong with our marriage?

By the time Brian had turned up at Tina's door, I was ready to run back into his arms and tell him I loved him. I wouldn't go for the promotion, I'd assured him, but I stood my ground: I wasn't prepared to give up any hours.

I TRIED IGNORING how much he continued to obsess over Tina and how she'd influenced me so easily. How unhappy I'd made him putting my friends and my so-called career first. At the time I was just pleased I'd stood up for myself, though deep down I knew he felt betrayed.

What I never expected, when I was back at school three weeks later after Easter, was for Brian to pick me up and tell me we weren't going home to our flat anymore. "Surprise! I've bought you your dream, Harriet," he'd said, clapping his hands.

"You've what?" I'd laughed. "What are you talking about?"

"We are moving, my love," he'd said, straight-faced

and carefully monitoring my reaction. "Everything is packed already, so you don't need to worry about a thing."

"But I like our flat," I'd told him, watching his face fall. "You're having me on, Brian." I giggled nervously.

"No, I am not. I've bought us a house by the sea in Dorset. We are starting again. A new life," he'd told me, a little more despondently than the conversation had started.

"But—" I began. "You mean you've sold our flat and bought a new house? You can't have." But I knew that was exactly what he had done, and because it was all in his name, he didn't need me to approve it. "Why?"

Brian looked at me carefully. "It's just going to be me and you, Harriet," he'd said. "Isn't that what you want?"

It took a long time for me to understand how threatened Brian had been, how close someone had come to seeing him for the man he was. Someone who, in his eyes, was turning me against him. I stood up to him. I refused to let my job go. It was Tina's fault; it couldn't have possibly been my decision.

Other friends had been more easily disposed of, but one of the reasons Brian disliked Tina was because she was so dogged. When Brian moved us to Dorset, he knew he couldn't let that happen again. He needed another way to ensure I wouldn't slip away from him. Having his daughter wasn't enough. He needed me to believe that without him I wouldn't survive. So he chipped away at me until I doubted my own sanity. How could I leave when I was so reliant on Brian or had no money of my own? How could I leave when he'd set it up so he could effortlessly prove I couldn't be trusted to look after my daughter?

As I pressed on toward Cornwall, I ignored the unsettling feeling Brian might have been right. If I could be trusted, I would know where Alice was right now. Instead I was heading to a place I'd only ever seen on the internet.

"It's dirt cheap," he'd told me, pointing to the pictures on the rental website. "It's tucked away on a lane that's pretty much deserted. There are only three cottages and no one bothers you. No one even goes down there."

I shuddered at the mismatched furniture and the old-fashioned stand-alone units in the kitchen. The backyard was long and much larger than Alice was used to, but it was also overgrown and untidy, and I couldn't imagine what she would have made of it when she was taken there from the fair.

But wasn't it also perfect, I had thought at the time. We'd needed a hideaway where no one would notice a little girl and a man appear one Saturday afternoon, before they were aware the country was looking for them. A place where no one would look for her.

Only now, all the things I had convinced myself were good about it made me sick. The secluded shack of a cottage was more of a threat than a safe house, and I was still more than three hours away from getting to it.

NOW

s there any news?" I beg.

They've told me so little of what's happening—all I know is that Charlotte's being questioned in another room somewhere down the hallway by the detective who'd turned up at the beach. But this isn't the news I'm after.

Detective Lowry shakes his head no. Behind his small, circular, wire-rimmed glasses and his light-ginger stubble, his face is the epitome of blankness. It has been since he introduced himself when I was brought into the station, his short legs scurrying up the hallway as I followed quickly behind.

I am desperate to get back out there and find out for myself what is happening. I'm sure the detective is keeping something from me. Maybe he thinks that by keeping me in the dark he can manipulate me to his advantage, use my fear to break me down.

I peer at the clock and then at the door, dismissing a crazed yearning to jump out of my seat and run toward it. Is it locked? Can I run out? I've not been arrested, after all. He's told me I'm here to help, and yet he's stepping around me like I might snap at any moment. Of course, I could physically walk out, but what would

I do then? Where would I go? If I did that, I'm sure they would haul me back inside in handcuffs. So even though I want to run, I know it's impossible.

I gaze toward the wall on my right and wonder if Charlotte is on the other side of it. She could be saying anything, and I have no right to ask her not to. I lost that luxury the day of the fair.

"Are you okay, Harriet?" Detective Lowry asks.

"Sorry?" I look up at him and he nods at my wrist. I hadn't noticed I'd been rubbing it. I pull my hand away. The skin is red but the searing pain has subsided and in its place is a dull throb.

"I think it's okay," I say, though no one has checked, but right now my wrist is the least of my problems.

He is still watching me, glancing at my wrist. He looks concerned as he strokes a thumb against his stubble, before he checks himself and looks down at his pad. Now he is moving on and is interested in my friendship with Charlotte. I tell him she was always a good friend to me.

"Charlotte knew I didn't know anyone in Dorset," I say. "She made me feel welcome." I was grateful for that, more than I would have ever let on. It had taken me three months to find a part-time job and settle in at St. Mary's primary school, and still I had no one I could call a friend. I'd seen Charlotte on the playground, huddled in her group of mums. She'd stood out from the others, with her long blond hair always swishing behind her in a ponytail, her skinny jeans, long gray cardigan, and sparkly flip-flops. I couldn't take my eyes off her, for no other reason than she attracted me like a moth to a light.

I would go into school in the mornings and look out for what she was wearing. I used to pull my own tangled mass of hair back into a ponytail and see if I could look like her.

Charlotte was the picture you stick on the fridge: the one that reminds you there's something to aim for. For me she epitomized everything I wanted in life: freedom and the ability to make choices without repercussion.

"Charlotte introduced me to her group of friends, but to be honest I didn't have much in common with the rest of them," I say.

"But you did with Charlotte?"

"Surprisingly, yes. We were both raised by our mums. We lost father figures in our lives at an early age. There was an understanding between us because of that, and not everyone gets it."

Detective Lowry looks at me quizzically, but I don't elaborate. Instead I say, "It just meant we had something in common. Something we could talk about," I add, even though I was never the one to talk.

I tell him more about our friendship, the hours we spent chatting on the bench in the park.

"Your friendship sounds a little . . ." Detective Lowry waves a hand in the air as he searches for the right word. "One-sided."

I look up at him.

"Don't you think?" he says, tapping his pen lightly against the desk.

"No, I think she wanted it too."

"Absolutely, Harriet. I meant it seems like she needed you a lot more than you did her."

I smile thinly because he could not have been more wrong.

"Or maybe I have the wrong impression, but it sounds like you were there for Charlotte a lot more than she was for you."

That might be true, but only because I made it that way.

"Do you think on some level she knows this now?" he asks, and his words sound shrill as they ring across the desk. I know what he's getting at, but he doesn't say it outright.

"It wasn't a matter of either of us needing each other," I lie, because surely that was the essence of our friendship.

"But why didn't you ever share anything with her, Harriet?" he asks. "Were you afraid she wouldn't believe you?"

No, that wasn't it.

At first I was afraid I didn't believe myself, and then I was afraid I would lose her. But I was also scared of what would happen, how far he would go. He had dispensed of Jane easily because I'd let him. He had moved our whole life because of Tina, but with Charlotte I couldn't take the risk, because I had Alice to think of too.

Wednesday, October 5, 2016

Brian told the doctor today that I am getting worse. He said that when he came home he found out I'd locked myself in a cupboard for most of the afternoon. He raised his eyebrows as if this were typical of me.

The doctor looked at me under his bushy eyebrows. I might have mentioned my fear of small spaces once. He asked me how I'd coped.

Brian butted in, saying he felt so sorry for me as I was claustrophobic. He added that I can't even lock bathroom doors and told the doctor that I'd once made him walk up thirteen flights of stairs because I wouldn't get in the elevator.

The doctor just nodded and asked if Alice was with me, but I still didn't get a chance to answer. Brian said she was as he shook his head, calling her a little mite and saying that she must've been going out of her mind. Then he said that he'd explicitly told me yesterday morning not to go anywhere near the cupboard because the lock was faulty. Apparently this is what worries Brian—that he tells me things and I don't remember.

I closed my eyes but I didn't speak.

The doctor said my name, waiting for my side of the

story, but what was the point? Brian would only contradict me. In the end I told him I couldn't remember. But I can. I remember all of it:

I woke, relieved when I realized Brian had left the house already, because I could start my day without having to look at my husband. Never mind it was raining heavily outside, Alice and I would stay in and watch TV and play games.

Alice was looking for something when I found her in the living room. Her toys were scattered over the floor and I remember thinking I'd have to tidy them before Brian came home.

Alice said she couldn't find the game with rockets—the one with the aliens and spaceships—and we looked through her toys together but couldn't find it. In fact, none of her board games were there, which was odd.

As I'm now in the habit of checking everything with Alice, I asked if we'd moved it, but she shook her head. I didn't think we had, and we'd even played it the day before. Alice pointed to one of the plastic crates and said she'd put the game back in there.

The only other place I could think it might be was the downstairs cupboard, which we rarely use, but it's the only place to store anything in this small house. I held the door open with my foot and pulled the light cord, but the light didn't come on. The box of spare bulbs was at the back of the cupboard so I squinted in the darkness until I just about made out a stack of board games shoved onto a shelf at the far end. Edging closer, my heel still against the door, I leaned in to grab it but couldn't quite reach. I shuffled a little more, and as I touched the box my foot slipped and I fell forward while the door slammed shut behind me.

I screamed out in the pitch-black. But with one hand on the game, I straightened and felt my way back to the door. It wouldn't open. I shoved at it, pushing as hard as I could, but the door remained jammed. My heart hammered as I shoved and shoved, banging on the door, though what use was that when it was only Alice and me in the house?

I heard her whimper on the other side of the door. She was asking where I was.

I called out that I was stuck in the cupboard, trying my best to keep the fear from seeping out through my words, but I was scared stiff. I asked Alice to try pulling the door from the outside and felt it give a little as she did, but still it didn't open.

I told her to turn the handle, but Alice started crying. I said everything would be fine and got her to stand back, then I shoved against the door with everything I had, but still it wouldn't move.

She needed to ask for help. This was a big thing for Alice—she'd have to go into the backyard and climb onto her flowerpot and lean over the fence to Mr. Potter's house. I knew she was scared, but I told her she had to be a big brave girl and go and see if she could get his attention.

Mr. Potter ended up climbing over the fence to come into the house with Alice. When he pulled and twisted the handle and eventually got me out of the cupboard, I sank into his chest and sobbed, pulling Alice toward me too.

He asked how long I'd been in there for. It felt like hours.

He started pulling on the handle and told me the lock was jammed, and then the whole thing came off in his hand. We agreed it was lucky that didn't happen a minute ago, because I would have been in there a lot longer.

Before he went I asked him if he could wait while I got the spare lightbulbs. I said the one in there must have blown already. But then Mr. Potter nodded at the ceiling and pointed out that there wasn't even one in there.

Except I know I changed it just a few days ago.

BEFORE

HARRIET

I didn't understand until last November, six months before the fair, just how deeply Brian had me under his control, but I also knew there was little I could do about it. Not if I wanted any chance of keeping Alice.

One morning last autumn I took Alice to the park in Chiddenford in a haze of despair. He had fooled everyone. Mostly me, but he'd managed to drag everyone else into his version of reality too. What chance did I, the crazy wife who put their child in danger, stand against him? Who would believe me if I told them my truth?

Charlotte was already at the park, and I slipped onto the bench alongside her, watching Evie run around with a bubble wand clutched in her tiny hand. Alice stood by my side, hesitant to join in until she was ready. Charlotte babbled on about her sister's wedding and, as I often did, I lost myself in the wonderful mundanity of her problems until she said, "There's still no news of that little boy, Mason."

"I know. The parents must feel awful. You just can't imagine what they're going through, can you?" I shuddered, and both our eyes followed Evie a little closer as she ran around. "I haven't read much about it," I admitted, even though his disappearance was headline news. Every time I thought of the little boy vanishing I felt sick.

"Hmm. I know this is a dreadful thing to say, but do you think the parents are involved?"

"No. Not at all," I gasped. "Why, do you?"

"I don't think so, but that's what some people are saying. I read this article online listing all these weird reasons the case doesn't stack up and it makes you think, doesn't it?"

"No, it's not them," I said. "I don't believe that for one minute."

Charlotte sighed. "No, I don't either," she agreed. "But isn't it awful that it gets so twisted by the media? His family's lives have been invaded. They can't do anything without the world watching them. It must be so hard." She fiddled with a scarf that lay across her lap. "But then I suppose if they do have anything to hide, they won't be able to for long."

That night I read everything I could about the Mason Harbridge case—the boy who vanished out of sight. It was an interesting thought: how someone can vanish completely. And Charlotte was right, the eyes of the world were on those left behind—Mason's parents couldn't put a foot out of place without someone picking up on it.

If they stripped back the walls that Brian had so skillfully built, what would they see? How long would he be able to deceive everyone? With the press poking into our lives, the police trawling our house: living with us, watching every moment, hearing every lie that came out of his mouth.

All I'd need was for everyone to see what I saw. Then Alice and I could escape him. And Alice wouldn't have to stay hidden for long. Just until the world recognized the monster I lived with.

After all, how clever is Brian, really?

CHARLOTTE'S THROWAWAY COMMENT about the Harbridge family never left me, and a few weeks after, in late November, I first saw a chance of turning the idea into reality.

I was cleaning the house one rainy Monday morning when the doorbell rang. I smiled at Alice who was painting at the kitchen table and, with a duster in one hand, answered the door to find a man on my doorstep. He looked as shocked as I must have been, and with one hand gripping the doorframe, he leaned slightly forward as if he were about to speak.

My eyes skimmed over his face. I shook my head nervously, took a step back. I didn't recognize all of him, but his large green eyes were so familiar.

"Harriet," he eventually said. It wasn't a question.

"No," I muttered, still shaking my head. "It can't be you." I looked up and down the road but there was no one around, then back to him as he awkwardly shuffled his feet.

He dropped his gaze to the ground, leaving me to stare at the patch where his white hair was thinning.

"What—" I said in a low breath. There were too many questions running through my mind. *What are you doing here? Is there bad news? How did you find me? Are you really who I think you are?*

"Do you think I could, erm, come in?"

I shook my head again. I couldn't let him in. What would I tell Alice?

"I don't need to stay long. I would just like the chance to talk to you."

I eventually opened the door wider and directed him through to the kitchen, telling Alice that if she watched TV in the living room, we could make a cake that afternoon.

She didn't need telling twice and as soon as Alice was out of the room, I gestured for the man to sit down while I stood against the kitchen sink and said, "Everyone thinks you're dead."

"You didn't believe I'd died, then?" My father, Les, played nervously with his hands, twisting a wedding band around and around. I watched those hands closely, trying to remember them picking me up as a child or playing a game with me, but nothing came to mind.

"No, I knew the truth," I said quietly. What I did remember was the first time I heard my mum tell someone in a store that my father was dead. I'd looked at her in shock, wondering when it could have happened, but Mum gave me a look and a small shake of her head and even at such a young age I quickly understood she wasn't telling the truth. It was another of her fabrications.

"So Daddy's not dead?" I'd asked her later when we were on our own.

"No, he's not," Mum had said, flapping about a large sheet that she was desperately trying to fold. In the end she rolled it into a ball and stuffed it into the linen closet. "But he is gone and it'll be a lot easier for Mummy if we tell people he is."

I hadn't liked the sound of it, but I went along with her because she was my mum. There was no one else I could turn to, to ask if what we were doing was right. It certainly didn't feel it, but I absorbed her lie and at some point over the years it became easier telling people he'd died than facing up to the fact my mother had deliberately created such a dreadful story. By the time I met Brian I didn't even consider another version.

As I grew older I understood Mum well enough to know she wouldn't have coped with the looks of pity, or neighbors talking behind her back, asking questions and wondering what it was that finally drove my father away. Or maybe what took him so long. I don't know if Mum blamed herself for his departure—outwardly she blamed him—but she would have assumed everyone else thought it was her fault.

All I was left with was a memory of him from an old crumpled photograph. Our faces pressed together with wide smiles as he held me in his arms, both sharing an ice cream.

Now I searched his face. The features I remembered were there, but hidden under skin that puffed in layers on his cheeks. The bright green eyes were watery now and drooped under his white eyebrows. The years had taken away the one picture I'd had in my head and re-placed it with this old man who looked so lost and out of place in my kitchen. Years I would never get back, I thought, as I turned away from him sharply and fussed with the kettle so my face wouldn't betray me.

His sudden appearance had brought a rush of unex-pected emotion that I hadn't even realized I'd been ig-noring. Had I actually missed him? "How did you find me?" I asked eventually. Not why. I didn't know if I was ready to hear the answer to that yet.

"I found you on that Facebook about a year ago." He had a gentle lull to his voice. "You were there under your maiden name and it said you worked at St. Mary's School in Chiddenford." I had set up a page once to stay updated on school news, but had never added a post or even bothered updating my details when I'd left.

"Bit of a funny story after that," he'd went on. "I have a cousin who lives down here. He knows the area well, told me where the village was."

"Yes?" I prompted.

"One day I thought I'd come down and have a look around. I didn't really think I had any chance of seeing you, but I happened to be walking past a park just around the corner from the school and—" He paused. "I recognized you straightaway. I never forgot your face. You had your little girl with you. She looks just like you," he said, looking up at me and smiling. "The image of you back then."

"So you saw me and then what?" I said harshly.

"Then I followed you," he said, dropping his eyes to the table.

"You followed me?"

"I know, I know, it was an awful thing to do, I just— Well, I should have talked to you but I didn't have the courage," he said. "I dithered for ages until you got up and started walking away, and I didn't want to blow it. I wasn't sure what I wanted to say and—" He laughed and broke off. "Now I fear I'm still not doing a very good job."

I dipped tea bags into the cups, poured in a splash of milk, then turned back to him. My dad fidgeted uncomfortably at the table. Had he come to tell me he was dying? I wondered. Would that matter to me?

"It's a shock for you, I know that," he said. "Seeing me on your doorstep."

"I think there was a part of me that always imagined it might happen one day."

"I hope I haven't upset you?" He looked at me with a glimmer of hope as he tried to meet my gaze, but he couldn't hold it for long.

"I'm more intrigued than anything," I said, trying to sound distant. Often I had looked at Brian and thought children are better off without their fathers, but mine had never given me the chance to find out.

I handed him the tea and he wrapped his large hands around the mug, pulling it toward him and studying the liquid inside. "I'm sorry," he said simply.

"What are you actually sorry for?" I asked, my back pressed firmly against the sink as I clutched my own cup tightly. A sudden desperate need to believe his apology surprised me.

"For the way it happened," he said. "For not seeing you again."

"I don't really know what happened," I admitted, watching him, wondering what it would have been like to have had a father around. If my life would have taken a different path and whether I'd have wanted it to. The quiet hum of a kids' TV show filtered through the wall and I knew that no, despite it all, I wouldn't have changed a thing. "Obviously Mum told me her version."

"It didn't happen quickly," he said. "It was never a light decision for me. When I first met your mum she was a beautiful young woman." His eyes sparkled at the memory. "Full of energy and plans, and I fell for her head over heels. We didn't have much money but we were happy for a long time. Over the years I began noticing she had a lot of demons, troubles I wasn't very good at handling. She worried about everything. Hated me leaving the house, convinced I wasn't coming back. Every night she made me get out of bed at least three times to check the locks. Always at me over some concern about something or other. I started drinking a lot." My father paused and nodded. "My way of blocking it out. One day I realized I wasn't living anymore, I was surviving, and I didn't want to do it any longer."

I pulled out a chair and sat down opposite him.

"I was suffocating, Harriet," he said. "Being in that house with her was too much. But I don't expect you to understand what I mean."

I didn't answer but I must have made a sound because he looked up at me and said, "I'm sorry. Of course you understand. You would have seen the way she was. I realize I don't know how it was for you after I left."

"Mum was fine," I said, and for the first time I realized I had been suffocated by someone my whole life. "She was who she was and I loved her for it."

"She loved you very much too. More than anything else in her world, so there was no doubt in my mind you'd be fine after I left, that you'd be better off with her. I never considered taking that away from her."

"But surely you didn't need to make that choice?" I said sharply. "You didn't need to get out of my life completely."

"I could have fought," he said solemnly. "It would have been a fight, though. I'd met someone else, you see. Marilyn. She was this light. She saved me from—" He paused. "Well, from many things, really."

"So you chose Marilyn over me?"

"It wasn't like that. Your mum knew about Marilyn

and made it very clear that if I didn't leave her I wasn't welcome in your life. I begged her, pleaded that she didn't need to stop me seeing you, but there was no changing her mind. If I'd stayed, it would have ended me, Harriet. Like I told you, I was already drinking too heavily and it was only with Marilyn's help I finally stopped.

"I tried to visit," he went on. "But she wouldn't even let me in the door. It was the seventies, there weren't support groups for dads back then. Then a week or so later I found out she'd told everyone I'd died. I didn't come back after that. Part of me thought it would be for the best." Les shook his head. "I didn't want to make things harder for you with people wondering why your mother had lied to them. I'm sorry, Harriet. If I could turn back time—"

"Then you probably wouldn't do anything differently," I said. "Are you and Marilyn still together?"

"She died six months ago but yes, we were." His eyes watered and I found myself reaching across the table and taking hold of his hand, feeling his rough fingers curling around my own. It may not be how I would have done it, but could I honestly blame him for needing to get away?

"I'm sorry," I said.

"So how was it after I left?" he asked.

"Well, I wish Mum wouldn't have hovered over me as much as she did, but I never lacked love. Why have you come looking for me now?"

"It was something I'd talked about for a long time. Marilyn kept prodding me to do it. She was the one who told me to try Facebook, but I never had the nerve. Then she passed away and now everything in life looks different. I'm an old man with no one left. I don't deserve to have you back in my life, but I wanted the chance to see you again. And your little girl, of course."

"Alice."

"That's a pretty name. How old is she?"

"She just turned four."

My father nodded. "I promised myself that whatever you wanted from me, I would do it. If you tell me to get lost, I'll go." He gave me a sad smile. "I just had to know for sure. I don't want any more regrets." He looked at me expectantly, but I didn't answer.

Eventually he pushed away from the table and told me he should probably be going. I didn't stop him because I didn't want to risk Brian coming home to find my father in our kitchen. But when my dad asked if he could see me again and spend some time with Alice, I agreed because I had nothing to lose. I wanted to find out more about him and I liked that he wanted to get to know us. And whether I liked it or not, there were similarities between us.

We arranged to meet the following week in a café in Bridport and I led him to my front door and said, "My husband thinks you're dead."

"Oh?" He looked shocked. "You told him that?"

I nodded. "I told everyone that," I said. "And I don't think I should tell him otherwise for now." He looked at me quizzically but I didn't explain. "It's better we keep this between us," I said. "I'd rather no one else know you're here."

"Apart from my cousin." He gave a small smile.

"Oh, right." I'd forgotten he'd mentioned a cousin.

"But you don't need to worry about him. He's practically a hermit," my father said.

"Well, please don't mention any more to him."

"Of course, if that's what you want." He smiled. "But

you may be surprised. If you tell your husband about me, you might find he's a lot more understanding than you're giving him credit for."

I shook my head. Brian would not be understanding in the slightest.

Monday, November 7, 2016

Brian grabbed two towels from the linen closet and ordered me to take off my clothes, yelling that Alice and I were both soaked and demanding to know what was going through my head.

I wrapped my arms tighter around the damp shirt that clung to my body. I hadn't expected the clouds to open. I hadn't taken umbrellas and our raincoats were packed at the bottom of the suitcase.

His mouth was close against my ear as he told me I was inches from the edge of the train platform when he found me. I turned my head away as he peeled my arms apart and shoved a towel against my chest.

A sob lodged in the back of my throat. I didn't want to get undressed while he was there. I didn't like the way he was watching me, waiting for me to take my clothes off.

Brian began unbuttoning my damp shirt, exposing an old, graying bra that bagged over my breasts. I recoiled from his touch, which made him suddenly stop. He asked if I did all these things on purpose. He's not happy that after everything he does for me, this is the way I treat him.

He said he knew I was leaving him and taking Alice. He didn't have to add that she was shivering when he got there, that her little body was drenched, but he said it anyway. Brian grabbed my arms and pressed his thumbs into my skin.

I cried out that I couldn't do this anymore. He looked at me like he had no clue what I was talking about. I said I couldn't live like this.

Brian asked me how I supposed I could live without him.

I didn't have an answer to that. When I'd packed a suitcase and hauled Alice to the station, telling her we were going on holiday, I hadn't thought through what we would do. Not long term. All I knew was that we needed to get away from Brian.

He reminded me that he'd found me and that he always would. He took a step back and said he couldn't shake the image of us both standing so close to the edge, and that he'd need to talk to the doctor about this and see what he suggests. Brian added that he'd hate him to say I needed a stay in a hospital, but maybe it was for the best. He told me again I was turning into my mother.

I can't stay but I don't know how to get away. I can't risk him having me put in a hospital. He'll be watching me even closer now.

HARRIET

In the lead-up to Christmas, as Charlotte became embroiled in the aftermath of her sister's wedding and plans to take the children away for the holidays, I found myself increasingly dependent on my father.

We met up in various places over Dorset, each time somewhere new. With him living in Southampton, he wasn't so close that Brian would ever bump into him, but he was near enough to see us for a day. I hid our meet-ups from Brian, always arranging them when my husband was at work. Seeing my dad was an escape from the downward spiral of life at home, and I began to look forward to watching his blossoming relationship with Alice.

There were times when I was resentful, particularly when I watched him running away from the waves with a squealing Alice or making her cars out of sand.

"Why didn't you try harder?" I'd asked, when he'd insisted on buying us ice cream in the middle of January. I had missed out on so many moments like this. I'd been fine not knowing what I hadn't had, but now that he was back in my life, a hole had opened up that I hadn't realized was there.

Then I would watch Alice curl up on his lap like a

contented cat, in awe of his card tricks, and I wondered if it really mattered what had happened in the past. It was more important that I didn't let it ruin the future. Alice had a grandfather in her life now, and one she doted on. And secretly I was excited at the thought of having my dad again.

Les felt like a world away from my real life and I began telling him snippets about the man I had married, certain he would never meet Brian. It was good to finally share the truth with someone, and even more when that person was my father. Eventually I told him how Brian had led me to believe I was crazy.

"I can assure you, you are not crazy," he said.

"He drops it into conversations that I'm like Mum."

"He never even knew your mother," my dad said angrily. We were sipping hot chocolates in the café of a National Trust house watching Alice play outside. "And she wasn't crazy. She just had a lot of anxieties."

I didn't tell him I was more like her than I liked, but it was what I was thinking.

"Besides," he said, "being like her is not a bad thing. She was a very good mother and in her own way she always put you first."

I dropped my head so he couldn't see the tears that had sprung into my eyes. "I can't see a way out," I said.

"There's always a way out."

"I have no money. Not a penny of my own. I don't even have my own bank account. If I walked out, I wouldn't be able to buy us our next meal."

"Well, I can help," he offered.

"Thank you, but with what? You've already told me your state pension barely gets you through the week." He didn't have his own house and was still in the rented flat he and Marilyn had lived in for years.

"So you need to go to the police," he persisted.

"And say what? I have no scars to show them," I said, rolling up my sleeves. "No bruises. I've no way of proving he's abusing me."

"But somehow you need to get away, take Alice and—"

"I've tried," I cried. "Brian finds me. He's done it before," I told him. "Somehow he manages to track me down and haul me home, and I know he'll take Alice away from me. He'll prove I'm crazy, that's the beauty of what he does," I said sarcastically. "Brian has it all worked out."

"You really think he wants to take her from you?" my dad asked. "I don't get the impression he has much of a relationship with Alice."

I watched Alice pick up a leaf and carefully tuck it into her pocket. "He loves her," I said. But I also saw the way their conversations looked awkward, that he didn't always know how to talk to her. That when the three of us were together, Brian often hung on the edge like an outsider. Surely he must have noticed that too, though I'm not convinced it would matter in the end. "I have no doubt he'd make sure she was taken from me," I said. "If he thought it was what he had to do."

"Let me help," my father pleaded. "At least come stay with me while you work things out. You can both have my bed and I'll sleep on the sofa. Let me do this for you and Alice, please." He took hold of my hand and squeezed it tightly. "I want to."

"But everyone thinks you're dead," I cried. "Don't you see? If I suddenly announce I'm off to stay with my dead father, who I've been seeing for the last few months, Brian will have a ball. I write 'mother and father deceased' on forms. My best friend thinks you died when I was five. If they find out I've been lying to them all this time, Brian will be shouting from the rooftops that this is exactly what he means."

"But there's got to be something I can do for you," my father said.

"Maybe there is one way." I took a deep breath and told him about the Harbridge family and the idea Charlotte had put into my head.

"You want me to *abduct* Alice?" He looked aghast.

"Shh." I looked around but the café had emptied out. "Let's go outside." We grabbed our coats and went out, waving at Alice who was still busy stuffing her pockets with leaves and twigs that she'd make into something later. "It would only be temporary, and you're not abducting her. You'd be keeping her in a safe house for me while I figure out a way to expose Brian."

"No, Harriet. I don't like it one bit."

"No one will suspect you because you don't exist," I went on.

"No." He shook his head. "Too many things can go wrong. The police won't see it that way."

"If anything went wrong I'd tell them it was all my idea," I promised him.

"It's ridiculous. You'd go to prison. Have you even thought of that?"

"Yes," I lied. I hadn't thought of much more than getting away from my husband.

"And how do you suppose it ends, Harriet? What are you planning? That you'll run away with Alice and live abroad?"

"No." I'd thought about that, but I couldn't contemplate us living the rest of our lives in hiding. In some ways it would be no better than what we had now.

"No," I said again carefully. "What I've been thinking is that when the time is right, you leave her somewhere. Somewhere safe where there are people and you could tell her to call the police." I spoke with as much conviction as I could. We both needed to believe it was a plausible outcome. "By then you'll have gained her trust and she'll know not to say it was you. All anyone will have is her description of the man who took her. She's four, they'd expect inconsistencies, they wouldn't expect her to know exactly where she'd been."

"Yes, she's *four*," my father said. "You're entrusting a toddler to carry this lie. It's so wrong, I can't believe I'm hearing it."

"Alice trusts me. And you," I add. "She's bright. She'd understand if we told her this was the only way to be safe."

"Oh, Harriet," my dad sighed, shaking his head. "This isn't the way."

"Do it for me," I pleaded, ignoring him. "If nothing more than because you owe me this."

"Don't put that on me."

"But that's what you said. The first time I met you, you told me that whatever I wanted you to do you'd do it. This is what I want," I said. "You can either walk away or be in our lives," I tried as a last-ditch attempt.

He walked away.

I HAD LOST my only hope of a future and my dad. He still turned up at the museum where we'd arranged to meet the following week as planned, but there was a distance between us. We reverted to being more like the strangers we were two months ago than the father and daughter we'd become.

Over the following weeks the gap widened. The only times I saw flashes of the father I'd grown to care so deeply about were when I watched him playing with Alice. He'd throw her into the air and spin her around and tickle her on the ground until she begged him to stop because she was laughing too hard. Only in those times did he look like he'd almost forgotten what I'd asked of him.

One Wednesday in mid-March we took a ferry to Brownsea, an island that sat in nearby Poole Harbour. I sat on a log while my dad took Alice to show her the peacocks, but when they came back he had a grave look on his face. "We need to talk." He joined me on the log as I watched Alice run across the grass. "If you're adamant it's the only way, I'll do it."

"Are you serious?" I gasped.

"There are many things we need to sort out."

"Yes. Yes, of course." I leaned toward him and wrapped my arms around his waist, though I felt him stiffen. "Are you sure about this?" I asked, pulling back.

"For what it's worth, I think it's very risky, Harriet. Many things could go wrong." He took my hands and peeled them off his waist. "And if anything bad happens, I need you to promise me something."

"Okay?"

"It's me who takes the blame. Not you."

"No way. I can't let that happen."

"That's one of my conditions," he said firmly. "It's up to you to ensure no one knows you had anything to do with it. I won't let Alice be taken away from you."

"But—"

"I mean it," he said. "If you can't promise me that, we don't do this."

"How would I ever be able to do that?" I asked him.

"Alice will say she knows you and then it'll be clear I've been meeting you for months."

"I'll come up with something," he said. "But for now it's best we don't see each other again."

I gaped at him. "Why can't we see each other?"

"We can't risk anyone seeing us together while we work out what to do. But I'm deadly serious, Harriet. You need to promise me you'll never let anyone think you had anything to do with this if it all goes wrong."

I stared at my father, whose eyes hadn't once strayed from Alice. "Okay," I said in a whisper. "I promise."

He nodded.

"What made you change your mind?" I asked.

"I just did," he said shortly.

"Dad? What is it?" I followed his eye line to where Alice played, running after an unsuspecting peacock. "Has Alice said something to you?"

He squirmed beside me, never taking his eyes off my daughter.

"If she has, please tell me."

"I said I'll do this, Harriet, so let's just focus on what we do now."

FROM THE TIME we agreed to this plan, I'd known there were many what-ifs. I was well aware everything could fall apart at the slightest crack, but by then I was desperate. I picked out parts that needed slotting together and forced them into place. I ran my fingers over the points where something could go horribly wrong and I knew I was taking a leap of faith, but faith was all I had.

"I trusted you, Dad," I said aloud as I drove on toward Cornwall, hands trembling against the wheel. "I trusted you."

But then, deep down, didn't I still?

Yet if I did, all I was left with was the unsettling worry that something must have happened to them to stop him from answering my calls.

HARRIET

F our days after Alice was taken I called the pay-as-you-go cell my dad had bought, as we'd agreed. I told Angela and Brian I needed to get some fresh air and stopped at a pay phone three streets away. My hand was shaking as I tapped in the numbers, praying I'd remembered them in the right order.

As soon as my dad said, "Hello," four days of tension flooded out of my body.

"Is she okay?"

"She's fine. She's asking for you, but she's okay."

"Oh, thank God," I breathed. "Can I speak to her?"

"She's outside but I don't think it's right that you do anyway. She's more settled today."

I tried to imagine Alice through the pictures of the house I'd seen online. It was my dad's idea to take her to Elderberry Cottage, a holiday home in the tiny village of West Aldell in Cornwall. He and Marilyn had stayed there twice and we were both comfortable that he knew the area. He assured me that they had never been bothered, that during both stays they'd barely seen anyone in the area, at least no one who took any interest in them.

"But she's okay?" I asked him. "She's well?"

"Alice is doing fine. I've told her it's a little trip. She thinks you're not feeling well, like we said."

"And how was she at the fair? She wasn't frightened?"

"No. She was surprised and confused, but I told her what we agreed, that I'd spoken to Charlotte and told her you weren't well. Then she was just worried about you, but once I assured her it was nothing serious—" My dad broke off. I felt our deception cutting through my skin and I knew he did too.

"It's so good to speak to you, Dad," I said.

"Right." He sounded flat.

"Dad? You sound strange, what is it?"

"It's nothing, Harriet."

"Tell me. What's the problem?"

I heard his large intake of breath. "Where do I start? You're all over the news. Alice is too. Her picture is everywhere. I worry about leaving the cottage in case someone sees her."

"I know, but it's not going to be like that for long," I said, sounding more determined than I felt. "You have to do this now, we can't turn back."

"I know that. But it doesn't feel right anymore. Hell, what am I saying? It never did."

"You're scaring me," I said, pressing my hand against the glass of the phone booth.

"I am scared," he said in a whisper. "And I have a very bad feeling this isn't going to work out the way we want it to. Listen, we need to keep these calls short. Just let me get on with it here and we'll keep our heads down."

"Okay, but I'll call you again next Wednesday as agreed."

"Fine."

"Keep her safe, Dad. Don't take her anywhere."

"We have to go out sometimes."

"Well, nowhere anyone sees you."

My dad sighed again. "We go to the beach, but that's all. Like I told you, it's deserted most of the time and the cottage has a fishing boat I can borrow, so I'm going to take her out on that."

"Okay. That sounds good," I said, thinking no one is likely to spot them in the middle of the sea. "Thank you, Dad. You know I couldn't do this without you."

I hung up, the tension already seeping its way back inside. It was a relief to know Alice was safe, but what if my father couldn't hold out?

I'd go through the motions until I'd arranged to call him again. Just to hear him tell me they were both okay was all I needed to get me through. If I knew then that when I called the following Wednesday he wouldn't answer, I would have driven to the cottage to get my daughter back straightaway.

I HAD JUST passed the halfway mark on my journey to Cornwall when a warning light flashed on the dashboard. The car started to slow and as much as I pressed my foot on the accelerator, I could feel it losing power until it stuttered to a stop three hundred feet from a gas station. Grateful for its proximity, I asked the assistant if he knew a number for a tow truck and waited in the stark light of the convenience store for an hour until help arrived.

The mechanic said he would tow me to a local garage, adding that of course no one would be able to look at it until the following morning.

"I can't wait until then," I cried out.

The mechanic shrugged as he wiped his hands on an oily cloth. "I'm afraid you don't have much choice. No one will be there tonight."

"What do I do?" I couldn't leave my car there and I certainly couldn't turn back.

"Well, if you want to come with me while I tow the car to the garage, I can take you on to my brother's bed-and-breakfast if you like?" he suggested. "I'll call him now and make sure they've got a room, but I'm sure they will," he added softly, eyeing the tears cascading down my cheeks. "Thursday night, so he won't be busy and he's very cheap. He'll take you to get your car in the morning."

It was the only realistic option. We left my car at the garage, where the mechanic posted a note with his brother's number on it. Then he drove two miles through narrow country lanes to the shabby B&B, which was nothing more than a house with a handwritten VACANCIES sign stuck to its latticed bay window.

As darkness crept in, the idea of being so isolated without a phone made me physically tremble. "It'll be warm inside," the mechanic said, mistaking my fear for cold as he pressed the doorbell.

I could never explain to him that this was so much more than the inconvenience of a faulty car. I had no idea what I'd walked away from and even less what I was walking into, and the thought of being trapped midway between the two was terrifying.

CHARLOTTE

On Thursday evening Charlotte stood at her bedroom window and watched Angela step out of her car, gazing up at the house opposite with its FOR SALE board attached to the gate. She knew what Angela would be thinking. There were a few coveted roads in Chiddenford and this was one of them. The pretty cul-de-sacs with their beautiful houses sat on plots much more generous than in other parts of the village. Eventually Angela turned and walked toward Charlotte's home.

Charlotte smiled warmly as she opened the door and tried to gauge the expression on the detective's face. "The kids are still playing outside. I should get them ready for bed, but it's such a nice evening." She looked at her watch. It was already 7:00 p.m. "Can I get you a drink?"

"Just water would be lovely, thank you," Angela said as she stepped into the hallway. "Wow, this is amazing."

"Thank you." Charlotte gave a small smile. Everyone commented on her grand hallway, and usually she was proud of it. But it seemed so small in importance now.

"So, how can I help you?" Charlotte asked, leading Angela to the kitchen where she filled a tumbler with water and handed it to her. "Please sit down." She gestured to a bar stool and Angela perched on it, resting her glass on the island in front of her, continuing to gape at the expanse of Charlotte's kitchen.

"Have you heard anything from Harriet?" Angela asked, taking a sip and carefully placing the glass down.

"No, not since I went to her house after the fair. Why do you ask?"

"I just wondered if she's come to see you, or spoken to you," Angela said.

Charlotte shook her head. "I haven't heard from her once."

"You see, she isn't at the house," Angela went on. "I arranged to be there at four this afternoon. Harriet's never not been in, especially when she knows I'm coming."

Charlotte pulled out a stool for herself on the other side of the island. There was obviously more bothering Angela than Harriet not being at home. The thought of her visitor the previous night was beginning to set off alarm bells.

"Brian was here last night," she said.

"Brian?" Angela looked surprised.

Charlotte shuddered at the memory of him waiting for her on the other side of her front hedge. "He was outside my house when I was going out. He wanted to speak to me in his car. He wouldn't come into the house, I don't know why."

"What did he want?" Angela asked, leaning forward.

"That's the strange thing. All he kept talking about was Harriet and how much he loved her. He wanted to know if she ever talked to me about their marriage, which she never did. It was an odd conversation."

Angela looked as confused as Charlotte felt. "Did you get the hint they'd had an argument?"

"I wondered that, but he didn't say as much. He was just a bit—" Charlotte gestured a hand in the air. "Weird. I assumed it was the stress of Alice and everything—but like I said, it was Harriet he was talking about, not Alice."

Angela sat back and reached into her handbag, pulling out a notepad.

"Has something else happened?" Charlotte asked, trying to see what the detective was writing but unable to make anything out.

Angela looked up. "Nothing in particular. But the house was a little disrupted when I got there this afternoon."

"How do you mean 'disrupted'?" The word made her cold. Harriet's home was always so neat and organized.

"It was a mess. Things had been disturbed," Angela said, pen poised in the air. "When I looked through the living room window, I could see all of Alice's toys strewn across the carpet."

"But what did Brian say?" Charlotte asked. "How did he explain it?" She'd always thought he was the one who liked it so tidy. Harriet never seemed to mind a bit of a mess, you only had to look in her handbag to see that. But still, there was no way Harriet would have thrown Alice's toys around.

"That's the strange thing," Angela said. "He wasn't there either. There's no sign of Harriet or Brian and I have no idea where either of them have gone."

NOW

The detective wants to know why I didn't tell anyone where I was going when I walked out of my house yesterday. He wants to know why, twelve days after my daughter had disappeared, I got up and drove off without telling my husband or Angela or my best friend, who is currently sitting in another room being questioned by his colleague.

I tell him the same story over and over, but each time he asks me again, only he frames the question slightly differently, hoping he might catch me in a lie. I fear he soon will.

Eventually Detective Lowry sighs and suggests a "comfort break."

"Is there any news yet?" I ask again as I'm leaving the room. "Could you find out for me, please?" I cannot bring myself to say the words.

He nods, and for a moment I see a fleeting look in his eyes that resembles compassion. He hesitates by the door as if about to tell me something. I hold my breath, but in the end he says nothing.

There is news. There is something he isn't sharing.

Detective Lowry heads one way up the hallway and I turn in the other direction toward the bathroom. It's been thirteen days since I've been with Alice. Before the fair, not thirteen hours had passed when I hadn't been able to look at her face and hold her in my arms. That's what tears me apart the most: not being able to touch her.

The air in the hallway becomes so thin it's hard to breathe. I reach for the wall to steady myself as a sharp pain splits across my forehead. The bright lights flicker and dim, and my vision narrows. I haven't eaten since breakfast, though they offered me a biscuit an hour ago. I should have forced it down but I couldn't, and now I regret it as I feel the pain of my empty stomach.

The thought of staying here a moment longer is almost unbearable. With one hand on the wall I feel my way along, a few more paces, until I reach the bathroom door. Pushing it open, I almost fall inside and clasp on to the basin's cool white enamel with both hands.

Eventually I pull my head up and focus on my reflection until I become clear. In some ways it seems like only yesterday I slunk out of my class and was staring at myself in the hotel mirror, waiting for news that my plan was under way. In others, it feels like a lifetime has passed.

I turn the cold handle and drench my hands, splashing water over my face until the sharp pain recedes. I have no choice but to pull myself together. No choice but to stick to my story, despite what Lowry isn't telling me.

BEFORE

HARRIET

I woke at seven thirty to find a note had been pushed under the door of my room to say the garage owner had called and my car would be ready in two hours. Finally, things were turning in my favor. By lunchtime I would be in Cornwall.

I wolfed down a breakfast of greasy eggs and undercooked bacon made by the owner of the B&B, and accepted his offer of a ride to the garage, where I waited longer than I'd been told. My car wasn't ready for another hour, but I was finally back on the road by ten thirty.

With the sun trying to break through the clouds as I headed west, I turned the radio up and allowed my thoughts to oscillate between what lay ahead and what was behind me.

Best case I would find Alice safe and if I did, I would turn around and go straight back to Dorset. Last night I'd decided I would tell Brian and Angela that I'd needed to get away from the house. That I'd needed one night on my own away from the prying eyes and invasive questions, where nobody knew me or my story. I'd tell them I drove without thinking about where I was heading and would give them the name of the B&B owner who could vouch for me. I didn't know if they'd believe me, but it was all I had.

With the rest of the journey passing without mishap, I soon approached the tiny village of West Aldell, where the familiar, unnerving surge of dread resurfaced. I had no idea what I was walking into: whether my daughter would be there; if anything had happened to her.

I turned off the main road and drove down the winding lane that eventually led to a short street of clapboard-fronted shops and cafés. Passing the White Horse pub, I slowed so I wouldn't miss the right turn that would otherwise lead me to the beach.

This lane was even narrower and lined with hedges as it climbed a steep hill, twisting to the left. There were two unloved houses on the right before I finally spotted a sign for Elderberry Cottage. The wooden name was stuck to a post and jammed at an angle into the bushes out front. I assumed that if I carried on, I'd wind up at a dead end at the top of the cliff, as my dad had told me.

It was 12:30 p.m. when I finally pulled up alongside the hedge opposite the cottage, wincing at the scratch of its branches against the side of the car. There was little space to park without jutting into the center of the lane.

So this was it. Sadly, it looked exactly like it had on the website.

I didn't bother checking the deserted road for oncoming cars as I crossed and passed through a gate hanging miserably on one hinge and leading to a cobbled path with overgrown grass peeking through its cracks. On the front door a bell dangled dubiously on a wire. I took a deep breath and knocked.

"Please be in, Dad," I muttered. "Please God, let Alice be here."

I knocked again, louder this time. Still nothing. To my right a net curtain partially hid the living room behind it, but I could make out the red velvet armchair and faded brown two-seater sofa I'd seen on the website. The cottage looked like it had been caught in a time trap. I imagined a thin layer of dust coating the china figurines that were lined up on the mantel like a row of soldiers.

I banged on the door again until my hand felt bruised. My heart echoed back with each thump I made on the peeling green wood. How had I allowed her out of my sight? Yes, she was with her grandfather, but she'd only known him six months. I barely knew him.

"Where are you, Dad?" I cried at the closed door, pressing my forehead against it in despair. "Where's Alice?"

When I pulled away I noticed the side gate was ajar. It led to the back of the house, weaving through tubs of withered plants that stood on a slab of concrete. Through the glass panel of the shabby blue back door, I could see the kitchen, with mugs left on the table, a few bowls stacked in the sink.

After I tried the handle, the door swung open and I tentatively stepped inside. "Dad?" I called out. "Alice?" The only response was the loud ticking of a grandfather clock.

My legs felt like liquid as I drifted through the house, one step at a time, climbing the staircase, its floorboards creaking beneath me. I called out their names again as I reached the top. Now the clock's ticking was much fainter.

They weren't here, I was certain of that. But had they been? Were they here this morning?

I glanced into a bedroom with a double bed neatly made, a purple quilt tucked over the top. Next to it was a small box room, half the size of Alice's at home. A single bed had a green blanket laid carefully over its end. Had Alice slept here?

My hand shook as I reached out to touch the sheet, frightened there'd be no evidence that she'd been here. One tug ripped the sheets back. "Oh God." I held a hand over my mouth as the other touched the corner of the fabric that peeked out from under the pillow. Pulling slowly, I found a neatly folded nightie dotted with pretty pink owls and a frilled hem. I pressed it against my face, breathing it in. There may have been the faintest scent of Alice, but I couldn't be sure I wasn't imagining it.

Exhilarated by that small find, I went over to the chest and pulled out its drawers one by one. Balled socks, a new pack of girls' pants, a couple of T-shirts. Then in the last one Alice's pink chiffon skirt with the embroidered birds and, neatly placed next to it, her little blue shoes with their pinpricked stars.

I let out a cry as I sank to the floor, a wave of nausea rushing over me. This was a good thing, I told myself. It meant she'd been here. My dad had at least brought her here as promised. And he had bought her a pretty nightie and new clothes. I had to take comfort in that, I thought, grabbing a handful of shells from the pile on the dresser. And now I was convinced I knew where to find them.

Racing down the stairs, I went back through the

kitchen and out the back door, leaving it unlocked like I'd found it in case they didn't have a key. I ran down the lane until it came to an abrupt stop at the top of the cliff. Only then did I pause and inhale deep lungfuls of air.

Over the edge of the cliff was a sheer drop. Below me waves rolled in, their white foam washing up on the sand before being dragged out again. The tide was out, revealing a small slip of beach, and while it wasn't windy it looked like there was a strong current.

I stepped back before I lost my balance and started down the steep, grassy path that wound down the cliff to my left. Intermittent stone steps had been laid in places where the ground was rough and I had to carefully find my footing. It was the type of walk Alice would've loved.

At the bottom the path joined the main lane that ran through the village. Opposite was a small deserted parking lot and to the right a wide path led onto the beach, which looked wider than it had from the top, and I wondered how much of it would disappear once the tide came in.

The beach was almost empty, as my father had said, apart from a little boy playing with a fishing net at the farthest edge of the cove, watched by a couple engrossed in animated conversation.

I looked one way, then the other. Had I really expected to find them here? Seeing the box of shells in the cottage had made me certain I'd find Alice and my dad on the beach. Only they weren't.

My feet circled and circled as I refused to accept that they weren't here. Everything started to spin and I fell to the sand in a heap of desperate tears. A sound escaped, but I wasn't sure it had come from me.

"Are you okay?" A voice drifted toward me but I

ignored it as I dug my hands deeper into the sand. Never had I felt so frightened or so alone.

"Excuse me?"

Go away.

Thoughts swarmed my head like locusts until they turned the sky black.

"Do you think we should call a doctor?" The voice was approaching. Nearer and nearer.

I buried my head into my knees.

Go away. Go away. Go away.

"Do you need help?" A hand touched my side, making me sit up. The light from the sun was harsh and I was forced to shield it with my hands.

"I'm fine," I said, my legs trembling as I forced myself to stand. "Thank you," I added, brushing the sand from my jeans.

"Can we get anything for you?" she asked. A man was right behind her, the little boy with his fishing net trailing reluctantly after.

"No, I'm okay," I said. "Maybe I had too much to drink last night." I attempted a smile. The woman nodded but didn't smile back, and eventually she allowed the man to take her arm and called the boy to follow as they walked away.

I waited until they had disappeared and then retraced my steps quickly back up the path, past the parking lot, and up the cliff path. Tears raced down my cheeks until I was sobbing great gulps of air that made me double over in pain. When I reached the top I looked out to the sea, mouthing my daughter's name.

What should I do? Alice was now genuinely missing, but there was no one I could tell. The police would say, "We know she's missing, Harriet, she disappeared nearly two weeks ago."

"Alice!" I cried quietly. "Baby, where are you?" I went back to the cottage on unsteady legs, letting myself in through the back door again. "Dad? Alice?" I screamed into the cold, silent air as I collapsed onto a wooden chair in the kitchen. "Where have you gone?"

CHARLOTTE

On Friday morning Charlotte placed the phone facedown on the kitchen table, having just hung up with the school. Molly was sick and asking to come home. She had claimed a tummy ache that morning, but Molly occasionally did that if there was a chance of staying at home. Usually it turned out to be nothing.

She told the receptionist she'd be there shortly, but it messed up her plans. Evie was in nursery and Charlotte was supposed to be meeting Captain Hayes at the police station in fifteen minutes. He had called her that morning asking her to come in "for a chat," admitting that neither Harriet nor Brian had returned home all night.

"I don't know any more than I told Angela," she said. "But of course I'll come in if you think I can help."

"I wouldn't be asking you if I didn't," the detective said. "I'll see you at two p.m."

Charlotte hung up. His sarcasm grated and it made her wonder if he thought she was lying and knew where Harriet and Brian were. Now she was going to have to call him en route to the school and explain that not only would she be late, Molly would be with her too. She could picture his exasperated face when she gave him the news.

Charlotte grabbed the car keys and picked up her purse. Rifling through it to check she had her wallet, she was just about to leave when her cell rang from the bottom of her bag, flashing a number she didn't recognize.

"Hello?" Charlotte cradled the phone between her ear and shoulder as she fiddled to close the zipper on her bag. It was forever jamming and she knew if she tugged it much harder the whole thing would snap.

"Charlotte?"

She froze. "Harriet? Is that you?"

"I need your help," her friend said stoically.

"Thank God you're okay. Where are you? Where's Brian? Why didn't you go home last night?" Her questions tumbled out.

"Charlotte, I need your help," Harriet whispered.

Charlotte dropped her bag and pressed the phone closer to her ear. Wherever Harriet was, it was difficult to hear her. "Harriet, what's happened? Is Brian with you?"

"Brian?" There was a short pause. "No, Brian's not with me." Another pause and then, "I don't know what to do," she cried.

"Oh God," Charlotte muttered, and all she could picture was that Harriet was planning something stupid. "Okay, tell me where you are and I'll come meet you. Are you nearby? I can be there—" Charlotte hesitated. She had already committed to be in two different places, but Harriet came first. She would call the school and ask them to keep Molly a while longer. No, she would call Tom. He would have to leave work and collect her. "I can come over straightaway, Harriet. Are you back at home or can you get there?"

"No. I'm not there."

"So tell me where you are. I'll come to you, wherever it is," Charlotte said.

"I'm in Cornwall."

"Cornwall? What the hell are you doing in Cornwall?"

"I never meant to hurt anyone."

Charlotte's grip tightened around her phone. "What have you done?" she asked slowly.

"I had to do it and I don't expect you to forgive me, but she's gone, Charlotte. I'm so scared. I don't know where she is." Harriet let out another sob.

"Slow down. Just tell me what's going on."

"I had to get Alice away from him, Charlotte, I had to. But it's gone wrong and now I don't know where she is."

"Harriet, what exactly are you saying?" Charlotte's fingers were beginning to feel numb she was clenching the phone so hard.

"I had to get Alice away."

"No." Charlotte stared at her spiral staircase. "No," she breathed again, shaking her head. "Did you . . . Did you have something to do with it?" With her spare hand she reached out for the hallway table, which shuddered under the strength of her hold.

"I had to," she begged through her sobs. "I had to get away from him. But it was never meant to be like this."

"No. This doesn't make sense. You're lying to me, Harriet."

"I'm not lying and I'm sorry. I'm so sorry, but I don't know where Alice is anymore. I did, but she isn't here and I can't find her—" Harriet's voice trailed off.

"But you made me believe she was abducted. You made me think a stranger had grabbed her."

"I'm sorry," Harriet cried, but Charlotte wasn't listening.

"You made me think it was all my fault, that I wasn't looking after her, but all along *you* did this?" she spat. "I don't believe it, I can't believe it."

"I know," Harriet said. "I know everything you're saying is true and I'm so sorry, but right now that's not important."

"Not important?" Charlotte let out a shallow laugh. "Are you kidding me? Of course it's important. I was accused of not watching her, Harriet," she cried. "Jesus, how could you do that? What kind of mother would kidnap her own child?"

"I had no choice," Harriet pleaded.

"Of course you had a choice!" she screamed. "No one abducts their own child."

Harriet was silent.

"You must have known how guilty I'd feel," Charlotte went on. "Surely you've seen what everyone's been saying about me; you can't ignore it. How could you have done this?"

"Charlotte, please, I'll explain it all," Harriet cried, "but I really need you—"

"Tell me what happened," Charlotte said, cutting her off. Her body was shaking with rage. "Where is she?"

"I don't know," Harriet sobbed. "That's just it, she's supposed to be here but she isn't."

Charlotte pressed the heel of her hand against her forehead. She couldn't understand what Harriet was telling her. It was unthinkable that her friend had done this.

"He was supposed to have answered my calls but he didn't," Harriet continued. "That was two days ago, and now I'm here and there's no sign of either of them."

"He? Who is he? The person who took her? I'm assuming you weren't at the fair." She tried to force herself into a state of calm so she could piece together the story that had so many holes in it.

Silence.

"Who took her?" she asked again, her voice rising.

"My father."

"But he's dead," Charlotte said, incredulous.

"No," Harriet said quietly. "He never was."

"*What?*" Charlotte choked the word out. "But you told me he died. Right at the beginning. In fact, the first time we met you told me your dad was dead and I felt awful because I'd been going on about mine walking out."

"I always thought of him as dead because that's what my mum used to tell everyone, but actually he left us. I hadn't seen him in over thirty years, but he turned up one day last year."

"This is crazy," Charlotte cried. "Why would you lie to me about something like that? Do you have any idea how this sounds?" Charlotte was trembling again and she had to sit down. Her balled fist lay gripped tightly in her lap. "This is—" she broke off. "Has anything you've ever told me been true, Harriet? Do you even know what that word means?" she shouted.

"Please," Harriet pleaded. "I know how it all sounds, I do."

"And he's taken Alice?" Charlotte went on. "I can't even believe this."

"I know it doesn't make any sense."

"You don't trust *anyone* with Alice," Charlotte said. "Why did you trust him? *Why* did you do this, Harriet?"

"We weren't safe," Harriet cried. "I had to get us away from Brian and he made it impossible for me to leave him."

"Brian? What do you mean, you weren't safe?"

"I was desperate, Charlotte. He tricked everyone. He would have taken Alice from me."

Charlotte recalled the first time Brian had turned up on her doorstep when he was worried about Harriet's state of mind and Alice's safety. She'd disregarded it completely. But what if Brian had been right? Just because Harriet didn't behave how Charlotte supposed someone would with postnatal depression, it didn't mean she wasn't capable of doing something stupid.

"How come you never told me?" she asked slowly.

"I was too ashamed," Harriet said. "He was making it seem like I was crazy, and for a long time I thought he was right."

Yet you've just kidnapped your own daughter, Charlotte thought, remembering Brian telling her he was worried because Harriet had left Alice in the car and forgotten all about her.

"You have to believe me," Harriet begged.

Charlotte rested the back of her head against the wall behind her. How could Harriet expect her to believe anything she said now?

"I've got no one else I can ask and I'm sorry but please, you have to help me find Alice."

Harriet's fear sounded genuine, but Charlotte didn't have any idea what to do. She listened as Harriet told her about her dad not answering her calls and the empty cottage where Alice should be.

"But they could be anywhere. How long have you waited?" Charlotte couldn't believe she was already trying to placate her friend, but the pain in Harriet's voice was very real.

"I know something's not right," Harriet said. "I can feel it."

"You need to call the police, Harriet. There's nothing I can do."

"I can't," Harriet cried. "If I call them I have to admit this is all my fault. If I do—" she broke off. "I could go to prison. Brian would have custody of Alice, and that can't happen, Charlotte. You have to understand, I *cannot* let him have my daughter."

"What are you asking me to do?"

"Come here. Help me find her."

"Seriously—" Charlotte broke off and gave a short laugh. She couldn't get embroiled in Harriet's plan any further. The very idea of driving to Cornwall to aid a friend who'd betrayed her was ridiculous.

"I'm in a place called West Aldell," Harriet was telling her, and began reeling off the address of Elderberry Cottage. "I've already looked at the beach, but I'll wait at the cottage for you."

"No, Harriet. You need to tell someone who can help you and it's not me."

"There is only you." Harriet sounded almost hysterical at the other end of the line. "Charlotte, I know you don't know whether to believe me or not, but you have to know by now that I would do anything for Alice."

"Please don't ask this of me," she said. There was silence at the end of the phone, and for a moment Charlotte thought Harriet had hung up. "Harriet? Are you listening to me?"

"I can't not ask," she whispered. "If I don't, then it's over."

CHARLOTTE

Charlotte pulled out of her driveway and to the end of the cul-de-sac. Her shoulders ached with tension. She'd have thought the weight of her own responsibility would have shifted now that she knew it hadn't been her fault, but if anything it was worse.

She couldn't get her head around the degree to which her friend had betrayed her. Her life had been pulled apart, everything she thought she knew about herself had shattered. Her friends didn't trust her, hell, she didn't trust herself anymore. Charlotte's happy existence had been ripped at the seams and it was all Harriet's fault.

She had only ever been a good friend to Harriet, taking her under her wing when Harriet needed it most. And *this* is what she did in return?

Everything rooted deep inside Charlotte told her to call Captain Hayes. She needed to extricate herself from this mess she'd already been unwittingly caught up in. As soon as everyone knew the truth, Charlotte's name would be cleared. And it was all Harriet deserved.

Charlotte pulled up at a red light and waited for it to turn green, slamming her hand hard against the steering wheel. She was already fifteen minutes late picking up Molly, but hopefully her daughter wasn't as ill as the school had implied.

She pressed the telephone button in her car, ready to redial Hayes's number, playing out the conversation in her head. He'd suck in his breath loudly as he listened to her tell him it was Harriet who had abducted her own daughter. Then he would badger her with questions she didn't have answers to while signaling for a raid of the cottage in Cornwall. Charlotte shuddered. She could picture Harriet waiting for her at the window, but instead of seeing her friend, Harriet would watch as a police car pulled up and officers marched to the door, ready to handcuff her and drag her to the station.

There had been a case recently where a father had escaped to Spain with his son. He'd pleaded that the mother had abandoned her child and he was taking him back to his own country to live with his parents. Regardless, the dad was locked up for seven years. Her heart went out to him when she saw a picture of the mother. She didn't seem remotely bothered by what her son had been through.

Charlotte tapped the steering wheel as she waited for a mother and daughter to cross in front of her, debating what to do. Charlotte's chest tightened as she took deep breaths. She knew as soon as she told Captain Hayes the truth, Harriet's life would be over.

Was that what she deserved?

In the crossing, the little girl had stopped, letting go of her mum's hand to pick up a gray teddy she'd dropped. The mother turned and scooped her into her arms, kissing the girl on the head as she carried her the rest of the way. Images of Harriet with Alice filled her head.

Charlotte could hear her friend begging her to believe her about Brian.

He'd been acting so odd two days earlier when he'd turned up at her house, and his focus on Harriet rather than his daughter had concerned her.

But could he really be the man Harriet had described? Capable of such hidden abuse, bad enough to make her stage such an elaborate plan.

And then there was the story Brian had told when he'd visited months earlier. When he'd calmly explained how Harriet had left Alice in the car while she renewed her passport at the post office.

Charlotte shuffled forward in her seat, rolling her shoulders. There was something niggling her, she thought, as she absently watched the mother and her little girl. Something in the corner of her mind, a fragment of a conversation that felt important. But she couldn't quite reach it.

CHARLOTTE CHECKED FOR traffic cops as she pulled up outside the school. She didn't expect to see any at this time of day, but it wouldn't be the first time she got caught parking illegally.

"I'm sorry, I got held up," Charlotte said as she ran into the office. Molly sat on a plastic chair at the far side of the room, with a bowl on her lap and a teaching assistant's arm loosely around her shoulders. Her face was ashen, apart from the skin under her eyes that in contrast made her look like a panda.

"Oh, Molly." Charlotte had obviously ignored how bad she'd been that morning in her rush to get out of the house. Her daughter fell into her arms, crying louder as she did. Charlotte hugged her tight and then, holding her at arm's length, looked into her face and wiped a stray tendril of hair away from Molly's eyes. "Come on, let's get you home."

"She hasn't been sick," the teaching assistant said, "but she feels very hot. You can take this with you," she added, handing her the empty bowl.

Charlotte placed a hand against Molly's forehead and agreed she was very hot to the touch. "Is there anything going around?"

"Not that I know of."

"I'll call the doctor," she said. She'd usually wait twenty-four hours, but Charlotte was leaving nothing to chance anymore. Not where the children were concerned. Picking Molly up, she carried her back to the car, snuggling into Molly's warm hair. She couldn't leave her like this.

On the way home Charlotte called the doctor's office and a nurse had rung back by the time she pulled into the driveway. "Just a bug, I expect. Give her some Tylenol and get her to rest, but keep an eye on her," the nurse told her. "If she gets worse, call back."

At home Charlotte laid Molly on the sofa, covering her with a crocheted blanket, and stretched out on the other one so she could watch over her for a bit while she decided what to do about Harriet. But no sooner had she lain down than her cell started ringing.

"Charlotte? It's Angela Baker."

"Oh, Angela, hello." She'd completely forgotten to cancel her appointment with Captain Hayes. "I'm sorry. I meant to call and say I wouldn't be able to come in." She looked over at Molly. "My daughter's sick."

"I'm sorry, I hope it's nothing too serious?"

Molly was sleeping soundly already. In fact, some color had already returned to her pallid cheeks. "No, I think she'll be okay. I just need to keep an eye on her," Charlotte said, realizing she'd need to go back to the school in a couple of hours to get the others. Maybe Audrey could bring them home.

"Well, I hope she's better soon. I'll let him know you can't make it, but he'll probably want to call you."

"Of course." Charlotte's heart was beating so loudly she wondered how Angela didn't hear it. She knew if she was going to say anything about Harriet, this was the time. Any later and she'd be—

"So, can I arrange another time for you to speak to Captain Hayes? Maybe he could come to your house if you aren't able to leave your daughter?" Angela said, interrupting her thoughts.

She needed to tell her now. If she ended the phone call without admitting what she knew, she'd be withholding evidence.

Yet there was still that thought niggling at her. Something wasn't right, and if she let them take Harriet away, then what would happen to Alice? What if her friend was telling the truth?

"That's fine," Charlotte said, her heart banging so hard it almost cracked through her skin. "I'll be able to come in later."

"Okay. Thanks. Before I go, have you ever heard of a friend of Harriet's named Tina?" Angela asked. "Harriet knew her in Kent."

"I don't think so."

Angela didn't answer, and Charlotte couldn't help asking, "Has she heard from Harriet? Do you think she knows where she is?"

"Possibly. She may have gone back to Kent. Somehow I don't think she's gone too far."

"Really?"

"She hasn't left the country, at least," Angela said.

The memory she'd been trying to grip on to felt closer. "How do you know?" Charlotte asked, but in that moment she already knew.

"Harriet's never had a passport," she murmured at the same time Angela spoke the words.

HARRIET

I waited at the cottage like I'd told Charlotte I would, though I didn't know if she would come. Five years I've had to confide in my only friend and I didn't, so I doubted I'd gotten across what I'd needed to in five minutes. I didn't know if she believed me—I couldn't blame her if she went straight to the police—but I had no other choice except to wait.

Had I made another grave mistake by calling her? My plan was already so feebly held together. I had proved that by the frantic way I was ripping it apart. I was becoming my own undoing and now that I'd reached out to Charlotte, I may as well have handed her the rope that would hang me.

But I needed help, and the only person I hoped I could trust was possibly the one person I should have confided in at the start.

The minutes ticked by on the grandfather clock as rhythmically as the metronome that had sat on my music teacher's piano at school. Back then it had lulled me into a trance where I'd waste large chunks of the class staring out of the window, dreaming of a different life. Now with each sharp tick, a fraction of hope evaporated.

Tick. You still don't know where Alice is.

Tock. The longer you wait, the worse it will be.

I fidgeted impatiently in the armchair in the living room. I got up and paced the floorboards in the kitchen. I went upstairs and looked out the front window onto the lifeless road below. Everything was morbidly still. Even the branches of the trees were immobile, captured in a moment of time.

How long would I wait? Hours? Days? There would come a point when I would need to do more than patter about the inside of an empty cottage. When I would need to call the police myself.

What would be the tipping point?

I stood at the front window, my hands splayed against the net curtains as they pressed against the glass. My heart burned with the crushing realization that whatever happened now, Alice would undoubtedly be taken from me. But all I wanted was to see her—I would risk everything to know my daughter was safe.

"Come back, Alice," I called into the silent room and, as if in response to my plea, a shard of sunlight pierced through the window and flickered onto the patterned carpet. In a moment of clarity, I knew I had to take back control and figure out what I'd say if the police arrived or it got to the point I needed to call them.

Searching in my bag for my notebook, I took out the Elderberry Cottage business card I kept in the back pocket. I turned it over and stared at the blank space. Then I grabbed a pen from a jar on the mantel and sat in the armchair, chewing on the end of the pen as I thought. Carefully, in an impression of my father's loopy scrawl, I wrote a short note on the back of the card.

It was crude and doubtfully sufficient, but as I read

over it I figured it was better than nothing. I tucked it into the back pocket of my jeans as the grandfather clock chimed six o'clock.

If Charlotte had walked out of her door the moment we'd hung up, she would have been here by now. Sitting up straight, I set deadlines. I would go back to the pay phone and call Charlotte again if she wasn't here by seven.

I would call the police and tell them everything if my father and Alice hadn't returned by eight.

AT HALF PAST six I peered out the window again, but the same quiet, motionless scene lay outside. The little street lined with bushes, the tall trees with the sun now dappling only the very top of them as it dropped behind the house. I wished something looked different, just so I could see there was still life out there.

My stomach grumbled with hunger, reminding me I hadn't eaten since breakfast, so I searched the sparse kitchen cabinets. There were a few tins and a loaf of bread, a half-eaten packet of crackers, and a variety box of cereal with three boxes missing.

I ran my fingers over the cereals, trying to work out which ones had been eaten. Had Alice had one that morning? When was the last time she'd been in the house? It could have been days ago, I thought, with a surge of sickness rising through my stomach and up into my throat. I slammed the cabinet door shut just as there was a loud rap on the front door.

Automatically I froze. It felt too good to be true that it could be Charlotte. But if it wasn't her, then who was it? The police?

Slowly I crept toward the front door, looking through

its obscured window, but not even a shadow flickered behind it.

I opened the door a crack and looked out, pulling it open wider. With a plummeting sense of disappointment, I realized there was no one there and that deep down I had thought it would be my friend. Closing my eyes to stem the threat of tears, a heavy sense of despair told me I should never have expected Charlotte to come.

I began pushing the door closed when I felt the slightest puff of breath against the back of my neck. The hairs on my arms pricked up, goose bumps splattered across my bare skin.

Someone was behind me.

I felt him. I smelled the woody scent of his aftershave. He was inside the house, standing in the hallway, breathing against my neck. I would have screamed if the sound hadn't frozen in my throat.

"Hello, Harriet," Brian murmured, his mouth so close to my ear I could almost feel the brush of his lips.

My hand shook violently against the doorknob as he reached over my shoulder to gently close it. "Surprise," he whispered.

Slowly I turned around. Brian's face was almost pressed against mine, skewed into a smirk though it couldn't hide the wrath emanating from his empty eyes.

"Brian? What—?" I tried stepping away from him but there was nowhere to go as he'd trapped me against the front door. He must have gone down the side of the house and crept in through the back.

"What am I doing here?" he asked with his head cocked to one side. "Is that what you want to know? But where did you think I would be, Harriet?" He reached up and took a lock of my hair, winding it slowly around his fingers as he stroked it with his thumb.

I shook my head with the slightest of movements. My heart pounded, reverberating in my ears. He must have been able to hear it too.

"Maybe I should be asking what *you're* doing here, don't you think?" he asked. He tugged gently on my hair, and even though it wasn't hard, I could feel its pull on my scalp. "Haven't found Alice yet?" He gave me a smile that felt like a knife through my chest.

"Where is she?" I exhaled the question in one tight breath.

Brian smirked. "What a funny question." His eyes traveled up to the top of my head as he tenderly stroked my hair. "How do you suppose I would know what's happened to my daughter?"

"What have you done to her, Brian?" I cried. "Where's Alice? Please, you're scaring me."

"I'm scaring *you*?" he snarled. His face contorted into the pained shape I had seen so many times. Every one of my questions was angering him more.

I wanted to turn away but I resisted the urge, keeping my eyes on him. "If you've done something to her . . ."

"You'll what?" he snapped. "Because the funny thing is, *you're* the one who's done something to her, aren't you, Harriet?" With a sharp pull on my hair, Brian twisted my neck down with it. The pain shot through my shoulders and up into my head. "You let me believe my daughter was kidnapped."

"Is she safe?" I pleaded. "Just tell me she's safe." The pain had shocked me because Brian had never been physical—but then I had never seen him this enraged before.

"Oh, isn't she here?" he said, arching his eyebrows, leaning back and casually looking around.

"Please, Brian—"

"Shut up, Harriet." He took his other hand off the door and pressed his palm flat against my mouth. "Stop your questions. Don't you think I have a few of my own?"

The sound of my breath was unbearably loud as I was forced to breathe through my nose. I didn't know how long I'd have to endure his torment before he'd tell me what had happened to my daughter. Or how he had found me.

When he removed his hand, Brian gently took hold of my bottom lip, squeezing it between two fingers. "And stop biting your lip," he said. "You'll make it bleed." He rubbed his finger across it and then let go of me and casually strode off, sitting down on the sofa.

He knew I wouldn't run; he knew I'd follow him and sit opposite in the armchair because he had things I wanted to hear and, as always, Brian was in control.

"I never thought you had it in you, Harriet," he said. "You took Alice and made me believe the worst." He shook his head, the light reflecting the moisture in his eyes. "Why did you do that to me? I was nothing but a good husband to you."

When I didn't answer, he carried on. "But it wasn't just you, was it? It was your daddy. Come back from the dead."

"How did you—?" I stopped. "Where's Alice?" I said again. It didn't matter how he knew so much, finding out what he had done to my daughter was more important.

"What did I ever do to make you hate me so much, Harriet?"

"You ruined my life," I said, turning my head so he couldn't see the tears in my eyes. "You manipulated me and made me think I was losing my mind. You told me you'd take Alice away from me." I couldn't let him get away with it anymore. Not if he'd done something to her.

"No, Harriet. I never did," he said firmly. "I would never do that."

"You're doing it now," I murmured. "Please just tell me where she is."

"I said if you ever left me I would find you, and look—" He gestured about himself. "I have." He forced a smile that made him look incredibly pleased with himself as he clasped his hands together between his knees. "I won't let you go, Harriet. I can't ever let you leave me. I love you. I love you both too much for that."

"No. You don't love me, Brian," I said.

"You, you think you're so clever," he snapped, his hands unclasping and waving in the air. "Trying to get one over on me. Well, look around you, my love. You're not really, are you? Because I've foiled your plan and look where you are now. Sitting in this god-awful cottage with no clue what's happened to your daughter.

"Did you hope I'd get arrested for it?" he went on. I shook my head as he snorted. "But you will now, won't you, Harriet? They'll lock you up for what you've done. I could have told you your stupid idea would never work."

"Where's Alice?" I asked him again. I knew by now I had no chance of fighting for my own freedom.

"Don't you want to know how I found them?" Brian said, still ignoring me. "Your notebook. A *little* bit stupid," he said, pinching his fingers together to emphasize the word, "to write so many things in there."

But I had never written my plan in the notebook. I'd only kept a record of the things Brian had told me and the way I believed them.

"I have to say, I'm quite surprised you allowed him to bring her here." He screwed his nose up as he looked around the living room. Then he turned and smiled at me. "Ah, you're wondering how I found the book, aren't you?"

I shook my head, not wanting to give him the satisfaction. Of course I wanted to know, I just needed to see my daughter first. "Just tell me what you've done to her. Tell me you haven't hurt them."

"You see, no one knows you like I do, Harriet. Since Alice went missing, there's been something about your behavior that hasn't quite fit. It was more than Alice; you were acting strangely, but I couldn't put my finger on it. Then two days ago I saw you pouring a pint of milk down the sink before telling me we'd run out and you needed to buy more."

I slumped back into the chair. Brian was always loitering in the last place I expected to find him.

"I followed you. I waited until you'd turned the corner at the end of the road and I came after you. When you went into the phone booth and came out again ten seconds later, I knew you couldn't have made the call you wanted. So as soon as you disappeared around the corner, I went in after you and hit the redial button."

My fists clenched tightly at my sides. How could I have been so stupid? I played back the memory in my head, but I knew I'd been so intent on calling my father I would never have noticed Brian following me.

"He answered thinking it was you. 'Hello Harriet,'" Brian said with a snarl, failing to imitate my dad's voice. "'I'm sorry I didn't pick up, but Alice was hanging upside down on a tree at the end of the yard.' When I said nothing, he spoke again, a lot more nervously this time. 'Harriet, is that you?'" Brian laughed and shook his head. "Eventually he hung up, and when I called back he didn't answer. So that, my love, is how I found out you knew where our daughter was."

"What makes you think it was my dad?" I said.

He chuckled. "Are you going to pretend it wasn't? Alice was calling out in the background. I knew it was her, I just couldn't work out what she was saying at first. Then I played it over and over in my head until I was convinced she was calling out 'Grandpa.' "

I held a hand over my mouth to stop myself from crying out. My need to see my daughter was so desperate.

"It made me think that whoever had her was some sick old man trying to make her think he was her grandfather, because supposedly she didn't have a real one, did she, Harriet?" Brian spat. "My father is dead, and allegedly so is yours," he said. "But then I wondered, what if yours wasn't? After all, you never went into much detail about him. Always clammed up when you mentioned his dying. Never gave me any detail; I'd no clue what had supposedly finished him off. And the more I thought about it, the more it made sense that he could still be alive." Brian paused. "Anyway, I did a quick online search and found there was every possibility of it because there was no record of his death.

"I knew I wouldn't get the truth out of you, so I watched you even closer. You don't always know when I'm watching you, do you? When you came back with your milk you protested you felt ill and asked me to get you a glass of water, which I kindly did. But when I left the room, after you accused me of swapping the photo of Alice, I didn't go downstairs like you thought. I waited for a while to see what you did next, how deep your deception ran."

"God!" I cried. "My deception?"

"I saw you fussing around on the floor next to the bed, moving your bedside table, then pulling out a notebook. You hid it under a floorboard, didn't you, Harriet? I found it when I looked there later. When you were downstairs I pulled it out for myself and read everything you'd ever written. I knew then for certain your dad was alive and it was clear you wanted to get away from me.

"I found the card for the cottage and called the number. I told the woman a friend of mine, Les Matthews, had recommended the place, and do you know what she said, Harriet? She said, 'How funny. Les is staying in the cottage at the moment.' That's your dad's name, isn't it, Harriet?" He tapped the side of his head with his finger, leaning in closely, teeth bared in a smile. "See, I remember the things you told me. The ones you don't lie about." He leaned back, savoring his words.

"I went to see your best friend that night," Brian said in a sudden change of conversation.

"Charlotte?" I asked, stunned.

"I thought she must've been involved too, but the poor cow doesn't have a clue what you've done, does she? I paid a visit to my old fishing buddy yesterday too, Ken Harris. What happened there, Harriet? Your dad manage to have a word with him and get him to withdraw his alibi?"

"No," I said. "No, my dad knows nothing about any of your fishing buddies."

"No, well, the man's a drunk anyway," he said eventually. "Doesn't have a clue who he sees and who he doesn't. The good news is he's making another statement for me. They'll soon know I was there after all that day, though it won't really matter now, will it, my love? Very soon everyone will know this is all down to you.

"How could you have done this to me, Harriet?" He stood up and paced over to me, taking both of my wrists and pulling me up too. "I've always loved you, but that was never enough for you, was it?"

The sound of a car pulling up outside made us both jump. Was it my dad and Alice? Or Charlotte?

Brian grabbed my arms and pushed me against the wall, out of sight of the window so I couldn't see who was coming. He arched his back to peer out, his eyes flicking back and forth. "Are you expecting anyone? I can see a woman in the car."

It had to be Charlotte. She'd come for me, but now I regretted making that call, involving her further, and I wished there was some way I could stop her from coming any closer. If Brian saw her he'd never believe she had nothing to do with Alice.

"I don't know," I said, though he would know I was lying. Brian always knew everything, that was clear enough now.

He pursed his lips. With a jerk he leaned back and grabbed my handbag, which was sitting in full view on top of the side table. He pressed it into my chest, forcing me to take it. Then with one finger against my mouth he leaned in close to my ear and told me not to make a sound while we waited for the inevitable knock.

The loud rap on the door still surprised me. Silence. Then another knock. I waited for her to walk away, when all of a sudden a key was pushed into the lock. Brian's face froze in panic as he gripped my arm, his fingers pinching my flesh hard.

It wasn't Charlotte. It must've been the owner of the cottage. In seconds Brian was pulling me through the kitchen and out the back. Behind us the front door opened, but by then we were already making our way down the side path toward the front gate.

Brian wouldn't stop running as he turned right and headed toward the cliff top. I yelped in pain as he raced down the hill, tugging on my wrist and making it burn. Each time I begged him to let go of me, his grip tightened. When we reached the cliff edge, he stopped.

The air was getting colder, the light beginning to fade. "Brian, tell me where she is," I cried.

"I'll do better than that," he sneered, his fingernails piercing into my skin. The wind picked up from the sea as it carried his words toward me. "I'll show you."

But as he stared out at the sea I recognized the same flash of fear I'd seen that day he'd taken me for a picnic on the beach. I followed his gaze. The waves were choppy, encroaching onto the sand as the tide came in. Brian hated even looking at the water.

"You're scaring me. Where are they?" I said.

With a shaking finger he pointed toward the horizon.

"Where are they, Brian?" I shouted. The feeling of helplessness almost drowned me.

"Out there," he replied, and nodded toward the water.

Friday, April 21, 2017

When I spoke to my dad on the phone today he finally told me what Alice had said to him on Brownsea Island when they were looking at the peacocks. Now I get why he changed his mind about my plan.

Alice had told him she wasn't a liar and my dad assured her of course she wasn't. He asked whatever had given her that idea.

She said her daddy thinks she makes things up to make him angry. She told my dad about an incident with an ice cream that I had all but forgotten. On New Year's Day, Brian had driven us to the New Forest. Alice hadn't wanted to go, she preferred playing on the beach, but Brian had been adamant we walk in the woods. I had noticed by then how he liked to make plans for the three of us almost as if he were marking his place in the family.

I'd been walking ahead with Alice when I'd slipped into a rabbit hole and twisted my ankle. Brian had muttered in my ear that I'd done it on purpose. I told him that wasn't the case, but despite his annoyance, I needed to go back to the car and rest it.

Alice hadn't wanted to leave me because she didn't like that I was hurt, but regardless Brian had dragged her

over to the river to make her look at the fish. I'd watched
through my side mirror for a bit as she agitatedly prodded
the water with a stick. Eventually I'd looked away, the
pain making me close my eyes and rest my head against the
seat.

Fifteen minutes later they'd come back to the car and
I'd noticed Alice's eyes were red from crying. I'd asked
her what was wrong and Brian had told me she was upset
because she couldn't have an ice cream from the van
parked up the road.

I'd smiled and told her it was too cold for ice cream. My
ankle was hurting and I'd been desperate to get home.

But Alice had given my dad her version of the story,
which went more like this:

Brian told her if she looked a bit happier he'd get her
an ice cream. As always, Alice wanted one that came in a
cone and he told her she could even have sprinkles, too.

They'd watched the fish even though Alice wanted to
ask me if my foot was better, just so she could have her
treat.

But when he'd said that they were going home she'd
asked again if they could go to the van, and Brian told
her it was too cold.

She said he'd promised her an ice cream, but he told her

flatly that he never had. Alice went on to say that he'd even said she could have sprinkles, but then her daddy crouched down until they were at eye level and snapped at her to stop making things up. He said that no one likes a liar.

Then he grabbed her arm and led her back to the car, telling her she was ungrateful. Before they reached me he turned to her and asked if she wanted him to tell me she was turning into a liar or if she'd rather they kept it between the two of them.

Alice told her grandpa that Daddy says I make things up too and that I lie for her, and Brian doesn't like it. She asked her grandpa if she could tell him a secret and he said she could tell him absolutely anything.

So she said that if she hides behind the sofa Brian can't find her, and then he can't get cross with her because she hasn't said anything wrong.

Surely whatever happens I am doing the best thing for all of us, right?

HARRIET

I don't understand," I shouted to Brian. "What do you mean they're out in the water? What have you done to them?"

Brian continued to stare out to sea from the edge of the cliff. "I haven't done anything to them," he said eventually.

"Then what's going on?" My voice shook as I took a step closer to him. I wanted to grab him and shake him, scream at him to tell me where Alice and my dad were. But I also knew I'd get nothing if I did. It took every ounce of strength I had to restrain myself.

"They went out in a fishing boat. I watched them get in it. Just before you showed up," he said, turning to me. "I followed them down to the beach and he took a boat that was tied up on a jetty by the rocks down there." I looked in the direction he was pointing but the rocks were high in places, and from where we stood I couldn't make out the jetty, let alone see if there was a boat tied up to it.

"You must've missed them by ten minutes," he said. "I saw you running down to the beach and watched you from behind the rocks. You didn't see me, but then you weren't looking for me, were you, Harriet?"

I stared at Brian, wondering what he expected me to say. Of course I wasn't looking for him.

"You were looking for Alice," he said frankly, and it crossed my mind, not for the first time, that my husband was jealous. "And your father, of course," he added flatly.

My dad had told me about the fishing boat, but they must've left hours ago now.

"The old man seemed very determined as he headed down there," Brian said. His jaw tensed. "Holding on to my daughter's hand as if he had every right to. It made me sick."

I turned back to the beach. The sky had clouded over and even though the rocks were still visible, I knew there would only be another hour of daylight before the sun disappeared. Surely they'd be back before it was dark? "I still don't understand any of this," I said. "You're telling me you watched them this morning. That you followed them to the beach and you let him take her in a boat and did nothing to stop them?"

"I've been watching the house all night, Harriet," Brian said calmly. "I got home yesterday and found you gone. When you still weren't back two hours later, I had a feeling you were on your way to find them. But when I got here last night, there was no sign of you." He turned, expecting me to tell him where I was, but I didn't answer. "I saw him though. Clear as day through the window, sitting in that armchair. I sat in my car and waited for you. All night I waited, but you didn't show up. I was beginning to think I'd gotten it wrong," he said.

"If you knew Alice was in the house, how could you just sit there watching it?"

"Like I said, Harriet," he snapped. "I was waiting for you."

I stared at him, incredulous.

"Do close your mouth up, Harriet," he said. "I could see Alice was safe this morning. There was no need for me to rush in. Not when I was still certain you'd be along soon. And here you are," he said, reaching out to stroke my hair. "You came in the end."

I pulled out of his reach. He hadn't seen his daughter in two weeks, he'd believed she'd been abducted for the most part, and yet once he knew where she was, he was happy to let her wait until he got what he wanted: me.

"I knew she was okay," he growled, as if guessing my thoughts. "If she was in any danger I would have gotten her, so don't try to say I'm not a good father."

"Oh my God," I muttered under my breath. Brian stepped closer and took hold of my wrist again. I winced as pain shot through it and up my arm from where he'd grabbed me when we ran out of the house.

"You weren't there, Harriet," he said, his words ice cold as his eyes flashed brightly. "And I need you to realize you can't take our daughter away. You have to know you can't leave me, Harriet."

When Brian let go of me, I rubbed the tender spot on my wrist, wincing as I flexed it up and down. Who knew what damage he had done? An X-ray might show me that, but it would never tell the real story. The one that lay deep beneath the skin where the scars are invisible.

Brian began walking along the cliff top, toward the path that led down to the beach. "I don't know why you let them get in the boat," I called as I followed him. He ignored me, but I knew his fear of the water would stop him from going any farther. "So what did you do when they left? Why didn't you come looking for me?"

"I waited for them to come back," he called behind

him. "I didn't think they'd be long." Brian started making his way down to the beach and I stayed close behind. He stopped and turned back to me. "Over five hours I waited before I came back to the house and saw you. They shouldn't have been gone that long, right, Harriet?" he said, his eyes drifting over my face as if he wanted to see me panic.

I shook my head. "No," I said quietly, "they shouldn't've." I had no idea what my dad thought he was doing. All I knew was this morning she was safe and all I could hope was that he was looking after her like I believed he would.

"So what happens now?" Brian said. "We go home, one big happy family?"

"Yes," I told him. "We can do that." Whether he was serious or not, I'd take the bait. "We can, Brian," I pleaded. "We need to talk about what we do next."

I'd do whatever I had to to make sure Alice was never out of my sight again. I'd stay with Brian forever if it meant he wouldn't tell the police.

He laughed softly. "You really think I believe that? That you'll happily walk back into our life together? Jesus, Harriet. How stupid do you think I am?" His dead eyes bored into my head, where he could always see everything that was going on. And then he turned on his heel and began down the path again.

Finally we reached the bottom. Brian strode off toward the beach. The tide had come in and was now covering nearly all of the sand. I wondered if it would come in farther still. I'd been to coves like this and watched the sea wash straight over the rocks, hitting the walls beyond when it was stormy.

To our left the rocks stretched ahead of us, but as soon as we started walking we could both see the jetty and a little fishing boat that must have been there all along.

"Is that it?" I cried. My legs felt like jelly as Brian grabbed me again and began pulling me toward the rocks. "Brian, is that the boat?" I believed it must be, the way he hauled me toward it. I strained to see past him and could just make out the outline of a figure in the boat.

As desperate as I was to see Alice, it was still a struggle to keep up with him, but then the nearer we got the more visible the figure became, until I was certain it was my father.

"Dad!" I cried, climbing over the rocks to get to him. He looked up as he stepped out of the little boat that bobbed on the water, glancing at Brian and then turning to me, his face dropping in shock.

"Where's Alice?" I shouted when I couldn't see her. Brian's grip squeezed tighter. "Where is she?" Panic coursed through me, my legs buckling with every step. We had reached my dad now and I could clearly see Alice wasn't in the boat.

"Alice is fine." My dad stepped forward as we reached him. "Harriet," he pleaded, "she's fine."

"Tell me where she is!" I shouted again. "She's not with you, so what have you done to her?"

"I haven't done anything." His eyes sought Brian out and then flicked nervously back to me.

"Dad, just tell me where she is," I said urgently. The need to hold her in my arms and know she was safe had become unbearable.

"He's been here all night," my dad said to me, his eyes wide with fear. I felt Brian tense at my side. So my father had seen him. He'd have known Brian was watching the house. No wonder he looked so frightened; he must have been worrying all night about what Brian would do. But that could all wait. Right now I needed to see my daughter.

"Alice!" I called out, and when my dad turned to his left, I followed his gaze toward a bundle of blankets on the rocks. I stepped forward but Brian yanked me back.

"She's sleeping," my dad said as the bundle stirred. "I took her out for the day because I didn't know what else to do. It's been a long day and she fell asleep on our way back, so I laid her out there while I finished up on the boat."

"Alice!" I shouted again, trying to pull away from Brian whose hold remained resolutely locked on my arm. I turned to tell him to get off me, but he wasn't even looking in our daughter's direction. He was glaring at my father.

"Mummy!" a voice called from behind me and when I looked back, Alice was awake and pushing herself to her feet.

"Alice, oh my baby." I held out my arm as far as I could reach, but Brian was sidestepping around me until he was between me and my dad and my little girl, who was now carefully stepping over the rocks toward us.

"Let me get to her," I cried, but Brian wouldn't budge.

I watched her find her footing in bright pink wellington boots that I'd never seen before. In my desperation to touch her and hold her, I tried to wrench away from Brian but lost my footing and stumbled.

"Mummy!" she called out again, panic rising in her voice.

"Mummy's okay." I was, but the searing pain in my wrist wasn't letting up.

I needed to hug her, tell her I would never let her go

again, but I also knew there was no way Brian would let me get to her right now, and I had to go carefully. He held too many cards in his hand and could still make sure I lost everything.

Beside him, my dad glanced nervously between me and Brian. He was rooted rigidly to the spot. Brian began edging toward him, still never looking at Alice.

"Dad, you should go," I said.

But my father didn't move. "He was here all night," he said again. "Just watching." He sucked in a breath and held it tightly.

"Dad," I urged. "Please just go." He was never going to win a fight with Brian, who turned and stared coldly at my dad.

When Dad eventually took a step back, he looked at me and said, "I meant what I said, Harriet. My one condition, you remember that, don't you?"

I nodded, praying he'd walk away as he stumbled on the rocks and I saw a flash of the fragile, old man he'd become since I'd last seen him. My heart fractured at the sight of him trying to stop himself from falling. Automatically I held out my free hand to steady him, but before I could, Brian pushed me back and lurched toward my father.

I stumbled and fell as Alice's cries filled the cold air. Brian grabbed for my dad, clasping his hands around his neck.

"No!" I cried out, as Alice screamed louder. "Let go of him, Brian."

But Brian wasn't listening. Amid Alice's screams and my own, I couldn't tell if Brian was saying anything to him as he shoved him backward. All I could see was the terror in my dad's eyes as Brian lunged for him and propelled him to the rocks.

"Leave him alone," I cried. "This isn't his fault. Please. He's an old man, Brian."

My dad steadied himself, but Brian held out a hand to block me from getting to him or Alice. I was helpless as I watched my father place his hands carefully in front of him, trying to get back up. Alice stood shaking and crying, "Mummy, make him stop."

But Brian wouldn't stop. I knew that. His back formed a solid wall between us and he had shut us all out.

Slowly my dad pushed himself unsteadily to his knees and eventually to his feet, holding his hands up in surrender as he struggled to catch his breath.

"Brian!" I begged. "Please don't hurt him." I tried pulling Brian away from my dad, but he thrust his arm backward and pounced once more, catching my dad off guard as he sank his thumbs into my father's neck.

I watched in horror as fear appeared in my father's glassy eyes and the skin on his thin neck rippled around Brian's fingers where they dug into his throat. "Don't do anything stupid," I sobbed. "Please. We can all just go home."

"You must know that can never happen now!" Brian roared, and with one last push he flung my dad to the rocks with such force that I heard the back of his head crack.

There was a moment of pure silence before the air was filled with screams. By then I could no longer tell whose they were: mine, Alice's—they blended together and rose deafeningly above us.

There was no sound from my dad, who lay motionless, as Brian swiftly turned away from him and back to me. His breaths were shallow and quick, his eyes so dark they were almost black. Every muscle in Brian's body was tight, and I knew he was still ready for a fight.

I could *see* how much he wanted to hurt me for what I had done.

Alice had now quieted into a whimper. I too had stopped shouting and the beach was eerily silent once more except for the rhythmic lap of the waves as they hit the rocks.

Brian's eyes didn't leave me. They devoured me, absorbed me. I could see his mind working overtime, wondering how he'd lost me and what he'd do about it. Then he snatched my injured arm and began dragging me toward the jetty. I called to him to stop. I reached for Alice as he swept me past her, but she was too far away.

"Brian, what are you doing?" I looked back at my little girl, whose lips were quivering in fright as she stood frozen to the spot.

He ignored me as he continued to push me toward the boat, though he paused when he reached it and I caught his flicker of indecision. Surely he wasn't planning on getting *in*? What could be going through his mind to make him put his greatest fear to the side?

"Brian, stop this," I said urgently. "We can't leave Alice. You don't want to get in that boat."

But Brian knew he had lost control and somehow he needed to get it back, even if he wasn't sure how. He shoved me into the boat. "Alice will be fine," he muttered.

I scrabbled to get back out, but Brian pushed me into the corner. "We can't leave her here," I cried. "And my dad needs help. Brian, you've got to stop." My father lay motionless on the rocks and Alice had inched toward him.

"Brian, stop." I tried pushing myself up, grabbing on to his shirt, gripping handfuls of the cotton and crumpling it into balls.

He ripped his shirt away from me and with one hand untied the rope that held the boat to the jetty then turned on the engine, which whirred into action. Winded, I lurched toward the side of the boat but now he had hold of my ankles, and as much as I tried to pull myself forward, his strength overpowered me.

Slowly we started to move away. Alice's arms hung limply by her sides, her little pink boots pointing inward, her mouth open wide—and in that moment I had never hated him more. Never before had I such an intense desire to hurt my husband.

With everything I had, I prepared to swing around and push Brian away when I saw a figure running down the beach. Briefly paused in my tracks, I watched the figure run closer until I could make out the long gray cardigan and the skinny jeans, with a ponytail swishing behind.

Charlotte?

My breath caught in my throat, relief washing over me as the woman I now knew must be Charlotte turned in Alice's direction. My hesitation meant we'd drifted further away from shore. If she was calling out I couldn't hear her, yet Alice must have because she'd turned away from the boat and had started carefully climbing toward her.

I pressed a hand over my mouth to stifle my sobs. At least my daughter was safe. And they'd call an ambulance for my dad, who as far as I could tell was still not moving.

Brian's hold on my ankles loosened. I glanced behind me and watched him staring out at the horizon, presumably not realizing Charlotte was there. I glanced over the side and thought if I acted quickly, I could jump out and swim back to the rocks. The water was shallow and it wasn't far. In minutes I'd be back with my daughter.

But Charlotte was there now. And as I looked at Brian, I knew that if I did leave him he'd follow me back and make sure it was over for me. I wouldn't ever get away with what I'd done.

Trapped in a moment of indecision, we continued drifting out to sea in the small boat as I weighed up my options. Each wave we bobbed over made the boat wobble, which in turn caused Brian to grab the edge to steady himself.

Back on the beach, Charlotte and Alice's silhouettes were fading into the distance. The light was dimming too now. Soon it would disappear completely. Already the sea was turning an inky black.

I realized that one way or another it was all over for me. I'd likely pay for what I'd done, and I figured that if there was any slim chance of staying out of prison, then maybe I should stay on the boat. And surely I had the upper hand on the water? After all, I could swim. He couldn't.

CHARLOTTE

Charlotte wrapped herself tighter around Alice to keep the little girl warm. For two weeks she had felt responsible for Alice's disappearance and now she was holding her in her arms, breathing in her smell as the little girl's head nestled into her chest. The relief was so intense Charlotte had to force herself to keep from sobbing. Alice was frightened and Charlotte knew how much she needed to keep it together for her, but it was getting increasingly hard.

"Where's Mummy gone?" Alice asked again. "When's she coming back?"

"Soon," Charlotte told her. "I promise you she'll be back soon." She didn't want to think about what was happening out on that tiny boat or where Brian was taking them. She looked down at the little girl whose body shivered against hers and pulled her closer. When she looked up again, the boat had disappeared completely.

"Is Grandpa going to be okay?" Alice asked.

Two paramedics now crouched on the rocks in front of them. She couldn't see Les. "They're doing everything they can," she whispered into the little girl's hair. She couldn't admit it didn't look good.

• • •

TEN MINUTES EARLIER Charlotte had arrived at Elderberry Cottage and was met by a woman who looked as confused as she felt. "Oh hello, I was looking for a friend, but maybe I've got the wrong address." Charlotte leaned back to see if she could see a house name, but she was sure the weathered sign at the front read Elderberry.

"Who are you looking for?" the woman asked. Behind her heavy, dark bangs and thick-rimmed glasses, Charlotte could barely see her eyes. "I own the cottage, but I have a guest staying here at the moment."

"Erm," she stumbled. She had no idea what Harriet's father was called and knew she shouldn't risk getting into a conversation about him.

"I've got a Les Matthews here, is that who you want?"

"Yes," she said cautiously. "This is Elderberry Cottage?"

"That's right. He wasn't here when I turned up earlier and still isn't now. I only came by again now because Glenda just called and told me there was someone funny lurking around last night. Glenda lives in the house on the corner." The woman pointed up the lane in the direction from which Charlotte had come. "She's nearly ninety."

"Oh. Right."

"We don't get lurkers. No one comes up here. I told Glenda it was nothing, but I promised I'd check anyway. To be honest, I don't think she likes me renting the cottage out. She'd rather have someone permanent living here, but what can you do?"

"I don't know," Charlotte said. "What did this lurker look like?" she asked.

"Oh, I don't know." The woman brushed a hand

through the air. "Male, apparently. Glenda doesn't have very good eyesight. That's why I always feel like I have to come check these things out whenever she calls me, but—"

"I'm really sorry to be rude," Charlotte interrupted, "but I need to find my friend. Can you tell me how I can get to the beach?"

"The beach?" The woman looked at her watch. "It's half past eight; no one will be down there this time of night."

"I'd like to check since he's not at the cottage. Can I get down that way?" She pointed toward the cliff top.

The woman shook her head. "No. It's far too dangerous to use the path at night. You won't be able to see where you're stepping. You're best going back down the road and through the village by car. But the tide will be in, mind. There won't be much of the beach left."

Charlotte thanked her. She would have preferred to get back into the car and drive home, but she knew she'd never forgive herself if she didn't at least look for Harriet on the beach.

She turned the car around in the narrow street, careful not to hit the cottage owner's Land Rover that was haphazardly parked, and drove back the way she'd come, turning right into the small village and following the signs to the beach.

As soon as Charlotte had seen Alice standing on the rocks, she'd realized it was her. No sooner had relief swept through her when Charlotte had noticed the fishing boat with two people in it, slowly drifting out to sea.

She'd climbed onto the rocks, yelling out Alice's name. The little girl turned around, tears streaming down her cheeks. "Alice, it's me, Charlotte. Come this way."

Gradually Alice took small steps toward her until Charlotte could reach her and pull her into her arms.

"Daddy took Mummy in the boat," Alice had cried. "And he hurt Grandpa. He threw him to the rocks," Alice sobbed as she pointed toward him.

"Jesus," Charlotte cried when she saw him. She took a step toward the body, but didn't want to get too close with Alice gripping her tightly. Reaching into her pocket, Charlotte had pulled out her phone and dialed 911. "Ambulance and police," she'd said urgently when the call was answered.

The police and paramedics had turned up, and once they'd obtained brief details from Charlotte, had called for the coast guard. It hadn't crossed her mind to ask for them, too, and she berated herself, hoping they would get there fast because already the light was taking with it her last dregs of hope that Harriet would be okay.

Charlotte talked to Alice, to drown out the noise of the two police officers and their radios, hovering nearby. "When the lifeboat gets here, it'll go out to find your mummy and bring her back," she said. As Alice hadn't mentioned her dad, Charlotte didn't either. "Now, tell me about what you did in Cornwall." She tried to keep their minds occupied even though her own kept drifting to Harriet.

She'd told the police Harriet couldn't swim. Had shouted it to them as they made their call to the coast guard. Alice had looked up at Charlotte strangely and she'd told the little girl not to worry, that her mummy would be fine. She should never have said anything in front of her.

But Alice continued to look at her, puzzling over something.

"What is it?" she'd asked. But Alice had shrugged and didn't answer, so she didn't pursue it.

"I don't want Grandpa to die." Alice's voice was so small she could barely hear it. Charlotte couldn't get the image of his body out of her head, skewed at an angle it definitely shouldn't have been.

She looked at the paramedics and wondered what was happening, then at the policemen, who'd question her shortly. And when they did, she'd have no choice but to tell them the truth.

HARRIET

B rian's face was screwed tight as he steered the boat into the darkness. I'd thought it was rage that drove him, but each time he turned I caught glimpses of his eyes that were now nothing more than dead, black holes.

There was nothing left of him. An empty carcass of the man I'd met, the one I'd allowed to control me since. Brian knew he'd lost me, but this meant he had nothing left to lose.

My poor, tragic husband. So coiled up in his own world where there was no room for anything but me. Not even Alice. His own daughter came nowhere close to the so-called love he had for me. I'd seen that tonight.

I needed to at least try and talk him down from whatever he was planning. Though I doubted even he knew what that was.

"Brian," I said gently, arching my back as I bent my knees beneath me. "I don't think you want to hurt me, you love me too much for that."

"Love?" He laughed softly. His shoulders tensed as his right hand curled around the edge of the boat. "There's no love left," he said quietly, his focus fixed on the horizon ahead of us.

"What are you planning to do?"

"Shut up, Harriet." His body tightened, his hand gripped harder onto the side.

"I know you don't want to lose me," I said, figuring he'd had his chance to call the police at any point in the last twenty-four hours. Brian could have already made sure I'd pay for what I'd done, he could have had me locked up and away from Alice, just like he was always telling me.

Only I knew now he wouldn't have done that. He didn't want Alice without me. Taking my daughter away from me was never more than a threat to ensure I stayed with him.

I could no longer make out any figures on the beach, but as the blue lights lit in the sky I knew help must've arrived. It was a relief that my dad would be taken care of, though I also knew the police would be questioning Charlotte. They'd know what I'd done by now.

I slumped against the side of the boat. Was it all over?

I couldn't let it be. I had to find strength from somewhere.

"Brian," I started, "we need to go back for Alice."

"I told you to stop talking," he snapped.

"I know you love her," I went on. Not in the way you'd want your child to be loved, but still I was certain he didn't want to hurt her. "Imagine how scared she must be."

"I said shut up." He swung around to face me. The boat tipped to one side, rooting Brian to the spot, and I saw his fear again—the precariousness of balancing on the water he so dreaded. "Don't say another word," he hissed, slowly turning back toward the horizon.

I didn't speak. Instead I crawled deeper into my side

of the boat and watched him closely, imagining the sensation our situation had caused. The franticness of the officers and paramedics on the beach, the questioning, putting it all together. In contrast, it was entirely peaceful out at sea.

We continued to drift farther away into nothing. I no longer looked back. I told myself a lifeboat would soon be on its way. Shortly it would race into the water, gathering speed as it approached. Would they reach us in time?

I hugged my arms tightly around myself. Now that the sun had disappeared, it felt so much colder. I buried my head into my knees, biting a finger to stop my teeth from chattering.

What if the coast guard didn't reach us? What if they hadn't even been called? There was no way of knowing for sure. My life hung in Brian's hands, as it always had, and as renewed fear bled through me, I knew that somehow I had to take back control. I couldn't give up. What kind of mother would that make me?

I shuffled my legs beneath me, pulling my finger out of my mouth where my teeth had been clamping down harder than I'd realized.

I couldn't trust Brian. If I let him keep dragging us out into the black sea he would win. I had to stop him once and for all. But did that really mean I had no other choice than the thought that had begun rooting itself in the corner of my mind?

Quietly I pushed myself off the floor and, still crouching, onto my feet. I had the upper hand, I told myself again. Brian couldn't swim and he didn't know I could. I repeated the words inside my head until they drowned out the part of me that knew what I was thinking was preposterous.

My heart pounded heavily as I rocked onto the balls of my feet. As soon as I stood, I would have to lunge forward and catch him off guard, but I feared my legs wouldn't move fast enough. Even as my mind formulated my next steps, I still couldn't believe I was capable of what I was about to do.

Taking a deep breath, I held it in my mouth, and as soon as I expelled it, I pushed up and leapt toward Brian, my hands grabbing his shirt. The boat rocked and Brian whipped around, his own hands reaching for my arms to steady himself.

"What are you—?" he began to scream, and with every bit of strength I had left, I pushed him backward toward the edge of the boat.

I knew that whatever happened, Brian would always take me with him. He'd keep his promise that he would never let me go. If he went over the side, I would too.

His eyes were bright with fear, flicking between me and the water beneath us that stretched for eternity. I filled my head with thoughts of Alice waiting for me. Brian's would be filled with the dread of falling into the icy darkness that lay no more than an arm's length away. I thrust forward and together Brian and I toppled over the side of the boat.

The sea was ice cold, stinging my skin the moment I hit it. With every breath, pain shot through my chest. Brian's eyes widened as he hit the water, his arms still grappling to keep hold of me. As he opened his mouth to scream, he bobbed under the surface, his mouth filling with water before he rose back up, choking and spewing it out.

I saw the horror burn its way deeper inside him as he struggled to hold on to me. He knew he would go under again and was prepared to take me with him, but his hands shook on my arms and already I felt them loosening.

It was a bittersweet moment as my husband thrashed, his limbs flailing uselessly as I kicked my legs as strongly as I could to tread water.

Still holding on to me, when Brian submerged, he pulled me down too. I had already inhaled a deep breath but he somehow managed to tighten his grip again and his frantic kicking took us deeper.

I needed air and, as I pushed us both back up to the surface, I wondered how many times I could allow him to take me down.

The beam of a flashlight curved in the sky above us, closer than the lights from the beach. It had to be a lifeboat, and when Brian's panicked eyes followed my gaze, searching for signs of help, it hit me how someone who might have been so prepared for us both to die looked like he wanted nothing more than to live.

I had the power, I told myself again. He had none any longer.

I looked at my husband and felt a fleeting pity for him. There were two things he'd been so scared of all his life: being left to drown and losing me. In some ways it felt like his life was coming full circle.

He didn't deserve to die.

Did he?

The lights were getting closer. The coast guardsmen would be with us soon.

My heart raced and I looked into his eyes. Cold. Dark. I'd fallen for those eyes once, had thought them powerful and protective, but I had seen them too many times in the years since, controlling me. Making me his.

Drawing up my legs as much as I could, I drove them into him, feeling his thighs against my feet as I pushed him away. His hands slid off my arms, his eyes searching mine as his arms thrashed above his head.

Did he realize I could swim? I wondered.

As Brian sank under the surface I waited a few seconds, all the time knowing I could dive under and save him if I wanted.

The tide was slowly pushing me away from him. I counted to five but Brian didn't reappear. Frightened, I swam forward to where the ripple of water spread in swelling circles.

The lifeboat was nearby now; its light swept across the sea and caught me in its beam.

Then finally I lay on my back and pushed myself away from Brian. They would pick me up in a moment. By then it would be hard to tell where my husband was.

HARRIET

Where's your husband?" The coast guardsmen were understandably frantic that they couldn't see any sign of him. I gestured vaguely into the water. I was struggling to breathe, the icy coldness had hit me hard and pain was spreading rapidly through my body.

"Over—" I tried, but it was hard getting the words out. The moment I'd been pulled out my body went into shock. I closed my eyes until their voices hovered above me in jumbled whispers. Adrenaline coursed through me, but just for a moment I wanted to blank everything out.

The voices made decisions. They would take me back to the beach, they finally agreed, another lifeboat was already on its way. "Don't worry," one assured me. "We'll find him."

I wanted to tell them not to bother, Brian couldn't swim. He'd be long gone by now. He only felt safe dragging us both out to sea because he didn't think I could either. But my breath came short and sharp and I chose to save it.

In minutes we were on the beach. A policewoman helped me out of the boat and wrapped me in a foil blanket as a paramedic ran toward us. Eventually my shaking body began to absorb the warmth and my head started to clear.

"Where's my daughter?"

"She's taken care of," the paramedic told me, ushering behind her to the far edge of the beach where an ambulance sat, brightly lit, with two or three people milling around it. "Can you tell me your name?"

I screwed my eyes up until Alice came into focus, sitting in the back of the ambulance. Charlotte was at her side, one arm around her shoulders while a man in a green uniform crouched in front. He waved some kind of instrument in front of Alice. I imagined I heard her laugh, which made me smile.

"Do you know your name?" the paramedic asked again, slower and louder this time as if I might not understand. Her fingers pressed into my wrist as they searched for a pulse.

"Harriet Hodder."

The commotion had drawn a small handful of onlookers who stood together in a huddle, pointing and nodding and drawing their own conclusions about the drama unfolding on the beach. We must have been an exciting surprise to their otherwise boring evenings.

"I need to see Alice," I said.

"And you will in a minute, but we need to make sure you're okay first." She fussed around me. "Do you know what day it is, Harriet?"

"It's Friday. I haven't seen my daughter in thirteen days."

"I understand, Harriet," she said to me. "And you will soon." She released her grip on my wrist and carefully laid my hand down at my side. The sand was damp beneath me. "Open your mouth, please," she asked. I obliged, allowing her to look, then take my temperature, until eventually I pushed her away and begged her to let me see Alice.

The paramedic looked up at the policewoman who stood beside us, silently deliberating for what felt like an eternity. "Okay," she said finally.

The two women each took an arm and helped me over to the farthest edge of the beach. My legs shook as they carried much of my weight. I was weak from a lack of food and drink, from the coldness of the sea, and the energy I'd used keeping myself afloat.

Alice cried out to me when she saw me coming, pushing herself off the seat.

"Sweetheart!" My voice broke as I pulled away from the women's hands and stumbled the last few feet to Alice, finally able to wrap my arms around my little girl as I sobbed into her hair. Every other thought ebbed away, and in that moment I didn't think about what had happened to my husband, or what the future held for me. It was enough just to be back with my daughter.

When I finally looked up, I caught Charlotte's eye. She was still sitting in the ambulance, anxiously balling the hem of her cardigan in her lap. Tears welled in my eyes at the sight of her. I opened my mouth to speak. I needed to thank her, but surrounded by people, what could I say? Charlotte nodded, a small movement of her head, but her expression was pained as she watched me.

A paramedic told me he still needed to check me, but I assured him I was fine, and as soon as he went around the side of the ambulance, I turned to Charlotte. "Thank you," I said at the same time she spoke.

"Brian?" she said. "Is he— What happened?"

I looked out to the water and shook my head. "I, erm, they're still looking for him. I think they—" I broke off and bent down toward Alice. "Are you okay, sweetheart?" I couldn't bear to think how much she was taking in.

Charlotte stood up and gestured to the seat. "Let's lie her down," she said. "I think she'd have fallen asleep if she hadn't been waiting for you." She pulled a rough woolen blanket off the seat and, as I picked Alice up and lay her down, Charlotte draped it over her. Crouching down on the floor beside Alice, I stroked her hair.

"They're going to want to talk to you," Charlotte said quietly.

I nodded, still watching my baby. Already her eyelids were fluttering. It wouldn't be long until she drifted off; she was obviously exhausted.

"Harriet." Charlotte spoke more urgently this time. "The police will want to speak to you any moment."

"I know," I said, standing until I came face-to-face with her. "What have you told them? Why do they think you're here?"

"They haven't spoken to me yet, but they will, and I don't know what—"

"Just say I asked you to come because I was scared. Say you knew nothing," I told her, thinking quickly. "That way there's nothing that links you. Where's my dad?" I said. "Is he okay? Is he conscious?"

Charlotte began scratching her wrist until bright red streaks appeared. I grabbed her hand and held it still. "Is he okay?"

"He was unconscious when the paramedics got here," she said. "I'm so sorry, Harriet, I know this isn't what you need to hear. He didn't make it," she said. "I'm so sorry, but—"

"No." I shook my head manically. "No, that can't be true."

"He wasn't in good shape, but he didn't know what was happening or was in any pain, and the paramedics did everything they could—"

"No," I cried out, clamping my hands over my ears so I couldn't hear what she was saying. If I didn't hear it, it might not be true. Just as I'd believed when I'd seen my mum's empty hospital bed.

My father couldn't be dead. Not when I had so much I needed to say to him.

"Harriet." Charlotte pried my hands away from my ears. "You need to be careful," she whispered urgently. "There's too many people nearby."

"But I haven't told him I'm sorry," I sobbed. "He'll never know."

He'd never know that if I could turn back time, I would in a heartbeat, and I'd go back to the day he walked back into my life. And this time I would never have asked of him what I did. I would never have put him in a position where he couldn't say no.

Grief balled in the pit of my stomach, expanding with every tight breath I inhaled. Not my dad. Not the man who'd put his life at risk for me and Alice. This was all my fault and now it was too late and there was nothing I could do to make any of it better. "He only took her to keep us safe."

"Harriet!" Charlotte said. "You can't do this. Someone will be watching."

I knew what she was telling me. The police would be monitoring my every move. I wasn't supposed to show remorse for the man who had taken my child. But I couldn't help it. Bile rose so quickly, so forcefully, that before I could stop myself I threw up outside the back doors of the ambulance.

Charlotte's arms were instantly around me, stroking

my hair, making me sit next to Alice, who had thankfully fallen asleep already. How much I wanted to lie down with her, have sleep take me away too, turn this into nothing more than a bad dream.

"You *cannot* break down. He took your daughter, remember," she said so quietly only I could hear.

"But it's all my fault," I whimpered. She knew that, of course, but still she continued to stroke my hair and tell me I needed to pull myself together.

Yet the pain wrenched at my insides, tugging them apart, scrunching them back together haphazardly until they felt like they weren't a part of me. A searing heat spread through me like fire until I could feel nothing else.

I couldn't let them think my father was responsible. Not now that he was dead. I lifted my head up, surveying the scene that stretched around me. Taking in the chaos; the panic; the pain. Everyone was only here because of me.

"How can I live with myself if I don't tell the truth?" I murmured.

"Harriet, look," Charlotte snapped, turning my head to the left. Alice was curled up in the shape of a peanut. Her breaths slow and deep. Oblivious—as she should be. "How can you live with yourself if you do?"

I COULDN'T UNDERSTAND how, after everything I'd done to her, Charlotte was trying to protect me, but I never got the chance to ask her why. Or indeed whether she would be prepared to lie for me. At that moment a police officer appeared at the back of the ambulance, introducing herself as Detective Rawlings, and while she murmured condolences for nothing specific, she asked both Charlotte and me to accompany her to the station where she and her colleague would ask us some questions. Another officer would stay with Alice, she assured me, as she led me to the car waiting in the parking lot. I never got the chance to tell Charlotte how sorry I was before she was led in for questioning. And I never got the chance to ask how far she was prepared to go.

NOW

From the moment my dad agreed to this plan, I'd always known there was every possibility I'd one day find myself lying to the police. I tried convincing myself he would get away with hiding her for me and tried not thinking about the many ways it could go wrong, but I knew, of course I knew, how easily it could.

Sometimes I imagined myself in an interrogation room—my only ideas of them conjured from TV dramas—and I'd stick to my story, persuading the police I had nothing to do with my daughter's disappearance.

What I never considered was that I'd also be lying about murdering my husband.

Is it murder? I left him to die, but I didn't actually kill him. Is there a difference? My fingers tap nervously on the table as I wait for Detective Lowry to come back into the room. I wonder what the detective was called away for and suspect there must be news of Brian.

Maybe he isn't even dead, I think, my fingers pausing as the door swings open. I move my hands to my lap so Lowry can't see them twitching. He doesn't look at me as he slides back into his chair and speaks into the microphone, well-rehearsed lines rolling off his tongue as he announces the interview has begun.

I have already told the detective how my husband abused me for years, that he dragged me onto the boat tonight against my will, leaving my daughter alone on the beach. I've told him Charlotte will vouch for this, as she found Alice on the rocks.

"What I don't understand, Harriet," he says, "is why you never thought to mention that your dad was actually still alive when Alice first went missing."

I look at him, silenced briefly, because I'd expected him to continue asking me about Brian. But his words fire into the room like a bullet, loud and sharp as they echo around my head.

I tell him the truth about my mother's lie, that my husband believed my father was dead, and that I never could have contradicted Brian when he told the police this because I was so frightened about what he might do. And when the detective wants to know if I've seen my dad since he left, in the last thirty-four years, I admit he turned up at my door six months ago.

Lowry raises an eyebrow and settles back in his seat, letting my admission linger between us. It isn't the answer he'd expected. He is either excited or nervous by the turn this is taking—he certainly didn't think I would so readily admit I'd seen him again, but I have no choice. Alice will tell them she knows him.

"Harriet," he says, pressing closer to the microphone. "Did you know your father had taken your daughter from the fair thirteen days ago?"

I close my eyes and bow my head, taking a breath, slowly and deliberately.

"Harriet?"

My father made me promise him I'd deny my involvement. Betraying him feels so much more unforgivable now. "No. I didn't know anything about it," I say, Charlotte's words reverberating in my head: How could I live with myself if I didn't lie?

Detective Lowry crosses his arms and leans back in his chair, cocking his head to one side as his eyes bore into me.

In the twenty-minute journey from the beach to the police station, I'd stitched together a fragile story made from fragments of truths, creating another version of reality that I needed to believe. I may have learned to make up stories when I was younger, but it was thanks to Brian that I'd acquired the gullibility to believe anything.

I take another sip of water, swallowing it loudly, and remind the detective what my husband was like and how scared I was of how he'd react.

"Right. Your husband," he says flatly. "Who no one else knew was abusive."

I ignore his tone. "My father was the first person I confided in."

The detective glances at my wrist. I've been rubbing it again, and a wide red circle now bands my arm. "It wasn't physical." I stop rubbing and gesture to my wrist. "Though he did grab me tonight. But no, what he did throughout our marriage felt much worse," I say.

"So what did your father say when you told him?"

I tell Lowry my dad tried persuading me to leave Brian, but that Brian had made it impossible. And then I tell him the story my dad came up with when he said he couldn't see me anymore. That he'd told me he moved to France and he was sorry he couldn't do more to help. I tell Detective Lowry that I hadn't seen him again until tonight.

Lowry is still incredulous that I mentioned none of this to the police two weeks ago. That surely I would have suspected my father could have taken Alice.

"Of course I wish I had now," I say. "I haven't seen my daughter in two weeks." Tears trickle down my cheeks at the thought of Alice and how desperately I want to be with her again. I wipe them away with the sleeve of my T-shirt. I would change everything if I knew I could save my dad.

"Are you sure there's no news?" I ask him again. "Did they find Brian?"

DETECTIVE RAWLINGS FOLDS her hands, one on top of the other, on the table in front of her. Her shoulders are taut, her forehead now has a permanent crease along the length of it. She can't hide her frustration as much as she tries.

"I'm sorry, I just don't buy that you didn't know anything about Brian."

"Christ!" Charlotte falls back into her chair and looks away from the detective.

"What's the matter, Charlotte?" Rawlings's interest is piqued.

"I just can't believe we are still going over this same thing. *I didn't know*," she says through gritted teeth. "Harriet never told me about her husband's abuse. I didn't know Harriet as well as I thought I did, I realize that now," she snaps. "I don't know why you're trying to make me feel worse about it than I already do."

Somewhere along the line, tiredness has bled into exhaustion. But Charlotte's heart is thumping, adrenaline is feeding her veins, and the more Detective Rawlings accuses her, the more Charlotte wants to shout, "Just bring it on."

"I'm not trying to make you feel bad," the detective says, her face still void of emotion. "I just want to get to the truth."

"I've been telling you the truth," she cries, feeling the blood rush to the surface of her skin. "And maybe I should have looked harder, but the fact is—" She falters. "The fact is, if you don't want someone to know, they won't."

The detective pulls back, her eyebrows pinched, seemingly amused by Charlotte's outburst.

Charlotte's chair screeches back across the hard floor as she stands up. She rips open her cardigan and pulls up her T-shirt with one hand, lowering the waistband of her jeans with the other. "This," she says, pointing to the puckered red scar on the side of her stomach, "is what *I* didn't want anyone to know."

She lets her T-shirt fall and uses her hand to wipe the tears across her face. Not one person knew the truth: that one night her dad's temper led to him ripping the hot iron off the ironing board, out of the socket, catching Charlotte as he swung it around in anger. It might have been an accident, but still, she never wanted anyone to know the truth.

"And they never did," she cries, falling back into the chair. "They never did. So don't you dare say that this is my fault."

"HARRIET, I KNOW this has been a distressing night for you, but I will tell you if there is any news." Detective Lowry looks up sharply when we are interrupted by a knock on the door. An officer pokes her head in and calls him out of the room again. "Bloody hell," he mutters, scraping his chair back. "Two minutes," he snaps, glancing back at me.

When he returns, he takes his seat and clears his throat, sitting slightly forward in his chair as his elbows reach out to find the table. "Let's continue," he says firmly.

"What happened?" I ask.

They found Brian. I know they did. He is still alive and telling them what I did to him.

"Mrs. Hodder, I'm the one asking the questions," he says as he shifts awkwardly and clasps his fingers together. "What made you come to Cornwall, Harriet?"

Another deep breath. Another lump to swallow down. "I got a note," I lie. "It came through the mail slot three days ago." I lean forward and from my back pocket I pull out the Elderberry Cottage business card I'd written on earlier this afternoon, glancing at it one last time before I push it across the table.

Lowry reads it aloud. "'I'm sorry, Harriet, but I'm doing this for you. You're both in danger if you stay.'" He turns the note over and reads out the address. "So you get this and decide to come to Cornwall and find Elderberry Cottage?"

I nod.

"Without even thinking to mention this to *anyone*?" He flaps the card in the air. "Not even Angela, who was practically living in your house at the time?"

"I just needed to get to my daughter," I say quietly. "I wasn't scared of my father. I believed Alice was safe, and I was worried that if I told anyone else, something would go wrong."

Though I'm well aware of how very wrong everything went.

"How much longer will I be here?" I ask him, draining the last of my water and letting him refill my glass.

Lowry glances at the fat watch on his wrist but doesn't answer me.

"Did you find Brian?" I ask.

Detective Lowry hesitates. "No, Mrs. Hodder," he says after a beat. "We haven't found your husband."

"Oh—" I sink back, trying to make sense of how the news makes me feel. I was convinced they had.

Is he dead? He must be.

Lowry is asking me more questions about Brian and what he did to me, in the same tone that suggests he doesn't believe my story, when all of a sudden a thought hits me.

"My diary," I say, jolting upright. "It's in my handbag. I left it—"

Where is my diary? I had taken my bag to the beach because Brian had shoved it at me when we were at the cottage. "I dropped it, somewhere." I shake my head, I can't remember. I must have dropped it when I saw my dad. Maybe it's still on the rocks. Or maybe it's been swallowed up by the sea.

"PERHAPS YOU'D LIKE to take a break, Charlotte?" Rawlings seems to think she's gotten me to admit something, but she doesn't know what.

Charlotte had never meant to have an outburst. She nods, and once outside the room, she turns left and heads for the bathroom. The detective walks off in the opposite direction.

When Charlotte emerges five minutes later, she spots Captain Hayes at the front door with Detective Rawlings and a man she doesn't recognize. She ducks into a doorway, out of sight, where she can only just make out the voices farther down the hallway.

"How's it going?" Hayes asks. "Progress?"

"I don't know about progress," Charlotte hears Detective Rawlings say. "But I don't think we'll get any more out of Charlotte Reynolds."

"And Harriet Hodder's convinced the husband's going to turn up," another voice pipes up. Charlotte leans forward and takes a better look at the short man with wire-rimmed glasses. She wonders if he's the detective who's been questioning Harriet. "It's rattling her."

"'Rattling her'?" Angela appears in the doorway and Charlotte pulls back before one of them spots her. "Do tell me what that's supposed to mean, Detective Lowry?"

"Well, I believe he'd have a very different story to tell us. One she doesn't want us hearing."

"Oh, dear God," Angela cries. "Are you kidding me? Harriet Hodder is scared. That woman's been abused by him for years. *Of course* she's rattled."

"We only have her word for it," Lowry says. "And I'm not sure I believe her version of what happened on the boat."

"Well, this makes for interesting reading," Angela snaps. "She's been writing this diary for the last year." She falls silent, and for a moment all Charlotte can hear is the blood swishing in her ears.

"Yet you didn't pick up on it?" he asks. "You were practically living with them and you didn't see that side of Brian Hodder?"

Silence again. *None of us did*, Charlotte wants to tell Angela. *None of us saw it*.

"I didn't," Angela says eventually. "You're right. At the

time I didn't see what he was doing, but look in this notebook. What he did was subtle. Brian Hodder was a clever, manipulative, patient man. He did it in a way nobody would ever notice."

"Well, whatever happened on that boat we might never know the truth—" Lowry says.

"Angela?" Captain Hayes speaks her name. Charlotte leans forward, chancing another glance at the four detectives. Angela is looking the other way. "Is there something else?" Hayes says.

"Angela?" he asks her again when she doesn't respond.

"No," she says firmly and looks back at the others. "Nothing else." But Charlotte's sure there was something else Angela wanted to say.

"DO I NEED a lawyer?" I ask when Lowry comes back. He has been gone for more than ten minutes and it's felt like a lifetime, wondering what he'll decide to do next, whether he's going to charge me or not. My chest is burning and I scratch at the thin cotton of my T-shirt until I feel my skin sting. "Am I under arrest?"

"No," he says, though I don't believe he's happy about that.

"Then I can go?"

He nods slowly and watches me warily as he says, "Yes. Though we'll need to speak to you again. And we'll need to talk to your daughter in the morning."

I can't believe it. I'm free to go? Does that mean they believe me, or at least have no evidence? Does that mean Charlotte lied for me?

"There's someone here for you." Lowry's voice is low and I look up to see Angela in the doorway. I stand up and fall into her arms as she hugs me, then slowly walks me out of the room.

"I'm really free to leave?" I say to her, my words no more than a whisper.

"Yes you are." She smiles as she maneuvers me down the hallway toward the reception area. "I'm taking you to a safe house for the night. Alice is already there," she says as she opens the front door. "She was fast asleep when I left her."

Outside, the chill of the night air hits me. Angela stops at the bottom of the steps and, when we're alone in the parking lot, turns to me and says, "Your bag was found at the beach. I read your diary, Harriet. Why didn't you tell me what Brian was doing?"

I stare past her. I'd wanted everyone to see what Brian was doing, no one more than Angela. "I wasn't sure you'd believe me. I needed you to see him doing it with your own eyes."

I feel Angela tense and I can't be sure if it's because she'd fallen for Brian's lies too, or because she's still not certain if she can trust me.

"He's very clever," I say. "I'd hoped with a bit more time you'd have seen what he was doing. I've no doubt you would have, it's just that things went wrong before then."

"Did you plug your phone in?" she asks. "The day it fell into the bath? You were adamant it wasn't you, but Brian was so—" She brushes a hand through the air.

"Convincing?" I finish for her. "No I didn't. That was him."

We pick up our steps again as Angela leads me to the taxi waiting at the far side of the lot. "He killed my father," I say. "He attacked him, completely unprovoked." After everything that has happened, I still feel numb.

Grief has rooted itself inside me, a part of me now, and it terrifies me that somehow I just need to accept it.

"I'm sorry, Harriet," she says. "I'm very sorry about your dad."

"I know what everyone will think of him, but what he did was out of love for me and Alice." It breaks my heart to be uttering these words. I have a feeling I will be saying them a lot in the future, but I suspect they'll fall on deaf ears.

"You know you'll be questioned again, don't you?" Angela says. "Detective Lowry wants to ask you more about what happened on the boat."

I nod.

"It's just—just make sure your story's clear, Harriet."

I glance at her quizzically. "I don't understand."

"He'll want to dissect what happened at sea between you and Brian." She pauses as we reach the taxi. "I know you said you couldn't swim," she says, "but I know that's not true."

"What do you mean?"

"I saw your swimming suit at the bottom of the laundry basket once," she says, shaking her head. "Don't answer; I don't need to know any more." Angela's eyes drift to my stomach and my hand that's rubbing it in circles. "I missed that, though, didn't I?" she adds.

My breath catches as my hand immediately stills. I look down at my feet.

"How many weeks?" she asks gently.

"Seven," I mumble. "There was one night." I feel the need to explain the time to her, to make her understand why I slept with my husband when the act itself had become such a blessed rarity. I didn't want Brian upset about anything so close to the fair, and feared saying no would have triggered doubts that everything was normal. "How did you guess?" I ask. "There haven't really been many signs yet." So far this pregnancy has been so different than Alice's that often I forget I'm pregnant, or wonder if I still am.

"A bit of guessing, but there was something in your last diary entry. You wrote, 'Surely I'm doing the right thing for all of us.' It's a small detail, but it stuck out because you usually wrote both of you. And you haven't stopped rubbing your tummy tonight," she adds. "I was looking for it though."

I found out about the baby two weeks before the fair and, as much as I've tried putting the fact I'm carrying his child to the back of my mind, I knew the timing meant I had to go through with my plan. If Brian found out I was pregnant, I'd have no chance of escaping him. Especially if it's the son he always dreamed of, the one he always hoped might turn out just like him. I shudder at the thought as Angela opens the door to the cab. I begin to climb in when I spot someone waiting by the far wall.

"Actually, can you hold on for just a moment," I say. "There's someone I need to speak to."

CHARLOTTE'S PALE FACE is lit against the dark sky by the harsh white light floodlighting the front of the station. Underneath her eyes the skin is red and smudged with makeup. She blinks rapidly as she looks at me and then away, and neither of us knows what to say, but I know I have to find something. "I can't begin to say how sorry I am. I should never have done what I did."

"No," she says plainly. "You shouldn't."

Angela is watching us and I angle myself so she can't

see my face. "Thank you. I didn't deserve you coming to Cornwall. I shouldn't have asked—" I stop, because even to me my words sound hollow.

"You should have always known I'd have done anything for you. You could have told me what was happening. I was your *friend*, Harriet. It's what friends do," she says, her voice tired.

I don't even know what to say. She's right.

"For the last two weeks I've been blamed for losing Alice," she goes on. "I blamed myself too. Tonight I've had to listen to them blaming me." She gestures toward the police station. "For hours they've been asking me why I didn't know my best friend was in trouble, why I didn't act as soon as you called me this morning, and I couldn't tell them, could I?" She shakes her head and looks away, her eyes glistening. "This evening I still felt guilty, can you believe that? I felt guilty that I hadn't been a good enough friend to you."

"No," I say, "don't ever say that. You've been the best—"

"Don't," Charlotte stops me. "I can't hear it. I just want to get back to my family."

"I'm so sorry," I say, reaching out for her, but she moves her arm away.

"I can't forgive what you've done, Harriet," she says quietly.

"I understand," I say, and I do. I truly do, but I can't help thinking this is exactly what Brian would have wanted.

ONE YEAR LATER

Audrey pours a hefty amount of red wine into Charlotte's glass, cradling her own. Charlotte waits, but she knows Aud has no intention of speaking first.

"I don't know what happened." Charlotte rubs the stem of her glass between her thumb and finger.

"This isn't the first time," Aud says. "You made an excuse to leave Gail's two weeks ago and obviously didn't want to be at book club. But tonight you drove off before you even made it through the door." Audrey sighs, taking Charlotte's hand. "Talk to me."

Charlotte takes a large gulp of wine and puts the glass back down on the coffee table, too heavily. *Well, Audrey, here's the thing. I feel like I'm on the brink of a breakdown.*

"There's this black cloud hanging over me," she says eventually. "I can't shake it."

"It's been a year now." Audrey's tone is a little softer.

"I know, and I realize I should have moved on, but I can't."

Audrey looks at her quizzically. Charlotte can't expect her to understand when she doesn't know the truth. "You still feel responsible," Aud says.

"I don't." Not for what happened to Alice, anyway.

"Then I don't get it. You don't like coming out anymore. I watch you on the playground and your mind's somewhere else completely. Charlotte, look at you. You look permanently panicked. And you've lost weight, too," she adds. "Too much."

Charlotte picks her glass up, swilling the red liquid around until she almost spills some. It's true, a lot of her clothes hang off her now.

"Talk to me," Audrey says again.

"You know when everyone found out Alice had been taken by her grandfather?" Charlotte says. "Within twenty-four hours every one of the people I'd felt had shunned me turned up on my doorstep, each of them telling me how wonderful it was that Alice had been found and how relieved I must be."

"But you were."

"Of course I was relieved she was safe, but only days before, they'd all distanced themselves from me, pulled their kids away from mine. Then they all got a neat resolution, which meant they could brush over what had happened and pretend like it never did. I felt like they were forgiving me."

"You're losing me." Aud shakes her head.

"Their forgiveness meant they thought I was guilty in the first place. And they'd been happy to victimize my children because of it too."

Audrey looks down at her glass but doesn't answer. They both know there's truth in what Charlotte says.

"None of them apologized because they didn't want to acknowledge that they'd acted horribly. And I never confronted them. I just let it go." Charlotte shrugs. "The elephant in the room is always there, though. The other day Gail started talking about that TV drama, *The Missing*, and I was genuinely interested, but then she just suddenly stopped, looked at me, and it felt like the air had frozen. Someone changed the subject and we were all talking about hairdressers or some other crap and I thought, it's always going to be like this, isn't it?"

"If this is what's eating you up, you should tell them how you feel," Aud says. "You can't expect them to understand if you don't."

"Oh, I don't know," Charlotte sighs. What would be the point anyway? She couldn't tell them everything. She couldn't tell anyone that.

"Is that what this is really about?" Audrey asks. "There's nothing else on your mind?"

Charlotte leans her head against the back of the sofa. She's often come close to telling Audrey the whole truth, but she's always stopped herself. She wonders how Aud would react if she knew Harriet had set her up and that Charlotte had perjured herself to save her.

Maybe talking to Audrey would help lift the black cloud, because recently it's been drawing so close she expects to one day wake up and find it's smothered her completely. It's not easy pretending life has returned to normal.

Yet there are no gray shades with Aud. She'd undoubtedly tell her to go to the police and tell them the truth. Harriet would be arrested and tried, Alice would be taken from her, and what would those same people say then? What kind of friend would that make Charlotte?

No. She made her decision a year ago and needs to learn to live with it.

"I'm thinking of going to see Harriet," Charlotte says.

"Good. I never understood why you lost touch, especially when she was so eager to see you."

"Well, she moved away—"

"Oh, don't give me that again," Aud says. "You pulled away from her before she moved back to Kent. You haven't even seen the new baby. Is that why you're going now?"

"That's part of it," Charlotte says. She doesn't add that the bigger part is to get things off her chest. To ask Harriet about something that's been bothering her since that night on the beach. "If I go next week, could you watch the children?" she asks.

A WARM PUFF of air explodes into Harriet's kitchen as she opens the oven door. She leans in and jabs a knife into the cake. It looks done but she hesitates, her head practically inside the oven as she decides whether to take it out or give it another five minutes. In the end she closes the door and glances at the clock, stretching her back and rubbing her stomach. It feels knotted. A feeling that comes and goes, but it's tighter today, which isn't surprising since Charlotte is due in one hour.

Harriet picks up the baby monitor and holds it to her ear. She can hear a faint babble, a heartwarming sound. As she places the monitor back on the windowsill, her gaze drifts to the yard where Alice is wandering alongside the small flowerbed with a watering can. The leasing agent told her the yard was a good size for ground-floor flats in the area, especially so close to the school. The moment she saw the place she said she'd take it. After the other fifteen, Harriet knew she'd struck gold and wished the agent had shown her this one first.

Moving back to Kent had been an easy decision. They couldn't stay where they were, in a house filled with memories where Brian still lingered in every corner. Each morning when Harriet woke, the first thing she imagined was her husband lying in bed beside her. And then the last memory she had of him, in the sea, would flood her thoughts and that equally wasn't a good way to start the day.

There was nothing left for Harriet in Dorset. Nowhere she could take Alice without crushing reminders of what she'd lost. Once she'd stood in the café of a National Trust house and felt herself sinking to the ground, the world evaporating around her as the memory of her talking to her father in that very same room blinded her. When Alice pulled at her sleeve, Harriet looked around and realized she was crying. A couple was staring at her from their corner table.

In that moment she understood they needed a fresh start, a chance to make new memories rather than reliving raw and painful ones every day. The flat in the tall Victorian semi around the corner from Alice's new school became the perfect base.

Harriet takes a deep breath as a waft of smoke fills the air. "Oh no," she mutters, pulling the oven door open. The cakes are burnt around the edges, a dark brown crust that she knows without touching will be crispy and hard. She throws the cake pans to the side and fights back tears.

"Mummy, what's that smell?" Alice comes into the kitchen, her nose screwed up as she drops the empty watering can on the floor.

"I burnt the cake."

Alice totters over and peers at the treats. "They'll still taste nice, Mummy."

Harriet smiles and ruffles her daughter's hair. "What are you doing in the garden?"

"Watering Grandpa's rose," she says matter-of-factly.

"Good girl." She pauses. "Have you watered your daddy's, too?"

Alice nods and Harriet changes the subject, asking if she'd like a drink. She has no idea if she's doing the right thing when it comes to talking to Alice about Brian. Counselors advise her not to ignore him, to make sure Alice knows she can talk about her father, ask questions whenever she wants. But she often wonders if it does either of them any good.

Harriet hadn't wanted to get Brian a rosebush. In the garden center, she'd originally only picked out one with the intention of planting it for her dad. It wasn't until they were at the cash register that the thought hit her that Alice should have one for her own father. "Let's go and choose one for Daddy, too, shall we?" she'd said, and Alice had followed her back through the store at least three paces behind. Harriet had pointed out pretty bushes until eventually Alice had agreed to one.

At first Harriet would pick a bud and put it in a bud glass on the windowsill. She told Alice that sometimes they were from Grandpa's bush and sometimes Daddy's, but over time she couldn't bear having anything of Brian's in the house and stopped picking flowers from his.

It's only a plant, she would tell herself. But it wasn't. It was a constant reminder that he was out there watching her, and one day she feared she'd end up ripping the damned bush out of the ground.

"Do you want to take this outside?" Harriet fills a tumbler of water and hands it to Alice. She still needs to tidy the kitchen and change her clothes and lay out the new napkins with the cake she'd bought as a backup. Make it all nice.

She hasn't spoken to Charlotte since telling her there would be no trial. By then this was no surprise, but the confirmation was still a relief. Harriet understood there was no evidence of her involvement, no proof that anyone but her father was involved, whether others believed it or not.

So she'd ended up letting him take the blame, just as he'd made her promise to if it all went wrong. And how wrong it went, she thinks, her eyes filling as they are drawn to his rosebush again.

Her dad was only in her life for six months, but he'd managed to change everything. She takes a deep breath and looks around, reminding herself as she often does that he gave her all she ever wanted. Freedom.

Over the last year Harriet has told him many times how sorry she is. She whispers it at night as she curls up in bed and the tears flow down her cheeks. She longs for one more day with him so she could relive all the magic he brought into their lives. They would build sandcastles and eat ice cream when it was cold and they would laugh until it felt greater than any pain.

Harriet presses her hand against the windowpane, covering the view of the rose. She can feel the hole in her heart stretching, tugging until she forces herself to look away. She needs to think about the day ahead. Charlotte will be here soon. Her stomach flutters and she allows herself to feel a little excited as she pulls a cloth out and begins to wipe down the kitchen.

CHARLOTTE SQUEEZES THE tea bag against the inside of the paper cup with a plastic spoon. Fields roll past through the train window. The carriage was empty until they'd pulled into the last station, where a handful of passengers shuffled in. Now there are at least a dozen of them, including a couple sitting at the far end of the car that keeps drawing her attention.

The girl looks barely seventeen. She's sitting next to the window and stares glumly out of it. Her boyfriend, who is at least ten years her senior, kicks a battered purple suitcase with a restless foot. Each time his foot bangs against it the girl flinches. Behind his scruffy beard and dark eyebrows there are steely gray eyes that flick around the train as if he's expecting or looking for trouble.

Charlotte feels the plastic spoon snap between her fingers and looks down, surprised to find she's broken it in half. She forces herself to look away from the couple and think about what she plans to say to Harriet. There are many things she needs to get off her chest that won't stop haunting her.

At first Charlotte was relieved when Harriet moved back to Kent. She wouldn't have to look over her shoulder every time she went to the park. Not that she ever went to that particular one anymore. But then as the weeks passed, relief turned to an anger, which settled in her gut and began to grow. She was angry with Harriet. So full of rage.

The papers called Harriet's story "tragic" and labeled her "brave." Charlotte swallowed the lies she read, and all the while her rage grew and grew. What made it worse was that she couldn't release it. Instead she had to sit back and accept she'd played a part in turning Harriet into the victim.

Some mornings Charlotte yanked back the curtains, wanting to open the windows and scream. Let the world know that it was she who should have their pity and admiration. Not Harriet. Where were the stories about Charlotte? What happened to the people who attacked her in the press? None of them retracted their slurs. No one seemed interested in what became of the friend, but then maybe she should be grateful they'd stopped talking about her. And that that awful Josh Gates's story about Jack had never been published.

Yet staying silent is suffocating. It feels like it's quite literally drowning her. After Harriet moved, Charlotte started imagining the life her old friend was now living: what her house is like, if Harriet's cut her hair, if she has a circle of friends who've accepted what happened to her. She's wondered about it to the extent that she actually hates Harriet for running away and setting up a new life, while Charlotte's been sinking lower and lower into her own despair.

She can't move past the fact that she lied to the police, but there's also something else. And if what Alice told her is true, then Charlotte needs to know what she's been covering up.

She sips her tea and checks her watch as they pull into another station. Hers is the next stop, and they're due to arrive in twelve minutes. The train pulls away again and she texts Audrey to check on the children, looking up as the boyfriend at the end of the car raises his voice. He calls his girlfriend a stupid bitch and slams his fist on the table and she is crying, her shoulders heaving and tears streaming down her face in black streaks from her smudged mascara. The other passengers keep their heads down or stare out the windows, except for a lady in her eighties who watches them, shocked by their public display of anger and hysteria. Now he is in the young girl's face, making her recoil with each word he spits.

Charlotte pushes herself out of her seat. There was a

time when she would've stayed out of other people's business, but she can't allow this behavior. As she strides down the aisle she can feel the nervous glances of the other passengers, who likely think she's mad for getting involved. But as soon as she reaches the couple, Charlotte stops short. The man is holding his girl-friend's face, kissing her on the nose and telling her he's sorry and how much he loves her. Choking back her sobs with laughter, she tells him she loves him too. Both of them are oblivious to Charlotte hovering, about to step in.

She could keep walking and pretend she was going to the bathroom, but she can't be bothered with that charade and instead makes her way back to her seat. An arm reaches out midway down the aisle, stopping her in her tracks. Charlotte looks at the old woman who says, "You did a good thing there, love. You were the only one prepared to step in."

Charlotte turns back to the couple. "I don't think the girl realizes she needs help." She feels angry that he's treating her like this. That girl is someone's daughter, and she knows she'd want someone to step in if it were Molly or Evie.

"No," the old woman says. "But she will one day."

"Maybe I should go back and say something," Char-lotte says, still watching them.

"I wouldn't," the lady says. "You don't always know when you're doing more harm than good. If she's not ready for help, then neither of them will thank you."

HARRIET'S PLACE IS easy to find. It's at the end of a pleasant street, where just around the corner there's a small row of quaint shops and across the road a lush park with a pavilion and a pond and a children's playground.

Charlotte hovers on the sidewalk outside. Suddenly the thought of seeing Harriet is far too overwhelming and she needs to force herself up the short path to the front door, ring the bell, and wait without running. Her heart is beating hard and she wonders if she might throw up when Harriet opens the door.

Harriet is wearing a long blue dress with a white cardigan. Her hair has been cut short and colored a much richer brown. Her mouth that sparkles with gloss breaks into a small smile as she steps aside to let Charlotte in. Charlotte mumbles "Thank you" as she passes and is walking to the kitchen when Alice rushes in, armed with a handful of flowers that she thrusts into Charlotte's hand.

"Oh, goodness," she says as she bends down to the little girl. "Thank you." The tears surprise her. She didn't expect to be so emotional at the sight of Alice, who's even taller than Molly now. Her hair has been braided down the back and tied with a huge yellow ribbon. The little girl is chattering about the garden, something about a rosebush and about how the new baby sleeps in a cot next to Mummy's bed, and is asking if Charlotte would like to see her bedroom because she's hung her butterflies in the window.

"I'd love to, maybe a little later?" she says, straightening up. Alice won't stop talking, excitedly telling her all about school, and now she is pulling a drawing off the fridge that she hands to Charlotte.

"That's my picture of the school rabbit," Alice says. "It's a real one."

Harriet is drifting around them, filling the kettle and sliding a cake onto a plate that she puts on the small round table sitting snugly in the corner. A pile of muslins are neatly folded on its edge and baby bottles are lined up in a row behind the sink. She wonders where the baby is as Alice carries on.

"I go to big school." Alice smiles proudly. "I go every morning five times a week." She holds up five fingers.

"That's very good counting. Do you like it at your big school?"

Alice nods eagerly. "The rabbit is called Cottontail and we can hold her at break time and yesterday it was my turn to feed her, but do you know you're not supposed to feed them too many carrots?"

"I didn't know that."

"It's because they have sugar and they can give the rabbits bad teeth. My teacher said that in assembly."

"You're a bright little button." Charlotte smiles at her.

"She is," Harriet says as she comes to stand next to her daughter, resting her hand on Alice's head. "She doesn't forget a thing," she adds, but in a way that suggests this isn't necessarily a good thing. "Alice, why don't you take a piece of cake and watch some TV?" As soon as she passes Alice a plate, the girl is out of the room.

"She seems very happy." Charlotte watches her go.

Harriet nods. "I hope so. But then you don't always know for sure, do you? Please, have a piece." Harriet hands her a plate. Charlotte takes it and sits down.

"George is asleep," Harriet says, frowning as she nervously checks her watch. "He's already been down two hours. He'll probably wake soon." Charlotte remembers those days like they were yesterday—she can't tell if Harriet's desperate for George to wake up or desperate for him not to. "I was pleased to hear from you," Harriet says. "But now that you're here I have a feeling this isn't a friendly visit." She tries to laugh but it's a nervous sound that comes out.

"No, maybe not," Charlotte admits. "I'm struggling."

Harriet nods. "Because of what you said to the police?"

"That's part of it."

"Do you think you did the wrong thing?" Harriet's gaze drifts away as she prods a slice of cake with a small fork, sending tiny crumbs flying across the plate.

Charlotte sighs. "I never thought I was capable of what I did. It makes me feel guilty. And afraid. I'm afraid that one day it will all catch up with me."

"That can't happen now," Harriet says.

"No, maybe not, but it doesn't stop me from thinking about it. I don't even know who I am anymore."

"What do you mean? You're still the same person."

"No," Charlotte replies flatly. "I'm not the same person at all. I do things now that are so out of character." Tom wouldn't believe her if she told him how she'd almost interfered in that couple's argument. "I'm so far from that person and it scares me, because I liked the old me."

"But what's actually changed?" Harriet asks. "Your life's still the same. You have the same group of friends and live in your lovely house with your amazing kids. What's so different?"

Charlotte lays her hands flat on the table and fiddles with the corner of a napkin. She imagines Harriet buying them especially for her visit and feels a flash of pity for such an effort. "Everything is different, Harriet. None of it is real. It feels like everything I do is a lie and I can't talk to anyone about it. My *best friend* doesn't even know what I've done." She doesn't mean to, but she finds herself emphasizing the words "best friend."

"You want to tell Audrey. Is that what this is about?" Harriet drops her gaze to her plate.

"Yes, I'd love to tell Audrey, but that's not what this is about. It's about me feeling so angry all the time. I have this rage inside me that has nowhere to go," she says, holding a hand against her stomach. "Can you imagine how that feels?"

"Of course I can. I felt exactly the same when I was told my dad was dead. I felt that way for most of my marriage."

Charlotte looks down. She knows how upset Harriet was about her father, but that wasn't why she's come here and she refuses to be pulled into Harriet's world today. "I'm sorry about your dad," she says. "But you need to tell me what to do with this anger." She can feel the heat bubbling inside her. "I'm angry with you, Harriet," she says bluntly. "I'm angry that you seemed to have moved on and set up such a nice life for yourself."

Harriet glances around the room with its tiny window and minimal cabinets, the gas stove with its rings that look dirty no matter how much she scrubs them.

"You have the life you always wanted," Charlotte says.

"The life I always wanted? What do you imagine my life is?"

"I don't know," Charlotte admits. "But you've started again and I'm left—" She isn't sure how to finish the sentence.

"You're left what?" Harriet asks.

Charlotte sighs. "I don't know. Dealing with it all."

"You think I'm not?" Harriet says. "Every day I expect to see Brian turn up on the doorstep. I open the door and imagine him standing there, that look in his eyes, his head cocked to one side, and I can hear him clear as day: 'Hello, Harriet. Surprise.'"

"That's not going to happen."

"His body was never found," Harriet says. "So it might be unlikely, but it's not impossible. The years of dreading him coming home, fearing I'd done something wrong or said the wrong thing. Wondering what I was going to be quizzed about next—none of that leaves me. I don't know if it ever will."

"Are you telling me that after everything that's happened, it's no better?" Charlotte asks.

"Of course it's better. But it doesn't turn magically wonderful. I'm happy once I've reassured myself he's not going to walk in the door any moment. Then I breathe again and I go back to living my life with the children. But I'm still dealing with it. And I doubt I have the kind of life you think I do." Harriet smiles sadly. "I don't do much with it but it's fine. It's what we need right now and that's what matters. Alice needs to feel safe. They both do."

Harriet places her fork carefully on the plate. "There's not a day that passes that I don't look back and wish I could change what happened. But at the time I was so desperate, I didn't know what else to do. I was living in a trap that Brian created, and honestly, I couldn't see any way of escaping him."

"But why didn't you ever tell me?"

"It took me a long time to realize what he was doing," Harriet says. "By then I felt like he'd convinced everyone around us that I was crazy. When I started writing in my notebook, I was already wondering myself if I was. I didn't—" Harriet stops.

"You didn't trust me?"

"No, maybe not," she admits. "But only because I

was so frightened. I didn't trust anyone. I believed him when he said he'd take Alice from me, and I thought that if I'd fallen for it for years, then how could I expect you not to. Can you honestly say you would have taken my word over his?"

"Of course I would've," Charlotte says, but Harriet hears the moment's pause that's just a fraction too long.

"Do you regret what you said to the police?"

Charlotte looks down at her untouched cake. "Actually I don't," she admits. "Because I don't think the alternative was a better option. But there's something else—" Her heart is beating hard. She isn't even sure she wants to hear the answer anymore. "I know you can swim, Harriet. Alice told me when we were on the beach. She said you used to take her swimming but that it was a big secret. She actually told me so I wouldn't worry about you in that boat."

Harriet continues to look at Charlotte and gives a barely perceptible nod. Her hand is shaking as it grips the fork again.

"What happened to Brian?" Charlotte says as a cry erupts from above them. "Did you—did it happen on purpose?"

Harriet looks up to the ceiling but doesn't move. The cry stops and she glances back at Charlotte, eyes wide in shock, and now Charlotte really doesn't want to hear her answer.

The crying starts again, this time a persistent wail, and Harriet hurries out of the kitchen. Charlotte slumps back in her chair. She shouldn't have asked.

Harriet comes back holding her baby, who is tightly swaddled against her chest, and gently peels the blanket away so Charlotte can get a better look.

Baby George has a head of dark hair and tiny features, and when he opens his brown eyes Charlotte sees the resemblance immediately. The baby is identical to Brian. She hopes she hasn't reacted badly as she runs a hand over his soft hair, but for a moment she can't breathe. "He's lovely," she says eventually, because of course he is, whether he looks like his dad or not.

Harriet presses her lips against her son's head and continues to watch Charlotte, who in turn is wondering if Harriet can see the similarities or whether she only sees her son. She prays it's the latter.

"The first time I felt protective over George was when I was on that boat with Brian," Harriet says. "Before then I'd tried to ignore the fact I was pregnant. I couldn't imagine bringing another child into our family the way it was."

Charlotte keeps looking at George as she strokes his tiny head.

"Brian had started controlling Alice, too," she says. "I couldn't let him do any more damage."

"Harriet, I shouldn't have said anything—" Charlotte starts, but Harriet interrupts her.

"He could have killed me. He would have taken me from Alice, and once he knew he had a son—" Harriet pauses and closes her eyes as she nestles deeper against her son's head. "Children are our priority, aren't they?"

Charlotte shuffles nervously in her chair, looks toward the door, then back at Harriet and her precious baby.

"Tell me what you would have done, Charlotte," Harriet murmurs.

"I really don't know," she says honestly. She'd never have been able to consider that she could be capable of murder, but then being a mother can make you go to extraordinary lengths.

"I know I've asked so much of you already and I have no right to ask any more." Harriet shakes her head as tears escape from the corners of her eyes. "But I beg you—"

Charlotte shakes her head, her heart in her throat. "You don't have to ask, I'm not going to say anything."

"Thank you," Harriet whispers. "Oh God, thank you."

"MUMMY! I'M HUNGRY." Alice runs into the room and falls against her mum dramatically, dropping a kiss on her baby brother's head. "Can I have another piece of cake?"

"No." Harriet smiles, rubbing her daughter's tummy. "You'll spoil your dinner. Will you stay?" she asks Charlotte.

"Thank you, but I need to get going." Charlotte pushes her plate away and gets up from the table. She's booked a hotel for the night so she doesn't have to go straight home, but for now she needs to be on her own.

"Did you know that when you told me you and Tom were splitting up, I was envious of you?" Harriet says as she gets up too and waits for Charlotte to pick up her bag and the flowers Alice had given her. "I know it sounds mad, but it summed up everything I wanted. I was also sad because I knew Tom was a good man, but you weren't happy and you *did* something about it. I craved having the ability to make a choice and live with it.

"I've started a gardening class," Harriet goes on.

"Really?"

She nods. "One evening a week. I have an elderly neighbor who watches the children. You gave us this security," she says. "And I'm sorry for the way I did it, I really am. It was wrong on so many levels, but I won't ever stop paying for it."

Harriet steps aside and follows Charlotte into the hallway. "I'm glad you came," she says. "I miss you."

Charlotte stops at the door, standing aside to let Harriet open it. "I know you're sorry," she says quietly. It would be so easy to tell Harriet she forgives her. Maybe one day she will, but for today she feels—well, a little bit lighter, she supposes. A little bit more like she can go home to those amazing kids she has and give them a big hug. Tell Aud she wants to dress up and go out for a few drinks, and, sod it, she'll even call Tom and say thank you. Because even though they didn't make a very good husband and wife, he's been a wonderful friend to her over the last year. She is lucky, she realizes. She's always been one of the lucky ones and she doesn't need more than what she has.

Charlotte bends down when Alice runs into the hallway behind them, allowing the little girl to come crashing into her legs for a hug.

"Alice is doing fine," she says quietly to Harriet when she pulls herself up. "She's doing absolutely fine."

Harriet nods, biting her lip, willing the tears not to start again, though she knows they will anyway.

"Bye, Harriet," Charlotte says eventually, and steps off the doorstep.

"Charlotte," Harriet calls out. She wants to ask her friend not to go, but she knows she doesn't have the right. "Take care of yourself," she says.

HARRIET WATCHES CHARLOTTE walk away, knowing she has no choice but to let her go. Just like she did with Jane. When Charlotte disappears around the corner, Harriet closes the door, thinking it's unlikely she'll hear from her again, but hoping that one day she might.

She can't imagine how Charlotte thought she could be living an untroubled life, but then she supposes no one can really understand.

I see Brian watching me from the bottom of the yard, Charlotte.

I see him every time I look into my son's eyes.

Whenever the phone rings, I expect someone to tell me Brian's alive, found washed up on some beach.

My father's dead and it's all my fault.

Some nights she wakes up drenched in sweat and reminds herself that apart from her children, she's lost everyone who has ever been important to her. She tells herself that for some reason she must deserve it and hates herself for what she's done.

Then Harriet creeps into her daughter's bedroom and sees her blond hair fanned around her on the pillow, an innocent smile on her lips, and knows in a heartbeat that she'd do it all again if she had to.

And now there is George, too. Whose little fingers grab on to her hand, wrapping tightly around her, letting her know she is his world and nothing else is important to him.

She took his father away before Brian knew he'd have the son he'd always wanted—the boy he'd hoped would turn out like him—and she can only hope she's saved her son in time. That there's nothing more in George than his father's brown eyes, but only time will tell her that for sure.

"Mummy?"

Harriet is still standing by the front door when she feels a hand on her arm. She looks down at Alice.

"What's for dinner?"

"Oh, honey, I don't know. What would you like?"

"Pizza. Have you been crying?"

Harriet rubs her sleeve across her face and smiles at Alice. "Mummy's fine," she says. "Didn't we have pizza yesterday?"

Alice looks at her in the way she does when she knows something isn't right. "Grandpa let me have pizza every day at the cottage," she says quietly. "Are you happy sad?"

"Yes." Harriet laughs. "I'm very happy to have such a wonderful daughter." She crouches down and pulls Alice in for a hug. "I'll make you a sandwich in a minute."

"And ice cream too? Grandpa also let me have ice cream every day." Alice pulls her head away. "You're making my hair wet, Mummy."

"I'm sorry!" She laughs through her tears as she tickles her daughter. She hopes Alice won't ever stop talking about the two weeks she spent with her precious grandpa.

"Mummy, can we paint a picture?" Alice asks. "Can we paint a big seaside to go in my room?"

"My darling," she says, "you can do absolutely anything you want."

ACKNOWLEDGMENTS

When I began writing this book, I had no idea how it would end, whether it would be any good or even if I'd finish it. I just knew I wanted to write it and if no one else liked it, well, then I suppose I would have started something new. It's been a three-year journey and one that's had a few bumps along the way, but it's thanks to many people for helping me reach this point. I know without a doubt I wouldn't have succeeded without them.

I can clearly remember the day Harriet and Charlotte's story started as a seed of an idea. Holly Walbridge, that was down to you. Thank you for then endlessly listening on trips to the park as I made you think dark thoughts about how it would feel if your children went missing. I hope I haven't scarred you!

The idea turned into a first draft and it was then thanks to Chris Bradford, who let me quiz him about all things police related, and for directing me toward an alternative, and much better, ending than the one I'd originally written. Chris, your knowledge is immeasurable, and any mistakes are entirely my own.

I am very lucky to have such amazing friends who not only read early copies of my book but then read subsequent ones and under very tight deadlines! Donna Cross and Deborah Dorman, you're the best—thank you for reading so quickly and for your invaluable feedback. And as always, Lucy Emery and Becci Holland, who read early copies and who are always there with support. To all my other friends and family who have shown a huge interest in what I am doing—it means so much to be asked how the book is going and to see your genuine excitement when there is good news.

To my wonderful group of writers who have become lifelong friends: you have picked me up when things weren't going so well and celebrated with me when they were. Cath Bennetto, Alexandra Clare, Alice Clark-Platts, Grace Coleman, Elin Daniels, Moyette Gibbons, Dawn Goodwin, and Julietta Henderson—writing would not be the same without you all.

Then along came Nelle. You picked my book off the slush pile and told me we were going to work hard and yes, we certainly did! It took a year of rewrites until I finally heard you utter those magical words—*Your book is ready to fly*. Nelle Andrew, I would not be allowed enough pages to harp on about how fantastic you are. I could not have wished for a bigger champion. Thank you so much for believing in me and for taking me on this incredible journey. And big thanks also to the wider team at PFD, including my wonderful step-agent, Marilia Savvides, and the fantastic rights teams: Alexandra Cliff, Jonathan Sissons, Zoe Sharples, Rebecca Wearmouth, and Laura Otal. You have all worked so hard to make this a success.

When we did finally let my book fly I was fortunate that two incredible editors fell in love with it. Emily Griffin at Cornerstone and Marla Daniels at Gallery—I am thrilled to be working with you both. Your observations and direction are spot-on and between you, you took the story to another level.

Finally my wonderful family. Mum, ever since I was eight you have been telling me I can write and you have never stopped supporting me since. I have never lacked love or encouragement. Whatever choices I have made, you've always remained unconditionally by my side and these are things that matter the most. I know how proud you are, and I know how proud Dad would have been too.

My husband, John—five years ago I probably wouldn't have taken the time to "see if I could write a book" if it weren't for you. Your belief in me has not once wavered and I needed this more than I've probably ever told you. Thank you for reading the book nearly as many times as me and for your editorial input. I'm always telling you you know too much but in this instance I appreciate it! You make me laugh every day and are the kindest man I could wish to have met. Thank you for being you.

And my beautiful Bethany and Joseph. My proudest achievements ever. You have turned my world upside down and I love you for it. My own words don't do justice to how much I adore you and so I have stolen yours: Bethany, I love you to Pluto and back infinity times, and Joseph, I love you more than infinity more times than the universe. Always follow your dreams, my little ones.

BOOK
CLUB
FAVORITES

READER'S
GUIDE

her
one
mistake

HEIDI PERKS

This reader's guide for Her One Mistake *includes an introduction, discussion questions, and ideas for enhancing your book club. The suggested questions are intended to help your reading group find new and interesting angles and topics for your discussion. We hope that these ideas will enrich your conversation and increase your enjoyment of the book.*

INTRODUCTION

When Harriet Hodder asks a favor of her best friend, Charlotte Reynolds, Charlotte is happy to oblige. Harriet's young daughter, Alice, will join Charlotte and her three children at the school fair while Harriet attends an accounting seminar. Since Harriet has never left Alice with anyone before, Charlotte encourages her friend to enjoy her time away.

But when Alice goes missing at the fair, the police investigating the case uncover conflicting evidence relevant to the girl's disappearance. Could Alice's vanishing have anything to do with the abduction of a young boy in a nearby village? Does the fact that Charlotte was looking at social media on her phone when Alice disappeared point to her unsuitability as a caregiver? Why doesn't the alibi of Alice's father, Brian Hodder, hold up under scrutiny? Is Harriet's absent-mindedness a figment of her husband's imagination, or proof of something more sinister at work?

TOPICS AND QUESTIONS
FOR DISCUSSION

1. Compare and contrast Harriet Hodder and Charlotte Reynolds. How does Harriet view Charlotte, and vice versa? In what ways does their friendship seem out of the ordinary?

2. How does Charlotte's momentary distraction implicate her in Alice's unexplained disappearance? How does her behavior appear in light of her willingness to supervise four children at a crowded school fair? In your opinion, to what extent does Charlotte seem deserving of the attacks she receives from strangers on social media, and, to some extent, her friends?

3. "It pained [Harriet] to be away from Alice. It made her heart quite literally burn, but no one under-

stood that" (p. 26). How does the intensity of Harriet's attachment to Alice relate to her own upbringing as a child? Given that Harriet has never before been separated from four-year-old Alice, how typical does her level of anxiety seem?

4. How does the specter of Mason Harbridge, the little boy missing from a nearby village, hang over Alice Hodder's disappearance? Why do the characters in the novel continually reflect on his alleged abduction?

5. "I need to know what [Charlotte] was doing when our daughter went missing . . . because she obviously wasn't watching Alice" (p. 64). To what extent does Brian Hodder's fury at Charlotte Reynolds seem justifiable? What does Alice's disappearance reveal about the nature of Brian's marriage to Harriet?

6. How does the author's decision to narrate the novel through both the present- and past-tense perspectives of Charlotte and Harriet complicate the story the reader must unravel? Of the two perspectives, which did you find more compelling, and why?

7. "Harriet liked having Angela in her life. She thought they could have been friends in very different circumstances" (p. 139). Describe Detective Angela Baker, the family liaison officer assigned to Harriet and Brian Hodder. How does Brian feel about Angela's presence in his home? What does Angela think of their marriage?

8. In what ways does Charlotte's friendship with Audrey differ from her friendship with Harriet? Of the two women, whom would you say is Charlotte's closer friend, and why?

9. The depictions of fatherhood in *Her One Mistake* span a spectrum from abject neglect to selfless sacrifice. In your discussion, compare and contrast the paternal instincts of Tom Reynolds, Brian Hodder, and Les Matthews. How do their behaviors compare to the book's depictions of motherhood?

10. At what point in the novel did you become aware of disputed facts that called into question the reliability of the narrator? Whose version of the truth did you find more credible? Why?

11. How does Brian's concern for Harriet's mental health undermine her self-confidence and sanity? To what extent does his ongoing characterization of events qualify as gaslighting? What possible motive would Brian have for this behavior? How else might one interpret the bizarre and inconsistent things happening to Harriet?

12. "Harriet read through her notes and the discrepancies between what Brian said and what he tried to make her believe, until she was confident she knew the truth" (p. 168). How do Harriet's entries in her journal enable her to reject her husband's version of events? To what extent is her contemporaneous written account persuasive for you as a reader?

13. Why does Harriet deliberately conceal her ability to swim and her father's existence from her husband?

14. To whom and to what do you think the "one mistake" in the book's title refers?

15. What does Charlotte's willingness to help Harriet in Cornwall, despite learning about her friend's ongoing deception, suggest about her character? What compels Charlotte to ignore her instincts to help Harriet?

16. "She'd never have been able to consider that she could be capable of murder, but then being a mother can make you go to extraordinary lengths" (p. 348–49). Discuss whether you believe Harriet is innocent or guilty of murder. Why does her unplanned pregnancy with George serve as the catalyst for her plan?

ENHANCE YOUR BOOK
CLUB

1. Trust is a recurring theme in *Her One Mistake*. Ask members of your book group to consider times in their lives when they have entrusted friends and family with significant responsibilities. Discuss whether they considered the many possible consequences or outcomes of those arrangements. You might want to use the central example of the novel—the disappearance of a friend's child on one's watch—as a starting point for your discussion.

2. Brian Hodder's repeated, deliberate attempts to manipulate Harriet's recollection of events and to compromise her ability to tell fact from fiction exemplify gaslighting, a word whose meaning was established in popular culture after the 1939 play

Gas Light by Patrick Hamilton, and two subsequent film adaptations. With members of your book group, discuss how Brian's efforts jeopardize Harriet's sanity and her personal integrity. If your book group wants to explore the subject further, consider holding a screening party of the 1944 film *Gaslight* starring Ingrid Bergman and Charles Boyer. Alternatively, ask members of your group to consider how the contemporary phrase "fake news" in social media connects to gaslighting.

3. Innocent or guilty? Ask your book club to imagine that Harriet Hodder is the defendant in a criminal trial in which she is accused of having caused the death of her husband, Brian. Divide members of your book group into two teams, one of which represents Harriet and the other of which prepares to prosecute her. What arguments or evidence from the novel would each team use to persuade the jury?

4. The friendship between Harriet and Charlotte gets irreparably damaged by Harriet's scheme. Encourage members of your group to reflect on friendships in their lives that have become broken. If they're comfortable being candid in sharing their recollections, collectively explore the sorts of problems that can commonly emerge in the course of female friendships. Your book club may want to distinguish between childhood and adult friendships in its dialogue.

Don't miss the latest "ingeniously plotted page-turner"
(*Publishers Weekly*) from Heidi Perks

THE WHISPERS

Coming soon from Gallery Books!
Keep reading for a sneak peek…

WEDNESDAY,
1 JANUARY

The body has been found on the beach. At the bottom of Crayne's Cliff, a spot that the people of Clearwater know all too well for the victims it has pulled over its perilous edge over the decades.

The detective stands on the stony coastline, not far from where a scattering of fishermen's huts are wedged into the base of the cliff. They are empty, of course, as is often the case at the height of the winter. He has always found their desolation in the cold months quite haunting, and never more so than today.

He shudders as he pulls himself away, giving the SOCOs space to do their job, and starts to walk back along the beach to where he has parked his car. It is on the other side of the stone wall, built to form a barrier against the waves that can rise high when the sea is rough. Today the sea is a mill pond. In a few hours' time there might be some hardy sailors or even a few crazy paddleboarders out for a New Year's Day jaunt, but right now the beach ahead of him is empty.

He hadn't been called to the scene, but as soon as he heard about it he had to see for himself. His first case, so many years ago, had found him standing on this very stretch of beach. Though that time it had been the body of a young girl that had gone over the edge. Not a woman: not a mother.

He remembers it like it was yesterday, but then, dead bodies are a rare occurrence in Clearwater. Incidents like this are a shock to the community, just like the one all those years ago had been.

As he reaches his car, he pauses and looks back at the cliffs, wondering if anyone else at the station will be asking themselves the question that he is taunting himself with. Could they have known something like this might happen?

Three weeks ago, Grace Goodwin had stood in the station and tried to report a crime, but the officers she spoke with had refused to believe she was right to be worried. And yet his first call this morning hadn't been to wish him a Happy New Year, but to tell him there was a dead body.

SEPTEMBER

FOUR MONTHS

BEFORE

The whispers started on the first day back of the autumn term. As was often the case at drop-off, a group of mothers from across year four had gathered in the playground to chat. Quite often it was the only time they came together, and it had been weeks since they'd last been here at the end of the summer term, so there was plenty to catch up on. They weren't all friends with one another outside of school, but they liked to drop in and out of the gossip, make sure they were kept in the loop of what was happening inside the school gates.

Today they were interested in the fact that there was an unfamiliar face hovering outside their children's new classroom. She had a honey-toned tan, sleek auburn hair pulled back into a ponytail, and wore white cutoff jeans that made her legs look incredibly long and slim. Even in her gold strappy sandals she was at least five foot eight. A little girl with dark pigtails was standing by her side.

It didn't take long for someone to approach her and make an introduction. And when she replied that her name was Grace Goodwin, she'd done so in the very soft twang of an Australian accent. This was enough to draw each of them over to her and, intrigued, they fired off questions at the new mum.

They soon learned she had moved back to England only three weeks ago from Sydney and that she had attended this very school as a child, as some of them had, too. There were a few murmurs that her name sounded familiar. Had she changed it? they asked. To which Grace confirmed she hadn't. But then it wasn't familiar enough that she might have been in their year group and it was too soon to be asking her age just yet.

Grace had lived in Clearwater until she was seventeen, when she and her parents had moved to Australia because of her father's job. Her parents had returned to England five years ago, apparently because of an aunt's ailing health. This was three years after her only child, Matilda, was born, and Grace had decided to stay behind in Sydney until this summer.

Matilda was going to be in 4C, the same class as many of their children. One of the mothers was already talking playdates and snapping out her phone to make sure Grace was included on the class WhatsApp group.

"You need to be on this," the mum was saying. "Anything you need to know about homework, assemblies, anything school-related—just pop on a message and someone will get back to you."

Grace had smiled in return and obligingly given her number, though her gaze kept drifting around the playground as if she were looking for someone else.

She was very pretty, in her midthirties, and looked effortlessly casual yet chic. It was as if she hadn't gone over-

board to make an effort for her first school run but managed to come out looking good, nonetheless.

"So do your parents live nearby?" another mum asked her.

Grace told the group that her parents had relocated to Leicester to be close to her father's sister. That after first the aunt and then her father died three years ago, her mum had made the surprising decision to stay put.

Someone suggested that maybe she'd move down to Clearwater now that Grace was back, but Grace replied that she just didn't see it happening, and they moved onto other questions like, "And what does your husband do? Is he local?"

"Actually, Graham works in Singapore," she said. "He's a project manager for a big pharmaceutical company."

"Oh wow, impressive! But that means you moved over here on your own?"

She had, it turned out, and she and Matilda were renting one of the Waterview apartments, the luxury wave-designed complex that took pride of place on the edge of the road to Weymouth, which made it clear that money wasn't a worry for her. Although the apartments tended to attract young couples, with the building's gym and bar, and weren't family-orientated, so surely it wouldn't be a long-term option.

But their attentions quickly returned to Graham and his job abroad, and the knowledge that funnily enough he'd been in Europe until the start of July. Grace told them this with a smile and a shrug, as if it were no big deal that her husband lived and worked so many miles away, but they already understood how hard it must have been for her, being in the throes of moving to England when he had been shipped off in the opposite direction, though it was probably too soon to delve deeper into this particular line of enquiry when they had only known her for five minutes.

Besides, she was professing that it was fine for him to be living abroad, and that Matilda had been very good about the whole thing, and so none of them probed further just yet, though later they would discuss in forensic detail what kind of husband would allow his wife to move across the world all by herself.

"So why have you moved back to Clearwater?" one of them asked. Clearwater was a small headland town that jutted into the sea on the south coast and was connected to nearby Weymouth by a single road. One way in and one way out, unless you went by water. It had a long stretch of shingle beach on one side, and small stony coves cut into the coastline on the other. It was beautiful, they could all give it that, but it was quiet and didn't attract many tourists, who preferred the buzz of Weymouth. It seemed an odd choice for Grace.

"I guess it still feels like home," she said, continuing to scan the playground.

"Are you looking for anyone in particular?" one of the mums asked her.

"Actually, I am," she replied. "Anna Robinson."

"Oh! Ethan's mum? Ethan's in 4C too. Do you know her, then?"

Grace nodded. "We were best friends for years. We met here when we were five." She gestured a hand around the playground.

"Oh wow, that's amazing," another woman exclaimed, although what she suspected they were all thinking was, Well, this is going to put the cat among the pigeons.

IN THE MINUTES that followed, they gathered some more basics: Grace and Anna had been inseparable until the day

Grace left for Australia. They were both only children—more like sisters than friends—and Anna had spent many nights of those many years at Grace's house.

By that point some of them had already spotted Anna at the gate, huddled, unsurprisingly, with her small circle of friends. They liked Anna. She had always been kind and friendly, and her son Ethan, a popular boy, had never uttered an unkind word to any one of their children.

Anna always turned up to school with a smile, and never bitched about anyone. But she was part of what they all knew to be a very tight clique: four women who had met each other on their children's first day of school and had been inseparable ever since. Most mornings they were huddled together, arms flung around one another, giggling, whispering. Much younger behavior than you would expect for women in their late thirties and early forties.

There was Nancy, a head taller than Anna, tightly squeezing Anna into her side as she rocked with laughter. And Rachel, in too-high heels and a black pencil skirt, dressed for her office job in Weymouth, who was also laughing as she was dragged up the path by her two sons. Beside them, Caitlyn had a hand over her mouth as she giggled behind it.

And now Grace was making her way towards the group, and it took a few moments for Anna to spot her. When she did, her mouth opened wide in surprise. Finally, her face cracked into a smile and she joined Grace in the middle of the playground, the two women hugging each other as the other mums looked on.

Later they would wonder among themselves how Grace's arrival might affect Anna's relationships with her other friends. And as the early autumn term slipped into a *biting winter, they would watch with a seesaw of faint amusement and a little pity for Grace.*

But it wasn't until the second week of December, when the children had almost broken up for the holidays, that things really got interesting.